There was a wailing s[...]
mingling with it, the [...]
whose mind had been hurled through the barrier
between sanity and madness. Benetan saw the
huge wing of shadow rushing towards him and
instinctively he flung himself to the ground as the
demon soared overhead. It was gaining height
fast, but as it passed above him Benetan saw it
clearly for the first and only time. A shape that
defied belief, changing and transmuting with
every instant, it was horse and pig and cat and
serpent and bird and a hundred other, unnameable things. Only the vast, black wings kept
constant form. The wings, and the face . . .

Benetan knew he would see that face again
and again in his nightmares. It was a human face,
many times human size, pure and perfect and
awesomely beautiful; but its skin had the
nacreous sheen of the grave, and it was eyeless,
and black flames burned in its open mouth as its
strange, grim, wailing laughter rang above the
tumult of the Warp . . .

SCIENCE
FICTION
FANTASY

LOUISE COOPER

Eclipse

The Star Shadow Trilogy Book II

HarperCollins*Publishers*

HarperCollins Science Fiction & Fantasy
An Imprint of HarperCollins*Publishers*
77–85 Fulham Palace Road,
Hammersmith, London W6 8JB

A Paperback Original 1994

1 3 5 7 9 8 6 4 2

A catalogue record for this book
is available from the British Library

ISBN 0 586 21724 X

Set in Linotron Sabon by
Rowland Phototypesetting Ltd
Bury St Edmunds, Suffolk

Printed in Great Britain by
HarperCollinsManufacturing Glasgow

This trilogy is warmly and
appreciatively dedicated to
June Hall, who, with her
guidance, insight and
acumen, showed a
directionless ditherer that
she should stick to her guns . . .
and by so doing, brought
Tarod and Yandros unequivocally
back to life!

CHAPTER I

He wouldn't have gone so far as to term it a disturbance as such, but Tarod, brother of Yandros and one of the seven great lords of Chaos, couldn't shake off the feeling that something was awry in the gods' realm.

What the cause of his disquiet was he didn't know. Overtly there was nothing untoward to be seen or sensed, and though he turned his far-ranging and powerful mind to a brief but thorough exploration of Chaos's many levels and planes, he found nothing to give him any clue. Yet still the conviction persisted that all wasn't entirely well.

He considered mentioning his doubts to Yandros but decided against it. Yandros frequently teased him about his over-vivid imagination and would doubtless dismiss this as just another example, amusing but of no consequence. Instead Tarod resolved to make a few further investigations of his own. Yandros wouldn't be troubled by his brief absence even if he should notice it, and as a useful adjunct it would also give Tarod an excellent opportunity to attend to another small but irksome matter that had incurred his displeasure.

At the Star Peninsula the first moon had set and the second was a thin, haloed crescent low on the western horizon when the door leading down to the castle's library opened and a solitary figure emerged into the courtyard. Dawn was a little over three hours away and there was a sharp hint of frost in the air, presaging a clear but cold day to come. The courtyard was deserted, all the castle's windows unlit. Or almost all, for in one narrow embrasure in the west wing a telltale blue-green glow showed dimly, barely brighter than the moon.

A faint vibration rippled through the bones of the castle as the newcomer crossed towards the main doors, and between the summits of the spires there was a shiver of occult energy. Tarod glanced up with a slight smile. As always, the ancient building sensed and responded to the presence of Chaotic power, but he wanted no ceremony to welcome him tonight and at a thought the phenomenon subsided.

The doors opened silently for him as he ascended the steps, and he walked into the dark, echoing vault of the entrance hall. No lights burned on the staircase or in the corridors at this hour, but he needed none. He climbed the stairs, turned left and walked noiselessly towards the west wing.

The light's thin illumination showed under the door of Vordegh's private apartment. In one sense Tarod was disappointed, for he would have preferred to find the First Magus asleep, but he pushed away the small, malicious thought as too petty to be worthy of him and approached the rooms.

As the iron-studded black door swung back and he stepped inside, a woman started up from a chair by the hearth. Her face was a study in shock and, for a moment, outrage that anyone would dare – or even had the ability – to intrude on the First Magus's privacy, and her mouth opened to hiss a furious admonition. Then she saw the high-collared black cloak, the black hair tangling like smoke around an unhuman face, the cool stare of impossibly green eyes. The reprimand was transformed into a gasp and she dropped to her knees, bowing her head almost to the floor.

'My lord!'

Tarod looked at her with detached interest. Verdice,

Vordegh's amanuensis, was the result of the unusual, and doubtless unwilling, usage of an enslaved human girl by two lovers, one human and the other a lower being of Chaos. The First Magus valued her qualities highly, and she was certainly quite a beauty in her own icy way, though her looks held little appeal for Tarod – and none, unless his ascetic habits had changed startlingly, for Vordegh.

'I'm glad to see that you recognize me without prompting,' he said crisply. 'Rise; I'm sure I don't need to remind you that we dislike shows of abasement.' Verdice got to her feet, though still keeping her gaze cast down, and he added, 'The First Magus is in the inner chamber?'

'Yes, my lord.'

'Good. Don't announce me. You may return to your own quarters; your master won't need you again tonight.'

He waited until she had bowed again and left, then with a small mental command he opened the door of the inner room.

Vordegh was at his desk. He had immediately sensed the arrival of an emissary from Chaos but was unaware of his visitor's identity until the door swung back. Breath caught in his throat and he snapped instantly upright, his dark eyes intense.

'My lord . . . this is a great honour.' The First Magus bowed with meticulous precision, making a religious sign over his heart. 'You are a hundred times welcome.'

Tarod didn't answer immediately, but gazed around at the room and its furnishings. Spare almost to the point of starkness; no tapestries or other decoration on the walls, the chairs uncushioned and unadorned, no personal effects or ornaments. Vordegh's new status hadn't changed his nature in the least, it seemed.

His emerald stare flicked at last to Vordegh himself. A handsome man in a saturnine way, though his eyes had not the smallest trace of warmth. A fearsome scar disfigured his

3

forehead, the mark placed on him by Chaos's representative during the old First Magus's death rite and the testing of his successor's suitability. The gods hadn't troubled to attend that small ceremony in the Marble Hall. Knowing what he knew now, Tarod regretted that oversight.

'You work late into the night, First Magus.' He took the least uncomfortable-looking chair and indicated that Vordegh should also sit.

'There is a great deal to attend to, my lord, and many matters which I prefer not to delegate to others.' Vordegh ventured a faint smile. 'I have trained myself to require only a modicum of sleep.'

'Very commendable. Then I trust you'll be in a position to provide me with the information I require.'

'I am at your service, my lord, in any and all things.'

'Very well. I'll waste no time with pleasantries, as I don't doubt you find them as meaningless as I do.' If the First Magus felt the malevolent edge to those words, Tarod noted, he had the self-possession not to show it. 'In recent days, you and your fellow magi have been more active than usual on the astral planes. Your purpose isn't relevant to this conversation, so I'll not trouble you with my opinion of your work at present.' Ah; that did unsettle Vordegh a little. 'But I wish to know if you have encountered anything untoward during your explorations.'

'Untoward, my lord?'

'Specifically, any disturbance in the fabric of the astral planes – any abnormality or discontinuity for which there appeared to be no cause.'

The First Magus frowned thoughtfully. 'I don't believe so, sir . . . Although there was one conjuration; an oracular communion which failed to produce a satisfactory result . . .'

Tarod raised a dark eyebrow. 'On which plane?'

'The fifth, my lord.'

'Oh yes, I recall it. You used a new-born child for the purpose, didn't you? We found that decision more than a little surprising under the circumstances.'

Vordegh tensed. 'It was a decision I made with great regret, naturally –'

'Was it?' Suddenly the Chaos lord's eyes glittered and an arctic aura flickered around his gaunt frame. 'I'm more inclined to believe, Lord Vordegh, that regret didn't enter into your equation until after a rare and potentially powerful life had been wasted to no purpose, and I find this sorrowful charade a little distasteful. I'm not concerned with the fact that the child died, or with the manner of its death; Chaos expects its servants to make their own judgement in such matters. But if that judgement becomes subordinate to more personal issues, I for one begin to have doubts about its validity.'

The First Magus sat motionless. His expression didn't change but Tarod saw the tightening of the skin around his mouth.

There was a long silence. Then, 'My lord,' Vordegh said at last, very carefully and very calmly, 'if we are speaking of misjudgement, then I believe you misjudge me.'

Tarod said nothing but waited for him to continue. Vordegh pressed the tips of his fingers together and appeared to study them. It might have been intended to imply a faint insult.

'Lord Yandros, your great brother and the ultimate liege of us all, has personally entrusted me with the honour and the responsibility of the First Magus's rank,' he said. 'I feel that responsibility very keenly for I am, to the exclusion of all else, a devoted servant of Chaos. And as Chaos's devoted servant I consider it my prime duty to ensure that nothing threatens the supremacy of Lord Yandros's rule.' He raised his gaze to look at Tarod once more. 'That, my lord, takes precedence over all other considerations. And

I am convinced that in the matter of the heretics my judgement is right.'

Tarod was astonished by the man's arrogance – and, though he was loth to admit it, by his courage. In all their history no magus had ever dared show such temerity to a Chaos lord. Though his tone was faultlessly respectful, even reverent, Vordegh's attitude verged on outright defiance. He had understood Tarod's implied reprimand and warning but he refused to be cowed by it, refused, indeed, to accept it. And Tarod knew why, for the First Magus had made the point – none too subtly – that his first allegiance was to Yandros and Yandros alone. While Yandros sanctioned his decisions and deeds, or at least didn't actively condemn them, he had an utterly free hand. As First Magus he was invulnerable; he was well aware of it and would not defer to anyone, even a god, who sought to challenge his position.

Tarod said, 'Your confidence is impressive. Thus far, though, I fail to see the evidence to justify it.'

Vordegh's mouth pursed. 'I hesitate to differ with you, my lord –'

'Not just with me, Vordegh, but also, I gather, with the great majority of your peers.'

The First Magus's eyes hardened abruptly. 'The magi know their duty, my lord, just as I know mine.'

'To obey their leader?'

'Their *chosen* leader. Yes. As – pardon my presumption, but I think I speak only the truth – as you obey your great brother, without dissent and without question.'

Tarod considered that for a few moments, then his thin lips curled faintly. 'The parallels aren't quite as close as you think, Vordegh. Yandros's authority in the realm of Chaos is absolute, but in practice his attitude differs somewhat to yours. My brother is not autocratic. He has the . . . well, let us say he has the insight to appreciate and respect the views of his lesser brethren, and to allow those views free rein without the need to refer constantly to him for sanction.' He paused briefly, then added with a fine sting, 'Which is why I am here to express my views, which aren't necessarily those of my brother. As a self-professed servant of Chaos, you might do worse than to bear that fact in mind when you claim Yandros's example as a precedent for your own conduct.'

Vordegh's pale cheeks coloured faintly. 'I am sensible of the honour you do me in proffering your . . . advice, my lord. I shall, of course, take heed of it.' His composure, which had wavered only a fraction, returned in full measure. 'However, as a mortal man I would never presume to aspire to the standards set by the gods. I am aware that my judgement is as fallible in this matter as in any other, but I am also certain that time and endeavour will prove me right, whatever certain of my colleagues may presently believe to the contrary. If that is so, then I think that the end will more than justify the means I use to achieve it.'

Tarod nodded. 'Very well, First Magus. You've made your views quite clear, as I think I have made mine.' He rose to his feet. There was nothing more to say, for he had precisely assessed Vordegh's attitude and disposition and that gave a surer answer to his questions than any words could have done. 'I'll follow the progress of your hunt for the heretics with great interest – as, I imagine, will the rest of your world.' He flicked back his long cloak, and for a moment the light in the room dimmed almost to blackness. 'I only hope – and trust – that your methods don't foster another kind of insurrection, either here in the castle or elsewhere. It would not amuse us to find that the gods were held to blame for the actions of one misguided man. I wish you a good night.'

For several minutes after Tarod's departure, Vordegh stood motionless where he had risen to make his bow. Both the inner and outer doors were still open, a faint, dark aura shimmering around them and marking the Chaos lord's progress. Verdice was absent, the apartments empty of any presence save his own. Then, at last, the First Magus sat down. At a gesture the doors closed quietly, and with precise, economic movements Vordegh began to tidy away the documents on his desk. His face was impassive, betraying no sign of emotion; to look at him, no one would think that the interview with Tarod had ever taken place. But in the depths of his dark eyes something stirred. Something implacable, hard as tempered steel. Vordegh believed that he had been a combatant in a small battle tonight. And he believed that he had won.

Tarod descended the main stairs, one shadow among many, and crossed the flagged floor of the entrance hall to the great doors. Emerging onto the steps he noted with a quick glance that the light in the First Magus's apartments had now been extinguished. If Vordegh chose to sleep tonight, he would have interesting dreams.

The double doors closed at his back. He walked down the sweeping steps to the courtyard ... then stopped. There was a presence in the darkness by the pillars that lined the walkway to the library, not visible, but there. Tarod considered for a few moments, sensing a troubled state of mind and aware that if he did what was desired of him it might not be quite the favour that the watcher hoped. But then perhaps not to respond would be a greater unkindness still ... and besides, he had never been one not to indulge his own whims.

He walked more slowly towards the pillars and, to reassure, allowed his footsteps to sound softly, breaking the silence about him. Five paces from the walkway he stopped and said quietly,

'Andraia. There's no need to hide from me.'

Andraia hadn't meant to do it, but the temptation had simply proved too great. She had been restless all day and sleep was impossible, but for once, perversely, none of her friends in the castle had been awake to talk or drink or play dice games with her to while away the small hours. And Benetan Liss wasn't there. That was at the hub of it, the frustration and the nagging worry she couldn't shrug off as she wondered where he was, how he fared, what he was doing. She had wanted him to take the First Magus's commission in the south; indeed she had been one of the prime movers behind it, for it was partly thanks to the plan that she and the castle's historian, Savrinor, had concocted between them that Benetan had been chosen. But he'd been gone three days now, and she missed him. Missed his laughter, his teasing, even the bickering and arguments that had been so much a part of their liaison for the past two years. And above all she missed his warm presence in her bed and the pleasures they enjoyed there.

Feeling lonely and sorry for herself, she had been sitting looking out of her window for the want of anything better to do when she saw the tall figure emerging from the library vault and moving noiselessly towards the main doors. Instantly her mind jolted back to the night of the First Magus's inaugural celebrations, when after the latest in a succession of furious quarrels she had left Benetan to drink himself insensible in the great hall while she climbed to the battlements and indulged in a self-pitying tantrum. She had wanted only to be left alone, or so she'd told herself, but someone had known otherwise. She had thought at first that the strangely tall, strangely serene black-haired man who had approached her in the chilly moonlight was some opportunistic outsider, seeing her alone and hoping to take advantage. But he had not been that. Never, *ever* that. *Black hair like smoke, curling on her naked shoulders as his mouth touched hers and seemed to consume her in ice and fire. Hands that made her burn, awaking her to a shattering pinnacle of delight and desire . . . And his eyes. Oh, his eyes . . .*

For several terrible, irrational minutes Andraia struggled inwardly, trying not to let herself believe that he had returned to the mortal world for her sake, to see her again and to offer her a second glimpse of a pleasure and an honour that were almost too much for her mere humanity to bear. She remembered the advice of her friend and mentor, the Lady Magus Pirane. *You have been granted a great and rare boon,* Pirane had said, *but for Lord Tarod it was nothing more than a moment's diversion. You must live with that knowledge, and never for one moment wish that it might be again.* Wise words, and Pirane had better reason than most to utter them, for it was rumoured that she and Yandros had been lovers once. But Tarod had returned, and whatever his motive might be, whether or not she had any part in his thinking, after one glimpse of him Andraia was lost. She paced her room, barely able to breathe, blood pounding in her ears, every sense alert for a sound at the door, a shadow on the threshold. But he hadn't come. She was wrong; she had been a fool. Doubtless his business was with the First Magus and he didn't even recall her name, let alone what else had sparked so briefly between them.

Then on the heels of bitter disappointment and self-reproach had come the reckless impulse. Perhaps he *would* remember. Perhaps if he saw her – if they should encounter one another apparently by chance – the spark would re-ignite, and she would . . . she didn't know what she would do, but it didn't matter. Just to see him again would comfort her soul. It wasn't disloyal to Benetan. How could it be? Tarod was a god, and the love she felt for her gods was of another order to the love she felt for her man. Benetan would have understood. He would have been *glad*

10

for her, for he loved the supernal lords of the world just as she did. Besides, she had made no pledges of fidelity to Benetan, or he to her. She was a free agent. They were both free agents. And he wasn't here, and he would never know.

All this and more Andraia repeated to herself, a tally of reasons to justify the impulse that now had become an irresistible compulsion, as she found her darkest silk shawl and changed her slippers for outdoor shoes. Then, terrified to pause even for a moment lest she should lose her nerve, she was running, running through the silent, unlit corridors to the stairs and the main door. She prayed that she would reach the courtyard before he returned, and it seemed that Yandros was amused by the irony of her prayers, for the main doors still stood open, suggesting that Tarod's dealings were not yet completed.

Then, when he finally emerged, her courage had failed her. Though she hadn't a psychic talent she sensed an ominous shift in the air as the tall, dark figure stalked down the steps, and like a frightened child she shrank into the shadows, trying to make herself small and insignificant and hoping that he would pass her by and go on his way. She had no right to intrude, no *right*. It was a terrible presumption, an enormous arrogance, a —

He spoke her name, and all her resolve collapsed.

'My lord . . .' she came forward slowly, timidly. For an instant her green eyes lifted to his as though in entreaty, then, shamed, she cast her gaze down. 'Please,' she whispered, 'forgive me. I thought only to . . .' But she couldn't finish.

Tarod knew — or at least guessed, for despite what many mortals believed, the gods neither could nor would have wished to read their inner minds — what she had thought to do. Under other circumstances he might have made a game of it, but something behind her eyes, behind the effort

11

she made to appear composed, told him that that would be cruel. Tarod despised cruelty as an unpleasant and unnecessary human trait, and he smiled at her.

'It's not the most congenial hour to be abroad. You must be cold.'

Andraia flushed. 'No, I – I'm not cold. I couldn't sleep. And then –' She desperately wanted to dissemble but couldn't summon the courage. It was impossible to lie to him. 'I saw you enter the castle,' she added miserably, 'and I – and I –'

'You thought to greet me?' The smile became a little more subtle but there was still no hint of mockery. 'I'm complimented.' He reached out, and one slender hand touched her cheek lightly, gently. His fingertips were warmer than the night air and an agonized, ecstatic shudder shot through Andraia's spine. She tried to ward off the effect his touch had on her, tried to remind herself that, to him, this was nothing, and took refuge in defensiveness.

'I think you're teasing me, my lord.'

'I assure you I'm not. You may find it strange, Andraia, but to know that among mortals there are a few – just a very few – whom I can count as friends is very gratifying.' With a more formal gesture he extended his hand towards her again. 'My business here is completed, and you are restless. Perhaps we might enjoy each other's company for a little while?'

Andraia's heart was thudding painfully under her ribs. She couldn't speak, only nodded and linked her arm with his.

He led her towards the library door. The spiral stairs beyond led down into absolute darkness, but a silver flame came to life in Tarod's hand, illuminating the way with a soft, eerie radiance. Their footfalls echoed as they descended, and underlying them Andraia imagined she could hear – or perhaps rather feel – a deep, subliminal

12

throbbing, like a slow pulse emanating from some unimaginable place beneath the castle's foundations.

The library at the foot of the long flight was chill and deserted. Unnatural shadows seemed to shift among the arches of the vaulted ceiling, and the pillars and benches and ranks of shelves were shrouded in brooding gloom. Andraia shivered as she gazed around, and felt Tarod's arm disengage from hers and slip across her shoulders. Stealing a quick glance at his face she dared to smile. 'It isn't only the cold. The library feels different, somehow. When the torches are lit and people are here, it's welcoming, almost friendly. But now . . .'

Tarod laughed softly. 'We needn't linger,' he said. 'I've more pleasant and more private surroundings in mind.'

He ushered her to the far side of the vault, where a small door was all but hidden behind the bulk of a row of bookshelves. It stood ajar; they passed through and were in a long, downward-sloping passage. As they began to walk along it Andraia suddenly realized where he was taking her, and her steps faltered.

'My lord, I can't . . .' The words tailed off.

'What's wrong?' Tarod queried gently.

She gestured ahead uneasily. 'This is the way to the Marble Hall.'

'Yes.'

'No one is permitted to enter without the magi's sanction. I have never —'

She was startled into silence by Tarod's laughter. He swung her round to face him, and she realized that for some reason he found her protest hugely amusing. Then his laughter subsided to a broad smile and he said, 'My dear Andraia, I don't think that while you're in my company you need trouble yourself about the magi's rules!' The smile took on a hard edge. 'Even the lofty

Vordegh doesn't quite presume to set his will above ours as yet. You are, if you care to put it in such terms, my guest.' Then suddenly the original grin was back and he added more prosaically, 'Besides, who will ever know? We can both savour the pleasure of defying authority without the risk of being found out!'

Her mouth twitched. 'You *are* teasing me.'

'This time, yes. But there's a grain of truth in it all the same.'

She was reassured but also more than a little daunted as he led her on down the passage. The Marble Hall was, she knew, the castle's foundation in more ways than one. Located deep among the stone roots of the ancient building and accessible only via this passageway, it was the magi's most hallowed sanctum and the repository of enormous power. To enter it was to step between and among dimensions, and though its structure was tangible enough its proportions defied spatial laws. Yandros, it was said, had created the Marble Hall with his own hand when the castle was built countless centuries ago. And within the Hall lay his greatest legacy – the supernatural gateway between the mortal world and the realm of Chaos.

Andraia knew that few secular mortals were ever permitted to enter the Marble Hall. Only on great occasions such as the inauguration of a new First Magus were the rules relaxed, and then the privilege was extended only to the highest-ranking officials. Andraia's father, Qenever, had been present to see Lord Vordegh receive Yandros's warrant and he had tried to describe the glories of the hall and the ceremony to her, but as she and Tarod approached the portal Andraia was in a ferment of excited and nervous anticipation.

To begin with she was disappointed, for at the end of the passage only a plain door awaited them. It had no latch or handle and was made of a dull, pewter-like metal that gave off a strange glow and seemed to drain all colour out of the surrounding air. Tarod touched the door with a light hand; it swung open . . .

And Andraia drew in her breath in a wondering gasp.

The Marble Hall was shrouded in a shimmering pastel mist. Eerie patterns, at once beautiful and disturbing, swirled among a forest of slender marble pillars which seemed to stretch away to infinity in all directions. Beneath her feet the floor was a mosaic of pale colours, flowing and twining. Cool air wafted into her face, carrying scents that she couldn't name but which tugged at her memory, and on the very edge of perception she thought she could hear a sound like soft laughter.

'It's so lovely.' She was almost afraid to intrude on the sublime peace of the Hall but she had to try to express her feelings, however inadequate the words might be.

Tarod smiled but said nothing; for all its marvels the Hall was a mere shadow when compared to Chaos's awesome beauty. Together they walked across the shining floor, until Andraia saw that a little way ahead the mosaic pattern was broken by a dark circle. It looked strange, out of keeping with the symmetry all around it, and instinctively she hung back.

Tarod said, 'Don't be afraid.' As he spoke she felt his arm tighten about her, then – she would never know whether or not an instinct within her anticipated what was to come by a split second – Andraia cried out in fear as from the black circle a column of light flashed upwards and outwards like earthbound lightning. She stumbled back; her skirt tangled in the folds of Tarod's cloak, and something vast and dark came rushing at her. Brilliance seared her eyes, her mind seemed to twist and invert and she felt herself falling. She screamed, and preternaturally strong hands took hold of her and held her against the colossal force trying to pull her down. Gasping like a half-drowned swimmer Andraia clawed and clutched; her fingers closed on nothing, yet still the hands held her. She couldn't see. Her eyes were open, she knew they were open, but she couldn't *see* – there was no light, no sound, no sense of her surroundings, only a darkness so intense and disorientating that it brought fear beating against her mind in dizzying waves.

Then there was a sound, though so slight that at first she thought it an illusion. A faint *hushing*, as though leaves – or fine silk – had moved nearby. And the soft sound of someone's quiet, steady breathing. Andraia's skin prickled as she sensed a presence close to her. Then the unseen hands released their hold and, so gently that the shock was all the greater, cool lips touched her mouth.

She uttered a tiny cry, which was suddenly stifled as Tarod's kiss became more intense. Now she could feel him, his warmth, his strength, the contours of his body beneath the dark shroud of the cloak he wore, and she reached out avidly. He drew her close, and momentarily she glimpsed the green fires of his eyes in the blackness. Terror and joy and longing and misery swamped her in a wave of confusion and she turned her head aside. 'I . . .' She tried to cling to her identity, to some sense of perspective, but words wouldn't come. Still she couldn't see the Chaos lord's face, but she sensed his smile, felt the slight shifting of his body against hers as he looked up. There was a flicker of disturbance as he exerted his will, then a dim radiance tinged with shades of deep blue and purple and crimson began to impinge on the darkness. Gradually, subtly, light filtered through the gloom; a thin golden corona sprang suddenly to life about Andraia, etching the contours of her face, her hair, her arms – and, as if the sun had abruptly risen after a moonless night, the scene around her lifted into brightness.

The Marble Hall was gone. She stood – or seemed to

16

stand, for she could feel nothing beneath her feet – on the surface of a limitless lake of mist. Currents of light flowed past and over her, motes of silver eddying in their drift, and she felt as if she was merging with the light, becoming one with it and losing all sense of self. Then, giddyingly, the illusion snapped and her consciousness spun back with a jolt that set every nerve in her body quivering.

Before her a shadow stirred. Andraia looked up, and her breath caught in her throat as her eyes focused on Tarod's face. Nothing, overtly, had changed – but he had quietly laid aside the mask of mortality, and what she saw in the stark sculpture of his features, the etched purity of nose and mouth and jaw, the eyes with their burning inner light, told her reeling mind that he had chosen to grant her an ineffable privilege. This deity, her lord, her lover, had unveiled to her a glimpse of his true self, and that self was the quintessence of Chaos.

Mesmerized, enthralled, quivering with a sense of rapture so eerie that it was almost sinister, Andraia felt herself devoured by the intensity of Tarod's unhuman gaze. Then with one calm movement a black fringe of lashes shadowed his eyes and they became mere slivers of molten emerald behind them. The enchantment cracked, though it didn't entirely break, and Andraia drew a shuddering breath.

He raised a hand, touched her face. Despite the constantly changing light his skin was ice-white, and a silver aura flickered along the length of his arm. Andraia felt the pulsing stab of a fervour she could barely contain and, suddenly afraid of the emotional chasm that was opening before her, fought to hold on to some last vestige of self-control. Twisting in his arms she looked wildly about her and struggled to speak.

'Lord Tarod . . .' She could barely compel her throat

17

and tongue to form the words. 'Have you brought me to
. . . to your own realm?'

Tarod bent his head towards her and his breath stirred
her hair. 'No.' His fingers traced the line of her neck, came
to rest on her shoulder; she felt her shawl slide away. 'This
is not Chaos, Andraia. We've simply moved into the Gate's
hinterland, to a dimension that is neither in your world nor
in mine. There's nothing to disturb us here, and nothing for
you to fear. Unless you're afraid of me?'

The question's unspoken implications hung between
them. At last Andraia found her voice.

'No,' she whispered. 'No, Lord Tarod, I'm not afraid of
you. Far from that. So very far from that. In truth, I believe
I —'

He knew what she was in danger of saying and he didn't
let her finish. This time his kiss wasn't a salute but a
demand, snatching her words away as he pulled her
fiercely, almost savagely against him. The shifting, spectral
river seemed to rise up, enfolding her; she was weightless,
floating, her body turning slowly and all sense of orienta-
tion falling away under the crushing, intimate power of
Tarod's embrace. His sheer presence overwhelmed her, he
was so real, so alive; and a mayhem of emotions – love,
fear, desire, terror – roiled in Andraia's soul. For a single
moment she poised floundering at the abyss of her own
passions. Then his mouth found hers again, his hands
moving urgently, hungrily now, black hair tangling and
flowing over her bare skin, and with an ecstatic fervour
she hurled all doubt and caution aside and cast herself over
the brink.

CHAPTER II

She could have lit one of the torches. Flint and tinder were set ready, as they always were, in a small alcove near the library door, and even in the darkness they would have been easy enough to find. But she didn't want light. Light would have forced her to face and accept the reality of her surroundings, and she didn't want that. Not yet. Not yet.

So she sat motionless on the bench, hands splayed loose and passive on the table before her, trying not to acknowledge the smell of polished wood and musty books and damp, ancient stone; trying, though in her heart she knew it was impossible, not to allow any emotion to creep through the shield she struggled to build around herself.

He had gone. She had watched the Gate closing, seen a last fleeting glimpse of his smile, and then she had walked slowly, numbly back through the shifting mists of the Marble Hall, back along the corridor, back to the library and the real world. Her loins and her back ached with the fiery aftermath of the joy she'd known, but his touch was only a memory now. And Andraia felt utterly, helplessly lost.

You must never for one moment wish that it might be again. Magus Pirane's words echoed in her mind but she couldn't accept them, couldn't endure that truth. Nor, she realized, could she ever allow herself the comfort, small though it would be, of confiding her precious secret to anyone. Pirane knew about her first encounter with Tarod, but this second meeting had been so much more, so much *more*. To speak of it would be to betray it, and to betray him.

She wasn't aware that she had begun to cry until the first tears splashed onto her outspread hands, and then she found she couldn't stop. The *loneliness*, that was the worst. Knowing he was gone, knowing nothing could ever come of it, knowing that he looked on her as a friend but that anything more was impossible and to hope for more was madness. With stubborn concentration she began to count the falling tears. It was a futile exercise but she was desperate for something, any mundanity, to fill her thoughts and keep the yearning at bay.

She had counted to twenty-six when the door to the spiral staircase creaked open.

Andraia started like a scalded cat, her head coming up before she could control the reflex. Light spilled from the stairwell and illuminated her stained face, and beyond the upraised lantern she saw pale, narrow eyes and the smooth sheen of fair hair.

'Andraia?' Savrinor, the castle's senior historian, an elegant, pragmatic schemer and her co-conspirator in the matter of Benetan's commission, stopped on the threshold and looked long and steadily at her. It was too late for her to turn away; he had already seen her unhappy condition and was doubtless putting his own interpretation on it.

But if she had expected Savrinor to react with his customary sardony or mannered world-weariness, she was mistaken. The historian frowned, then, treading lightly, came towards her. He set the lantern down and leaned over the table, not so near as to encroach on her but close enough to give the impression that his concern was genuine.

'My dear, whatever's wrong?'

She couldn't answer that, and this time she did look away.

Savrinor reached out to touch her hand very gently. 'This isn't some small matter, is it? Your business is your own and I've no wish to intrude, but won't you tell me about it?'

His tone disconcerted her, for it wasn't the Savrinor she knew. She had never really liked the historian, much less trusted him although she was well aware that his code of honour, if peculiar, was highly scrupulous by the standards he chose to set. But she also knew that in one matter and one alone Savrinor's allegiance could not be bought at any price. He was utterly dedicated to the gods, and no power in this world or any other could shake his fidelity. For that reason, perhaps he of all the living souls in the castle was the only one who would understand why she had done what she had done, and why it had broken her heart.

He said softly: 'I think your sorrow has nothing to do with Benetan.' Not a question but a statement. He knew she loved Benetan fiercely, but he was also perceptive enough to be aware that this grief went beyond such worldly concerns.

'No.' Andraia found her voice at last. The single word came out as an ugly sob and she felt something give within her soul. *No, don't, don't cry again, don't lose control* –

The pale hand withdrew but Savrinor was still looking keenly at her. 'I know I'm far from an ideal confidant, but if this is something . . . arcane . . . then it's possible that I might offer you at least sympathy, if not direct help.'

Without knowing why – perhaps it was simply that she needed an outlet, a target for her hurt – Andraia was goaded. 'I already owe you enough favours, Savrinor. I don't want to add yet another to the tally on your slate!'

Immediately she regretted saying it; it was unkind and uncalled-for. But Savrinor didn't take offence. He sensed that she was retaliating as any injured creature might retaliate, blindly and without true malice.

'If you want me to go,' he said, 'I'll go. But this has no place on my renowned slate, Andraia. It's simply an open-handed offer to a soul in torment.'

He started to move back towards the door, and suddenly Andraia knew that she couldn't bear to be alone with her emotions any longer.

'No! No, please, Savrinor – please, don't leave. I didn't mean what I said.'

'I know you didn't.'

She gulped a harsh breath. 'It was just that I couldn't – couldn't bear to . . .' Then her vision blurred and the tears started to fall in torrents. Silently, wretchedly, Andraia railed at her own weakness, but the tears streamed down her face, one after another after another, and there was nothing she could do to stem them.

'He was so –' She didn't know what she was saying, couldn't control the words. 'He was – he took me to – but he's gone, he's gone back, I saw him go through the Gate, and I thought I was going to break apart – And now . . . now, I . . . I can't forget. I can't *forget!*'

Savrinor felt a clenching, freezing sensation in his stomach as he realized what she was telling him. It had happened before, he knew; there was Pirane for certain, and doubtless many others. But Andraia . . . She wasn't a magus, she didn't have a magus's resilience or understanding. Yet Yandros or one of his brothers – he didn't know, and would never, *never* ask her to tell him – had come to her, and loved her, and honoured her. *Sweet gods,* he thought, *no wonder she weeps! Such joy, and now such loss . . .*

He moved closer, made to touch her again then balked, afraid that she would misconstrue his meaning. Yet surely she must know him better, must realize that no mortal man would dare to presume that he might take a god's place?

22

At last, tentatively, he stretched out a hand, touched her hair.

'Oh, Savrinor!' Andraia's voice broke and she turned to him, reached for him. Savrinor lapsed awkwardly onto the bench beside her, and suddenly she was sobbing stormily, helplessly against him, while he, not knowing how to find words of comfort, rocked her in his arms as though she was a very little child who had fallen down in the midst of a joyous game and grazed her hands and knees on unyielding stone.

Savrinor entered his quarters silently, but the heavy thud as he dropped the books he was carrying onto the table in the outer room alerted Iselia. She tensed, then, realizing that her brief private hiatus was over, slid the parchment she had been reading under her pillow and climbed quickly out of bed. Wrapping a robe about herself, and taking care that she was well covered, she ventured to the door that divided the apartment's two rooms.

Savrinor looked up at the slight sound of the door opening. 'Ah, you're awake.' She couldn't judge from his tone whether or not he was in a good mood. He sat down at his work-table and opened one of the books.

'I heard you leave.' Iselia slipped through the gap of the door. 'Have you been to the library? You could have asked me to run the errand for you.'

'You'd have taken too long to find the books I need,' Savrinor said dismissively but without overt rancour. 'Besides, you wouldn't have been welcome in the library this morning.'

Iselia began to feel uneasy, and was thankful that he wasn't looking at her lest her expression should give her away. 'Not welcome? Is there some trouble?'

'What?' Savrinor was paying only the most cursory attention; he looked exasperated as her question dragged him back from his thoughts. 'No. Nothing that's any of your concern. A purely private matter.' Andraia distraught and crying, sheltering a secret she couldn't bear to keep. Under the circumstances, he thought, Iselia would most certainly *not* have been welcome in the library, for Andraia had developed a dislike for his protégée that was nothing short of ferocious. And perhaps with good reason.

Savrinor had at last persuaded Andraia to leave the library. She was chilled through, shaking and exhausted; he'd picked up the books for which he had come and then shepherded her back to her own room. Others in the castle were up and about by this time and on the way one or two advanced with solicitous inquiries, but Andraia turned her face away and a sharp look and meaningful shake of the head from Savrinor had stifled any questions. In her room he had made her drink a large cup of wine before leaving her, he hoped, to sleep for a while. Others might have thought it wise to alert someone to her plight, but Savrinor knew better. Until and unless she chose otherwise, what Andraia had told him would remain a close secret.

Iselia had fallen silent now but he was aware of her gaze on him, the hesitant, slightly fearful gaze that at times he found disarming but which occasionally irritated him. It irritated now, though the reason was no fault of hers, and Savrinor had a sudden powerful urge to get away from her, away from these rooms, and divert his mind with something other than work. Something within him ached and it wasn't a physical malady but one of the spirit, almost of the soul. Something *lacking*. He could have blotted the feeling out in any one of several ways, wine or drugs or an hour or two in intimate privacy with Iselia, teaching her another new twist to his sexual desires and satisfying his body if not his soul. But for once he didn't want that. It wouldn't be enough, and at this moment there would be something grossly repugnant about it. What he really wanted, Savrinor realized, was to be alone.

'My dear.' He swung round in the chair, amused on a shallow level to see that he had taken her by surprise.

She blinked, her blue eyes wide, and ventured, 'Yes . . . ?'

'There's little to be done today, and nothing that can't wait. I have some research I wish to do which entails some tedious and solitary reading, so you may as well have the day to yourself.'

That did surprise her. Since Savrinor had taken her under his wing, as he chose to term it, free hours had been infrequent and free days almost unheard of. Iselia could barely believe her good fortune.

She said: 'If you're sure . . .' For a moment, knowing him, she wondered if this could be the prelude to some new and intricate game he had devised. But there was no sly insinuation in his eyes, none of the lazy, half-mocking speculation which she had learned to dread. He meant it.

'Th-thank you.' She rushed the words out, terrified that he would change his mind. 'Then if I may be excused . . .'

'Of course. Amuse yourself with whatever takes your fancy. You needn't return before sunset. There's to be some festivity in the dining-hall later tonight to mark someone's birth-anniversary and we'll be expected to put in an appearance, but until then I'll have no need of you.'

A lesser man, he thought, might have been offended by the alacrity with which Iselia retreated to the bedroom, dressed and returned ready to enjoy her freedom, but Savrinor shrugged it off. He thought it unlikely in the extreme that she had any secret liaisons; the only source of potential trouble in that direction had been Benetan Liss, and Benetan was miles away – probably several hundred miles by now. Nonetheless, as she made to leave he rose and crossed the room, taking her by the shoulders. His fingertips pressed hard into her flesh, hurting her.

'Enjoy yourself.' He spoke lightly, but when he kissed her his teeth nipped her lip. It was a small warning, she knew, and her gaze slid away.

'Thank you, Savrinor. I – shall try.'

Was there someone? Savrinor wondered as the door closed behind her. Impossible to imagine who it might be, unless she'd taken a fancy to one of the lowlier servants – and that would be a little too close to home, for these days she preferred not to be reminded of her origins. Besides, what did it matter? She was as near his property as made no difference, and if there was anything going on behind his back it was no threat to him. Quite amusing, in fact, for whatever else he might be, Savrinor was not a jealous man.

Or never had been in the past.

That thought took him by surprise and made him feel suddenly and unexpectedly uncomfortable. He pushed the sensation away; it was a nonsense and not worthy of attention. This morning's events had made him feel unhappy and out of sorts. Let the little trull go, if that was what she wanted. It didn't matter. Nothing mattered.

Depression was a rare malady for Savrinor and didn't sit easily on him. He returned to his table but, instead of sitting down, paused for a minute or so, staring at the open book but not seeing it. His expression was stony. Then he uttered a small sigh and walked to an ornate cabinet that stood against one wall of the room. The key . . . damn, he'd left the key in the bedchamber –

But the cabinet door wasn't locked, and at a slight touch it swung open. Savrinor's shrewd, narrow gaze flicked towards the inner room. Through the door, which Iselia had left ajar, he glimpsed a small cup standing on a table beside the bed and his suspicions were confirmed.

A brief but efficient check of the drugs and concoctions that lined the cupboard's shelves showed him what Iselia had taken, and his mouth twitched in a hard, private smile. Be it on her own head. He had warned her about the dangers of addiction to that particular nostrum; he was prepared to do no more. And – as he seemed to recall saying to her at the time – he was hardly in any position to preach.

His fingers skimmed the array of phials and bottles and found what he wanted. Sharp euphoria without the wrong kind of after-effect. He would be fit to appear in public by tonight, and even if he wasn't, and drifted through the festivities with his mind half in another dimension, it might wring a modicum of interest out of the general tedium.

A wine flagon stood on the table beside an empty cup. Savrinor reached for it and began, meticulously, to measure out the dose he required.

If he had known the real reason for the relief and anticipation Iselia felt as she made her way through the castle's labyrinthine corridors, Savrinor would have been very surprised. Her destination – quite contrary to his suspicions – was the library, which she now had permission to visit freely and officially as his assistant. Today, though, her mission was entirely personal.

She had retrieved the parchment from under her pillow and hidden it in the folds of her shawl before she left. There was no real reason to conceal it from Savrinor; it was simply a key to aid translations of an old linguistic form and as such a perfectly legitimate step in her efforts to improve her scholarship. But Iselia didn't want Savrinor to know the exact direction her studies were taking or how far they had progressed, for if he did, he might begin to wonder about her purpose. And if her purpose – her *true* purpose – should ever be discovered by any living soul in the castle, Iselia knew that she wouldn't survive to see another dawn. For, slowly but surely, she was learning about the castle, about the magi, and about the scope and nature of the sorcery that the magi practised in the name of Chaos. How she would use the knowledge she was gaining she didn't yet know; it was too early and she was as yet too alone. But that would change. Her belief, which she held to with a savagery that sustained her through the private hell of her life as Savrinor's possession, was that one day, not yet but soon, *soon*, word would come from her husband, in hiding now in the south with their friends. She should have gone with him, but on the night of their clandestine marriage the Chaos riders had smashed their plans and dreams when they swept through her village in search of candidates for the castle and she had been caught up in their net. But one message had reached her from Kaldar. He knew she was alive and relatively safe, and she in her turn knew that he would make contact again when he could. *When*. He had promised that, and Iselia clung fiercely to that promise. Word would come. Kaldar had the power; he was a skilled sorcerer and once he was safe among their friends he would be able to use his abilities to help her.

And if luck was with them, Benetan Liss would be their courier as he had been before.

Thought of Benetan gave Iselia a small frisson of guilt but she pushed it away. To use him was not to hurt him, and besides he surely owed her a debt, for the Chaos riders who snatched her from her home had been under his command. However old their friendship, whatever they might have been to each other in adolescence before he was taken to begin a new life at the Star Peninsula, she would never forgive him for that. And if she could play on those old ties and use them to further her cause, she would do so.

She *must* do so, for in the fight against Chaos and its servants there could be no room for scruples.

She reached the library door, and briefly, before ducking under the low arch, paused and looked up to the sky. She dared not speak the name of her god aloud but in her mind she formed a silent prayer and willed it away over the black rampart of the castle wall, over the harsh mountains of the mainland beyond the castle stack and on into the south.

Sweet Lord Aeoris, if you have any power in this world, help Benet to succeed in his mission! Help him to find Kaldar – and please, please, let Kaldar know what to do!

The sky, blank with a thin cloud-layer that promised later rain, offered her no response: from a high window in the west wing where the magi's apartments were located a burst of wild laughter rang down on the courtyard. Iselia shivered violently as the sound seemed to penetrate to her marrow like spikes of glass, and hurried through the door to the library stairs.

CHAPTER III

Five days on the road had broadened Benetan Liss's horizons in more ways than one. As a Chaos rider he had seen a great deal of the world during the past decade or so, but his previous journeys had been brief and arbitrary, leaving him with nothing more than cursory, detached impressions. This sojourn was different – and it was rapidly opening his eyes to the depths of his own ignorance.

He had left the Star Peninsula via the Maze, arriving on the mainland at a point some fifty miles clear of the northern mountains, and had picked up what was in effect the only road worthy of the name, heading southward. Thus far the weather had been reasonable, and he had encountered a fair number of other travellers; well and good, as for the time being it suited his purpose to be seen and noted. And noted he would be, for a solitary man wearing good clothes and riding a highly bred horse was a rare sight in the lawless, brigand-haunted areas between settlements. He would arouse curiosity and comment, and that was precisely what he wanted.

The fact that he had not as yet been waylaid by brigands was, Benetan knew, simply random good luck, but if an attack came he had little to fear. His fighting abilities, honed to the magi's exacting standards, were more than a match for any untrained force, and if the worst should come to the worst he had subtler weapons than the heavy sword and two lethal knives he carried at his belt. Hidden beneath the fur coat he wore was the full regalia of his rank – and no brigand would take on a Chaos rider, unless he was willing to consign his soul to the Seven Hells.

So with nothing to threaten him he had both the time and the leisure for other concerns as he rode on his way. To begin with, the novelty of his surroundings had been a pleasant diversion and had lifted his spirits. But the mood hadn't lasted, for his mind was filled with a turmoil that made it impossible to concentrate for long on any distraction. And at the heart of the turmoil, eating at him like acid, was Iselia.

Again and again he had tried to tell himself that he wasn't in love with her. The past was over and done with, the ashes of that old fire long cold and blown away. Iselia was married to another man, while he had found fulfilment with Andraia. When he left the castle he had believed that this respite, away from them both, would clear the confusion in his mind and make him realize that the pangs he felt were only the final, feeble echoes of an adolescent love which he had outgrown long ago. But he had been wrong. His old love for Iselia was not an illusion, and it was not dead. Twelve years had passed; they were no longer callow children but adult, matured. Yet the fire had kindled again and was burning in him, and this time it would not be smothered.

And Iselia herself? What did *she* feel? Benetan's conscience was tearing him apart, for even to ask himself such a question was a betrayal of others; Andraia, who loved him, Kaldar, who trusted him. But strive as he might, he couldn't forget what Iselia had said to him at their last, clandestine night meeting on the beach below the castle stack. *Did you think I could change so much?* she had asked him. *Or that Kaldar could ever truly take the place that you once held?* Those words had seared into Benetan's mind and nothing could dislodge them. Neither he nor Iselia had the power to change the course their lives had taken — but the words had been spoken. The thing had been said. And Benetan was lost.

31

Now as days passed and he experienced more of the world beyond the castle, the confusion of guilt and divided loyalties was taking on a further dimension. He encountered no trouble on the road – but neither did he encounter anything approaching goodwill. Indeed, all who saw and recognized the trappings of his rank reacted with fear or hostility or both; they turned their faces away, steered their animals off the track and steadfastly refused to acknowledge his presence in any way. As a boy Benetan had shared the common dread and hatred of the Chaos riders, but twelve years among the castle's elite, cushioned and remote from the outside world, had all but erased the memory of those old fears. Now they were sharply recalled, but for the first time he was seeing them from the privileged side of the great divide between the people and their masters – and learning what it was to be a pariah.

Feeling, as he did, like a man in limbo, caught between two inimical worlds and a misfit in both, Benetan's perspectives were beginning to change. And his discomfort was increased by a deep, cold sense of foreboding which settled in his gut as his journey progressed. There was an ominous mood in the land, strong enough in places to taint the atmosphere like a pall. The countryside was *too* quiet, demesnes and settlements *too* peaceful. It felt like the sinister calm before a colossal thunderstorm. Benetan believed he knew the cause but he was trying not to dwell on it, or on the unpleasant connections with his more personal troubles, until circumstances should force his hand.

Matters came to a head on the seventh day when he reached the first village worthy of the name. It sprawled across a valley between two hills, from the higher of which the local overlord's fortress glowered down, and although it was for the most part a ramshackle affair it did boast a rough meeting-ground flanked on one side by a stone-built tithe house. Benetan had intended to pass it by, but an encounter with the keeper of the tollgate at the village boundary changed his plans. The keeper was young, burly and thought a great deal of himself; a well-dressed traveller was a rare bonus on the road and, squaring himself aggressively in the middle of the track, he demanded five times the overlord's set fee. There was a sharp exchange, quickly terminated when Benetan pushed his coat back to reveal the silver insignia on his black tunic and the heavy black belt with its complex buckle. Bravado turned instantly to terrified servility as the keeper begged "My Lord's forgiveness" and pleaded to be allowed to carry word to the overlord's stewards that their district was to be graced by a visit from a high emissary. Any castle-bred man, Benetan knew, would have ignored the grovelling soliloquy, kicked the keeper into the dust where he belonged and ridden on his way undisturbed. He could not, and so resigned himself to the formalities that would be expected of him.

It began to rain as the toll-keeper hurried before him towards the village, a thin, cold, driving rain with more than a hint of sleet. The daylight was fading but the day's labours hadn't yet ended. Herders were at work with their animals on the sere valley slopes, and a heavy eight-wheeled cart with two horses and three men pulling it was making painfully slow progress towards the tithe-house, which was guarded, Benetan noticed, by four armed men. Dim lights shone from the windows of a few of the buildings but most were already shuttered against the weather and the coming night. A woman crossing the meeting-ground with a pannier on her back paused to look curiously at the stranger, then hunched her shoulders and hurried on her way. In the distance a dog was barking, sounding lonely and hopeless.

The toll-keeper veered towards the tithe-house. Benetan reined in, watching as urgent words were exchanged with the guards, then one turned and ran pell-mell towards a drinking house some thirty yards away. The toll-keeper came back, begged "My Lord's" indulgence and said that the Overlord's head steward would attend him instantly. With "My Lord's" honourable leave he would now return to his post, and with a good deal of obsequious bowing he turned and hastened back towards the road.

The steward emerged from the tavern moments later, flailing his arms into his coat sleeves as he hurried out. He was a tall, fair-haired and sturdy man, middle-aged though his face was prematurely lined. Reaching the waiting figure on the black mare he looked up, and as he recognized Benetan's rank a look of sheer horror flicked across his features. Crushing it – and it clearly took considerable effort – he made a sharp, martially formal bow. 'Sir, I beg pardon that I wasn't here to greet you on your arrival. I thought – we were told that –' A muscle in his throat worked convulsively. 'I didn't know that we were to expect you tonight.'

Benetan frowned. He wasn't aware that he had been expected at all, and he said, 'No one's at fault, steward. Your overlord wasn't warned of my visit; I'm here by chance.'

'By chance?' The steward was clearly nonplussed, and Benetan had the impression that the man thought – or feared – he was playing some kind of game. Then, avoiding Benetan's eyes, he bowed again. 'Yes, sir. Then if you'll permit, sir, I'll take you up to the hold at once.'

Benetan flicked wet hair out of his eyes. 'I'd appreciate it.'

A horse was being led out from a shed beside the drinking house, and the steward mounted and led the way at a brisk trot out of the village and towards the fortress on its hill. He didn't dare to say any more, but now and then when he hoped Benetan wasn't attending he glanced back over his shoulder, his expression one of deep apprehension

34

mixed with bitterness. Benetan had expected little else, but the intensity of feeling he sensed in the steward surprised him. It was almost as though the man had some personal grudge against him. Had the riders carried out a sweep in this district in the recent past? Guiltily he realized that he didn't know; but if the steward had had a son or daughter taken in such a foray then that would explain a great deal. Yet again Benetan felt acutely conscious of the gulf separating him from the world at large, and the impossibility of bridging it. He wished he could offer the steward some word of reassurance, but there was nothing he could say.

Their arrival at the fortress caused a furore. Guards – there were a good many of them – scattered in search of their master, and Benetan was quickly conducted to a hall within the stronghold's keep, where a fire blazed in a vast grate. Clattering footsteps announced the arrival of the overlord, a squat man with a choleric look and small, furtive eyes that glittered as though permanently watering. A tail of servants followed in his wake and at his agitated command began to shake up cushions and clear tables and fetch wine. The keep hall wasn't well furnished by the castle's standards but the overlord clearly didn't stint on what comforts he could get for himself. From the ornate chair to which he was ushered Benetan noted the extraordinary array of ornaments in the place, and also the amount of jewellery the overlord wore; rings on every finger, armbands and brooches, even a circlet set with gems. Imagining what Savrinor would have had to say about such vulgarity Benetan took a glass of wine and tried to appear gracious in the face of the overlord's fawning welcome speech. The overlord's name was Tanneler, and if His Excellence would permit the liberty he liked to believe that he was known to the exalted magi at the Star Peninsula as a keenly diligent servant and upholder of his duty to the gods and their avatars. His Excellence might recall that the last tithe from his demesne had been nearly half again that which the noble magi in their graciousness required, and only two months ago he had received word to the effect that his acumen and efficiency had been praised by no less a personage than Secretary Qenever himself. Benetan's mind shut out the deluge of words; he was, however, uncomfortably aware that the steward who had conducted him here had remained in the room, standing by a table in a shadowy corner and mutely radiating disquiet.

Tanneler was still striving to ingratiate himself, but abruptly Benetan realized that his efforts were sidling round to a new tack.

'. . . that it is a matter of great personal regret and anxiety to me, Excellence, for even though your visit is a little earlier than anticipated – I imply no criticism, of course; far be it from me to presume to do such a thing – but I was given to understand that we would have more *time*.'

'Time?' Benetan tried to grasp what the man was talking about, but failed; he simply hadn't been listening. Tanneler licked his lips, leaving an unpleasant moist sheen.

'Well, Excellence, you see, I am sure you see and will understand, it is a matter of *resources*.' The emphasis now had a faintly desperate edge. 'This is a small demesne, thinly populated. I am greatly hampered by the lack of reliable men, and with the tithes to be gathered and my own property to be protected there simply aren't enough hours in the day to ensure that all is as it should be–'

'Wait one moment,' Benetan interrupted. 'You run ahead of me – ensure that what is as it should be?'

Tanneler blinked rapidly. 'I refer of course to the First Magus's recent instruction, Excellence.' And, seeing that Benetan's expression was still blank, 'The *edict*, sir. Concerning the . . . the heretics . . .'

Abruptly it slipped into place. Benetan's memory flicked back to a bright, chilly morning in the castle; Andraia standing by the window of his room and watching with detached interest as Vordegh's supernatural messengers left on their errand. At the time he had not known the nature of their mission. But later, Iselia had told him . . .

Tanneler had begun to sweat profusely, clearly convinced that Benetan's silence boded ill for him. 'The edict said, Excellence . . . it said that we should have *time*, you see. Forty-nine days, it said, before the Chaos riders would honour us with a visit and inspect our findings. Yet it has been only . . .' he began to count on his fingers but gave up the attempt. 'Not as long as that, Excellence. Nothing *like* as long. We have followed the First Magus's command in every detail – our twenty-one chosen captives are securely held, and I can give you my personal assurance that we have stinted nothing – but I'm sure you'll agree that as yet it is too early to have the information we hope to garner.'

Twenty-one captives. Twenty-one men, women and children chosen at random – or at the overlord's whim – to be held hostage against a stark and simple ransom. The price of their freedom was information that would lead the magi to the heretic followers of Aeoris and his demon-brothers of Order. And if such information was not forthcoming in the time allotted by Vordegh, the hostages were to be publicly burned alive.

He understood their terror now, and though he had taken an instinctive dislike to Tanneler, understanding brought a measure of sympathy. The overlord was beginning to talk again, explaining, apologizing, excusing. Benetan held up a hand and silenced him.

'I think, Overlord Tanneler, that there has been a misunderstanding,' he said. 'I'm not Lord Vordegh's emissary. My presence here has no connection whatever with the edict; it's simple coincidence.' He forced a smile. 'Albeit an unfortunate coincidence.'

Behind him the steward made an inchoate sound which he quickly disguised as a cough. Tanneler's gaze darted quickly from one man to the other, then settled uneasily on Benetan again.

'No . . . ah . . . connection?' he repeated hopefully.

'None. In fact if it hadn't been for the zeal of your local toll-keeper, I would have ridden through this demesne without troubling you at all. He insisted that I should accept the honour due to me by making myself known at your gate.'

Irony was lost on Tanneler. Effusive with relief, the overlord at once began to shout anew at the servants now huddled in an uneasy group by the door. Their noble guest must be entertained with the best of everything; the best room must be prepared, there would be a feast, nothing would be stinted or he would know the reason why. Benetan was given no chance to demur and reluctantly resigned himself to the prospect of a night under Tanneler's roof. At least, he reflected, he'd sleep on a dry bed and wouldn't be faced with the prospect of trying to light a fire with wet wood and wetter kindling. And it was possible that he might learn something from his sojourn here.

Benetan did learn from his sojourn, but it wasn't a pleasant lesson. With the initial misunderstanding cleared up Tanneler proved an insistent and tireless host, anxious to impress his guest with his taste in everything from precious gems and metals to women. While the hastily-planned banquet was being prepared he conducted Benetan on a tour of the fortress, every room of which seemed to be crammed with objects that supposedly reflected his wealth and status. Benetan experienced several sharp flashes of childhood memory, recalling an overlord who had regularly

38

demanded all manner of 'gifts' from the craftsmen of his own district. His predations had reduced more than one family from poverty to outright destitution, and the sight of Tanneler's proudly displayed trophies invited ugly comparisons.

The tour was finally completed, or so Benetan thought, and they were walking back towards the main tower when the overlord suddenly turned and indicated an archway that opened onto a dark stairwell.

'Before we dine, sir, I'm sure you will wish to see for yourself that the noble First Magus's orders have been carried out exactly as he would wish. Naturally I'm confident that you will agree I've been as efficient in this as in all other areas, but,' he uttered a false laugh, 'your inspection and approval of the arrangements will set my mind at rest. One simply can't be too careful in these matters, and the expert judgement of a Chaos rider will reassure me that I've done all that could be expected of any man.' His smile as false as his laugh had been, he shifted the focus of his small eyes. 'Gefen! Where's the cellar key?'

The fair-haired steward, who had followed them at a discreet distance throughout the tour of the fortress, came forward. His gaze was fixed on the stone floor as he fumbled with a leather purse at his belt, but Benetan glimpsed a hard and terrible glitter in his eyes as he held out a heavy iron key.

'Bring a light.' There was an edge to Tanneler's tone, a suggestion of challenge. Wordlessly Gefen took down a torch from the nearest wall-bracket, and for one instant Benetan thought that he was going to swing the burning brand and slash it across the overlord's face. *Or,* came the sudden disquieting afterthought, *across mine.* But the tension faded as Gefen abruptly brought his emotions under control and, still without speaking, stepped through the arch.

The stairs wound in a tight, steep spiral down into the fortress's foundations. Gefen led the way, Tanneler on his heels and complaining about the light's inadequacy, and Benetan followed with one hand touching the hilt of the longer of the two knives he carried. It was hard to believe that he would meet trouble from an unarmed steward, but he was certain now that Gefen was harbouring some kind of grudge, not only against his master but also against his master's guest. Or against what his master's guest represented . . .

The stairs ended at an old and rusty iron gate which, at a word from his master, Gefen unlocked and pushed open. As the grinding echo of the hinges died away Benetan saw by the torchlight that Tanneler was sweating, and instead of stepping through the gate the overlord gestured for the others to go first. 'The air down here.' He tapped his chest theatrically. 'Not of the best; the odours don't sit happily with my constitution. Gefen will lead the way.'

The steward turned abruptly and walked off, Benetan following and Tanneler falling in a few paces behind them. Like most such buildings the fortress was riddled with cellars, connected by narrow, tunnel-like passages such as this. Doors were set into the walls at intervals, each one secured by a bar and heavy chain; doubtless the rooms where Tanneler stored the overflow from the tithes he collected so assiduously. But they passed these doors, penetrating further into the maze, and gradually the condition of the tunnel started to change, taking on a dank, claustrophobic feel that caught in Benetan's nostrils and throat. Moist stalactites hung from the roof, and the walls sprouted poisonous-looking fungi. The doors were fewer, half rotten with damp in places, and the air was so thick and cloying that the flame of Gefen's torch sank to a dull, sulphurous flicker.

At last the steward halted. A few paces ahead Benetan

saw a glimmer of stone as though the tunnel had been walled off, though the poor light made it hard to be certain, and to their left was a solitary door, larger and in better condition than those they had already passed. Gefen turned and made his odd, martial bow.

'As Overlord Tanneler says, sir, the air here is not of the best. I trust it doesn't trouble you too greatly?'

Something in his voice; and by the waning torchlight Benetan saw a hard glint in his eyes. 'No,' he said composedly. 'I've known worse.'

'The outer door only!' Tanneler's voice echoed out of the darkness. He had stopped some way back and seemed reluctant to come any closer. 'Don't unlock the inner gate, Gefen – remember your orders!'

Gefen said nothing but moved towards the door. A key grated, a lock turned. The door swung open – and a new stench, far worse than the mingled stinks of the tunnel, hit Benetan like a physical assault.

The door gave on to a small ante-chamber in which a brazier burned, casting a dull, feverish glare that reminded Benetan unpleasantly of the glow from the deep underground fumaroles that had been a hazard of his early mining days. The light reflected hotly on the bars of a heavy iron gate at the chamber's far end. Beyond the gate, from the confines of their tiny dungeon, human faces stared back at him.

He didn't need to count their numbers to know who they were. First Magus Vordegh's twenty-one hostages, gleaned by Tanneler in obedience to his master's will and held in this foul, stinking place to await their fate. Some had risen as the outer door opened and had come to look out between the bars, but most were too weak or too devoid of hope and merely sat or lay in the litter of straw and their own filth. But every head had turned, every pair of eyes was staring fixedly, and for a terrible moment

41

Benetan thought he was going to be sick. They knew what he was – without a coat to cover him, his regalia gave him away instantly – and the surge of mute hatred that assailed his psyche was far, far worse than the physical stench of the prison. Appalled, he swung away. And saw Gefen's face.

The steward was oblivious to his reaction. Instead he was staring at the cage and its pitiful contents, and his eyes were full of pain and hunger. His throat worked violently, swallowing again and again as he struggled to control his emotions, and quickly Benetan looked back to the dungeon, following the direction of his gaze.

The woman was one of those who had come to the bars. She was perhaps forty or a little younger, and her hair was probably fair though beneath the filth it was impossible to judge. But her face ... Benetan was no physician but he knew she was ill, not through the deprivations of her captivity but from some deeper and older cause. She alone of the captives paid no heed to the Chaos rider in their midst but was staring back at Gefen with a hunger and desperation that matched his. She made no sound, but Benetan thought he saw her lips move in some silent plea or prayer. Then, so quickly that he almost missed it, her right hand made a small movement and her thumb and middle finger formed a circle.

Heat and ice shot the length of Benetan's spine. It was the sign Iselia had revealed to him and told him to look for in his search for Kaldar. The secret sign of the followers of Aeoris.

'Gefen!' Suddenly Tanneler's voice rang querulously from the tunnel outside. 'Remember what I said! Don't unlock the –'

His cry snapped Benetan out of his paralysis and he turned sharply. 'There's no need for concern, overlord. The gate is securely locked.'

42

A shadow moved beyond the door, and Tanneler, handkerchief held to his nose, peered in. 'I'd advise you not to stay too long, sir. The air –'

'Isn't of the best. I know.' Benetan steeled himself to look at Gefen again but the man didn't return his gaze. The steward's face looked as dead as a stone carving. More quietly Benetan added, 'I've seen all I need to see. Thank you, Gefen.'

The bitter, hopeless faces still stared at him. He would see those faces in his dreams, he thought, for a long time to come.

Shame and misery making him sick to the pit of his stomach, he turned his back to them and walked out of the chamber.

Tanneler knew that the Chaos rider was displeased, and as the meal progressed and his efforts to determine the cause met with failure he grew more anxious with every minute. His guest only picked at the food, barely touched the wine and showed not the slightest interest in the women at the table – including Tanneler's own three concubines and four daughters – who had been told in no uncertain terms to make it clear that it would be their honour and pleasure to fulfil his every wish. For the first hour the overlord had tried to keep up a flow of light and, as he saw it, entertaining conversation, but eventually even he could no longer maintain the pretence and the meal continued in strained silence.

As the last dish, an elaborate and sickly confection of which Tanneler was especially fond, was brought in, Benetan abruptly pushed his plate away. He was well aware of his host's discomfort and the reason for it, but Tanneler's feelings and fears were of no interest to him. He had other preoccupations, and as a nervous servant approached him with the new dish he held up a hand.

'No more food.' His instinct was to add "thank you", but he remembered in time that neither the Star Peninsula's refinements nor the common courtesies of the peasantry had any place here and thanks were not expected from one of his rank.

One of Tanneler's women leaned towards him. 'Perhaps some more wine, sir? It is a very good vintage —'

'No.' He glanced quickly around to confirm that the steward, Gefen, was not in the hall. Well and good . . . 'Overlord Tanneler,' he said. 'I would like a word with you about your captives.'

Tanneler was so startled that he bit the rim of his cup. 'The . . . ah . . . the captives, Excellence?' Terror glimmered in his damp eyes. 'I hope nothing's wrong, sir? I assure you that every precaution has been taken, every security measure observed —'

Benetan ignored his words. 'I noticed a woman among them; forty years old or thereabouts, fair-haired as far as I could tell. She looked ill.'

'Ill?' Tanneler paled a shade further. 'Well, Excellence, of course the conditions in the secure rooms do leave something to be desired. But, as I'm sure you appreciate, my resources here are limited and I have not been able to provide the — ah — required hostages with the best of facilities; not if — as is, of course, the case — their security must take priority. I confess that there have been some instances of sickness, but my own herballer —'

Again Benetan cut brusquely across the flow. 'You misunderstand me, Overlord. I'm talking about the one captive in particular, and I suspect her illness has nothing to do with the conditions in which you're keeping her.'

'Ah.' Tanneler nibbled at his lower lip. 'Yes, Excellence. I understand.'

'Well? What's wrong with the woman?'

'It's a sorrowful matter, Excellence, a very sorrowful

matter. In truth, to number her among the hostages was an act of kindness, you see; the act of a –'

'Kindness?'

'To my steward, sir. The woman is his wife.' Tanneler sighed with exaggerated delicacy. 'You are quite right about her condition, Excellence, though naturally such insight is only to be expected from a man such as yourself. Gefen's wife – he is a peasant, you understand, and he favours their peculiar custom of taking only one woman – is ill. A wasting disease. Doubtless your own physicians at the castle would understand its nature in a moment, but here we are not blessed with such skills, and,' he shrugged, 'we cannot cure her.'

Benetan stared at him in disbelief. 'You're telling me that you have imprisoned the sick wife of your own steward, and you consider that a *benevolent* act?'

Tanneler looked wounded. 'Benevolence, sir, was my sole purpose! The woman has perhaps a year to live, or two at very best if our Lord Yandros wills it, and the nature of her sickness means that she will fail slowly and painfully. Gefen is inordinately fond of her, and I reluctantly concluded that it would surely be better not to prolong her suffering and his any longer than need be.'

'So you mean to hasten her end?'

Another heavy sigh, and Tanneler nodded slowly. 'It was a decision that caused me untold personal grief. But I feel it will be for the best.'

It was all Benetan could do not to reach out, pull the overlord off his feet and smash his self-satisfied face into the table-top. He couldn't guess at the real motive behind this cruel and spiteful manoeuvre – it was even possible that Tanneler believed his own warped reasoning – but the charade of it disgusted him. He forced himself to quell his reaction. There was a better way to deal with Tanneler. His mind had been wrangling over it during the meal, fighting a

45

battle with his conscience which argued that by righting one injustice he would only be perpetrating another. But conscience had lost to pragmatism. In this, he had no choice.

He stretched out a hand, rested his fingertips on the table and stared at them. 'So,' he said, quite equably, 'the woman is dying and you consider it an act of charity to hasten her end. Therefore you have found a convenient way to perform that act – at the First Magus's expense.'

Tanneler was drawing breath to agree emphatically when the sting in Benetan's last words suddenly registered. Mouth open and eyes widening, he stared at the Chaos rider in consternation, and Benetan returned the stare with icy disdain.

'You consider then, Overlord Tanneler, that Lord Vordegh's edict may be interpreted to suit your own requirements. That you may use his order as an easy means to rid yourself of the sick, the worthless, the general dregs and flotsam who have outlived their usefulness and become a drain on your resources.'

Tanneler's face was grey. 'Excellence, I – I – that was not –'

Benetan tapped a finger on the table, silencing him. 'You know the terms of the edict, Tanneler. Twenty-one commoners, to be held for forty-nine days and then, if the required information has not been forthcoming, to be publicly executed. If the example is to make its mark on the populace, that means twenty-one living, healthy individuals.' His voice rose sharply and he clenched his hand into a fist, thumping it down on the table. 'Not a cage filled with corpses!'

Tanneler flinched back and his own hands came up before him as though to ward off a blow. 'Excellence, please – I didn't know, I didn't think –' With a vast effort he swallowed. 'Wh-what can I *do?*'

'I would have thought that was obvious to a man of your intelligence.'

Panic spread across Tanneler's face and his gaze flicked rapidly from side to side as though seeking either escape or inspiration. No one else at the table met his eyes and, taking some cynical pleasure from his disarray, Benetan said, 'Well?'

'I – I –' Then suddenly inspiration came, and with desperate relief Tanneler sputtered out, 'Sh-she will be replaced! I'll make another choice, someone fitter, healthier. A man, one of my own guards –' His chair grated piercingly as he pushed it back and scrambled to his feet. 'It will be done at once, sir! This was a mistake, only a foolish oversight; it simply didn't *occur* to me . . .' The flood of words tailed off and he looked beseechingly at Benetan. 'Excellence, need this matter be reported to the First Magus? I made a mistake, a simple mistake, and now that you have so wisely pointed it out to me . . .' His lower lip quivered. '*Please*, sir . . .'

Benetan toyed with a sliver of quartz set into the cuff of his sleeve. 'I would be neglecting my duty, Tanneler.'

'But sir, it is such a small matter! An unwitting error –'

'Well . . .' There was nothing to be gained from prolonging the torment, Benetan thought. Savrinor might have made a sadistic game of it, but he wasn't Savrinor. He allowed his face to relax and smiled faintly. 'Very well. It was, as you say, a simple mistake, and can be overlooked. Providing, of course, that you put matters right without any more delay.'

'Yes! Yes, sir, of *course!*' Tanneler let out his pent breath with a hoarse sound, then swung round and snapped his fingers at the nearest servant. 'You! Send Gefen to me.'

The steward came in. He looked wary and suspicious, as though he expected some new mischief from his master.

Tanneler didn't look at him but said curtly, 'Gefen. Our noble guest informs me that the First Magus expects those held under his edict to be strong and in the peak of health. Your woman is not a suitable candidate. She is to be released and I will find someone else to take her place.'

Gefen stared at him. 'M . . . my lord?'

'What, what?' Tanneler jerked round irritably, glaring at him. 'Are you deaf, man? Didn't you hear? Take four guards, unlock the cellar cage and take your chattel out! She is no longer required. She is not *good* enough. Don't you understand plain speech?'

The emotions that chased each other across Gefen's face were painful to watch. Uncertainty, hope, fear, and above all an inability to believe what he was hearing. Benetan spoke up.

'What your master says is perfectly true, steward. Lord Vordegh wants only the fittest. I understand your wi— your woman is ill, so I have ordered her release.'

He leaned forward as he spoke, resting his elbows on the table and folding one hand over the other. And as the bewildered steward looked towards him he moved his thumb and finger, covertly but clearly, to form the sign of Order.

Gefen's face froze, but only for an instant before, with considerable presence of mind, he collected himself and bowed.

'Excellence, I . . . I thank you!' Hastily he turned to Tanneler. 'And you, my lord!'

Tanneler grunted disdainfully. 'Don't waste any more of my time. You're dismissed for tonight. Get the woman out of my house and back to the village before she infects the rest of us with her disease. And think yourself lucky that I find you useful, or you'd be the one taking her place!'

Gefen bowed again and headed for the door. On the threshold he paused, looking back. Tanneler had turned his attention to the sweet concoction, his women were prudently looking down at their own plates, and only Benetan caught the steward's eye. He received a look that was both heartfeltedly grateful and deeply enigmatic. Then Gefen was gone, and the door closed quietly.

Benetan did not see Gefen and his wife depart. He was in bed – Tanneler had sent one of his concubines and two of his daughters to the guest room but he had turned them away – and had drifted into fitful, dream-ridden sleep. He rose at dawn, feeling drained and spiritually unclean, and left after exchanging no more than the necessary courtesies with his host.

As he joined the road again and the fortress and its surrounding settlement fell behind him, he was unaware that from a vantage point on the slopes of a nearby hill a silent, thoughtful figure was watching him. The woman was a herder but she was also something more, and at dawn this morning when she drove her flocks up from their night fold to the grazings, she had found Gefen waiting for her with a strange story to tell. Now, though she dared not use her full skills in the daylight, she sensed that Gefen's tale had some foundation. But one question, the vital question, could not be answered. Was the man with his black hair and black clothes and black horse a true friend? Or were matters even worse than they feared, and had their Sign become known to the magi?

Warn them, Gefen had pleaded. He was right; they could take no chances. The risk involved in sending that warning would be greater than it had ever been; with the threat of execution hanging over twenty-one innocents, people were desperate for the chance to unmask a traitor. But it had to be done.

The rider was almost out of sight. The herder shut her eyes briefly and offered a silent prayer to Aeoris to lend her strength tonight. Then she turned and, feeling a weight of fatalism pressing down on her shoulders, began to drive her flock on towards the higher slopes.

CHAPTER IV

The raucous din of the gong – a makeshift of three old shovel-blades roped together and suspended from a post, but effective for all that – was the signal for the day's work to end and the communal evening meal to begin. Men, women and children came hurrying from the half-built houses of the new village, from the fields and gardens where food-crops were grown and animals husbanded and, as word was passed along the chain, from the natural harbour on the island's north coast where the construction of the quay and jetties was all but completed.

Kaldar Alvaray was among the last to arrive at the cleared square in what would eventually be the village centre. He and four other men had been digging foundations for another new house but, with typical rigidity, Kaldar had insisted on staying behind to finish his particular trench before allowing himself to rest. The sun was low in the west, throwing his long shadow before him as he crossed the square, and torches had already been lit to brighten the sullen crimson glare of evening. The serving of food had begun, and people were queuing at the spits and open hearths before sitting down with filled plates on the dry ground of the square itself or under the branches of the many shade-trees.

Kaldar's back and arms ached fiercely but it was the ache of work well done, and under other circumstances he would have found it satisfying. Yet as he awaited his turn he felt the old frustration nagging at him again, the sense that, for all its apparent worth, this kind of labour had no meaning. There were nearly two hundred and fifty people on the island now, their numbers swollen during the past seven days by the arrival of three more boats from the mainland. They all shared a single fealty and a single cause; they were the core of the rebel movement, and – as Kaldar knew from his own shattering experience on the White Isle – they had power. But although their power had forged the first link with the gods of Order, it wasn't great enough to destroy the barrier that had held Aeoris and his brothers in exile for so many centuries. They had breached the dam, but the breach was small as yet and to sweep away the dam entirely would take untold effort – and time. Kaldar felt that too much time had already passed. He struggled constantly to be patient but all too often he failed miserably. And his fear for Iselia's safety was another poison corroding his mind. She was still trapped on the Star Peninsula, in Chaos's own stronghold and under the 'protection' – though Kaldar didn't know and was afraid to speculate on what that might mean – of one of the castle's high-ranking secular officials. Kaldar still dreamed about her plight, nightmares which even the most rigorous mental exercises couldn't keep at bay, but he could *do* nothing. And the strain of inaction was becoming almost too great to bear.

He swore under his breath as the thoughts crowded in on him, and the girl serving food at the rough table looked up with quick curiosity. She was a newcomer; Kaldar knew her face but not her name and he avoided her gaze, pushing sweaty tendrils of his red hair back from his face as he took his portion of roast fowl and root vegetables. He didn't want to talk to anyone, and walked away to an unoccupied spot by a half-built house, sitting down with his back against the outer wall.

He had been there for perhaps four or five minutes, eating mechanically and staring blindly at the ground between his feet, when a shadow fell across him.

'Kaldar.' Against the sunlight's dying glare the figure of a fair-haired, middle-aged woman stood looking down at him. 'I thought I saw you in the queue.'

Kaldar looked up, then with a combination of defensiveness and habit started to get to his feet.

'No, no; sit down, my dear.' Shammana Oskia Mantrel, who had been his travelling companion on the dangerous road south, settled herself on the ground beside him and gave him a long, assessing stare. 'You look exhausted. How many hours have you worked today? Ten? More? You shouldn't drive yourself so hard. There are enough men here now to share out the heaviest work.'

With the hand that wasn't holding his plate Kaldar made a dissenting gesture. 'There aren't enough; there never could be enough for everything that needs to be done. Anyway,' he hunched his thin shoulders and flicked an unquiet glance towards a long, low building, one of the few finished structures in the village, that stood a short way off, 'work stops me from thinking too hard about other matters.'

'Fretting and brooding, don't you mean?' Shammana's expression grew sympathetic and she touched his arm. 'Everything that can be done *is* being done. You know that, my dear.'

Kaldar nodded, though his hair had fallen forward and Shammana couldn't see his face. 'Yes,' he said. 'I do know.' Then abruptly he added, 'But knowing doesn't help.' His head came up sharply and his blue eyes glittered with emotion. 'You were *there*, Shammana. You were with us on the White Isle, you took part in the rite and you looked on our Lord Aeoris's face. We achieved so *much* that night, but since our return we've done nothing but wait.'

'That's true, and I know how hard it is to be patient . . . especially at your age.' She saw the quick, angry reaction that he tried to suppress, and added, 'I'm not trying to make light of your frustration. But I think the gift of patience is one of the few advantages that we older folk have over you young ones.' A wry smile softened her mouth. 'Though the gods know it's taken me long enough to learn it.'

Kaldar returned the smile, but bleakly. 'I wish you could teach me the secret.'

'I wish I could, too. You'd suffer a lot less for it.' But, Shammana thought privately, perhaps it was in Kaldar's nature to face suffering and even to court it. He drove himself so hard and so uncompromisingly, and his hatred of Chaos was like an open wound which he constantly probed as though afraid that it might otherwise heal. He had stopped eating now, the food only half finished, and was staring at the ground again. Shammana watched him for a few moments, then said gently,

'We're opening the first cask of apple brew tonight. It'll be new and raw, but drinkable. Shall I fetch us both a cup?'

Kaldar looked up, about to refuse, then stopped as a quick movement near the roasting hearths caught his attention. A girl of seventeen or so, long dark braids bouncing on her shoulders, was running from the direction of the low central building.

'It's Nanithe.' Kaldar sprang to his feet, dropping the plate and heedless of the food spilling to the ground. Hope and fear lurched in him in a sharp mixture. 'She's heading in this direction –'

Shammana knew what he was thinking. Nanithe Lowwe, raped and left for dead three years ago by the same brigands who had murdered Shammana's husband and sons, had been rescued and cared for by the older woman, and they had become as close as any true mother and daughter. When Kaldar first encountered them both,

54

the mental scars of Nanithe's ordeal had been starkly clear; she never spoke and she was terrified of strangers and of unfamiliar surroundings. But since their arrival on the island she had begun to change. She was still mute – Shammana privately believed that she might never regain the power of speech – but her introverted timidity was fading and a new confidence taking its place. Nanithe was happy. And at the heart of her happiness was the rapport she had formed with their own leader, Simbrian Tarkran. Despite the great difference in their ages a bond had grown between them, and throughout each day Nanithe was almost constantly at Simbrian's side. Now, her sudden appearance quickened Kaldar's pulse. Since the day of their return from the White Isle their sorcerers and psychics had kept a perpetual vigil in the long-house, taking turn and turn about as they strove to maintain their tenuous contact with the realm of Order and also with human friends on the mainland. Simbrian was on watch at this moment, Kaldar knew, and as Nanithe saw him and raised an arm to wave he started forward.

'Nanithe –' He caught her by one elbow as she ran breathlessly up to him. 'What is it? Has something happened?'

Nanithe nodded, pointing back towards the building, and Kaldar cast a rapid glance over his shoulder.

'Shammana, I'm wanted at the long-house. Something's afoot.' Nanithe had already started back across the square and he didn't pause to hear Shammana's reply but ran after her. His heart was thumping with apprehension as he reached the building. Nanithe was waiting for him, hovering outside the door, and at a gesture from her Kaldar ducked under the low lintel.

Firelight and the fading sunset gave way to the paler but dimmer glow of rush-lights in the hall, and Kaldar blinked as his eyes adjusted to the change. To begin with, the single large room was a blur of shadows, but he heard the steady hush of breathing and after a few moments made out several silhouetted figures sitting cross-legged on the floor. A single flame of cool light that had no visible source hung suspended in the air between them, but apart from the quiet susurrus of their breathing there was no other sound.

A shape loomed close by and a hand touched his arm.

'Kaldar.' Simbrian Tarkran had been waiting for him. His huge bulk blocked the light from the rushes as he moved closer and indicated the door. 'Best if we talk outside, then we won't disturb the others' concentration.'

Kaldar looked uneasily at the silent figures. 'Is something wrong?'

'No. But there has been a new development, and I think it may concern you.'

They stepped out into the dusk. Nanithe was still hovering and Shammana had joined her; Simbrian spoke briefly and quietly to the older woman, then bent to kiss Nanithe's cheek.

'We won't be long, my dear. Kaldar . . . ?' He beckoned to the younger man, and led the way round the building and away from the square to where the ground rose in a small ridge crowned with sapling trees. A number of people saw them go – the sorcerer's huge, bearded figure was unmistakable – and curious eyes watched their progress, but no one followed and they climbed to the top of the ridge, well out of earshot of those below. As they reached the shelter of the trees Simbrian stopped and turned to face Kaldar.

'We've had news from the north,' he said.

Kaldar felt as if a fleshless hand had taken hold of his gut and twisted it. *Iselia* –

'No.' Simbrian saw the terror in his face and raised a hand quickly, forestalling his thoughts. 'Not about your wife – at least, not directly.'

Kaldar turned his head away. 'Sweet Aeoris, I thought –'

'I realize, and I'm sorry. I didn't mean to alarm you.' Simbrian started to lean against one of the saplings then thought better of it as the tree creaked in protest. 'One of our friends in a northern demesne has made contact with me through the psychic link we maintain. She's a talented seer, leader of a small group in the area, and she tells me that there's been a strange development involving a Chaos rider.'

Kaldar's eyes grew suddenly intent. 'A Chaos rider?'

'Yes. Apparently the man was travelling south and broke his journey overnight as the local overlord's guest. While he was there he performed a very great kindness for the overlord's steward. Now, that steward is also a secret servant of Lord Aeoris, and the seer trusts him implicitly. He's told her that the rider indicated to him that he is also one of us.'

'*What?*'

'I know. It sounds like an impossibility.' Simbrian smiled grimly. 'I'd have dismissed it and begun to mistrust the source of the tale, but for one thing. The seer saw the Chaos rider for herself and she described him to me. He's about your own age, a tall man with long bones and the hard look of a northerner, and with black hair which he wears in a single braid.' Simbrian paused. 'Does that sound familiar?'

'Good gods.' Kaldar stared at him. 'It's Benetan Liss. It *must* be!'

'Your friend from the old days. Yes, that's what I suspected.'

Kaldar had told Simbrian the story of his meetings with Benetan; the first, fraught encounter when he had gained entrance to the castle unnoticed and the later rendezvous in the northern mountains. Simbrian knew, too, that Kaldar had tricked Benetan into carrying a coded message back to Iselia, urging her to use the Chaos rider in any way that she could.

'Kaldar, listen.' Simbrian leaned suddenly and urgently towards him. 'We need to be as sure as is possible about his identity. From my understanding, there are more than seventy Chaos riders at the castle –'

Kaldar interrupted. 'What colour horse was he riding? A black?'

'Yes. Yes, it was.'

'Benetan's mare. I've seen the animal myself and I doubt if he'd ride any other from choice. It *has* to be him.' Kaldar was frowning now, thinking hard. 'Was he alone?'

'Quite alone. That's another mystery; those riders usually hunt in packs, as we all know. One solitary man travelling southward without even a raw recruit for company is all but unheard of.'

'What happened at the overlord's house?' Kaldar asked. 'What was this service that the rider performed?'

Simbrian repeated the account as the seer had heard it from Gefen, but when he mentioned Benetan's surreptitious but clear signal in making the Sign of Aeoris, Kaldar interrupted sharply.

'No, Simbrian, there's something wrong there. Whatever else he may be, Benetan isn't a devotee of Order. He blindly reveres Yandros and his demon brothers and won't hear a word spoken against them.' His lip curled. 'We didn't exactly come to blows over the matter when we last met, but he made his loyalties very clear. Whatever he might have pretended to the steward, I'd take any odds that he hasn't truly changed allegiance.'

Simbrian nodded. 'In which case he was deliberately trying to mislead the man. But he had no need to justify his actions; in fact to make such a pretence could put him in considerable danger.'

'He'd be aware of that,' Kaldar said.

'Quite; the magi don't appoint fools to high military rank. So why did he do it?'

Kaldar suspected he knew, but he was reluctant to voice his thoughts, firstly because he was wary of Simbrian's reaction and secondly because he didn't want to acknowledge the spark of hope this news had kindled within him. He looked away through the trees and down the slope of the hill to the pastures spread out below the ridge. Full darkness had fallen now – he was still disconcerted by the swift change between day and night in this southern latitude – and a faint ground-mist gave a pearly cast to the gloom.

'The obvious answer,' Simbrian said quietly, when it became clear that Kaldar wasn't going to speak, 'is that your friend was attempting to lure the man into revealing *his* true loyalties. But you don't believe that, do you?'

'No,' Kaldar replied after a few moments. 'No, I don't.' He hesitated, marshalling his thoughts, then, 'To begin with, that ploy wouldn't work. Any of our followers who received the Sign from a Chaos rider would have done just as the steward did; feign ignorance or simply pretend not to notice. Benetan must have known it would achieve nothing.'

'True.' Simbrian watched him steadily. 'But there are many ways to spring a trap. Your friend's intention might have been to lure us to him by more devious means.'

'Such as?'

'Such as deliberately arousing the steward's suspicions. As you say, no man in his senses would believe that a Chaos rider could be one of us. He would – and did – instantly suspect trickery. But that might be part of your friend's subterfuge. A snare within a snare, so to speak.' Simbrian smiled cynically. 'The magi teach their servants subtlety among many other crafts.'

'Benetan wouldn't resort to that,' Kaldar said sharply. He glanced at the other man, saw his expression and, discomfited by it, turned his head away again. 'I know what you're thinking, Simbrian. Benetan and I grew up together, so you suspect that those old ties have clouded my judgement and persuaded me to look for good motives where they don't exist.'

Simbrian raised his eyebrows expressively. 'I won't deny that it seems likely.'

'Well, you're wrong.' Abruptly Kaldar laughed, a short, bitter bark of a sound. 'You're making one fundamental mistake when you keep referring to Benetan as my "friend". We never were friends in any real sense. We might have come from the same district and known the same people and even worked for a while in the same mine, but we were never *friends*.' He looked round again, his eyes angry. 'I didn't even like Benetan Liss; in a lot of ways I still don't. He was always the popular one when we were children, while I was the boy with the awkward temper who didn't fit in. Then there was Iselia. I told you, didn't I, that she and Benetan were all but betrothed before he went to the castle? That rankled with me for a long time after he'd gone, the thought that I was second best for her.' Abruptly his face relaxed a little. 'I know now that it wasn't true, but I took a lot of convincing in those early days. So you see, Simbrian, when you call Benetan my friend you're a little wide of the mark.'

The sorcerer continued to look at him for some time. Then he said, 'Yes. Yes, I see that I am. But you understand, don't you, why I had doubts about your judgement?'

'Of course.' Kaldar stared at the nearest tree-trunk.

'So if you have no reason to like Benetan Liss, why do you trust him?' Simbrian hesitated. 'Forgive me for saying this, but your wife, whom he once loved, is now in the castle. If he still harbours any of his old feelings for her –'

'Oh, he does. There's no doubt of that.' Kaldar saw Simbrian's surprise and laughed again, a little less harshly though still with an edge. 'But I'm not afraid of that, because although I may not like Benetan, I *know* him very well.' He glanced over his shoulder, to where the lights and fires of the village flickered below them. 'Whatever his faults, Benetan Liss is honourable. So honourable, in fact, that it's almost painful to witness. He's always been that way, and even twelve years with the scum at the castle haven't changed his nature, as I discovered when we met again. Yes, he and Iselia are both in that damned castle, and yes, he still loves her. But he won't take advantage of her. He won't even try, because to his mind it would be a betrayal of his honour.'

'He sounds an unlikely candidate for the Chaos riders.' In the darkness Kaldar couldn't see Simbrian's expression but he heard the scepticism in the sorcerer's voice. He sighed.

'I know I sound like a man desperately trying to persuade himself that night is day,' he said. 'But if you met Benetan – if you could use your skill to read him, as I've done – then you'd understand. I won't pretend that I know what this new development means, what kind of mission Benetan is engaged on, who sent him or what he means to do.' He looked up quickly. 'But knowing him, and knowing my wife, I'd be prepared to wager on a guess.'

'Ah. So the wheel comes round again to our original conundrum.' Simbrian nodded slowly. 'All right. What's your guess, Kaldar?'

'That Benetan is looking for us. Or more specifically, for me. And that, whether he knows it or not, he's carrying a message from Iselia.'

'I see.' There was a long pause. Then: 'Even if your surmise is true, you must realize that your fr– that Benetan can't be acting entirely under his own volition. He's a senior servant of the magi; he *must* be travelling at their behest.' The sorcerer stared at his own hand, which he had clenched unconsciously into a fist. 'Kaldar, we both know that the First Magus is intensifying the search for us. This latest edict from the castle is only the tip of a very long and very deadly sword. I think . . . forgive me, but I can't trust Benetan Liss's motives, and I think that if we allow him to find us, or even come close to finding us, we'll be putting our entire cause in terrible danger.'

'So what do you think we should do?'

Simbrian hesitated, then decided that he had no choice but to be blunt. 'The surest safeguard is to have him killed before he gets much further south.'

'No! We can't, it would –'

'Kaldar, listen to me. We *daren't* trust this man. He could jeopardize everything we've striven to achieve. He could lead the magi straight to us. For all our efforts, Lord Aeoris doesn't yet have enough power in this world to protect us from the forces of Chaos – we'd be destroyed, Kaldar, and our gods would be hurled back into exile!'

'Benetan wouldn't take the risk of exposing us to the magi!' Kaldar protested vehemently.

'You can't be sure –'

'I can! Because he knows that if he betrayed us, he'd betray Iselia, too. And I don't believe that any power in the world would persuade him to put her life at risk!'

Simbrian opened his mouth to say that there could be no guarantee of that, but suddenly he realized that the argument was fruitless. They were both entrenched in their views, and he had no more hope of swaying Kaldar than Kaldar had of swaying him. He couldn't blame Kaldar for his attitude. Terrified as he was for his wife's safety, his trust in Benetan Liss's high principles was a lone spar in a particularly stormy ocean. But however great his sympathy, Simbrian couldn't rely on such an uncertainty.

Wanting to ease the tension between them the sorcerer reached out as though to lay a hand on the younger man's shoulder. Then, knowing Kaldar's likely reaction to anything that might smack of patronage, he drew back and instead said in a level voice, 'Then what would you do?'

'Make contact with Benetan. Bring him here and find out what he wants.' *And*, he told himself silently, eagerly, *find out what news he brings of Iselia.*

'No.' Simbrian shook his head emphatically. He didn't like having to fall back on his authority but he was acutely aware of the grave responsibility resting on his shoulders; responsibility for all too many people's lives. 'I can't allow that. You know how we work and why we've so far been successful in hiding ourselves from the magi. We've maintained small but active groups who have no knowledge of each other's numbers or whereabouts. If one group is unmasked the rest aren't imperilled, and only we, on this island, know the full extent of our network. Break that rule by having Benetan Liss brought to us, and you forge a direct link between us and the servants of Chaos. I won't permit it.'

He heard the hiss of Kaldar's quick, taut breathing. Then the young man said explosively, 'You can't kill Benetan! He could be so valuable to us!'

'But he could as easily send us all to the Seven Hells!' Simbrian rarely lost his temper, but in the face of Kaldar's stubbornness he felt his patience and tolerance ebbing dangerously away. 'Sweet gods, Kaldar, don't you think I *want* to believe you? Don't you think I know the potential worth of an infiltrator in Chaos's own stronghold? But you said yourself that Benetan Liss is devoted to Yandros!'

'Only because he knows no better.' Kaldar drew air sharply between clenched teeth. 'We could teach him, show him the mistake he's made. Or if we couldn't, Iselia could.'

He met Simbrian's gaze challengingly. 'I'm willing to stake that if it came to a choice between her life and loyalty to that demon Yandros, he'd choose her.'

Was it possible? For a heady moment Simbrian found himself wavering, lured by the possibility. If Kaldar was right about Benetan Liss's feelings for his wife, then . . . well, he had seen often enough the power a woman could wield over a man, for good or for ill. And if the Chaos rider was truly decent and honourable – as the incident with the steward, though a small thing, seemed to suggest – then his loyalty to Chaos could surely have no real foundation. As Kaldar said, he simply knew no better.

Then, like the sudden slap of a cold wind on a summer day, reason returned. Possible or not, the risk was monstrous. If he let himself believe for one instant that it could be worth taking, he was no longer fit for his role.

'No,' he said. 'No, Kaldar. *No.* I won't do it. I won't take the chance.'

For what seemed a very long time they were both silent. At last Kaldar shifted his position, moving out of the trees' shelter towards the night-drowned pasture. He rubbed at a stone with his foot, staring into the darkness. At last he spoke.

'Then you're resolved? You've decided that we have no option but to have Benetan killed?'

He sounded bitter and Simbrian understood why, even though he couldn't condone such an attitude. 'I'm sorry, Kaldar,' he said heavily. 'But I can't see any other safe course.' He paused. 'Though there is one possible compromise.'

Kaldar's head came round quickly. 'Compromise?'

'To wait; at least until we have some better idea of the purpose behind Benetan's mission and where it's taking him.' Simbrian rubbed at his beard, frowning. 'That in itself might be a risk, but at least it's a small one. We could send word to some of our more southerly friends to watch out for him and report anything they learn. In the meantime, the rites we're performing are having an effect on our links with the realm of Order, and giving our Lord Aeoris greater strength. It may be that before long he will be able to offer us not only his guidance but also his direct help.'

Kaldar's eyes lit keenly. 'Do you think that's possible?'

'I don't know. But – for Iselia's sake and perhaps even for all our sakes – the gamble might be worth taking.'

For several seconds Kaldar said nothing. Then, hesitantly and awkwardly, he turned and laid a hand on the sorcerer's arm.

'Thank you,' he said indistinctly. 'Thank you, Simbrian. You see, I –' He snapped the words off and the hand drew back to brush quickly at his own face. His voice had been filled with emotion; abruptly then it changed, becoming harsh as though he was determined to suppress the feelings aroused in him. 'It's ridiculous, isn't it? Why should I give a damn for Benetan Liss's safety? He's nothing to me, and in principle I don't care whether or not he survives to see another dawn. But until I can reach Iselia, until I can get her *out* of that damned place, he's the only friend she has. Knowing that, I think that if he died, you see, if he . . .' Something caught in his throat and his voice shook involuntarily. 'If that happened, I don't think there'd be any hope left for her.'

CHAPTER V

'Andraia.' Lua stepped back from the ornate mirror that hung on the wall, and subjected her daughter's back view to a long, hard look. 'Have you heard a word I've been saying?'

Andraia turned from the window with the air of apathetic lassitude that had persisted for the past few days and troubled Lua more than she cared to admit. 'I was listening, Mother.'

'Were you? I see. Then what did I say to you a few moments ago?'

'You said that . . .' But Andraia realized then that she couldn't remember, that her mother's words had only skimmed over the surface of her mind without registering. She sighed and looked away again. 'I'm sorry.'

Lua frowned. 'It's not your apologies I want, Andraia, but your *attention*. And, perhaps more to the point, a change in your attitude.' Suddenly both her posture and her voice softened and she crossed the room to the girl's side. 'Child, you *must* stop this constant moping and brooding. I know you miss your lover, I understand your feelings perfectly, but you're doing yourself no good at all by languishing your time away.' She paused, then added with a candour which she privately felt was long overdue, 'He really isn't worth it.'

A sharp, angry retort came to Andraia's lips but she forced it back, knowing that, even if she could have explained the real nature of her unhappy confusion, her mother wouldn't 'understand perfectly' as she claimed. Lua *couldn't* understand. Better, then, that she should continue to mistake the real reason for her daughter's mood.

Lua was beginning to repeat the lecture that had gone unheard the first time. 'You've taken no part in any pleasures to be had; no games, no recreations, no parties – you pleaded a headache to avoid Clavan's birth-anniversary festivities, you no longer even spend any time with your friends. And now look at you. Your hair is a sight, your face unpainted and you might as well be wearing a scullery-drab's shift for all the care you take over your clothes. It really isn't *good* enough, Andraia. People are starting to notice. Even Lady Magus Pirane has commented on your absences.' She pursed her mouth. 'And it is *not* a wise idea to displease Lady Magus Pirane.'

Andraia was looking out of the window again by now, and the stubborn set of her shoulders reminded Lua suddenly and strongly of her father, Qenever. 'Staring like that won't make Benetan Liss miraculously appear in the courtyard,' she added a little tartly. 'He's a long way from the castle and, though I don't like to say this, it wouldn't surprise me in the least if he hasn't already had a dalliance or two to console himself. Why you can't be sensible enough to do the same is quite beyond me.'

'Benetan wouldn't do that.' Andraia spoke firmly, ignoring a small, jealous inner voice that added, *unless her name happened to be Iselia Darrow.*

'Then more fool him – and more fool you for letting him influence you into adopting his nonsensical peasant customs. An affair or two needn't *mean* anything; it would simply help the time to pass. And the gods know you've enough would-be admirers to choose from.'

'Thank you, Mother, but I don't *want* any admirers,' Andraia said resolutely. 'I only want –'

'Your beloved Benetan Liss. There's no need to stress the point; I'm well aware of it.'

67

Andraia's mouth tightened into a hard line. 'What I was about to say, Mother, was that all I want is to be left alone to order my life as I choose.'

Andraia might have inherited her wilfulness from her father, but Lua had determination to match hers; it was one of the shared qualities which, years ago, had sparked the attraction between her and Qenever.

'Whatever you do or do not want,' she said, 'you have certain obligations which you simply can't evade. There's to be another celebration in the great hall tonight and you are specifically required to attend.'

'Mother, I don't *want* to attend any festivities! I'm perfectly well as I am, and —'

'The celebration,' Lua said, 'is hosted by Lady Magus Pirane, and she has instructed me to tell you that you *will* attend and enjoy the night.' She paused. 'Do you wish to argue the matter with her?'

Her words had the desired effect. Andraia knew that Pirane's command couldn't be ignored, and Lua was grateful that the magus had been willing to collude with her in this matter. Seeing her daughter's stricken face and seeking to leaven the mood of the conversation a little, Lua added, 'It's sure to be very pleasurable, Andraia. We think, though she hasn't confirmed it, that this is a particularly special occasion for Lady Pirane, commemorating a great event in her life. What that event is I can't say, but I've *heard*,' she paused for emphasis, 'that there may be guests from Chaos.'

Andraia's heart seemed to twist and turn over under her ribs. Guests from Chaos . . . could that mean . . . ? Then fiercely she thrust the wild surmise down and with it the stab of mingled excitement and pain, turning her head away so that Lua shouldn't see her expression. 'Very well, Mother. If that's what Lady Pirane has said, of course I'll attend. And I'll try to enjoy it, to please her.'

'And me?' Lua asked drily.

Andraia gave in. Lua was, above all things, persistent. 'Yes, Mother,' she said. 'And to please you.'

Pirane had instructed that the festivities should begin at second moonrise, which tonight was shortly after midnight. Andraia could hear the strains of elegant but lively dance music from the great hall as she changed her gown for the fourth time and posed before the mirror to ensure that, at last, she was satisfied with her appearance. Lua had already gone to the hall with her two current paramours; she had tried to persuade Andraia to accompany them but Andraia preferred to follow in her own time. She told herself that she had no reason for wishing to arrive alone, no reason at all, but as she finally finished dressing and stepped out into the torchlit corridor she felt keyed-up with an excitement that was part hope and part dread.

The great hall was a glittering fantasy of light, sound and movement. Virtually every castle-dweller of rank had been invited, and the crowd ebbed and flowed like a living tide under the hall's shifting spectrum of light. Pirane had conjured elementals from the fire and water planes – their innate contradictions posed no problems for a skilled sorcerer – and the air shone and rippled with shades of blue and green and purple, creating the illusion of an underwater world, while streamers of cool fire danced between the walls and among the rafters. Servants wearing elaborate masks and with their bodies painted silver moved silently among the throng, bearing trays of wine and food, and under the eerie, ever-changing light the vast chamber was like something from a strange, drug-induced dream.

Crossing the hall's threshold between the open double doors, Andraia paused to allow her eyes and mind to absorb the scene. A silver figure glided to her and with a mute bow proffered a tray; she took a thin-stemmed glass, neither knowing nor caring what it contained, and gazed around. Pirane was at the far end of the hall, a statuesque and spectacular figure with her silver-tinged skin and blue-black hair; she was surrounded by admirers but seemed to have no particular consort tonight. Lua was among her party and had attracted a third young man; a short way off, Andraia's father, Qenever, was deep in discussion with Physician-Magus Croin, and their laughter as they shared a joke rose briefly above the music and its counterpoint of murmuring voices. Most of the other magi were here, too, with the exception of Vordegh himself, who disdained frivolity and preferred the austere solitude of his own apartments. Then among the crowd Andraia glimpsed unhuman faces and forms, and sharp excitement clutched at her and brought a tingling chill to her skin. *Was it possible?*

'Andraia.' A familiar voice spoke to her right and she turned quickly to find herself face to face with Savrinor. The historian was dressed entirely in white and the light playing across him and draining the colour from his pale hair made him look corpselike, almost spectral. A few paces behind him Iselia, in contrasting black and with her hair elaborately dressed, stood watching. The two women's eyes met and clashed briefly.

'Good evening, Master Savrinor.' Andraia bowed and Savrinor's eyebrows lifted a fraction, a silent comment on her formal attitude.

'Are you well?' he asked.

'Very well, thank you.' She sounded stilted, artificial; she sensed genuine concern behind his polite question and the fact that he *was* concerned made her irrationally angry. They hadn't met since the unhappy episode in the library and now the memory of that last encounter embarrassed Andraia deeply. She regretted having unburdened herself to Savrinor and wanted him to forget or at least ignore her lapse, as she was trying to do. Her gaze slipped sidelong, avoiding his steady scrutiny, and she waited for him to make his excuses and return to Iselia. But Savrinor had something more to say. He raised an elegant hand towards his mouth as though to suppress a cough, then the hand changed direction and he caught hold of her fingers before she could evade him. Resentfully Andraia's gaze flicked back to him and he smiled.

'You look very beautiful,' he told her. Then abruptly the smile vanished and he added in an undertone, 'And very sad.'

Andraia had been about to make the conventional response to a meaningless compliment, but this caught her completely unawares. She stared at him, and for a moment was on the verge of a furious rebuttal before she realized that whatever she might say would make no difference. Savrinor knew too much, and was too shrewd an observer, to be convinced by any pretence she might make, and Andraia's shoulders sagged as her anger and with it the combative impulse died.

'Sad?' She made herself smile at him. 'Well, perhaps. But sadness is only a transitory emotion, isn't it? It passes soon enough.'

'Like happiness?'

'Not necessarily.' She drained half the contents of her glass, realizing as she did so that it was a wine she didn't like. No matter. The effect would be the same, whatever the taste. Then, wanting to steer Savrinor away from dangerous waters, she asked carelessly, 'Do you know if there has been any word from Benetan?'

'None that I'm aware of.' A pause. 'You must miss him.'

'Yes.' For a few moments Andraia wrestled silently with herself, then abruptly, and more sharply than she'd intended, she added, 'My mother believes that Benetan's absence is the only reason for my . . . small travails. I don't want her – or anyone else, for that matter – to think that there might be any other considerations involved.' Now she looked at him, her eyes candid and challenging. 'I think you understand what I mean, Savrinor.'

'I understand. And of course you may rely on my discretion.'

She nodded. 'Thank you.'

He released her hand at last and took a step back. 'Perhaps I might claim the pleasure of a dance later?'

'Yes. Of course.' Again she waited for him to go but he still seemed reluctant, and she perceived that there was something else, something he was, perhaps, hesitant to say. Then suddenly the carefully neutral mask of his expression changed to a look that was acutely serious and, she realized, genuinely sympathetic. 'Andraia.' His light eyes held hers, intensely. 'I'm probably speaking out of turn, and if I am then I'll deserve anything and everything you might say to me. But if you had hoped to see . . . someone in particular tonight, then as a friend I'd advise you not to build on that hope.' He touched her hand again but gently this time, the lightest brush of his fingers. 'The Gate is open, but I don't think these festivities will be graced with the presence of those whom we both crave to have the privilege of meeting again.'

He knew; he had read her as though her mind were the pages of an open book. Andraia snatched her hand away and turned, quivering with rekindled anger and also with shame and the bitter sting of disillusionment.

'I'm sorry,' Savrinor said quietly, and she didn't know whether his words were an apology or referred to something else entirely. 'I thought only to save you pain.'

'As a friend?' Her voice was savage.

'As a friend.'

She heard the slight hush of his silk coat as he moved

72

away, but she counted slowly to fourteen before turning her head again. Savrinor had merged into the crowd by this time, but instead of following him Iselia had hung back. For the second time her gaze and Andraia's met. Iselia's eyes looked unnaturally bright and she wore an extraordinary expression in which curiosity, pique, dislike and something resembling contempt were all blended. Andraia felt a retaliatory stirring of anger as her old jealousies and uncertainties about Benetan and this girl abruptly surfaced, and suddenly, in the wake of Savrinor's misplaced attempt at kindness which she still didn't entirely trust, she felt intemperately spiteful.

Tilting her chin and giving a disdainful flick to the serpentine swathe of her close-fitting green gown, she moved gracefully towards the centre of the hall, cutting across Iselia's path and obliging her to step back. Briefly and obliquely she gave the fair girl a searing look, and her voice carried clearly to everyone in their immediate radius.

'How demure you look tonight, Iselia. I must say that black is a little ageing on you . . . but I imagine Savrinor does tend to have that effect on his women, while they last.'

She had the satisfaction of hearing someone suppress a snort of laughter, and didn't look back at Iselia's face as she walked away.

When Iselia trod on his foot for the third time and then swayed violently, Savrinor knew that matters had gone a little too far. With a world-weary air he led her out of the dance and beckoned a servant to bring wine.

'Drink this.' His voice was brusque.

She shook her head. 'No – no, thank you –'

'Drink it. I won't tell you again.' His eyes added cold emphasis to the warning and she reluctantly took the glass and forced herself to sip at its contents. Keeping his voice low, Savrinor added, 'I know what you took before we came to the celebration, and you've let it get out of hand. The wine should antidote it to a degree; enough at least to stop you from making a complete public spectacle of yourself.'

She gazed at him over the glass's rim. Her eyes didn't seem to be focusing properly. 'I'm so *hot* . . .' she said unsteadily.

'You would be. It's a common side-effect during the early days of addiction.' Savrinor wasn't in a mood to unbend but suddenly the deeper feelings underlying his indifferent façade got the better of him. 'Are you really such a fool?' he demanded in a harsh whisper. 'I warned you about the consequences of Moonwrack when you first started helping yourself to the contents of my cupboard – and I credited you with enough intelligence to listen!'

Iselia blinked slowly. Contrary to what he had told her, the wine was making matters worse. Something was wrong with the dimensions of the hall, and the music and the cool elemental flames seemed to be swelling and fading by turns.

'It . . .' she said, lost the thread of her thoughts, pulled them back together with an effort and tried again. 'It's no more than you indulge in yourself, Savrinor.'

'Don't use that piteous tone; you know I find it irritating. Yes, I indulge as you do, and a great deal more. But I'm fifteen years your senior, and I'm also intelligent enough and skilled enough to keep my pleasures under my own control! I am *not* a half-fledged and half-witted trull who needs to put her fingers in a fire to find out whether or not fire hurts!'

Iselia said, '*Hurts?*' then to her horror realized that she had been about to hurl the truth at him, to shout in his face that she *needed* the drugs she took, needed their numbing euphoria to make her life with him, and the things he demanded of her, bearable. For one terrifying moment as

74

she floundered to a halt she thought that she had given herself away. But quickly she realized that though Savrinor's eyes had narrowed and he was staring hard at her, he had put the wrong interpretation on her smothered outburst.

'Yes, *hurts*,' he said savagely. 'You may not know it yet, you may be too naive and too ignorant to understand, but what you are doing, and the way you're doing it, will hurt you if you don't start taking greater care. More to the point, it will damage you. And I'll warn you now, I have no interest in goods that are damaged beyond repair!'

That stung her, he saw immediately, and to his own surprise Savrinor instantly regretted saying it. The barbed words had come with a calculated ease born of long habit, and his peers, who knew him – and knew his tongue – would have shrugged them off. Perhaps by now Iselia also knew him well enough to realize that his cruelty didn't run deep, but all the same he wished he had kept silent, and the realization, and what it might imply, threw him.

'Damn you,' he said. 'Finish your wine and drink my glass too. It's souring on my tongue.' It was near as he could bring himself to an apology; he was angry with her and with himself. 'When did you last eat?'

'This morning,' she answered in a small voice.

'I see. A basic lesson – don't swallow your pretty potions and then neglect food. It's a dangerous habit and one to be avoided.' His eyes raked her briefly. 'You're becoming thin. It doesn't suit you.' A pause. 'Are you feeling any better?'

She shook her head.

'Then you'd best sit down for a while. Over there, where there are chairs.'

'I'd rather go outside –'

'No. Sit where I tell you, fill a plate with food – anything, it doesn't matter – and eat it. *Make* yourself eat it, or you'll answer to me. Do I make myself clear?'

Feeling too weak and disorientated to argue, Iselia inclined her head in silent acquiescence. Savrinor watched her slow progress across the hall, saw her stop a servant and take a dish from his tray. Then, satisfied but very far from content, he turned and walked away in search of someone or something to divert him from his innermost thoughts.

She didn't touch the food, but she drank two more glasses of wine and after a while they gave her at least an illusion of improvement. The celebration was still in its early stages; no one was flagging yet and so to her relief the other seats ranged under the tall windows remained unoccupied. Iselia pressed her head back against the wall's cool black stone, closing her eyes and trying to will her spinning mind back to an even keel. She had known she was taking a risk tonight by drinking a second dose of Moonwrack, and moreover she had augmented it with a pinch of a brown powder – she didn't know its name – that had power to dull the physical senses. She had no idea what effect the two drugs might have together and hadn't cared at the time, for she had known what Savrinor had in store for her. Usually when there was some revel in the castle he preferred to wait until they returned from the festivities before taking his pleasure with her, and sometimes, especially if she succeeded in plying him with more than he usually drank, he was too tired and too indolent for anything more than sleep. Tonight, though, he had locked the outer door of their rooms shortly after sunset, and when he coolly told her what he wanted from her she had turned first to the Moonwrack and later to the powder as a desperate resort. Now she remembered little of what had taken place, but she was paying the price for that comfort. She felt so sick that even the faint smell of the food which she had set down on an empty chair beside her made her stomach churn, and she tried to distract herself with the sounds around her in an effort to force the nausea away. Voices and music flowed past her in waves; their effect was hypnotic and oddly soothing, and after a few minutes she began to drift towards sleep. She was poised on the edge of a dream when an abrupt burst of laughter close at hand broke the spell and wrenched her mind back to reality with a jolt that set her stomach lurching again. Iselia opened her eyes . . . and froze.

Several gorgeously-dressed people had just swept elegantly past her chair. It was their laughter that had roused her but Iselia didn't even notice their amused glances in her direction. What arrested her was the sight of the tall and disturbingly handsome man who walked alone a few paces behind them. The mane of hair flowing over his shoulders and down his back was the colour of pure gold; he wore a sea-green cloak which seemed to move with independent life, and his face above the cloak collar had an unhuman edge in the eldritch light. He wasn't looking in Iselia's direction but suddenly he seemed to become aware of her shocked stare. His head turned, and quick curiosity lit his vivid blue eyes.

Then he smiled faintly, and the colour of his eyes changed first to crimson and then to black.

Savrinor had once taken Iselia to a revel attended by Yandros of Chaos but she had been unaware then of the god's presence and so did not recognize him now. Yet in a deep, atavistic part of her mind she knew the nature of the man – the *creature* – who met her gaze with such mild but ominous interest. In that one instant she felt that her soul's innermost secrets had been plundered, and terror punched up into her consciousness. *If he could see all that she was, then he would see all she had done and all she planned to do –*

Terror became panic, and on panic's heels the nausea

came back and hit her with enormous force. Iselia careened to her feet, knocking her untouched plate of food sideways as her world turned to a reeling turmoil of uncontrollable sickness. Stumbling, her face stark white, she groped towards the doors. People made way for her and surprised faces swam before her eyes, but she registered nothing beyond the desperate need to get out of the hall.

The doors stood open and a draught of cool air met her as she staggered over the threshold and into the corridor. A few revellers watched, but their interest was brief; on these occasions there were always a few who misjudged their capacity for drink or other stimulants, and one young fool's undignified flight was nothing remarkable. Savrinor, by now at the far end of the hall, saw none of it, and Yandros only augmented his smile with a faint snort of amusement. He neither knew nor cared who the girl in black with her pinched, taut face might be. She had caught his eye for a moment but his interest didn't extend beyond an acknowledgement of her presence and, now, a flicker of condescending pity. Having decided on a moment's whim to attend Pirane's celebration, he had more diverting business here.

But as Yandros turned away, someone else was still observing. Andraia was among a group of her friends, making an effort as she had promised her mother but still feeling distracted and, after the encounter with Savrinor, ruffled into the bargain. Glimpsing the small commotion she looked up in time to see Iselia running from the hall, and her interest abruptly quickened. Something amiss with little Lady Purity? She glanced around but saw no sign of Savrinor. Not his doing then but something else, and the old suspicions which Andraia had never quite resolved and never quite banished reared their heads again . . .

Iselia was vanishing through the double doors. Andraia didn't pause to examine her reaction too closely – if she was motivated by anything beyond simple curiosity then she didn't want to acknowledge it at present – but made a quick excuse to her companions and left them, threading her way through the crowd in the fair girl's wake. Qenever saw her and waved to attract her attention but she ignored him, reached the doors and slipped through just in time to see a flicker of black skirt disappearing into a side passage. That way, she knew, led only to a small door giving on to the courtyard, and Andraia set off in pursuit.

The flame of a nearby wall-torch dipped and guttered in a sudden draught, and as she turned the corner Andraia felt a rush of cold air that told her the door at the far end had been opened. She proceeded more cautiously, alert for any sound or movement, but when the door came in sight after another sharp turn there was no sign of Iselia.

Andraia slowed her steps and halted, feeling faintly ridiculous. She couldn't imagine what she had hoped to accomplish by following Iselia; couldn't even imagine, now, why she had given way to the impulse at all. Whatever was wrong with the girl was no concern of hers and could be no concern of Benetan's, either, since Benetan was hundreds of miles away. Better if she returned to the celebrations now, before she made a fool of herself.

She turned – then stopped again as her ears caught a sound from beyond the door. An ugly retching, muffled as though someone was trying to disguise or suppress it. And a word – a name – gasped out in a desperate plea.

'*Aeoris . . .*'

The name rang a sharp little bell in Andraia's mind and she tried to recall why. Iselia's mysterious husband? No, for not even Savrinor seemed to know his name. But it *was* familiar.

And then she placed it.

Her skin crawled and suddenly she knew that she was not being foolish. She kicked off her shoes, snatched them up and began to move quickly but warily towards the door. It stood wide open; beyond it the courtyard was stippled with night-shadows as the two moons gleamed dimly through a thickening overcast, and on silent feet Andraia reached the door and peered cautiously out.

Iselia's pale hair gave her away in the darkness which might otherwise have hidden her. She was huddled against the courtyard wall, clinging for support to a conduit-pipe that ran down from the roof to a drain, and her shoulders heaved as she retched helplessly and fruitlessly over the drain-hole. With every spasm she moaned, and Andraia heard her voice gasping out a miserable litany.

'*Aeoris ... oh, sweet Aeoris, help me ... oh, dear gods ...*'

Very, very slowly Andraia withdrew from the doorway. Her pulse was racing thickly, so loud in her ears that she feared Iselia would hear it. *Aeoris* – the heretics' patron, ruler of the exiled demons of Order. Oh, she knew about Aeoris, she had heard of him many times during her years of schooling and, later, from her father when he talked of his work. First Magus Vordegh had embarked on a ferocious campaign to unearth and eradicate the followers of that evil power – and now it seemed that one of their number was in their very midst, in the person of Savrinor's little paramour.

Wildly Andraia swung round and started to run back towards the great hall. Her instant urge was to find Savrinor and tell him everything, but as she reached the main corridor a new thought slammed into her mind and made her stop dead. Iselia was a heretic – but who else might be implicated in her schemings? Not Savrinor himself; that was an impossibility, for Savrinor was the gods' most loyal servant and couldn't know that he was harbouring a traitor. But there might be others. Or *one* other.

The idea of it sent a wave of dizzy sickness through

Andraia and she leaned hard against the wall, colour draining from her face under the cosmetics she had so carefully applied. Not Benetan. Yandros, please, not Benetan! He couldn't be so blind, so *mad*, as to have become entangled in that web –

'He *can't!*' She uttered the denial aloud, startling herself and thankful a moment later that there was no one in earshot. But the lapse had the effect of bringing her mind sharply back into focus. *Be rational*, she told herself. Benetan was no heretic. She knew him too well, she would have seen the signs and he wasn't a good liar. Unlike Iselia. But was Iselia using him in some way? Might she have manipulated him without his knowledge? Suddenly Andraia remembered the circumstances under which Benetan had taken his present commission. It had been her own idea, a chance to put distance between Benetan and Iselia in the hope of dousing the rekindled fire of his old attachment. But Savrinor had connived with her. Why? Who had persuaded the historian to help, when he had so little to gain from the scheme? It was a wild surmise, a straw in the wind, but suspicion was piling on suspicion now and Andraia's mind raced on down that road. Iselia, influencing Savrinor – who against all reason seemed to be besotted with her – to get what *she* wanted for Benetan, then using her wiles again to persuade Benetan himself to . . . to what? Carry a message? Perform some task? Or, wittingly or not, warn the heretic leaders of the First Magus's plans?

Andraia didn't believe that Benetan knew of Iselia's secret allegiance. He might suspect, but he couldn't *know*. But if Iselia were unmasked, no protestations of innocence would be enough to protect him. One word to Lord Vordegh, one hint of a link between the heretic girl and the Chaos riders' captain, and Benetan would be judged as guilty as she was. Andraia knew something of the methods the magi used in dealing with transgressors, and sweat broke out on her skin and trickled coldly down her body under the sheath of her gown. Not only Benetan would be condemned but Savrinor too, as Iselia's mentor – and perhaps even she herself would fall with them, damned by the mere fact that she and Benetan were lovers.

'Oh, gods –' Then Andraia choked the words off and put a hand to her mouth. There was no one she could turn to. Not her father, not her mother, and certainly not Magus Pirane. Only Savrinor might have the skill to help her. But to convince him of the truth was more than she could hope to do –

'Andraia?'

The voice was so unexpected that Andraia squeaked and almost tripped over the hem of her skirt as she spun round.

Savrinor was standing behind her. Andraia's eyes widened and she stared at him as though he were an apparition. Her mouth worked but no sound came from her throat.

'My dear, are you ill?' Savrinor was nonplussed by her reaction and started forward, extending a solicitous hand. 'Is something wrong?'

'No!' The word came out sharply and at a high pitch. Andraia snatched back her self-control and did her best to disguise the lapse as a cough. 'No,' she repeated more calmly, though she knew her voice was shaking. 'Not at all.' She forced an artificial smile. 'I might ask you the same question. Are you tired of the festivities already?'

Her performance was unconvincing, and normally Savrinor's curiosity would have been aroused and he would have pursued her with further questions. But he had other preoccupations.

'I'm looking for Iselia,' he said. 'I gather she left the hall in some haste.'

'Yes . . .' Andraia glanced back in the direction of the courtyard door. 'Yes, I saw her. She seemed unwell.' She nodded towards the passage turning. 'I think you'll find her in the courtyard. She'll probably need help.'

Savrinor's mouth compressed into a hard, angry line. 'I see.' He made a bow; it wasn't in his nature to forget the courtesies under any circumstances. 'Thank you,' he added, and walked away towards the passage.

Andraia was watching from a vantage-point near the hall doors when Iselia was helped from the courtyard. She was apparently barely conscious, sagging between two expressionless servants, and the front of her dress was stained. Savrinor, tight-lipped and clearly furious, walked ahead of the small procession, but the cause of his anger was obvious and the small hope Andraia had been harbouring died. Even in extremity Iselia had clearly been too wary to let anything slip, and Savrinor hadn't divined her secret. The four figures disappeared in the direction of the upper floor and with a small sigh Andraia returned to the hall.

Savrinor was gone for some while, and when he returned the pupils of his eyes were unnaturally enlarged and there was a faint beading of sweat on his forehead. The celebration was becoming more tumultuous by now, though Magus Pirane was nowhere to be seen, and Savrinor found Andraia looking isolated and a little lost in the midst of the revelry. He went up to her and put a hand on her shoulder, his fingers tracing the graceful curve of her neck with a familiarity he would not have risked without the new stimulus of his drugs.

'I think we both need a little comfort tonight,' he said.

Andraia sensed the complexity of emotions behind his quiet statement; anger still, and disappointment and worry, and a measure of new bitterness underlying all. It struck an answering chord in her and she set her plate down and leaned fractionally back towards him, a gesture that invited his hand to stay.

'Dance with me,' Savrinor suggested gently.

'For the show of it?' She turned to look at him and her smile let him know that the question stemmed from empathy rather than challenge.

'Something like that.' Savrinor returned the smile, and under the dreamy look induced by the narcotic she saw that there was deep, suppressed pain in his eyes; the pain of something that he couldn't quite grasp and couldn't quite understand. 'As you said so perceptively a little earlier, sadness is a transitory emotion and passes soon enough. Perhaps we can both persuade ourselves to believe that for a little while.'

They joined the more sedate of the dancers at the far end of the hall. As they became part of the pattern, moving gracefully and privately to the strains of the slow music, Andraia rested her head on Savrinor's shoulder and gazed with a curiously blind stare at the sea of light and colour shifting around her. This new intimacy with Savrinor wasn't the comfort she wanted but it was comfort of a kind, and she sensed that he felt as she did. The knowledge made her ache inwardly, a feeling of loss and yearning that she couldn't comprehend but which brought tears pricking hotly. She shut her eyes, refusing to give way to emotions which could have no foundation, and pressed her cheek closer against Savrinor's hair. Pale hair. Pale, not black. Not black, like Benetan's and like . . . like . . .

Her lips formed a name, but silently, and she prayed for the music and the movement and the gentle hypnosis of the dance to carry her away.

CHAPTER VI

'Away?' Lua looked at Andraia with blank incomprehension.

Andraia smiled innocently back at her. 'Yes, Mother.'

'But *where?*'

Andraia shrugged. 'I've nowhere particular in mind. I'd simply like to see a little more of the world, and with Benetan gone this seems like a good opportunity to indulge my fancy.'

The words 'indulge my fancy' went some way towards allaying Lua's suspicions, as Andraia had anticipated, and her mother made a small, careless gesture.

'Well, if that's what you want, my dear, then I have no reason to object. Although I can't imagine what you should be so eager to *see*, unless you've suddenly developed an inexplicable fascination for landscapes. They're about all the rest of the world has to offer, and I'd hardly call them worthwhile entertainment.'

'I'm sure that's true, Mother. But a number of my friends have been travelling lately. It's becoming quite fashionable, and I don't like to feel that I'm being left behind.' She smiled at her own unintended pun. 'Literally or metaphorically.'

Lua hadn't heard that there was a new vogue for travel and wondered if Andraia was being disingenuous. But then again, it was almost impossible to keep abreast of the ever-changing fads and fancies of the young generation. Doubtless this was some small infatuation which would run its course within a month or two.

Unless Andraia had another motive?

She turned away, touching her hair to see that it was smooth, and asked with apparent casualness, 'Well, go then, and with my blessing. Do you mean to travel alone?'

'I . . . don't know yet. Does it matter?'

'No-o. I simply wondered if you had a companion in mind.' Lua turned, lifting her eyebrows to add an interrogative, and Andraia realized instantly the direction in which her thoughts had turned.

'No, Mother,' she said. 'I don't think Savrinor will be coming with me.'

'Ah.' Lua couldn't quite hide her disappointment. She had seen Andraia and Savrinor dancing together last night and had hoped that it might herald the start of a new diversion for Andraia. She couldn't say that she liked the historian — few people actually *liked* him — but Savrinor was high-ranking, witty and cultured. Handsome too, in his own fastidious way, and even if his predilections were a little strange that would present no problem to a girl of Andraia's sophistication. Above all he would be a *suitable* lover; far more suitable than that vulgar Chaos rider. But she knew better than to press Andraia on the subject and so only said, 'It's as you please, of course. I merely thought that you might find it a little less tedious to travel with a companion than alone.'

'I'm sure I shall manage. Besides, I don't intend to be away for long.' Andraia made a play of stretching her arms and pretending a yawn. 'It will simply be a change. And I feel that a change will do me good.'

Andraia was deeply relieved when at last she was able to escape from her mother's scrutiny and questions to the sanctuary of her own room. She knew very well that Lua hadn't been entirely convinced by her protestations, but she hadn't raised any objections to Andraia's plan and that was all that mattered.

86

In truth, Andraia had no intention of allowing anyone to accompany her on her planned journey. She would have to make some concessions to propriety, of course, such as ensuring that suitable accommodation was found for her under an overlord's roof; not to do so would be unthinkable for the sake of her own safety if for no other reason. Her mother would probably also insist that she should take a personal maid to see to her needs. But a maid would do what she was told, while Andraia's rank and manner were enough to deal with any overlord who might try to curtail her activities. She had a plan and it was simple. She intended to follow the road Benetan had taken, and find him.

She had made the decision in the early hours of the morning as she lay alone in her bed, wrestling with her confused emotions. The brief empathy she had shared with Savrinor had led to nothing more; they had both known at the time that it would not and neither of them had considered any other possibility for a moment. But the encounter had been a catalyst of a kind, and in the cold, bleak silence as she waited for dawn to break, Andraia had known that the time had come for the conflicts and uncertainties to be resolved. Benetan, and Benetan alone, must be told the truth about Iselia. *If he loves me,* she had said to herself, *he will help me to find a way to unmask her without putting himself and our future in jeopardy. And if he loves her more than he loves me . . . well, then I'll know the worst. And that, surely, must be better than continuing to live an illusion.*

For all her fiery nature, Andraia was not good at hating. Her temper was quick and her angers fierce, but they rarely endured for long and she forgave as readily as she vilified. But the feelings she had for Iselia *were* feelings of hatred; a deep, savage, wounding hatred that nothing could assuage. Iselia was no mere rival; she was a bane, a cancer, eating at the foundations of all that Andraia held dear. Iselia cared nothing for Benetan — how could she when her life was devoted to the foul heretic cult? — but she was using him, twisting his mind and heart, leading him into terrible danger and not caring what might become of him as a result of her scheming. Savrinor, too, was entangled in the web she was spinning, and Iselia would doubtless cast aside his life just as carelessly when it suited her purpose. If all else failed, Andraia thought with a knife-twist of bitterness, if Benetan would not help her and Savrinor stayed blind to the truth, then she believed that she hated Iselia enough to overcome scruple and aversion and kill the blonde girl with her own hands.

Either that, or turn for help to the one being in whom she might dare to put her absolute trust.

Last night Andraia had tried to pray to the gods. But any words she might have used had died on her tongue as, with an icy shock, she realized the terrible paradox inherent in what she was about to do. How could she pray to the seven lords of Chaos when she had known one of those lords as a lover? Though she still revered and loved the gods as deeply as any true servant of Chaos, with Tarod she had tasted another kind of intimacy. He had closed the gulf between worshipper and worshipped, and to pray now would be to recreate that gulf and put a distance between them once more. However foolish, however futile, Andraia couldn't bring herself to take that step. But even if she was incapable of asking the gods' help through prayer, surely she might still turn to Tarod in her trouble, without jeopardizing Benetan's life?

She had put the possibility and its implications out of her mind, too uncertain — and perhaps too afraid — to allow herself to consider it. But the thought of how Tarod might deal with the matter of Iselia kindled a small and savagely comforting flame inside her as she began to make her plans for the journey south. An afternoon with her father, Qenever, provided her with details of the major over-lordships and their locations, and she requisitioned a junior clerk to work out how far Benetan was likely to have trav-elled since his departure. The answer she received pleased her, for it seemed that within a few more days Benetan was likely to reach one particularly large demesne that lay under the control of one of the land's wealthiest overlords. This overlord owned an imposing mansion, commanded what amounted to a virtual army of militiamen, and had a reputation as a highly convivial host. It would be hard to make a better choice or one more likely to allay Lua's suspicions. A servant could be despatched via the Maze to forewarn the overlord of her arrival, and she herself would follow in ... she calculated the time needed to prepare and pack ... say, three days. All things considered, matters couldn't have worked out more conveniently.

But she had reckoned without Magus Pirane.

It was Lua, of course, who told Pirane of Andraia's plans, at the same time confiding her own disappointment at the lack of any further developments between her daugh-ter and Savrinor. Pirane, who knew many more of Andraia's secrets than Lua did, was neither disappointed nor surprised and told Lua so, adding with some asperity that anyone who tried to inveigle either Andraia or Savrinor into anything against their wishes was a fool or an opti-mist, or more likely both. Pirane suspected that Andraia's desire to travel was prompted as much by the wish to get away from her mother's efforts to pair her off as by anything else, and she sympathized. So when a new report from Secretary Qenever's office was sent to her for attention the magus decided to kill two birds with one arrow, so to speak, and offer Andraia something a little more entertaining than a sojourn under a mere overlord's roof.

When she received Pirane's note, Andraia didn't at first believe that chance could have played such a vicious joke on her. Again and again she read the message and its invitation, but no amount of willing could change a word of it or rescue her own plans from ruin. A small matter, Pirane said; some temporary and doubtless greatly exaggerated outbreak of subversion in a fruit-growing district a little west of Andraia's intended destination. But the local overlord was entreating the magi for help and so it was necessary, if tiresome, to investigate. Pirane had decided to visit the area in person, creating a citadel for her private use, and she would be delighted if Andraia would consent to accompany her.

The word 'consent' was, Andraia knew, a matter of form and nothing more. The magi rarely travelled, and when they did they scorned any lodging that the overlords could offer but instead used their sorcery to conjure the citadels. Part palace and part fortress, the citadels were created from the Chaotic fabric of the castle itself, and anyone housed within their walls could enjoy all the familiar luxuries of the Star Peninsula. To be invited into a citadel was a great honour, and anything other than immediate acceptance was out of the question. Perhaps Pirane only thought to do Andraia a kindness or perhaps she had a deeper and more astute motive, but either way Andraia's plans were in ashes. She composed her reply, forcing herself to express a gratitude and eagerness she didn't feel. A servant was dispatched to carry the note to Pirane, and when the girl had curtsied and left, Andraia clenched her fists and pounded the writing-table until the force of her frustration sent an ink-pot skidding off the surface to upend on the floor. For what seemed like a long time but was in fact no more than a few seconds Andraia stared at the resulting black flood as her rage collapsed into mute, helpless misery. Then, knowing that she could only bow to the inevitable, she rose to her feet and went slowly to her clothes-chest, to begin her preparations for the journey.

For all his strange tastes and stranger reputation, in all his life Savrinor had never hit a woman. Engendering fear and pain was a refined art which, when perfected by a subtle mind, gave the shadowy depths of pleasure an entirely new dimension, but Savrinor's predilections were sly, delicate, sophisticated, and governed by his own singular but unwavering code of ethics. To strike out in anger was an unthinkable travesty – and the shock that went through him as Iselia recovered her balance and put a hand to her bleeding mouth jolted him to the core.

Yandros, what had he *done?* The fury had surged so fast that there had been no time to stop it, let alone analyse what lay behind it. Her face, pallid and drawn by the after-effects of sickness and the drugs, her eyes dull and haunted; above all the foolish, reckless *ignorance* that had lured her like a moth to a flame, tottering in pursuit of the narcotic dreams that were fast becoming the only reality she craved. He had tried to reason with her, thinking that the aftermath of last night's excesses would at last have taught her the lesson his words had failed to teach. Hadn't he warned her so many times, so *many* times, not to play with fire unless she first learned how to quench the flames if they threatened to get out of control? He could have helped her, would have, and gladly. But no; she thought she had no need of advice or guidance or protection. And it was as he uttered the word *protection* that Iselia, who until that moment had shown no interest and no reaction, laughed.

It wasn't the laughter itself that had been the catalyst. Savrinor would have shrugged that off as easily as brushing a speck of dust from his sleeve. It was the timbre of her voice that triggered the frustration and the fury and the fear within him; the shrill, hollow *emptiness* of it, like something insensate responding by reflex alone to a stimulus which it neither understood nor even truly felt. Without any conscious command from his brain, Savrinor's arm came up and he struck her, back-handed, across the face.

She hadn't cried. He had expected her to, had even hoped for it, not because it would have pleased him but because it would at least have been a human reaction. But she only rocked backwards in the bed, then steadied herself and covered the trickle of blood at the edge of her mouth, turning her head away so that he couldn't see her expression. She said nothing but he felt the psychic shrinking, the invisible barrier that put her beyond his reach, and suddenly he knew that he couldn't let it stay at this or it would fester in his blood and bones like gangrene.

'Iselia . . .' His voice had aged twenty years. She didn't respond in any way. She was like a statue, utterly self-contained. 'Oh, gods . . . I didn't mean it, Iselia. Iselia, my . . . my love, please . . . forgive me!'

Iselia turned her head then and looked at him. Her lip was cut; an emerald ring on his middle finger had caught her and Savrinor wanted to tear the ring off and grind it to dust under his heel. Her eyes, vast and unnaturally bright in the white oval of her face, regarded him steadily, and for a moment he thought he saw a terrible challenge in her gaze. But it was an illusion – could only have been an illusion – and it vanished.

'Of course,' she said softly. 'Yes, of course. I forgive you, Savrinor. And I understand.'

He hadn't touched her. He had only sat on the edge of the bed, gazing back at her, his pale eyes hunted and – something new, quite new in her experience of Savrinor – bewildered. And in that moment Iselia knew that at long last she had trapped him. He loved her. She hadn't dared to be sure of it until now, but this burst of real and desperate anger, and the plea for forgiveness that followed, was final proof. *My love*, he had said. Words that in all likelihood he had never uttered before in his life. Savrinor was caught, and now she could use him as she was already using Benetan, to further the cause that was her sole reason for staying alive. And for Savrinor, she had a special place in her heart. Two others already dwelt there; Kaldar, whom she loved with the same fierce passion with which she served her gods, and Benetan, as an old friend who might still be swayed from the evil that had infected him during his years in the castle. But Iselia had other plans for Savrinor. One way or another, by whatever means she could devise, she wanted *revenge*.

Kaldar forced himself not to listen to his conscience as he crested the ridge and began to walk down the last, long path that would lead him to the harbour. The sky was cloudless tonight and the first moon hung close to the western horizon, its light diffusing the sharper glitter of the stars overhead and showing him the way without need of a lantern. A breeze was blowing off the land, carrying the scent of dry grass, and the sea below and before him was a quiet, dark mirror broken only by the occasional white lick of small waves breaking as they found their way inshore.

It still felt strange to be walking alone at night without the constant fear of challenge at the back of his mind, and stranger still to see the stone harbour and the ships beyond unguarded. Kaldar had lived most of his life under the constant censorious gaze of authority in one form or another and still couldn't entirely accustom himself to the freedoms of Summer Isle. Freedom was a heady wine, and even the knowledge that he was in one sense about to abuse that freedom, and the trust that went with it, couldn't banish the excitement that stirred within him.

There were twelve vessels moored in the harbour now, from a three-master with sails furled and rigging stark against the sky to a tiny, one-man craft that even to Kaldar's inexperienced eye looked barely seaworthy. He had made his choice after an earlier observation, and now moved to where a long-snouted cutter with a single mast and boom rocked on the tide's slight swell. In his short time here Kaldar had learned enough about the rudiments of sailing to feel sure that with a calm sea and following wind he could handle this boat well enough for his purposes, and the fact that tonight's conditions were little short of perfect gave him additional confidence in the venture. Reaching the cutter, he paused and looked back. From here he could see to the crest of the hill. The path was deserted and the skyline unbroken. Good; his departure had disturbed no one, and by the time the first early risers woke he would be long gone.

He wished that he hadn't had to deceive Simbrian, but there had been no other way. The sorcerer was adamant about the matter of Benetan, and no amount of reason or pleading would persuade him to change his mind. Caution was vital, of course, but Kaldar, who knew Benetan well, was certain that Simbrian had made the wrong decision. And even if he took no action, as he had agreed at least for the time being, Benetan was still in danger. It would take only one zealous devotee, one swift attack; a solitary man, however skilled a fighter, would make an easy target. In Kaldar's view Benetan had too much potential value to the cause for such a risk to be taken – and the fact that he was also Iselia's only friend in her present predicament added a sharper urgency. Kaldar had no choice, he felt, but to take matters into his own hands.

It had been easy enough to discover Benetan's

whereabouts, for scrying was one of Kaldar's strongest talents. The Chaos rider was at present heading towards a certain district in the south-west; perilous territory for him, as Simbrian and his followers had a particularly strong coterie of friends there. And there was a further complication, for time was now running out in the matter of the First Magus's ruthless edict. In another eight days the reports would be collected and presented at the Star Peninsula, and for every overlord who had no information to give, twenty-one innocent people would be burned to death. Kaldar was enough of a realist to know that Order's servants could do nothing to avert this savage barbarity; but when the executions were carried out, as they surely would be, Benetan's chances of survival would become slimmer still. Kaldar only hoped that he could travel fast enough to find his old friend before anyone else did.

The tide was low and still ebbing, and a rough ladder led down from the jetty wall to the water level. Kaldar dropped the bag he was carrying – just a few provisions; he'd need nothing more – into the cutter and climbed down after it. He untied the mooring rope, then unshipped one of the long oars and used it to fend the boat away from the jetty. As the slight swell drew the craft towards open water he looked back again, his eyes intent in the darkness. What Simbrian would do when he found out about this he didn't know and preferred not to speculate. He had left a note explaining as much as he felt was judicious, but it wouldn't go far towards assuaging the sorcerer's wrath. Well, he'd cross that particular river when he came to it. In the meantime he felt that what he was doing was not only right but necessary, and he would defend his actions before Lord Aeoris himself if he had to.

There was a strong current just beyond the harbour and the cutter nosed into it, beginning to pick up speed. Kaldar hauled up the sail and, with one hand on the tiller and the other holding the ropes, settled himself in the stern. A pattern of stars near the horizon gave him his bearings; he turned the boat north-westward, and offered a prayer to Aeoris for protection and good fortune as the sails began to fill.

CHAPTER VII

Benetan knew that he was walking an increasingly narrow path between safety and disaster, and with every day that passed it was growing harder to maintain his fragile balance. And on nights like this, as he sat in the small room under the eaves of the drinking-house, the thought of the gamble he was taking and the price he would pay if it failed brought him out in a shivering sweat that nothing could allay.

Time was running out. In just a few more days Lord Vordegh would send the Chaos riders on their mission to collect the overlords' evidence against the heretics, and then the executions would begin. When that happened, Benetan knew that he would be hard pressed to keep his own skin intact.

He had no doubt now that the number of heretic sympathizers was far greater than the magi dreamed. The clues were small but legion, and the further south he travelled the stronger the sense of unease and the undercurrent of tension in the land had become. He had heard of incidents – minor, and quickly crushed, but numerous enough to be significant. Tithes resisted, tolls refused, quiet reprisals taken against the servants of oppressive overlords . . . the gathering storm that he had sensed so sharply further north was beginning to bring a little rain. Counted among the disaffected were not only peasants but traders, farmers, even a few militiamen whose consciences rebelled against their masters' worst excesses. And for the first time their grievances had a single focus, in the form of the shadowy and mysterious sorcerer who was mustering both power and disciples to the cause of Order.

Benetan had heard the sorcerer referred to by five different names, all of them known to the magi and all of them false, and he had also heard rumours that he was presently in the far west, the far east, the heartlands and a dimension beyond the world and beyond the reach of the forces of Chaos. All those tales were untrue, as was the legend that on the day decreed for execution of the hostages the rebel leader would rise with a great army and smash the regime of the magi and their overlords. Iselia had told Benetan that Simbrian Tarkran had no such power and no such intent, but the stories were like kindling, feeding the embers of sedition. The executions could be the spark – quite literally, Benetan thought with an inward shudder – that ignited the embers into flames.

And if Order's devotees wanted vengeance, and were ready to take it where they could, their hunters had one quarry already in their sights. For Benetan was known to them. And he knew in his turn that he was being followed.

The shadows had been a constant presence in the background since he had left Overlord Tanneler's demesne. Not one single follower – whoever had set this surveillance in train knew their art too well to make such an elementary mistake – but a succession. A man on horseback, face obscured by a loose-brimmed hat, who overtook him as though in a great hurry only to be glimpsed loitering a mile or two on. A wagon loaded with bales of straw, plodding creakily in his wake while the youth on the driver's box fixed him with a blank stare that wasn't as half-witted as it seemed. Others, some riding, some on foot. Benetan had checked each one by means of a small subterfuge and in each case was left in little doubt of their purpose. Thanks to the incident with Tanneler's steward he had made contact, however tenuous, with Simbrian Tarkran's followers.

He should have been elated by this development – it was, after all, what he had wanted – but under the present circumstances Benetan's feelings were closer to fear than to triumph, and the reassurances that Iselia had given him that night on the beach below the castle stack now rang a little hollow. There would be no risk, she had said; but that was not true. At this moment, alone as he was and without the sorcery of the magi or the sheer physical presence of his own riders to call on, Benetan knew that he was in danger. With feelings running high and ready to erupt, it would be a grave mistake to assume that the heretics were interested only in tracking his movements, and it would take only one word, one command from some secret headquarters in the district, for a swift ambush to be mounted and his life to be ended by an arrow in the back or a knife-blade across the throat.

He could take no chances. Since leaving the Star Peninsula he had spent a good few nights camping in the open, but that was out of the question now. His options were either a lockable room at a drinking house or, if the distance between settlements was too great to cover in a day, a makeshift eyrie in a tree where no one could approach him silently as he slept. So far he had been reasonably lucky and had only suffered two such wakeful and uncomfortable nights. But this was the heartland, well populated and relatively civilized. Further south, as the nature of the country began to change again, matters would be very different.

To complicate matters further, First Magus Vordegh would be expecting a report from him before too long. There was, in theory, no time limit on his mission, but Benetan knew very well that Vordegh wasn't the most patient of men. Several times he had thought of writing a message but on each occasion had realized that, without something more concrete to say, any account would look at best unsatisfactory and at worst suspicious. And now, with Order's devotees watching him, any attempt to communicate with the magi could be downright hazardous into the bargain.

The tavern was busy tonight, and the rumble of voices from the taproom directly below seemed set to go on into the small hours. Earlier, Benetan had ordered a meal to be brought to his room, and the tray was still set on the table in front of him. He'd hardly touched it, for the meat was tough and the vegetables had had the life boiled out of them, but his stomach was gnawing with hunger as well as tension, and after drinking the best part of a jug of sour wine he was reaching the stage where any food was better than none. Picking up a piece of meat and fastidiously shaking off the scraps of soggy greenery that clung to it, he got to his feet and, chewing mechanically, went to the window. There was a curtain of sorts, and he lifted it aside to look down into the stable yard.

The bay horse was still there. Benetan pulled a shard of bone from between two teeth and let the curtain fall again, satisfied that the man who had followed him tonight intended to stay at the tavern for as long as his quarry did. For a moment he was sharply tempted to go down to the taproom, pick the man out — which would be easy enough — and suggest that for the sake of his own skin he might care to move on. But he forced the impulse down, reminding himself yet again that this tenuous contact was his only link with the heretics and that if he alienated them now, the promise he had made to Iselia would be impossible to fulfil.

Abruptly Benetan swung away from the window as, with the forming of Iselia's name in his mind, the old ache came fiercely back. Every night he told himself that he wouldn't think about her, and every night the resolution was a dismal failure. Now he could see her face again, as clear in his mind's eye as though she were with him in this room.

And he saw again the haunted shadows behind her eyes, her mute desperation which tore at his conscience . . . and something else. Something that he dared not name, except in his most private dreams.

He looked at the narrow bed in the corner, the straw palliasse, the rough pillow, the unwashed blankets. To imagine her here, in that bed, in his arms, was a travesty. But it was what he wanted. At this moment, tired and strained, a little drunk, more than a little lonely, it was *all* he wanted — and it was a betrayal of every principle he had tried to cling to throughout his adult life. He mustn't think it; mustn't yearn for it. This desire he felt for another man's wife was the careless wantonness of the castle's influence, not his own true nature.

And an inner voice said: *Liar.*

He was at the door in three strides and across the landing in two more. Woodsmoke and an overpowering smell of beer drifted up from below; Benetan looked over the banister and shouted through the fug for the landlord.

'Send up another jug of wine,' he said curtly when the man's jowly, acquisitive face looked up at him from the noisy dimness. 'And I want a girl. Tell her she's to stay until dawn and I'll pay her well. And make sure she's clean.' He threw a coin over the rail. The landlord caught it, blinked in delighted astonishment as he saw that it was a whole silver, and hurried away.

The girl who tapped at Benetan's door five minutes later was a thin little creature of about thirteen. By sheer chance her sallow looks and a certain way in which she tilted her head reminded Benetan sharply of the child-lover currently favoured by Andraia's father, Secretary Qenever, and the twisted connection almost made him change his mind and turn the girl out. But instead he told her to drink as much wine as she wanted, took three more cups himself and promised that he'd do nothing to hurt her.

101

The promise wasn't kept, because she was a virgin. A servant's child, perhaps, or maybe even the landlord's own daughter; for a whole silver's commission the man wasn't going to stint his guest anything. She didn't seem to know what was expected of her or what a man did when he took a woman to his bed. But Benetan told himself that at someone else's hands her initiation might have been a good deal harsher.

And anyway, he was past caring.

Though for caution's sake he sent regular reports to the Star Peninsula, Overlord Leyan scorned any possibility that the murmurings of insurrection in his demesne would develop into anything more serious. Sedition was nothing new among the common herd, but brave speeches declaimed in drinking-houses lost their bite when it came to translating words into actions. And even if the peasants should be foolish enough to rise against him, his efficient and well-trained militia would deal them a short, sharp lesson that would be remembered for a long time to come. Any trouble would be crushed as easily as a man might swat a fly.

Like his fellow overlords throughout the land, Leyan had obeyed the First Magus's edict and taken his cull of twenty-one hostages. No information about the heretic cult had been forthcoming as a result, but Leyan had expected none; if the heretics had been active in the district he was confident that his own network of informers would have rooted them out long ago. Lord Vordegh's word was law, however, and Leyan wasn't about to jeopardize his own position by quibbling. The hostages would die on the day appointed – and, thanks to a little foresight at the time of their selection, he would be rid of some of his most bothersome tenants. All in all, a highly satis-factory arrangement. Until, five days before the executions were to be carried out, the rumours which he had so contemptuously dismissed erupted into reality.

The spark was a small one and under normal circumstances the fire might not have ignited. But as time began to run out for the hostages, emotions were reaching a pitch. This was a tight-knit community and almost everyone in the main village near Leyan's fortified mansion had a friend or acquaintance, if not a blood relative, among the imprisoned ones who awaited their grotesque fate. And in their midst, quietly but zealously, a cell of Order's devotees had been active. Their leader was young, inexperienced – and a little too impatient to be content for long with the caution and secrecy which Simbrian Tarkran strove to instil in all his followers. Now, news had reached the group that Simbrian and his fellow sorcerers had at last broken the barriers and made contact with Aeoris and his brothers of Order, and the young leader couldn't contain his enthusiasm. Their gods had returned from exile – the great uprising, rumoured and awaited, was surely about to begin. So, without Simbrian's knowledge and certainly without Simbrian's consent, the group began to set their plans in train.

Five of their members were among the long, docile queue of farmers, smallholders, artisans and others who lined up outside the doors of their overlord's largest tithe-house in the village square. This was not a Claim Day, but from time to time Leyan chose to exact an additional tithe beyond his monthly due, ostensibly as punishment for some general and invented misdemeanour but in reality to pay for some new personal indulgence. No one had yet dared protest about it, but in private resentment was strong and increasing. And when an impatient militiaman pushed a pregnant woman who was moving too slowly for his liking and sent her sprawling in the dust, resentment flared into violence.

Within two minutes a bloody fight was in full swing.

The farmers and smallholders had no training and few weapons, but the outburst was so sudden and unexpected that it took the militiamen completely by surprise. Their swords inflicted some fearsome wounds but they were outnumbered by ten to one and, amid a hail of swinging staves and flying stones, the tide of the conflict soon turned against them. Formed now into a tight but frightened group they were encircled, then forced further and further back until the tithe-house doors blocked any further retreat.

There was a pause in the fighting as the crowd realized that their enemies were cornered. The tithe-house doors opened outwards and had been built to withstand a heavy assault; the militiamen could neither kick nor cut their way through into the building to escape through the smaller door at the back. For the first time in living memory the overlord's men were at the mercy of those they had bullied for so long. Suddenly a hush fell, a stillness far more frightening than the mêlée, as a sea of righteously angry faces stared at their long-time tormentors and realization dawned in a hundred pairs of eyes. The militiamen stared back but dared make no move. One nervously shifted a foot; the sound was loud and harsh against the background silence.

Then a stone hurtled through the air from somewhere at the back of the crowd. It hit the tithe-house door above the trapped men's heads and ricocheted harmlessly away – but it was the trigger for which, subconsciously, the crowd had been waiting. A new sound began to rise, a chant, a growl, swelling to a roar as more and more throats took it up and found the rhythm. There were no words, only the inchoate, long-pent rage of frustration against years of injustice as the last barriers of fear broke down. As one the mob surged forward, and the slaughter began.

*　　*　　*

'. . . And if we fail now; if we fail in our courage, in our conviction, in our resolution – even in our *faith* – what then?' The orator's voice, high-pitched with excitement and emotion, carried across the market square like the screech of a bird of prey. 'What future will there be for us? There will be *none*, for our oppressors will crush us as they have crushed us before, like insects beneath their heel! They will burn our homes and take our lands, and they will herd us like sheep to the slaughter-pens, all in the name of rightful retribution! But if there is a right to retribution – and there is, my friends, be in no doubt – that right is *ours!*' He looked wildly about him at the throng, which was swelling by the minute as news of the conflict spread and people came from every direction to see what was to do. 'I say we must claim our right, and claim it *now!*'

A huge shout of approval went up, and the orator – and his fellow devotees of Aeoris who stood with him on the cart that was their impromptu stage – knew that they had won the crowd to their cause. It had been a gamble, all the more desperate because they had had no time to plan and prepare, but the fight and its aftermath had offered them a chance which might never come again. Ten dead militiamen lay in front of the tithe-house's red-stained doors, and the crowd's blood was charged with the adrenalin of their success. They had tasted vengeance, tested and proved their own power. Now they needed no reasoned persuasion but only a rabble-rousing speech to whip their confidence to new heights, and the young heretic had provided it. It didn't matter that less than half the crowd knew his face and fewer still knew his name. He was a focus, a leader, and they were ready to follow him.

'How many are we, and how many are our enemies?' the young man shouted, hoarse now as he strove to make himself audible in the farthest corners of the arena. 'We are hundreds, my friends, *hundreds*, while the scum who rule us and intimidate us and bleed us can count their numbers only in handfuls! How many men does the over-lord send to rob us of our produce? How many to guard the tithe-houses? How many to bully us in our own homes and on our own land? *And how many keep him safe in his fortress?*'

A rumble like distant thunder swelled among the throng as they began to realize what this impassioned challenge implied. The orator smiled a grim smile.

'Oh yes, my friends. Oh, *yes. We* have the strength. *We* have the power, if we will use it! And I say we *must* use it! I say it is time to rise from our knees, to throw off the yoke that our self-appointed masters have put on us. Lord Leyan rules us through fear alone, but if we see through that fear, see it for the illusion it is, then *he has no power!* He *cannot* stand against us, for *we* are the greater force! And I say let us *end* his tyranny! Let us *end* our slavery!' He flung one arm out, pointing towards Leyan's house foursquare on its hill in the distance, and his voice rose to a bellow. '*In the name of freedom and justice, let us end this evil once and for all!*'

The cheer that rose then was like the breaking of the storm.

By sunset, Overlord Leyan knew that this rebellion was too great, and already too advanced, for his servants to have a hope of crushing it. News of the rioting had reached him two hours after the killing of his men – it would have come earlier, but a small detachment sent out to investigate early reports of trouble had failed to return – and by the time he realized the need to muster all the armed force at his disposal, it was too late. Word of the uprising had blazed like fire throughout the district and the zeal of its leaders was contagious. The crowds began by smashing open tithe-houses and dragging out their contents before the empty buildings were put to the torch; a militia group striving to prevent the outrage succeeded in killing only four or five rebels before they themselves were torn to pieces by a yelling mob. The insurgents then turned their attention to rooting out others known or believed to be in the pay of Lord Leyan, from clerks and toll-gatherers to suspected informers. More than two dozen men and women were dragged from their hiding places to face summary justice; five died at the vengeful crowd's hands while the rest were left battered and unconscious. New skirmishes broke out in streets and buildings and across the farmlands as the ripples spread wider and wider, and when at last Leyan's men-at-arms were mustered and marched out in full force, they were met by a screaming horde, jubilant with success and ready for a pitched battle. The fighting lasted five hours before the militiamen were overwhelmed, and the survivors – less than half their original number – retreated to the fortress and hurled up the barricades. By the time the sun set bloodily in a crimson sky, the hot glow of twenty separate fires was visible from Leyan's highest tower. An eerie silence hung about the fortress; with the militia driven back, the rebels had no interest, yet, in the stronghold, and instead had withdrawn to their own territory. But Leyan knew that the hiatus wouldn't last. He had expected an all-out attack on his walls and the fact that it hadn't come chilled him, for it meant that the rebels had a strategy of their own. This was no impetuous and haphazard riot, simply dealt with by a brief show of force. *Someone* was behind the uprising, organizing and directing it; and the frantic reports brought to Leyan as the trouble spread had told of a name, a battle-cry, to which the insurgents were rallying. *Aeoris of Order.*

Leyan's stronghold was well-defended but it was not impregnable. It was only a matter of time – perhaps days, perhaps longer, but either way inevitable – before the rebels, through sheer weight of numbers, would succeed in storming it. And if, as Leyan feared, they were led and inspired by a power greater than their own massed will – the power of a long-exiled demon – then only the magi could hope to turn the tide.

Direct contact between the overlords and their masters at the Star Peninsula was rare. The magi issued decrees and received tithes and reports through their efficient network of secular officials, and did not trouble themselves with the trivialities of the world. But in dire emergency it was possible to cut through the usual channels and appeal directly to the heart of the castle hierarchy. Such a thing had never been done in Leyan's time, nor in his father's or grandfather's, and Leyan feared the prospect for he knew the penalty for any overlord who took this extreme measure without good reason. But his fear of the rebels was greater, and that night as the second moon rose he took a lantern and climbed to the top of the fortress's high central tower, where he unlocked a small door. The lock was stiff with disuse and the room beyond smelled damp and musty; the only furnishing inside was a solitary table, and on the table stood the artifact that Leyan sought.

It looked like a plain candlestick, made of pewter or some similar dull metal and with a shallow bowl. Leyan stared at it for a long time while the light of the moons and a hotter, uneasy glow from the distant horizon carved shadows out of the darkness. Then, drawing a deep breath, he stretched out one hand and laid it, palm down, over the bowl.

Light flared under his fingers and speared up in a livid green shaft. Leyan flinched back as though his hand had been stung, and the light coalesced and narrowed into a searing beam that forced him to shield his eyes. Slowly the beam began to pulse, and a dark aura formed around it. Sharp heat then intense cold washed over Leyan in waves, and a voice, not human, not even of this world, seemed to crawl out of the light and insinuate into his mind.

'*Address the magi. You shall be heard.*'

A shudder ran through Leyan at the thought of what manner of creature this might be; elemental or demon or something yet stranger. He clenched his hands in an effort to steady them, and ran his tongue over lips that were cracked and dry.

'My lords . . . My lords, I am in desperate straits. I beg your help, my lords, before it is too late . . .'

'It's inconvenient,' Pirane said. 'I greatly dislike being hurried and it would have suited us both better to make our preparations at leisure. But it seems the situation is a little more serious than the early reports led us to believe. Besides,' she smiled at Andraia, not entirely troubling to disguise the rancour she felt, 'it would not do to drag our heels when Lord Vordegh himself is taking an active interest.'

Andraia returned the smile but knew better than to make any comment. She had said her goodbyes to both her parents, and she and Pirane were now crossing the courtyard towards the great gates and the Maze beyond them. A group of servants followed in their wake, carrying bags and trunks, and the small procession passed under the black arch, which echoed to the sound of their footsteps, and emerged onto the smooth sward of the castle stack. The day was bright and a stiff wind was blowing from the sea. Andraia's nostrils flared appreciatively – it was easy to forget how musty the castle could become, especially as winter closed in – but Pirane only made a moue of distaste and pulled her cloak a little more closely about her shoulders before walking towards the rectangle of lusher, greener grass that marked the Maze's location. The supernatural gate was already open; as they neared it Andraia could see a tell-tale nacreous shimmer above the sward and the faint distortion of shape and colour in the landscape beyond. She shivered with a mixture of cold and anticipation, and stepped a little closer to Pirane.

Their trunks were set down on the grass, and with a curt nod Pirane dismissed her attendants, who would not be needed in the citadel. Then, telling Andraia to stand immediately behind her and close her eyes if she wanted to minimize the disorientation, the magus took what looked like a crystalline cylinder from her reticule and settled it in the palm of her hand. There was no preamble, no ceremony; she simply raised her arm and spoke seven words in the old, unhuman tongue known to every castle sorcerer. Her fingers clenched and there was a sharp *snap*, audible above the wind, as the crystal cracked in half.

The sun turned black. Andraia, who hadn't closed her eyes, gasped as she saw it, but before the sound could leave her throat her breath was snatched away and the world about her suddenly and violently inverted. She flailed wildly, clutching for support that wasn't there as her body seemed to twist and spin. Then unhuman laughter cut across the maelstrom, there was a wild, shrill gibbering – and lastly a soft, exquisitely musical sound, like the striking of a sweet-toned gong. Then, silence.

'You can look now.' Pirane's voice, dry with amusement, seemed to float towards her from a great distance and Andraia realized belatedly that she had, after all, shut her eyes tightly when the disorientation hit her. Feeling a little foolish, she blinked them open once more.

Their luggage had disappeared, and she and Pirane stood alone on a circular, semi-opaque black surface. Light filtered up from beneath them, casting grim shadows, and the shadows merged into a surrounding deep gloom. Andraia thought she saw sinister forms moving there and she looked away quickly, unable to shake off the conviction that the darkness was sentient.

She shivered, and Pirane saw the shiver. 'We are between worlds at the moment,' the magus said quietly. 'What you see has no real presence as yet but has simply been created from the substance of Chaos. Don't stray from this circle, and take great care not to touch the darkness. In a few moments the citadel will become more corporeal – and less unsettling.'

Andraia returned her smile pallidly. 'I understand, madam.'

'I doubt if you do, my dear, for I doubt if even the First Magus understands more than a fraction of the powers the gods allow us to play with.' She turned, looking ghostlike and ominous in the gloom, and the tone of her voice changed as she spoke again in the ancient, alien language. The shadows dipped convulsively and the darkness pulsed outwards at them. There was a sensation of rapid and violent movement, but so brief that later Andraia wondered if she had imagined it, then suddenly they were standing on nothing and surrounded by blackness. Andraia swallowed hard, but before her fear had time to take hold of her Pirane's voice rang out crisply.

'*Light.*'

There was a *hushing* sound, like velvet sweeping across stone, and the citadel materialized around them.

Andraia could only stare, bereft of words. They stood in a seven-sided hall with black walls that undulated as though formed from cascades of water. Seven tall windows, each reflecting a different gem-like colour, shimmered in the walls, and the light flooding through them pooled in incredible patterns on a stark mosaic floor beneath their feet. A filigree of stairs and balusters that looked no more substantial than snow curved around the walls and upwards to be lost in mist, while at the hall's centre a single clear red flame hung above another staircase spiralling downwards into absolute darkness.

Pirane studied the flame for a few moments, frowning. Then, signalling Andraia to stay where she was, she walked quickly towards one of the windows. Andraia thought she glimpsed something moving outside, but the image was too faint for her to discern any detail. For perhaps a minute Pirane's tall figure was etched against the window – then the magus swore sharply.

'Madam?' Andraia looked quickly at her but Pirane gestured for silence. Her posture was tense now as she continued to gaze out; then abruptly she turned and stalked back to where Andraia waited.

'Someone has been either criminally careless or criminally stupid.' Her voice was baleful and Andraia was taken aback by the anger in her eyes. 'How this situation could have been allowed to deteriorate so far . . . great Yandros, I *despair* of these overlords. Can they do *nothing* for themselves?' She paused, then with a visible and ferocious exercise of self-control her tone became merely businesslike. 'This will demand more time than I had anticipated. I'm so sorry, my dear. I'm afraid you must find your own amusements for a little while, but I'm sure the citadel can provide enough to distract you until I've completed what needs to be done.' The flash of anger had passed now, and turning to the centre of the hall again Pirane raised her hands towards the hovering red flame and clapped twice. Something moved in the dark well below the flame, then there was a soft sound and a small, wraith-like figure came skimming up the spiral stairway. Its shape was human but it had no face, and from its shoulders a cobweb-like membrane fluttered and rustled like folded wings. Andraia stared at it in fascination and Pirane smiled.

'You'll find this creature more useful than any human

servant, as it's highly intelligent as well as being obedient. Ask it for anything you require – oh, but don't venture outside the citadel. It isn't advisable, at least for the time being.'

Andraia's stomach lurched queasily as she wondered quite what Pirane meant. 'Are you saying, madam, that this might be dangerous?'

'Dangerous?' Pirane's eyebrows almost lifted into the shimmer of her black hair. 'Oh no, you misunderstand. There's nothing dangerous in our situation.' She smiled fondly. 'But the next few hours may be a little distasteful, and I see no reason why you should be needlessly discomforted. Now; we'd best not delay any longer than necessary. Close your eyes again if you feel disorientated, and I shall move us to our destination.'

She turned away, concentrated her will. A faint, eldritch aura sprang up around her body, hurling shadows across the mosaic floor. Once again the words she uttered were in the alien tongue but this time, though she couldn't begin to comprehend them, they struck dread into Andraia. The jewel-vivid light vanished from the windows. There was a sound, small but menacingly emphatic . . .

The rebels had finally stormed Overlord Leyan's house in a startlingly disciplined assault that no militia could hope to withstand. Leyan himself fled – no one yet knew how or where – taking with him four bodyguards, three female concubines and his eldest son; the rest of his household was left to the mercy of their attackers. Within an hour the fortified mansion was ablaze as the triumphant horde set light to anything that had belonged to Leyan and would burn. And from Leyan's cellars, twenty-one dazed, weak but thankful prisoners were brought into the smoke-stained daylight to freedom.

In a noisy and exuberant pack the rebels left the house

to burn and marched back towards the village and the market arena, where they found a great crowd waiting for them. With the overlord's power smashed, the people no longer feared reprisal or punishment; everyone from the oldest crone to the smallest child had turned out to welcome their heroes, and the arena was packed to over-flowing with cheering people. Many wanted to celebrate this new and decisive victory by breaking open wine and beer barrels seized from the tithe-houses and drinking themselves insensible. But a more level-headed faction, led by the young heretic and his friends, argued that Leyan and his party must be found and detained before any cele-brations began. While the overlord still lived he was a potential threat, and they could afford to take no chances. Debate became dispute, and the dispute was beginning to grow heated when suddenly a colossal flash lit the square. Like a single entity the crowd jolted and looked up at the sky. Storms were frequent hereabouts and often gathered quickly, but no one had noticed this one approaching and there was consternation as they anticipated the first assault of stinging rain.

But no thunder followed the flash. And as they stared upwards, the crowd realized that the sky overhead was cloudless.

'What was it?' An older man, his voice sharp with alarm, caught the sleeve of the heretic leader. The leader opened his mouth but had no answer –

Then the shock hit them, a soundless concussion of energy that blasted across the arena from beyond the empty tithe-house. The stunned crowd saw the building's walls warp and twist; then the tithe-house crumpled like paper and collapsed. Where it had stood, a vast spectral image shivered, towering over the now terrified throng. The air around the phantom turned crimson, then green, then purple, and streaks of livid silver crackled across it, spitting and sparking. Among the crowd there was a sudden and violent surge backwards, people pushing and thrusting and scrabbling to get clear as terror swept through them. Some fell and were trampled, others were swept up in the tide and carried willy-nilly; the heretic leader was shouting but his voice was inaudible and the wagon on which he stood rocked wildly as the crowd surged past. Suddenly it gave way to the pressure and overturned, pitching the young man and his companions into the maelstrom of panicking humanity – and at the same instant a second gale of power swept across the square, and with it a sound, a single musical note, painfully sweet yet so deafening that it paralysed the senses. The towering phantom flicked into sharp focus, became solid. And thirty people who hadn't been able to fight their way clear in time were annihilated as Pirane's citadel, black as the castle and with lightning crackling across its walls, materialized at the edge of the square.

CHAPTER VIII

Smoke from Overlord Leyan's burning mansion was visible from four miles away, and when he first glimpsed it Benetan reined in his horse and stared hard towards the distant horizon. His road lay well east of the smoke-stain, but the plume in the sky was growing thicker and darker and it was obvious that whatever was burning was something more than a hayrick or barn. Instinct and experience told Benetan that here was real trouble.

His mare pawed the ground, puzzled by the halt and impatient to walk on. Benetan checked her, still staring westward as he debated whether to investigate or leave well alone. It was possible – no, more than possible, it was almost a certainty – that this was rumour translated into reality; an uprising, albeit on a small scale, against whatever overlord ruled this demesne. To ride into the middle of it would be foolhardy. But it might also be his only chance to break the hiatus between himself and the heretics who were watching him.

The mare started to dance on the spot, tossing her head restively. Benetan glanced over his shoulder, at the same time shortening rein. No one in sight. There had been another follower but he had disappeared an hour or so ago. Now, perhaps, Benetan knew why.

Rough country, including a belt of deciduous woodland at least two miles wide, lay between him and the fire, but there were tracks through the wood which would be easy to follow. He turned the mare's head, tapping her lightly with the ends of the reins as she briefly objected to the new direction, and set her at the trees.

The mare came out of the wood at a fast trot, and Benetan pulled her up sharply as the full spectacle of the burning mansion came suddenly and shockingly into view. High on its hill beyond a sweep of open fields the house was completely engulfed in flames, a huge, macabre beacon rivalling the setting sun. Benetan had no doubt that this was the local overlord's stronghold. But there were no human figures to be seen; no one near the mansion, no one in the surrounding fields. And below the hill stood the jumbled buildings of a good-sized village which looked unnaturally quiet and deserted.

Suddenly from his left came a thump of hoofbeats and an outcry of voices.

'There, look! By the track –'

'Is it Brend?'

'Not his horse. But a good one –'

And, hailing him more directly, 'Hey! You there! Who are you?'

Without thinking, Benetan turned in the saddle. Ten yards away and approaching were half a dozen men. They were mounted on heavy farm horses and each one carried a makeshift weapon of some kind; pitchforks, spades, staves. Benetan's coat was open, and the small procession stopped dead as the men saw the distinctive black clothes, the ornate belt, the all too familiar insignia.

'*Seven Hells!*' The high colour drained from the leading rider's face and he yanked hard on his horse's reins, slewing it to a halt. Benetan realized, belatedly, the mistake he had made, and one hand went to the hilt of his sword, though he hoped to Yandros that he wouldn't need to use it.

The other riders had swung out in a semi-circle, barring the way forward. They stared at him, and Benetan saw their expressions change from puzzlement to realization, shock – and rage.

'Gods blind me, it's one of those devils from the castle!' Benetan had never heard such venomous hatred in a voice.

'*They know!*' someone shouted fearfully.

The leader turned sharply. 'Rot you, Parlo, they can't know! This is something else.' He faced Benetan again, aware of the sword and watching it obliquely. 'Chance. Pure chance.' He smiled, and started to edge his horse slowly forward.

Benetan wasn't prepared for this. Hatred, yes; he was accustomed to that, knew how to deal with it or at least how to ignore it. But hatred had always gone hand in hand with fear. That was the difference. These men weren't afraid of him, for he was only one to their six. And, for the first time in his life and probably in theirs, the fact that he was a Chaos rider made no difference whatever.

'He's only human. As human as any of us.' The leader was still smiling. 'And he's sweating. Look at him.'

Benetan could feel his heart thumping sharply under his ribs as he met the man's gaze and saw the imminent prospect of his own death. But that moment of silent exchange was a catalyst, and abruptly his years of training snapped into focus. His eyes were steady and he didn't move as the leading farm horse stepped closer. After only a brief hesitation the others followed suit, tightening the cordon, and Benetan's mind calculated rapidly. No point in speaking; these men no longer recognized the old order and his supposed authority would count for nothing. He was aware of a slickness between his palm and the sword-hilt, and a detached part of his mind told him that his hope of resolving this without bloodshed had no foundation.

The men's leader took a tighter grip on his spade. The blade, Benetan noticed, had been newly sharpened.

'Don't hurt the mare. 'Tisn't her fault who her master is, after all.'

'But him . . . ?'

A pause, but momentary. Then: 'Kill him. And don't waste any time.'

They had nothing to match Benetan's skill and experience, but it was as though some greater force moved and directed them to act in concert. Benetan was almost — but not quite — surprised by the swift efficiency that brought them at him in a pack, and for one moment as they closed in he believed that he had grossly underestimated them. But then the old lessons surged: one word to the mare and she rose on her hind legs, raking high and catching the first farm horse across the muzzle with a flailing hoof, and at the same moment Benetan's sword slid from its scabbard and he heard the crisp singing of air as the blade cut the leader's body from shoulder to gut. The man made an abysmal sound and slumped, and a bloody mess spilled from his corpse over the saddle as his horse shied away in terror. A second face loomed, an arm swinging and the tines of a pitchfork spearing down; Benetan's own arm moved without conscious will and there was a whining *thwack* as the sword, not quite edge-on, sliced off half the youth's left ear and sent him sprawling under trampling hooves.

But for all his superior abilities they were still four to his one, and when the mare reared again she was screaming, out of control as the bigger animals lunged and jostled with their frightened but resolute riders still astride. Suddenly Benetan couldn't control her, and his blade was swinging wildly but meeting nothing. He glimpsed a shovel-blade coming at him from the left, fast, lethal —

And suddenly the horses were rearing and screaming in terror as the sky lit with a gargantuan flash.

Benetan lost his grip on the sword, and only a wild

grab for a handful of mane stopped him from pitching backwards out of the saddle as his mare collided with the biggest of the farm horses, staggered on her hind legs and almost fell. His assailants were yelling; a stave whirled wildly through the air and missed his head by a hand's width, and he struggled to snatch the reins and pull his mount out of the pandemonium. Another collision, horses squealing; someone else lost his grip and plunged among kicking hooves. Then suddenly they were clear of the mêlée and the mare bolted, ears flat to her head and foam whipping from her muzzle. She headed straight across the open fields towards the village, and Benetan knew better than to make any attempt to stop her; instead he regained his stirrups, gathered the reins and let her race where she would. If nothing else, she was putting a distance between him and his attackers which the slower horses couldn't hope to close.

The village lay ahead and they were less than a quarter of a mile from it when the shock-wave of Magus Pirane's spectacular arrival met them. Benetan saw it coming, saw the storm of dust, bushes uprooted by the blast and the crackling violence of power in the air, but he could do nothing to avoid it. It struck them like a hammer-blow and they crashed to the ground, the mare's hooves flailing as Benetan rolled clear. The shock-wave crashed over them and onwards, and Benetan climbed to his feet, shocked and winded and feeling as if every bone he possessed had been shaken out of its proper place.

He knew, at least in essence, what had happened. Only sorcery could have created such an onslaught, unless the gods themselves had decided to take a hand in human affairs. This rebellion had attracted the attention of the magi . . . Benetan swayed on his feet, wiping dust from his eyes. His mare had struggled upright before him and was now cantering away with her reins trailing. He shouted, but though she looked back she was too frightened to obey his call. And when he stared westward to the village he saw something which moments ago hadn't been there. A towering structure, dark, and enveloped in a darker corona that glittered balefully against the crimson sky.

A *citadel*. Shock registered violently in Benetan's mind; he knew the magi's citadels and knew the level of power that could be wielded from within them. And it took little imagination to picture what would happen in the village as that power began to do its work.

From behind him came a sudden pounding and yelling. *'There! There he is!'*

He spun round and saw the farm horses galloping over the rough ground towards him. Three had riders, the others running loose beside them, and one of the riders was waving his own sword. Benetan swore, turned and ran. No time to call his mare again; he couldn't take the gamble that she would answer. His initial sense of alarm at the citadel's appearance vanished as he realized that, whatever menace it might pose to the villagers, it was his only hope of sanctuary. A slim hope at that, for though he was a fast runner the odds were against his reaching the citadel before his pursuers reached him.

Air rasped in his throat as he raced on. He didn't have the breath to call to Yandros for help, and doubted anyway if Yandros was sufficiently interested in his survival to notice his plight let alone answer. Nor did he look back; there was no need, for he knew that the men must be gaining on him, and fast.

He was at the outskirts of the village when suddenly he registered noise. Somewhere ahead, though muffled by the intervening buildings, the village was in uproar. For a moment Benetan faltered as he realized that he could be running headlong into a far greater danger than his pursuers presented. One look at him, at his clothes, and every man, woman and child in the place would be out for his blood; he would never reach the citadel alive. But there was nowhere else, no other haven. He *had* to try – and if the worst came to the worst he still had his knives . . .

The commotion grew louder and clearer as he dodged into the first of the village's twisting streets; not just an incoherent jumble now but a mêlée of individual voices and sounds. Men shouting, children screaming, dogs barking; the shriek of a terrified horse and the throatier bellowing of herd-beasts. Benetan could see nothing of the fray as yet but he was oppressively aware of the huge phantasm of the citadel towering over the village's centre and blotting out half the sky, its aura spilling black light over the scene and turning day into night.

With his lungs feeling as if they were about to tear apart Benetan ran on through the network of narrow streets. Still there was no one in sight, though the noise from the market-place was getting louder with every second. Then suddenly a figure appeared, rushing towards him. His hand went instinctively to his knife, but she was only a child and anyway she was oblivious to his presence and darted past him, vanishing in the gathering dusk. Moments later a woman and a man followed, hurrying hand in hand; they too ignored him. Then behind him Benetan heard a shout and a horse's shrill whinny. Gods, his pursuers – the fleeing villagers must have run straight into them, which could only mean they were almost on him –

To his left was another street, little more than an alley-way between the rough-built houses. With luck it would prove too narrow for the farm horses, and Benetan dived down it and forced his aching legs to run faster. Almost immediately the alley began to twist, taking him, he realized, nearer to the village's heart. The market-place must be only a short way ahead – then the alley gave another turn and he glimpsed the arena. There were flickers of movement in the gloom; the noise abruptly swelled to a din . . . Benetan struggled the last few yards, and burst out into bedlam.

On the far side of the market-place Pirane's citadel towered into the darkening sky, and its arrival had devastated half the arena. A spectral corona shot through with silver fire shimmered around it, throwing the black walls into stark relief, and its myriad windows, glaring like harsh jewel-eyes, blazed down on the scene below. By the light of the supernatural flames the arena was a seething turmoil of confusion. There must be several hundred people here, Benetan thought wildly, a swarm of human figures surging like ants around a demolished nest. They had clearly tried at first to cluster together, seeking safety in numbers, but now it was dawning on them there was no safety to be had and the edge of the throng was turning into a chaotic brawl as some fought to reach the edge of the arena while others struggled to pull them back. A few succeeded in breaking free and fled into the darkness of the surrounding streets; others fell or were drawn back into the central maelstrom, where a knot of men seemed to be trying to assert a semblance of command. Benetan could hear a hoarse voice yelling above the wider din; he made out one syllable, an order among the hysterical flow of words, and realized to his astonishment that some madman was trying to rally followers to attack the citadel. Incredibly, his exhortation was having an effect; the men around him were gathering, raising weapons, starting to yell in concert and no longer in terror –

Then with a sudden, violent motion the body of men moved, cleaving into the crowd and forcing their way towards the towering fortress. They had gained perhaps five yards when the silver fire around the citadel flicked into momentary dazzling brilliance – and a black portal materialized in the blank wall and smashed open.

Eclipsing the clamour, a sound that struck through Benetan's flesh and bone to his marrow rang out. A lone, unhuman voice rising in an unearthly howl that shivered between two horrifying, discordant notes before falling away. The echoes of the voice died, and for perhaps ten seconds there was profound silence. Benetan stood transfixed, feeling the last reverberations of that sound in the pit of his soul. Then, a blacker shadow against the black portal, something moved slowly and with dire purpose.

Benetan recognized it instantly. Twenty feet high at the shoulder, its huge, silver-furred body tapering to long, thin legs that gave it a horrifying grace, it lowered its bearlike and monstrously beautiful head almost to the ground and its muzzle swung this way and that, testing the atmosphere. The contours of the citadel were clearly visible through its frame but this was no phantasm, for the fires of Chaos burned like earthbound stars in its eyes and the fangs that filled its open jaws were more deadly than any sword. Four times Benetan had ridden out with such a being and its brothers, when the magi had sent the Chaos riders on a punitive sortie. He had coaxed the creatures, directed and controlled them, developed a brief but compelling rapport with them that was almost symbiotic.

And he had seen the havoc they could leave in their wake.

The monster raised its head and a second unearthly howl rose chillingly to the sky. The entire crowd was paralysed, panic arrested, bravado collapsing; they couldn't move, couldn't utter a sound. Then without warning the great head darted down like a snake striking. There was a shriek, a dull *crack*, and the creature tossed the two halves of a severed human body into the air. The remains fell. For a moment the dreadful silence held. Then the spell of helpless terror that had immobilized the villagers shattered, and there was pandemonium as the entire throng tried to run from the arena.

The section of the crowd nearest to Benetan erupted like a dam bursting, and a mass of scrambling bodies surged at him. Benetan leaped to one side, pressing himself against the alley wall, but as the spearhead of the terrified mob reached him he was buffeted back, swept up in a tide of wild-eyed, open-mouthed faces that threatened to carry him with them. Hardly aware of what he was doing he pulled a knife from its sheath and lashed out with it, forcing a clear space and fighting against the momentum of the villagers' headlong flight. Time and again he felt the blade bite but he didn't know and didn't care whether anyone was hurt or even killed. All that mattered was to get free of them, get through, fight his way to the citadel, *survive* –

Suddenly he was clear, stumbling out of the alley with a staggering lurch that carried him several yards across the arena. Figures whirled past him, but ahead the makeshift army was trying to rally again, a press of men yelling as they brandished staves and farm implements above their heads. They were between him and the citadel, screaming defiance at the phantasmic monster as it began to stalk slowly and ominously forward. It would kill them, Benetan knew – for all their show of courage they had no weapons that could prevail against it – and it would kill without partiality, mechanically, indiscriminately, simply annihilating anyone reckless enough to stand in its path. If he tried to break through and reach the citadel, the creature would not trouble to distinguish between friend and enemy and he would become only one more unheeded corpse. Unless . . .

Benetan thrust the knife away and reached into his belt-pouch. *Thank Yandros,* they were there, not in his saddle-bags – he pulled the long black gauntlets out, dragging them onto his hands, feeling the tingling change course through his fingers, as though his skin and the gloves were becoming one. Suddenly his hands were no longer human but something else, something *more*, and the silver claws that tipped each finger of the gauntlets picked up the baleful fire from the citadel and glared into life.

Drawing all the breath his lungs could muster, gathering his concentration, Benetan raised his left arm high and shouted a word the magi had taught him long ago, a word of command that rang across the arena.

Light flared from his fingertips, hurling stark shadows over his face and figure. Across the arena he saw the huge head come up and the Chaotic fire in the being's eyes burn more intensely. He had time, too, to register that it was turning from its path and moving in his direction – then behind him there was a shout and a rush, and something slammed violently into his back. Benetan lurched forward, losing his balance and almost falling; but within a second he had collected himself and spun around to face the assault. He had anticipated this, known it must come – but they had reacted faster than he'd thought they would, almost catching him off guard, and as he looked into the eyes of the man who had struck him Benetan suspected that he had taken the gamble too early.

There were four others at the villager's back, and there could be no doubt that they knew Benetan for what he was. His assailant, who was around his own age, was breathing hard and held his stave before him like a club. Benetan's eyes flicked quickly to it. Solid wood, thicker than the man's forearm ... The first blow had been a glancing one, perhaps deliberately. The second, if it found its target, could kill him.

Very slowly he started to reach for his knife again. He didn't know what might be happening behind him and it seemed that his opponents too were oblivious. This was the eye of a private storm, and the clamour beyond it meant nothing.

'Don't touch it.' The villager's voice was guttural; the stave shifted menacingly. Benetan gauged how long it would take the man to strike, hesitated – then snatched for the knife's hilt.

'*I SAID, DON'T TOUCH IT!*' The stave swung at his head and he ducked, rolled, was on his feet again in one movement, and the knife sheared towards his assailant's throat.

It didn't find its mark, for he'd made the mistake of underestimating the fury and the fear that drove them. They were on him in a pack; the knife was wrenched from his grip and went spinning, and then he was falling backwards, landing hard and awkwardly with two of them bearing down on him. He made a desperate grab for the second knife, but before his fingers could grasp it the stave swung again and a stunning pain shot through his right arm. Above him light flared on metal and he saw a pitchfork, tines sharpened to glittering daggers, poised over his head. There was a noise, an inchoate yell of hatred and rage, and the yell transmuted into a howl that dinned in his ears as the pitchfork speared down towards him –

The air blasted into searing fire and then into blackness, and Benetan lost his hold on the world.

'. . . and change the dressing on the shoulder in the morning. Another day should see him fit enough.'

The woman's voice was vaguely familiar but he couldn't quite place it. Whoever she had addressed didn't reply but there was an odd rustling sound and the sense of someone – or something – moving away. Then the voice spoke again. 'And you, child. There'll be time enough to talk to him later.'

Someone else departed. It was very quiet and that disorientated him. There had been noise, confusion, people shouting . . . and though he hadn't yet opened his eyes he sensed that he was enclosed by walls, which surely was wrong.

Abruptly remembering his knife Benetan tried to reach for it, and the shock of pain in his arm was so great that he almost vomited. Instantly the voice said,

'Keep it still, Captain, or it won't mend.'

Great gods, now he recognized that tone. Benetan opened his eyes. He was lying in a bed, under blankets that felt and looked like warm smoke, and the walls surrounding him — if they could be called walls — rippled with colours and shadows that formed soothing patterns. Above his head a cool, clear sphere of light hung motionless in mid-air, giving off a soft illumination. And Magus Pirane stood looking down at him.

'*Madam* —' Horrified at his lapse of protocol he pushed himself upright in the bed, and this time he was sick, couldn't stop himself. Pirane said something under her breath and handed him a small silver bowl which she seemed to pluck out of the surrounding dimness. When the spasm passed she set the bowl fastidiously aside and poured a cup of some dark liquid from a flask beside the bed.

'Drink it all. And have the sense to take it with your *left* hand,' as he reflexively made to move the injured arm again. 'One mishap is quite enough, thank you, Captain Liss.'

Benetan fought to bring his voice under control. 'Madam, I can only . . . only apologize for . . .'

'It's of no consequence; I'm not perturbed by human frailties,' Pirane interrupted dismissively. There was, he thought — and hoped — a faint trace of grim humour underlying her apparent impatience. 'If nothing else, you've provided a small diversion in the midst of some very tiresome business.'

He frowned. 'I can't recall . . .'

'What happened to you? Probably not; you took a blow on the back of your skull as well as the one to your forearm and a pitchfork through your right shoulder for good measure. I'm surprised that a trained Chaos rider should be so inept. Or did a section of the mob surprise you?'

'I . . . don't know, madam.'

'Mmm, well; the whys and wherefores are hardly relevant now. At least it seems you had the wit to call on our little pet from Chaos to help you.'

Benetan's memory was trying to piece itself together, and a picture of sorts began to form. The howling – and there had been something else just before he lost consciousness, something like the snap of bones breaking, and a sense of a vast, looming presence. *Coaxing, directing, controlling, a brief but compelling rapport . . .*

'It brought me to the citadel?'

'Yes, fortunately for you. Now, your wounds have been attended to and none of them are serious enough to warrant your returning to the Star Peninsula for Magus Croin's attention, so you might as well sleep through the rest of the night and I'll have your report of how you came to be involved in this fracas in the morning.' Pirane glanced disdainfully across the room to where the outlines of what Benetan took to be a window showed faintly, though he could see nothing but a dark void beyond it. 'The area's quiet enough now and the overlord is safe, which I suppose is what counts for the present.' She looked at him again. 'Settle yourself comfortably, Captain Liss, and I'll speak to you tomorrow. Your injuries will largely have healed by then.' She turned to leave. 'I'll tell Andraia that you're little the worse for your skirmish.'

Benetan was startled. 'Andraia?'

'Yes. Her room is adjacent to yours; though you may put any ideas that gives you out of your head – you need rest, and your pleasures can wait another day.' A pause.

'She came with me on this little expedition. A happy coincidence, don't you think?'

And she was gone before Benetan could answer.

Andraia had never before disobeyed an order from Pirane, but her need to see Benetan was too urgent for her to wait until morning. It took her some while to find his room, for the dimensions of the citadel were volatile and tended to shift bewilderingly and without warning, but at last she located him and, relieved to find none of the spectral servants on watch, entered through the murmuring oval of light that served as a door and hastened to the bed.

'Benet.' Her voice was soft. 'Benet, are you awake?'

He was, but Pirane had added a soporific to the wine she had given him and his mind was growing fuddled. He was, however, cogent enough to recognize her, and he reached out with his uninjured hand.

'Andraia . . .'

She sat down among the smoke-like coverings. 'Lady Pirane says your wounds aren't serious.'

'Nnh.' Then he wasn't quite sure if he meant no or yes, so only squeezed her fingers. 'What are you *doing* here?' he asked.

'Looking for you.'

'What?' He didn't understand, and in her frustration Andraia wanted to shake him. If only she could have slipped away earlier she might have been able to talk to him before this damned soporific took effect.

She cast a quick glance over her shoulder, half afraid that Pirane might walk in at any moment. 'Benet, listen to me, *listen*. I *had* to find you; this couldn't wait until your return to the castle. You're the only person I can tell, the only one I can trust – and you're involved, though you don't –' She stopped, looked more intently at him. 'Benet, did you hear me?'

He opened his eyes, which weren't focusing properly, and smiled at her. 'Of course I heard. You said you couldn't wait until my return to the castle.' His eyelids began to droop again. 'But if Magus Pirane finds out –'

'*Ohh.*' She shook her head, the mane of her hair flying. 'No, Benet, *no*, that wasn't what I *meant!* For the gods' sakes –'

But she realized then that nothing she might say would make any difference. His eyes had closed again and his mind was wandering over the borders of sleep. The hand clasped in hers relaxed, fell back on the bed, and slowly Andraia stood up. For perhaps half a minute she stared down at him, irrationally hoping that the drug's effects would suddenly be reversed, and in that moment she thought how pale his face looked under its wind-tan. Lady Pirane had said that he'd been very lucky. Another few seconds, another strike with the pitchfork, and even the Chaos being couldn't have saved him. It shocked her – especially in the light of all that had happened since they last met – to realize that the thought of his dying was unbearable.

She rubbed savagely at her eyes, smearing the luminous gold tint that she had applied so carefully before leaving the castle. 'Damn you, Benetan Liss!' There was fear and misery and, still, a savage edge of anger in her low-pitched voice. '*Damn* you!'

CHAPTER IX

Andraia had planned to wake early the next morning, hoping that she might be able to see Benetan alone before anyone else was about; but the chance slipped through her fingers. She overslept, and when she did finally rouse she found a message awaiting her from Pirane, to the effect that her servants were presently attending to Captain Liss and that if Andraia wished to see him – as she doubtless did – they could meet at breakfast.

Pirane hadn't slept, nor felt the need to. Despite her initial irritation at the inconvenience which the 'small trouble' of the uprising had caused her, one look at the situation had mollified her. Overlord Leyan, it seemed, had not exaggerated; if anything he had underplayed the seriousness of the situation, at least from the viewpoint of a man with only physical weapons at his disposal. Besides, for all its pleasures life at the castle had been uneventful lately, and a challenge – even a minor one – was stimulating.

It had taken her less than an hour to impose peace on the district. Her method was simple and pragmatically effective. She summoned a small legion of lower-plane entities and instructed them to put word out to the local populace that they had a straightforward choice: lay down their weapons and obey the will of their overlord, or face the magi's own form of retaliation. She didn't know and didn't trouble to find out how many had submitted and how many had died; commoners' lives were of no interest to her, and provided that the creatures from Chaos conjured to deal with dissenters did their work as directed – which they did – she was satisfied.

When the sun rose the village was silent and the view over the market-place wasn't altogether pleasant, so Pirane created opaque patterns of light in all the windows to avoid any unnecessary distress to Andraia and to the additional guests who had arrived during the night. One of the Chaos beings had located Overlord Leyan and his companions in the small hours, and brought them to safety in the citadel. There had been some ado over that, for one of the concubines had been so terrified by the transfer that she had suffered a heart seizure, and though Leyan himself was made of sterner stuff, it seemed only the mildest courtesy to spare him any further alarm. Besides, the man would need a clear mind today, for while Pirane's task was all but completed his was only just beginning.

She arranged for meals to be served to Leyan and his party in their rooms while she began her breakfast alone in the heptagonal chamber, lit now by a ring of cool fire at ceiling level and with a large, circular table where the central stairwell had been. Andraia arrived half way through the meal. She had taken great care with her appearance – Pirane would have expected nothing less – but she looked brittle and uneasy. As she came down the filigree staircase and crossed the floor, the magus rose from the table and drew her to a chair beside her own, kissing her cheek as she sat down.

'My dear. Didn't you sleep well?'

Andraia managed a pallid smile. 'Well enough, madam, thank you.'

Pirane didn't believe her but let it pass. 'Your Captain Liss should be joining us at any moment. I gather he's recovered barring a few bruises and a scar. That's just as well – I'll want him to make a report, of course, but if we can dispense with that this morning then he'll be yours for

133

as long as you want him.' Abruptly her eyes narrowed. 'Assuming that you *do* still want him?'

Andraia flushed. 'Yes, madam. Yes, I do. In fact, I wondered if . . .' She hesitated.

'If?' Pirane raised an interrogative eyebrow and there was a faintly impatient edge to her tone. Abruptly Andraia realized that the request she had been about to make – that she might have a private moment with Benetan *before* he made his report – would not be well received, and quickly she dissembled.

'No, madam, it – ah – it was nothing. Just an idle speculation, and now I think about it . . .' She let the sentence tail off and focused her attention quickly and intently on the hot drink which one of the faceless servants had set in front of her.

Benetan joined them a few minutes later. He looked pallid, and the prospect of taking breakfast with a magus had made him tense and reticent. Andraia noticed that his injured arm was very stiff, but in Pirane's presence she didn't like to ask about the details of his skirmish, so the meal progressed against a background of stilted small-talk punctuated by long, awkward silences. At last Pirane brought the ordeal to an end by rising from her chair.

'Well, if you've both eaten your fill – and I might say you've touched little enough – we'd best get the tedious formalities over and done with. Overlord Leyan should be ready by now, and I'd like you, Captain Liss, to join me while I interview him. If you'll kindly follow me . . ?'

Benetan only gave Andraia a quick, pallid smile as the magus led him away. He hadn't seen her surreptitious signals and would probably not have registered them if he had, for his mind was preoccupied by unquiet and unpleasant thoughts. He knew the essence, if not the details, of Pirane's method of putting an end to the rebellion, but every window in the citadel had been opaqued, making it impossible to see the aftermath of her work. However, it took only a little imagination and a few memories of past incidents to picture how the market-place probably looked in the light of day.

He wondered how many insurgents had died. Probably comparatively few, for no magus was ever less than scrupulously efficient; but enough, certainly, to ensure that none of the survivors would think of further rebellion for a long time to come. A few months ago Benetan would have felt little sympathy for them. Regret, yes, that the uprising had not been quelled without bloodshed, for contrary to what his old training-sergeant had called 'the prejudices of the prejudiced', a Chaos rider had the same human sensibilities as any sane man, and most castle-dwellers shared the commoners' dislike of overlords as a breed. But defiance of the overlords was defiance of the magi, albeit at one remove. And the magi were the direct avatars of Yandros. That was the logic, and throughout his life Benetan had never questioned it. Until now . . .

They had climbed the vertiginous crystal staircase and were walking through a corridor that twisted into the heart of the citadel when Pirane's voice impinged suddenly on his thoughts.

'This business shouldn't take up much of our time, Captain Liss,' she said briskly. 'It's simply a matter of reassuring the overlord that he can now take control of his own demesne again without fear of any further trouble – and of reminding him that but for his laxity there would have been no trouble in the first place.' She flicked him a sharp-edged smile. 'It does these people no harm to be pulled up for their shortcomings once in a while, and the presence of a Chaos rider will spice the rebuke with a little extra emphasis. I'm sorry to make such mundane use of you, but these devices are very convenient when we're obliged to deal with ignorant people.' She paused. 'How is your arm this morning?'

'Stiff, madam, but well enough apart from that,' Benetan replied.

'No lasting harm done, then. Good. Oh, by the way, your mare was found grazing in one of the fields outside the village. I ordered her to be brought into the citadel. She's uninjured, so you may have her back whenever you wish.' Pirane saw his expression lighten with relief at the news, and laughed shortly. 'My dear captain, from the look on your face anyone would think that you can't wait to be reunited with the animal and riding away from here! I assure you, there's no need for that; you're welcome to stay in the citadel until you're fully fit.' Another pause, barbed this time. 'That will please Andraia. She really hasn't been herself since you left the castle.'

Benetan's gaze slid away from hers as his conscience stabbed him. 'I – I'll stay, madam, of course. If it isn't inconvenient to you.'

'If it is, I'll tell you so. Now, when we've finished with this wretched little overlord I'll have whatever details you can give me about yesterday's disturbances, and then if you've a report for the First Magus you may also entrust that to me.' She looked keenly at him. 'I'm sure he'll be eager to hear whether your investigations have borne any fruit.'

'Yes, madam.' Benetan hoped to all seven of the gods that his cheeks weren't flushing as he spoke. He thought not, for he had expected this line of questioning and had prepared his response – but Pirane was shrewd even by the magi's high standards, and he had a poor talent for acting. 'To be honest, madam, I've nothing of any real value to report to Lord Vordegh as yet. The lack of progress is very frustrating – in fact, my purpose in coming here was to –'

'To see if this little trouble might produce a first taste of the elusive fruit?' Pirane raised her elegant eyebrows. 'Mmm. That's an interesting theory and could well have

136

potential.' Ahead of them the corridor took another twist and ended in a swathe of velvet curtain; Pirane made a small gesture and the curtain swept aside of its own accord. 'I hope you *are* right, Captain Liss. I wouldn't care to think that your long absence will serve no purpose – and I imagine that Lord Vordegh will share my feelings.'

Andraia was in one of the topmost rooms of the citadel; a round chamber adorned with silver stalagmites that seemed to change their number and positions each time she looked at them. The effect was disorientating and added to her agitation, so she had ordered one of the unhuman servants to play a dice game with her in an effort to distract herself. Andraia was a skilled player and had, in theory, won a good deal of money, but as the faceless being had no concept of wealth the entire exercise was academic, and she was nearing a pitch of frustrated boredom when at last Benetan came looking for her.

'Benet!' She got to her feet, knocking the dice aside and off the table. 'Thank the gods! I –' Then she remembered the servant.

'You are dismissed.' She nodded to the creature and tried to contain her impatience as it made its silent exit, its cobweb wings floating behind it. As soon as it had vanished over the threshold Andraia whirled to face Benetan. She opened her mouth to speak – but he forestalled her.

'Andraia, listen!' He crossed the room, gripped her upper arms. His face, she realized suddenly, was haggard, and he was as agitated as she was. 'You have to help me! I *must* make Magus Pirane understand – she's fond of you; if you speak to her she'll take heed –'

'Benet, you're hurting me!' She wrenched herself free, startled and irrationally angry that he should have preempted what she saw as her own more urgent need.

'I'm sorry, I'm sorry.' He let go and scrubbed distractedly

at his face with both hands. 'But Andraia, I can't stand by and let this man make havoc! It's revenge he wants, nothing more, and he doesn't care how he achieves it or how many suffer as a result! This is pure spite — it isn't right, it isn't *just!* But Lady Pirane refuses to intervene —'

'Benet, wait — calm down!' Despite her own state of mind Andraia realized that his distress and the fury underlying it were genuine and deeply felt. 'I don't know what you're talking about, and your efforts to explain aren't making much sense. Here, come and sit, and try to tell me about it rationally.'

'*Rationally?* There's nothing rational about this!'

'I can't judge that, can I, until I know what "this" is?' She steered him towards a couch that floated an armslength above the floor. 'There. Sit. And for the gods' sakes, Benet, don't take all day about it, because *I* need to talk to *you* — and that's more important than anything to do with Lady Pirane or some petty overlord!'

Benetan stared at her, white-lipped. 'You think so? More important than the slaughter of half the people in this demesne and the ruination of the rest?'

Andraia's temper was always volatile, and at this she flared up furiously. 'Damn it, Benet, what's done is done, and you can't change it! And anyway, who do these peasants have to blame but themselves? If they hadn't —'

'I'm not *talking* about what's already happened!' Benetan shouted. 'I'm talking about what *will* happen, *now*! Now that this — this monstrous apology for a human being has been given back his power and a free hand to do as he likes with it!'

Andraia knew nothing of the meeting, nothing of Overlord Leyan's savage diatribe in which, to Benetan at least, he had revealed himself as a small-minded and malevolent despot whose sole desire in the wake of the uprising was to teach the people he ruled a lesson which they — or at least those who survived his vengeance – would never forget. Leyan had described his planned reprisals in detail and asked Pirane for the magi's help in carrying them out, but Pirane had refused. The uprising had been stopped, she said, and the populace made aware that any further attempt to overturn authority would not be tolerated. That meant that there was now no danger to Leyan or his remaining servants, and nothing to prevent the overlord from taking up the reins of power once more. That much Pirane had been prepared to do, but she did not consider it appropriate for her to intervene any further in the affair. If Leyan wished to carry out mass executions or any other form of punishment, that was his privilege. The Star Peninsula, however, had no further interest in the matter.

Benetan had tried to protest, tried to make Pirane realize that the free hand she was giving to Leyan was a death-sentence for a very great number of innocent people. The rebels' ringleaders were dead and the uprising had been quashed so swiftly and effectively that there was no chance it would flare up again. From his own experiences as a Chaos rider Benetan knew that the great majority of individuals involved in any affray were bystanders who could not, in all justice, be held accountable. To take reprisal on all for the crimes of a mere few was – he had used the words and Leyan had been enraged, though the overlord hadn't dared show his feelings too overtly – the act of a fool or a coward.

He might have said a great deal more, but Pirane had silenced him at that point with a fearsome warning look, and when the overlord left shortly afterwards she had made it clear that Benetan had spoken out of turn and she was very far from pleased by his behaviour. Benetan had made one more faltering attempt to appeal to her sense of justice, but Pirane was unmoved. How the overlords chose to manage their demesnes was entirely their own affair, she stated aloofly. Leyan was obviously a coward, and certainly a fool; but the magi and their servants had far better things to do than worry over petty details, and it would be a fine how-do-you-do if they were expected to demean themselves by becoming involved in such trivialities. Now, assuming that Captain Liss had nothing more constructive to say on the subject of Overlord Leyan, Andraia would doubtless be awaiting him eagerly.

As the whole sorry tale came tumbling out, Andraia realized that she had never seen Benetan so deeply and emotionally angry. Furious, yes; during the quarrels that were so much a part of their relationship he could give as good an account of himself as she did, and it was one of the qualities that made him so attractive to her. But this was more than mere fury. This went far deeper. And she didn't understand it.

'Benet.' She hadn't interrupted him before now, but the flow of words was diminishing at last as he realized that he was beginning to repeat himself. 'Benet, wait.' They were sitting together on the couch and she took hold of one of his hands. For a moment it seemed he would pull away, then he relented and, encouraged, she continued. 'I know you're upset – no, all right, that's an understatement, I see it's far more than that. But haven't you rather lost your sense of perspective?'

Benetan instantly tensed again and his eyes narrowed. He didn't speak, however, and for once Andraia misjudged the implications of his silence. She smiled reassuringly, cajolingly. 'My love, you can hardly hold Lady Pirane responsible for what an overlord does or doesn't choose to do! She's quite right; the magi have far more important matters to concern them. Besides – as I tried to say a few minutes ago – these people aren't blameless, not by any means. They tried to *murder* their overlord. They burned his house, they killed his militia . . . you don't condone that, do you? No, of course you don't! And now they have to be *shown*, Benet. They have to be shown that insurrection won't be tolerated. Good gods, if nothing's done, then how long will it be before trouble flares up again?'

'It won't.' Benetan's voice had a dangerous edge.

'But it *could*. If the ringleaders aren't brought to justice —'

'I'm not talking about the ringleaders! Damn you, don't you ever *listen?* I'm talking about the innocent ones, the ones who committed no crime, the ones who are too old and feeble or too young and unknowing to have had anything to do with this! Children, Andraia! This creature means to execute *children!*'

'Children grow up. And if their parents were among the insurgents —'

'Then the crime of the sire is the crime of the son?' With a violent movement Benetan wrenched his hand from her grasp and stood up, backing away from her as though from a snake. 'Is that your idea of justice?'

Andraia looked baffled and a little hurt. 'It isn't my place to dispense justice. It's the magi's right and privilege to decide such things, and if Lady Pirane is content then I must be too, because Lady Pirane is wiser than I am. It's as simple as that, Benet. The magi know what's right and they will do what's right, as they always have done.' She paused, frowning. 'Besides, does it really matter how many of these people live and how many die? It's nothing to do with us, and there's no reason why it should affect us.'

For several seconds there was silence. Then, speaking slowly and incredulously, Benetan said, 'I can't believe this. I can't believe it.' He drew a racking breath. 'Are you really so blind and stupid and arrogant that you think you can dismiss this vicious madness as nothing, simply because

141

we're not obliged to soil our hands with it? Yandros help me, your mind must be *diseased!*'

Andraia's temper, which she had been struggling to keep under control, erupted. 'How *dare* you say that to me!' She too was on her feet, blazing, her voice shrill. 'How *dare* you, you puppy, you oaf, you – you obnoxious *nobody! Who do you think you're talking to?*'

'I'm beginning to find out who I'm talking to! A cold-hearted, self-absorbed bitch who doesn't know the meaning of human decency!'

'*Ohh!*' Without even pausing to think Andraia snatched up an ornament, a small, abstract figurine, from a nearby table. Her arm swung back –

'Throw it,' Benetan said, 'and I'll break your wrist.'

Cold shock went through her, snapping the hold of her rage as she realized that he meant it – and following fast came a second realization. For two years she had been convinced that Benetan was an open book to her. Since their liaison began she had always been able to manipulate him by one means or another, and she had slipped comfortably into the assumption that she knew all there was to know of him. But that assumption was disastrously, over-whelmingly wrong. This was an aspect of Benetan's nature which she hadn't dreamed existed. And in revealing it, he had suddenly become a stranger.

Very slowly she lowered her arm. She didn't want to; every instinct screamed at her to hurl the figurine at his head and follow it with anything else she could lay her hands on. But if she did, he would hurt her. She was certain of it, the promise was in his eyes. At this moment he looked as cold and implacable as Lord Vordegh, and Andraia was frightened.

She let the ornament go, heard it fall to the floor. 'I don't know you any more.' Her voice was shaking with emotion but the words were barely more than a whisper. 'Something's happened to you. Something's *changed* you.' She knew what it must be. She *knew*. Gods, had it truly gone that far? Had that pallid trull, that evil little schemer, injected her poison so deeply into Benetan's veins that he was now one with the heretics? The accusation quivered on her tongue and she wanted to hurl it at him as she hadn't dared to hurl the figurine, confront him, dare him, challenge him to deny it. But the words wouldn't come. She couldn't bring herself to say them, for she couldn't bring herself to face the possibility that they might be true. But the other thing, the other goad . . . oh, for that the words *would* come.

'I understand.' Her voice was savage with bitterness. 'There's a new influence working on you, isn't there, Benet? A new light in your life.' Her mouth distorted. 'Suddenly you're the peasants' champion and a paragon of compassion. Suddenly you have conveniently set aside your rank and your duty and your privilege – and all because some blue-eyed trollop has emerged from the dungheap of your past and flaunted her charms under your twitching, gullible nose!'

'*Don't say that about Iselia –*'

'I'll say what I please! Your precious Iselia's nothing but a whore! Just ask Savrinor – after all, he knows her *intimately!*' That hurt him and she was glad, and wanted the knife-point to stab home further. 'Or perhaps you don't need to ask him? Perhaps when his back has been turned you've already had a second-hand taste of what she can offer? Is *that* why you're so besotted with her, Benetan? Has Savrinor taught her new tricks, and does she perform them for you?'

Benetan's face was white, and for a moment Andraia thought she had gone too far. He might be her inferior in theory but that didn't change the fact that he had twice her physical strength and had been trained to use it. If he chose to, if something within him snapped, then he could do far worse to her than merely breaking her wrist.

But he didn't. Instead, to her astonishment, he turned his head away.

'There's no point in this.' His tone was flat. 'If you can only hurl insults at someone who can't defend herself, then there's no point in my listening and no point in your saying any more.' He looked at her again. 'Think what you please about me. I know the truth, but I'll keep it to myself. You see, truth is like justice and mercy and decency. A spoilt child can't understand the concept, so it isn't worth the trouble of explaining.'

'That is a *contemptible* thing to say!'

Benetan lifted his shoulders. 'Then it puts us on an equal footing, doesn't it?'

He wasn't even angry now, she realized; he was simply utterly uninterested. That shocked her, and it also wounded her far more viciously than she had wounded him. If she needed proof of his feelings for Iselia Darrow — and but for her own stubbornness, Andraia thought bitterly, she would have seen the truth a long time ago — she had that proof now.

'Well, it seems we understand each other.' Her fury, like his, had suddenly gone, replaced by arid misery and desolation. 'You're quite right about me, and I freely admit it. I *am* blind, and I *am* stupid — I must be, to ever have taken up with a two-faced creature like you! I'm very sorry, Benetan. I'm sorry that I let you crawl into my life, that I let you creep into my bed; that I ever troubled to treat you with anything more than the scorn which you deserve!' Her lip was beginning to quiver and she couldn't force it to stop. Anger might be absent but hatred was not, and hating him was fractionally more comfort than hating herself. 'You had the effrontery to call Leyan a coward, but he's worth fifty of you. He must be, for you're worth *nothing!* Go away, you hypocrite — get out of this room, get out of my life! Go and sniff round the heels of your village harlot, and I wish you joy of her! I never want to set eyes on you again, I never want to hear your name spoken again – and I swear to all the gods, if you ever so much as *attempt* to –'

'*Andraia.*'

The flood of words broke off in a squeak of shock as the new voice cut across the room, and Andraia spun round.

Pirane stood in the doorway. She raked them both with a glare which made Andraia, at least, feel as if she had been flayed to the bone, then came in and closed the door very quietly behind her.

'Andraia. Your voice is audible through half the citadel. If you wish to quarrel, kindly do so at a more civilized volume, or conduct your brawl elsewhere.'

Andraia looked down at the floor. 'I'm sorry, madam.' No *buts*; Pirane didn't brook excuses. Suddenly, to her consternation, a tear squeezed past her eyelids and dropped.

The magus saw it and turned to regard Benetan. 'Captain Liss,' she said curtly, 'I think it will be as well if you leave us.'

'Madam.' He started towards the door, his back like a ramrod.

'You'll find your mare on the citadel's lower level. Ask a servant if you don't know the way.'

Benetan stopped, stared at her, and she gave him a very cold smile.

'I seem to recall, Captain, that I said I would inform you if your presence here should be inconvenient. It is inconvenient. You have a journey to continue, and I believe it will suit us all better if you continue it without any further delay. I will forward your report to the First Magus, and I wish you good day.' She made the sign of the gods towards him, though it was a mere formality with no warmth. 'Yandros speed you, Captain Liss.'

Even if he'd wanted to say anything to Andraia – even if there had been anything he could say now – it was too late. Pirane would not give him a second chance. Benetan squared his shoulders, nodded, made a correct bow to the magus and left the room. Pirane listened until his footsteps had faded, then looked at Andraia.

'Child. If there is anything you want to tell me . . .'

For a moment Andraia almost did. It would be so easy; Pirane was not only her mentor but also her champion and friend – she would believe the truth about Iselia Darrow, she would understand Andraia's terrible dilemma, and above all, she would know what to do for the best.

But the best might lead Benetan to the execution block . . .

'Thank you, madam.' She fought to make her voice steady. 'But I think I would rather not. I think I would just . . . just like to go home.'

She wished that she could have travelled by road rather than through the Maze, for that would have given her time to think. But Pirane wouldn't hear of such a thing; and anyway, a part of her longed to be back amid the comfort of the castle's familiar surroundings as soon as possible.

Pirane didn't accompany her – she had one or two minor matters to oversee before she left, the magus said – but she sent word on ahead to warn Lua of Andraia's arrival. And when she was home, and Lua's curiosity at her sudden return had been assuaged with a little subterfuge and evasion, Andraia did at last have time to think and come to a decision. There was only one person she could turn to, and that person was Savrinor. She had been tempted to tell him the truth once before, but cowardice and fear for Benetan's safety had got the better of her. Now, though, everything had changed, and she needed a mind like Savrinor's – clear-cut and intelligent and above all pragmatic – to help her. She could trust him, and if he could be persuaded to promise secrecy, at least for the time being, she knew that promise would be kept.

Escaping at last from her mother's well-meaning but unwanted attentions, she went to her room and methodically destroyed everything she could find that reminded her of Benetan. Items that were small enough to burn went on the fire; the rest she bundled up in the folds of a gown she had had made especially to please her erstwhile lover, and gave the bundle to a servant with strict instructions that it should go straight into the kitchen furnaces. Then, telling herself that she felt cleansed and free and was *not* in danger of bursting into tears, she sought out the historian.

She found him in the dining hall. It was early evening and there weren't many people in the vast chamber as yet; looking about as she stood on the threshold Andraia saw Savrinor's pale-haired, elegant figure at a table near the fireplace. He was alone, and eagerly she started towards him –

And stopped as she saw that someone else would be there before her.

Savrinor turned as Iselia approached him, and Andraia saw him reach out, take her hand and draw her down onto the bench beside him. One arm went possessively around her shoulders, and something in the way he moved told Andraia that he was under the influence of a strong and doubtless highly pleasurable drug.

Andraia felt as though something within her had withered. She couldn't approach him. His preoccupations were obvious, and no ploy would be enough to get him away from Iselia. And it put an end to Andraia's hopes, for she knew herself well enough to be aware that her resolve wouldn't last. If she didn't confide her secret now she would not be able to summon the courage to confide it tomorrow. She had had one chance, and now it was gone.

Neither Savrinor nor Iselia had seen her. Andraia moved back, out into the corridor once more, then turned and ran towards the main staircase and the sanctuary of her room. With only the fire to light it the room was full of shadows, and they crowded in on her, renewing memories that she didn't want to recall.

She lit as many lamps and candles as she could find, set them around her bed and cried herself to sleep amid the protecting circle of their light.

CHAPTER X

'*Kaldar. Kaldar.*'

The walls of the long-house seemed to absorb the name as he repeated it, soaking it in and smothering it in silence. Simbrian paused, eyes closed, mind striving to reach further into the spaces between dimensions and forge the link that still eluded him.

'*Kaldar. Kaldar.*'

Nothing. Only a sense of emptiness, of a barrier that refused to be breached. Wherever Kaldar was – and that begged the darker question of whether he was even alive – he either could not or would not answer.

Simbrian knew that he would have to give up. His mental faculties were so depleted that his concentration was beginning to wander, his body ached from immobility and there was a gnawing in the pit of his stomach. He needed sleep and he needed food; for five days now he'd had the barest minimum of both and the strain was taking its toll. A quick meal, perhaps an hour or two's rest, and he would be in a better state to try again.

He opened his eyes, blinking as his vision adjusted to a longer focus. The contours of the room were dimly visible, which meant that dawn must be close. With luck, no one else would be up and about yet and he would be able to feed himself without the complication of inquiries and questions. He didn't think he had the energy left to face questions at this moment, however well-intentioned they might be.

Both his legs were seized by cramp as he tried to move,

and with a grimace he rocked back again and began to rub at his calves to ease the ache. Then, in mid-motion, he froze.

There was a light in the room. It was faint and uncertain, and at first he thought it must be either a first reflection from the rising sun or, more likely, a hallucination brought on by weariness. But even as he struggled to make sense of it, it began to glow more brightly, forming into a tall, narrow oval that wavered and flickered through a spectrum of strange colours like an earthbound rainbow. And at the heart of the oval a face was taking form; the face of a starkly handsome man with golden, pupil-less eyes, set in a frame of cascading silver-white hair.

The shock of recognition obliterated all thought of his own discomfort and Simbrian's mouth opened. For several seconds he couldn't find his voice, and when at last it did come he knew that no words could be adequate to express what he felt. Mind reeling as astonishment, elation and awe threatened to swamp him, he stammered, 'M-my . . . my Lord Aeoris!'

'Simbrian.' The great god of Order's voice had an eerie timbre, as though he were speaking across a very great distance, and the sorcerer had to strain to catch his words. 'This link between our worlds is weak and I cannot maintain it for long. But I wish to speak with you.' The oval of light glowed brighter and the face with its strange golden eyes became more sharply focused. 'Concerning Kaldar.'

Simbrian was stunned. He knew that the power he and his sorcerers raised during their vigils was giving strength to their exiled gods, but he hadn't dreamed that that strength could be enough, yet, to allow Aeoris to manifest without a full ritual to pave the way.

Aeoris smiled, and the smile softened the unhuman contours of his serenely handsome face. 'Chaos's barriers are weakening, my friend. We are rapidly regaining our power, and with each day that dawns we are able to make the breach a little wider. But for all its value, this achievement does not – and will not – provide us with the means to challenge our enemies and prevail. To accomplish that, we need something more. We need Kaldar to succeed in his search.'

Simbrian gazed at the god in astonishment and chagrin. 'To *succeed*, my lord? But he intends to –'

'I know what he intends, Simbrian, and I am very well aware of the risk he is running.' For a moment a note of censure crept into Aeoris's voice and the sorcerer bowed his head, abashed. 'I'm also aware that Benetan Liss is no friend to us, and Kaldar's fond belief that he can persuade the man to our way of thinking is, to say the least, naive. Liss is a Chaos rider and has had years of indoctrination under the magi's regime. But while Kaldar's motive may have been misdirected, his action will serve us very well, for in one sense Benetan Liss has great potential as an ally of Order.'

Simbrian shook his head. 'Forgive me, my lord, but I don't understand. I see only the dangers – if this man is brought to the island, if he becomes privy to our secrets –'

'There is no need to take so great a risk. I have another and better rendezvous in mind, and even there he will learn nothing that we don't wish him to learn, for I and my brothers are strong enough now to shield you from any investigations that Chaos or its servants may attempt. This man must play his part, Simbrian. He holds a vital key – and we need that key, whatever the hazards involved.'

'As you will it, my lord.' Simbrian bowed his head humbly. He couldn't entirely shake off the fear that Kaldar's rashness would end in disaster, but neither would he dream to question his god's wisdom. For all his misgivings he could only acquiesce.

151

'Find Kaldar,' Aeoris said. His voice was more gentle, for he understood Simbrian's misgivings even if he did not share them. 'Make contact with him through your friends on the mainland, make your peace with him and tell him that his mission has his gods' blessing.' He smiled. 'And I hope you will feel able to tell him that it has your blessing, too.'

Simbrian hesitated, then ventured to look up and, slowly and a little sadly, returned the smile. 'Yes. I'll tell him that. But my lord, will Kaldar be safe?' His mouth was very dry; he swallowed. 'If he has misjudged Benetan Liss and they meet under the wrong circumstances . . .' He swallowed again. 'If anything were to happen to him, I could never forgive myself.'

'Rest assured, Kaldar will come to no harm,' Aeoris said. 'As we shield you we also have the power to shield him, and we shall do so. For all his faults and weaknesses, we too have no wish to lose him. As for forgiveness . . . that isn't a responsibility you need take upon your own shoulders. Be at peace with yourself, Simbrian – your work is onerous enough without adding to the burden.' The oval of light flickered again, and when it steadied its radiance was less bright. Aeoris paused briefly, as though perceiving something beyond the reach of mortal senses, then spoke again.

'I shall take my leave of you now. For all our safeguards, there is always a risk that Chaos might detect my presence in this world, and as yet it would not be wise to prolong my visits unnecessarily. When Kaldar has found the Chaos rider, tell him that the man is to be carried to the White Isle. We can maintain greater secrecy there, and the gateway between our worlds is better secured. Take Benetan Liss to the crater, and await further word from me.'

The oval dimmed again, and convulsively Simbrian scrambled to his feet as he realized that the god's image was fading. There was so much more he longed to say, so much more he needed to know, and his voice had a desperate note as he called out, 'Lord Aeoris, please wait –'

The words came back to him as though echoing across the breadth of a still valley. 'I cannot wait, Simbrian. But there will be other times. Many other times. Our blessing goes with you, good servant and friend.'

He had one last glimpse of Aeoris's eyes, twin points of light like golden stars shining through cloud, before the bright oval faded, faded, and merged into the dusty gleam of dawn breaking beyond the long-house's easterly window.

Very slowly Simbrian turned. His body ached with exhaustion and he was shaking, could barely keep on his feet; he managed to reach the door and leaned against the jamb for a few moments to steady himself and regain his sense of balance. His emotions were in turmoil, the joy of having been face to face with the greatest of his gods warring with the pain of loss now that that god had departed. He yearned to sleep, yet at the same time he was filled with a wild desire to climb onto the highest roof in the settlement and shout the news of Aeoris's visitation to everyone on the island. He wanted, *needed*, to communicate what he had experienced to another human soul, someone who would understand the depth of his emotion and perhaps, even at one remove, be able to share it.

He smiled wryly as he listened to the silence outside the long-house. No one about yet, no one to be his audience, and by the time they did wake, his weariness would have got the better of him. The smile was followed by a faint, private sigh, and Simbrian opened the door and stepped out into the cool of the early morning.

Nanithe was waiting, sitting on the dusty ground with her back against the stone wall. How long she had been there he didn't know, but her face lit as she saw him and she got to her feet, approaching with one hand tentatively extended. Simbrian took hold of her fingers, lifted them to his lips and kissed them. Then, answering the mute question in her eyes, he said,

'All's well, little one. All's very well. And Kaldar is safe.'

Her look became radiant, then abruptly changed to a motherly frown that made him want to laugh because it was so reminiscent of Shammana. She touched his arm and with her other hand made a gesture that clearly indicated someone lying down. Quelling his laughter so as not to offend her, Simbrian nodded.

'Yes. You're right; I am tired and I should rest. I will, Nanithe. Just for a few hours, and then I'll have much to say to everyone.' He bent forward, his bulk dwarfing her, and kissed her mouth very lightly. 'Tell Shammana about Kaldar.' She had her own ways, he knew, of communicating what she wanted to say. 'Then, if you will, sit by me while I sleep.' He paused. 'It will give me more comfort than I can express to know that you're there.'

Benetan knew that he should have tried to do something to stop the madness, but he also knew that the voice of one man, however passionate, could achieve nothing. As he left the citadel the first 'tithe' of human victims was already being herded into the square, and he felt the massed hatred emanating from them like a violent physical force as he rode away. He couldn't look at their faces, for to look would be to accept their contempt and condemnation. Nor could he meet the cold gazes of Leyan's militiamen, who despite their depleted numbers now had the district under iron control again, thanks to Pirane's warning about the consequence of any further resistance. They held him in contempt of a different kind, for word of his outburst against Leyan's plans for retribution had spread, and Benetan knew that but for the protection of his rank it was unlikely he would have reached the edge of the village unscathed.

But he did reach the edge of the village, and as the last straggle of buildings fell away behind him he shortened rein and dug his heels viciously into his mare's flanks. She jerked up her head, snorting a protest, and he swore savagely at her, lashing her with the ends of the reins so that she leaped forward into a gallop, careering towards the forest that spread like low-lying smoke in the distance ahead. Benetan's vision was blurring with tears but he could still see that away to the south where the forest gave way to fields there was another haze, real smoke this time as a farmstead and its surrounding livestock pens burned.

This was just the first. How many more would be turned out of their homes and made destitute, all for one man's spite? The wind carried sounds from the blazing steading, sounds Benetan didn't want to acknowledge and fought not to hear; trapped animals shrieking, dying . . . Before the sun set again there would be human deaths, too; men and women, the young and the old, culled at random to pay the ultimate penalty with no appeal and no hope of reprieve. And Pirane did nothing, and Andraia shut her eyes and her mind and pretended there was no injustice.

'Damn them! *Damn* them!' Benetan lashed at the mare again, blindly, venting his frustration and anguish on the only target available and not even knowing whom he truly wanted to curse. The mare screamed and tried to buck; he hit her again, then suddenly woke up to what he was doing. It wasn't her fault – she couldn't know his feelings, couldn't understand his violence. If she had been Pirane, if she had been Leyan, Vordegh, Andraia, *any* of them – but she wasn't, she was only an animal, an innocent bystander like so many others.

They were almost at the forest's edge and to Benetan the trees were a haven that would shroud him and shut him

155

away from the insanity that was about to be perpetrated in Chaos's name and with Chaos's tacit consent. He allowed the mare to slow at last and turned her to where a track led into the woodland. They entered the forest at a trot, and when they were deep enough among the trees for the open land to be invisible Benetan halted and slid out of the saddle.

'I'm sorry.' He stroked the mare's neck. 'I didn't mean to take it out on you. I didn't mean it.'

The mare turned her head to regard him and suddenly he pressed his face against the rough tangles of her mane, closing his eyes and trying to control the ragged breaths that hurt his lungs and throat. His conscience was tearing him apart and his treatment of the mare was only a tiny fraction of it. He could have done something to stop Leyan. Surely, *surely*, he could have done something? He had power, he had rank; for all the gods' sakes, he was leader of the Chaos riders!

But the magi are your masters, a cold inner voice reminded him, *and the magi's word is law.*

'No.' Benetan spoke aloud, startling the mare who tossed her head and sidestepped. 'No.' He straightened, wiping a hand fiercely across his face. His right arm was hurting; he could feel a prickling sensation on his back and suspected that the shoulder wound had opened again, but in his present mood he wouldn't have cared if he'd been bleeding to death. 'Not the magi's word. Yandros makes the law. Not the magi. *Yandros.*'

A calm, aquiline face, framed by hair too vividly gold to be human; eyes whose colour changed with every moment and a smile that conveyed enigmatic amusement . . . Benetan had been drunk at the time and hadn't realized the stranger's identity until afterwards, when Savrinor berated him for his stupidity, but now he could conjure Yandros's face in his mind again as clearly as if the god had stepped out from the trees to confront him. A surge of confused emotions roiled up and he turned his face to the sky, though he could barely glimpse it through the leaf canopy. Did the gods listen to their worshippers? Could Yandros hear the voice of one solitary mortal, and if he could, would he respond? Benetan didn't know the answer but he had to believe that it was possible, for if it wasn't, then nothing made sense any more.

His hand closed around the star-shaped amulet on its chain at his neck and he lowered himself to one knee. He hadn't prayed to the gods in this way for many, many years – the prayers of Chaos's servants were personal, spontaneous, and could as naturally be whispered from the warmth of a curtained bed or shouted joyfully on horseback at full gallop as proffered in any formal fashion. But Benetan was weighed down with an ache of remorse and grief that no power of his own could remove from him, and this obeisance, this gesture of submission that, he felt, placed him at the feet and in the hands of Yandros was a small comfort. His mind reached out, striving to touch a dimension beyond the confines of the mortal world, and in words that came haltingly but with great intensity he entreated the Chaos lord to intervene and stop the murder and ruin being perpetrated in his name.

Sunlight played on his bowed figure and cast glints in his dark hair. The wind rustled the leaves above him and faintly, penetrating through the green scents of the wood, the acrid tang of smoke drifted from the east. Benetan didn't know how long he stayed there, how many times he repeated his desperate plea, but finally the last dregs of psychic and emotional energy were gone from him and he knew that he could do no more.

He rose to his feet, feeling light-headed and disorientated, and looked around. The forest was quiet. There was no sense of an unearthly presence, no feeling of calm or succour within his mind. Only a distant fuss of birds squabbling somewhere deeper among the trees and the irregular sound of grass blades tearing as his mare grazed. If Yandros had heard his prayers he had not deigned to answer them, and suddenly desolation descended on Benetan like a stone weight. He still didn't believe that the lords of Chaos could truly sanction what was happening in the demesne, but it seemed that even if they did not sanction, neither were they prepared to intercede. At this moment that felt like the final betrayal of everything he had held dear.

He rubbed at his eyes again, angry with himself for such a childish reaction. In honesty he knew that it wasn't the gods his mind railed against, but Andraia. Andraia, and her unwillingness to face truth and responsibility. Perhaps she couldn't be held to blame, for she was a child of the castle and it was unfair to expect her to cast off such a heritage easily. But wherever the fault might or might not lie, Benetan couldn't forgive her and that was what hurt, for he still loved her. And love couldn't be conveniently snuffed out, like snuffing a candle-flame, if the object of that love was suddenly found wanting.

He didn't want to stay in this district. His lost weapons had been replaced and his provisions replenished; Pirane had seen to those details with her usual scrupulous efficiency. His report would be conveyed to the First Magus. There was nothing to keep him here, nothing he could do to right the wrongs – great or small – that had been perpetrated. And nothing but enmity on all sides.

He walked to where the mare was still cropping hungrily, and made the *tiss*-ing sound that would attract her attention and tell her it was time to go. She lifted her head, nudged playfully at him as he mounted – a trivial gesture but one of forgiveness, and that hurt, too – and, as he gathered up the reins, moved eagerly towards the track and the southward road.

*   *   *

Lord Vordegh rarely slept and had no concern for the convenience of others, so Savrinor wasn't entirely surprised to be woken in the dead of night by a messenger telling him that the First Magus required his presence. Iselia didn't stir as he was dressing, which irrationally piqued him, but the heaviness of her breathing and the dark shadows under her eyes told their own story. Hers was a drugged sleep, and nothing short of a violent physical shaking would bring her out of it. He would have to do something about her before long, Savrinor reflected, and squashed the uneasy frisson that assailed him whenever his mind strayed along that path. Though he was very reluctant to admit it he was growing afraid for Iselia, for what had begun as a pleasant occasional diversion was now in his opinion a fully-fledged addiction. She would deny it, of course – inexperienced fools always did – but he knew the signs too well to mistake them. It was largely his own fault, he knew; he'd introduced her to Moonwrack in the first place, and had found perverse pleasure in the fact that she seemed to take to it as readily as he had done when he first experimented with it nearly twenty years ago. But he had studied the art of self-control and learned to keep his own addiction within bounds. Iselia didn't have that ability, and Savrinor knew what lay in store for her if her dependency wasn't checked before it got out of hand. Weaning her off the stuff wouldn't be a pleasant experience for either of them, and the worst prospect of all was the knowledge that a part of her would hate him for it. But if it came to a choice between that and her safety there would be no choice, for he didn't want any harm to come to her. Above all, he didn't want that.

He tried to stop the problem from preying on his mind as he gathered up his small case of writing materials and left the apartment. It would be unwise in the extreme to allow anything to distract him while he was in Vordegh's presence; especially so if the most recent whisperings were true. Four days ago, time had run out for the hostages held under the terms of the First Magus's edict, which meant that unless a good deal of information about the heretic cult leaders had been forthcoming from the demesnes, the mass executions had by now been carried out. Savrinor hadn't yet seen any of the reports which the Chaos riders had brought back to the castle and so didn't know what they contained, but rumour suggested that the exercise had achieved nothing and a lot of people had died to no purpose. If, as Savrinor suspected, that tallied with Vordegh's expectations, then the First Magus would be ready to begin the next stage of his stratagem. Hence this abrupt summons; Vordegh clearly intended that the castle's archivist should play a part in the second move of the game as he had done in the first. And that, if Savrinor was not very careful indeed, could lead him into trouble.

Savrinor was well aware that the First Magus did not like him. His talents were appreciated, and indeed on more than one occasion Vordegh had directly complimented his acumen, tact and efficiency, which from such a man was high praise indeed. But the personal level was another matter entirely. Vordegh eschewed pleasures of the flesh; he didn't drink, ate little and plainly, and as far as anyone knew had never laid hands on a woman – or a man, for that matter – for any purpose, nor ever wished to. Savrinor's appetites were no secret, and for that Vordegh despised him and would tolerate him only for as long as he made no wrong move in his official dealings. But each such dealing was a test. Just one error of judgement, one whiff of dissent, and the First Magus would take cold pleasure in breaking him. The knowledge of what such a fate would mean made the now familiar knot of fear tighten in Savrinor's stomach as he walked through dark corridors towards Vordegh's apartments.

The First Magus was waiting for him. No Verdice to show him in tonight, only a terse 'Enter' in response to his knock at the outer door. Vordegh sat at his desk in the inner room, the customary neat stack of papers before him. There was no fire and the room felt as cold as the northern sea-bed. Savrinor bowed formally and waited, trying not to shiver.

'Master Savrinor.' When the First Magus spoke at last it was impossible to gauge his mood; his voice was simply detached and perfectly controlled. 'As you are no doubt aware, the time limit specified in my edict to the overlords passed four days ago. A little over one thousand commoners have been executed, and the riders' sergeants have brought back seventy-eight reports for my edification.' He raised his eyebrows slightly at the word *edification* but there was no humour in the gesture. 'As I anticipated, the reports contain nothing of any worth whatever.'

Savrinor cleared his throat. 'I'm sorry to hear that, my lord.'

Vordegh looked up, his dark eyes intent. 'Don't belittle both our intellects with platitudes, if you please; you know as well as I do that this is a perfectly satisfactory outcome. And it has already borne its first fruit. You'll have heard about the attempted uprising in one of the south-western demesnes?'

Silently cursing himself for not having been more careful, Savrinor nodded. 'Yes, sir. I don't know precisely what happened, but –'

'Magus Pirane dealt with the matter and will give you details if you require them. For the present, all you need to know is that the rebellion took place and was suppressed, and that I am of the opinion that it has had the desired effect.'

Savrinor wasn't quite sure what the First Magus meant by that, but he also knew that uncertainty was another human failing of which Vordegh disapproved. Gambling

161

that his judgement was right he ventured, 'You mean, my lord, that the rebels' failure will have weakened support for the heretics?'

Vordegh smiled his wintry smile. 'You are as perceptive as ever, Master Savrinor. I understand that a small heretic faction was involved in this mischief, and when the trouble began they had considerable support among the peasantry. However, by the time overlord . . .' he consulted the topmost paper of the stack, '. . . Overlord Leyan has completed his reprisals, a great many of those who rallied so eagerly to the rebels' call will, I think, be reconsidering their views. And of course the tales will fly from district to district, and grow with re-telling.' Vordegh sat back in his chair and regarded the historian levelly. 'The common people are not altogether stupid, and when the noble principles of the heretics fail to save a man's family from the pyre, or his house and chattels from destruction, those principles tend to lose their appeal. I anticipate, therefore, that the *next* reports I receive from the demesnes will be of a very different calibre to the first.'

Something deep inside Savrinor contracted with a tight, unpleasant sensation, and cautiously he said, 'Do I take it, my lord, that you require me to prepare copies of a new edict?'

'That is precisely what I require, Master Savrinor. However, this time I shall not leave the implementation in the hands of the overlords. I intend to take a more direct and personal interest.' He picked up the sheaf of parchments on his desk and handed the pile to Savrinor. 'The overlords have been instructed to deal with the questioning and execution of their suspects; you will need only to collate these reports and add them to the castle archives. The topmost sheet is the text of my message. It is to be sent to the larger demesnes, as before, with the instruction that its content is to be made public.'

Savrinor looked at the parchment. There wasn't time to take in more than the gist of the edict, but the gist was enough.

'Yes, my lord.' He hoped to all seven of the gods that his voice didn't betray his thoughts.

'I will require the copies by midnight tomorrow,' Vordegh said levelly.

Savrinor bowed, then, as it seemed this last command had also been a dismissal, began to turn towards the door. But he had taken only one pace when the First Magus spoke again.

'One more matter, Master Savrinor.'

Quickly Savrinor turned back. 'My lord?'

'I wish you to perform another small task.' Vordegh's glacial eyes regarded him impersonally. 'I take it that at present we have no candidates in the castle awaiting designation?'

'None, sir. The last gleaning was on the night that the old First Magus died, and with –'

'With Captain Liss at present in the south there have been no further sorties during his absence. Mmm.' Vordegh's eyelids half-closed, putting Savrinor in mind of a snake. 'Well, I haven't the time to wait for another gleaning to be organized. You will make the choice from among the servants instead. I shall require twenty-one individuals, preferably young. Consult one of the junior secretaries for suitable nominees, and choose those whose removal won't affect the smooth running of the castle's domestic affairs.'

Savrinor swallowed. 'Yes, my lord.' He hesitated. 'If I may beg to enquire . . . to aid me in my choice . . . what the – ah – purpose . . . ?' His voice tailed off.

Vordegh's expression didn't change. 'Your choice, Master Savrinor, is a matter for your own discretion. But to satisfy your insatiable curiosity, the nominees will be used in a rite I intend to perform.' Abruptly his gaze lost its focus, as though he had flicked his consciousness into another, less tangible dimension and was issuing a monstrous challenge to what he saw there. Then, smoothly, the moment passed and he was his emotionless self again as he added detachedly, 'Their bodies and souls will constitute the proper fee to be paid in such an undertaking.'

Savrinor couldn't answer. It wasn't the words, nor even the carelessness with which Vordegh had uttered them; there was nothing unprecedented about an order like this. But the look he had glimpsed, briefly, in the First Magus's eyes sent a white-hot stab of sheer horror into him. It was unclean, rabid; *evil*. The look of a man who had calmly and deliberately chosen to cast reason to the four winds – and to open his mind and his soul to titanic and all-consuming madness.

Savrinor made a bow so deep that Vordegh could not see his face. Then, feeling as though a dead hand was trying to tear his gut from his body, he turned and left the room.

The morning was half over when Iselia woke. Her eyes were sore and her temples throbbed and there was an evil taste of stale wine in the back of her throat; she pulled herself out of bed and stumbled through to the outer room, fumbling for a drinking vessel – anything, it didn't matter – on her way. Savrinor no longer locked his drugs cupboard; he had abandoned that after the night when, having hidden the key in an effort to keep her cravings in check, he himself had indulged in such a cocktail that he couldn't remember the key's hiding place and had been obliged to break the lock to satisfy his own needs. The splintered door had been mended – he couldn't abide imperfection, even in an item of furniture – but the key remained lost. So Iselia mixed her customary dosage of Moonwrack, added a stimulant which she hoped would ease the ache that seemed to suffuse her entire body, and drank the concoction. Almost immediately her head began to swim, but she was used to the reaction and knew it would pass within a few minutes. Provided she could avoid being sick . . . though that had only happened twice since the disastrous night in the great hall; a sign, she thought, that her tolerance to the Moonwrack's side-effects was improving. Swaying a little, but convinced that she already felt better, she returned to the bedroom . . . and saw Savrinor.

He was lying prone in the bed, face turned sideways but obscured by his hair, one arm hanging limply with the hand trailing on the floor. In her haste to find the Moonwrack Iselia hadn't even noticed his presence, for he tended to be an early riser and logically should have been gone from the apartment and about the castle on his day's business long ago. But instead here he was, apparently dead to the world.

She felt a sharp thrill then at the thought that possibly he *was* dead, but it was short-lived, for as she moved closer she could see that he was breathing, though irregularly. There was a wineglass on the floor inches from his fingers, and an empty triple-flagon lay on its side a foot's length beyond that. The flagon was surrounded by a dark stain but by the look of it the spillage had been small. That vessel had been here when they went to bed and neither of them had touched it then . . . little wonder he was comatose now!

Iselia's mind was clearing, and with clarity came curiosity. What could have provoked Savrinor to drink himself insensible? He had been content enough when he allowed her to sleep – she pushed away the memory of what had contented him – and nothing had disturbed their rest afterwards.

Or had it? There was a fleeting recollection at the back of her mind, something she had glimpsed in the other room just now but hadn't heeded. She turned quickly and went back to the outer chamber. Yes – on his desk. Some papers that hadn't been there last night . . .

She crossed to the desk on silent feet and looked down at the pile of parchments. Most seemed to be lists of names, none of which were familiar, and at the end of each list was an overlord's official seal. Gradually Iselia began to understand the lists' significance, and a chill settled on her that had nothing to do with the cold of a winter morning. These were the names of Order's suspected devotees. Or rather, the names of those whom it was expedient to accuse for the sake of satisfying the First Magus's edict. Were any of these people truly followers of Aeoris? Or had they simply been given at random, chosen because it was better to denounce a neighbour than to let a loved one die? She knew what must have happened by now in demesnes throughout the land. She had even dreamed of it, and in her dreams the stench of roasting flesh had choked her. That was what had brought about the uprising and the short-lived hopes that one magus and her citadel had crushed so thoroughly. How many had died? Impossible to know, for the overlords' messages said nothing of the executions. There were only the endless lists of names.

Iselia set the papers down again and struggled to clear her mind. Whatever her own reaction to these lists, they would have had no effect on Savrinor, she thought bitterly. So what else was here? What else, that could have made him want to seek oblivion in wine? She started to rifle through the documents again – and realized abruptly that the last two papers in the sheaf were not lists but something else.

The top sheet bore Savrinor's handwriting, and the brief note he had made was cryptic. The figure 21, and beneath that, scrawled as though in great haste – or great stress? – a single word: *Expendable*.

She didn't understand. She set the paper down and looked at the second sheet. It was in Vordegh's hand, and it was a text of a new edict. Iselia read it, and when she had finished she set the page down slowly and carefully. The First Magus was very specific, very clear, very concise. And what he intended made her feel sick to the core of her soul.

She stood up, and straightened the papers until each edge was precisely aligned just as Savrinor had left them. Then she turned and walked steadily back into the bedchamber. Savrinor hadn't stirred, and as she stared down at him Iselia wondered if, contrary to everything she knew of him, he had a conscience after all. The idea made her lips twist cynically – yet wasn't this evidence, of a kind? The First Magus's new plan, it seemed, was too much for even Savrinor to stomach, and had moved him to some excess of emotion. Almost as though he had a human streak.

Savrinor's trailing hand twitched and he began to snore faintly. For a moment Iselia was touched by something that was almost compassion, then ruthlessly she quelled it. Her only feelings towards Savrinor were those of hatred and contempt. He was chief among her enemies, and for an enemy there would be no quarter.

She turned away, slipped out of the silk nightgown that had been his gift to her, and began to dress.

CHAPTER XI

Tarod paced to the end of the hall and swung round, the abrupt movement causing a ripple in the atmosphere that spread beyond the emerald walls and ended in a thunderous grumble far in the distance. For a moment a crimson aura sparked around him, and the tiny, jewel-like elementals that had been dancing close by scattered and fled. These mindless, drifting entities were always attracted to the Chaos lords, but anger frightened them – and Tarod was very angry. He also knew that Yandros was perfectly well aware of his mood, and that increased his ire for it meant that this whole display had probably been put on simply to humour him and keep the peace between them. Though his temper could outmatch any of his six brothers when it suited him, Yandros quickly grew bored with disharmony and Tarod suspected that his boredom threshold had now been reached.

But that didn't change the situation, and when he spoke at last Tarod's voice was suffused with a fury that he held only barely in check.

'You may find the whole matter a source of amusement,' he said, 'but I beg to differ! It's gone beyond a joke – *too* far beyond. And it's in danger of getting out of hand!'

Yandros leaned back in the carved chair, which bore a passing if sardonic resemblance to the First Magus's throne in the castle, and stretched his long legs elegantly out under the table. 'I didn't say that I find it amusing, Tarod. I most certainly don't; only a mortal could have a sense of humour quite *that* warped.' He turned the translucent cup he held between his fingers, studying the effect of the light on the wine in the bowl, then took an experimental sip from it. 'This is good. You should try some – or any of these.' An expansive gesture took in the dozen or so flasks on the table.

'If you want to divert yourself by finding out how mortals feel when they get drunk, that's your affair,' Tarod snapped. 'But if this charade is for my benefit you can dispense with it now. I've more important matters on my mind than the trivia of human pleasures.'

'Well, that makes a change.' Yandros raised an eyebrow, then grinned broadly at him. 'Or is that what lies at the root of all this? Is it simply a ruse, to give you an excuse to pay a further call on Secretary Qenever's daughter?' He saw Tarod's aura flare again and made a pacifying motion with his free hand. 'Calm down. It was just my joke; I acknowledge it was in bad taste and I apologize for it. But really, when you're in this frame of mind it's hard to resist the temptation to provoke you. Come out of your private storm-cloud, Tarod. I mean no slight to the lady Andraia, and I mean no slight to you.'

The affinity between them was such that Tarod took his words to heart. He relaxed a little. 'You'd be a hypocrite if you did,' he said, and there was faint if reluctant humour in his voice.

'I know. But Pirane and I go back a long way in her terms . . . even in our terms, come to that. And there's no danger of any misunderstanding where she's concerned. Which, incidentally, is a subject I've been meaning to discuss with you, though perhaps this isn't the time or the place.'

'It isn't.'

'All right, all right. But I don't want any complications. It would be tiresome for us and unjust to the girl if –'

Tarod interrupted him. '*Unjust?* Yandros, injustice is

precisely what I've been trying to bring to your attention, and I'm not talking about misguided infatuation on the part of one mortal woman! I'm talking about the acts that are being perpetrated, in our name, on an entire world!'

For a few moments Yandros looked at him, his expression inscrutable. Then he sighed. 'Oh dear. So you're dredging that up again, are you?' He made a pass with one hand, palm downward. The table vanished and the towering, shimmering green walls of the hall he had conjured dissolved into a void of dark, quietly shifting cloud. The tiny elementals had ventured to return; Yandros gave them a brief, warning glance and they flittered away again, vanishing into the gloom.

'Very well.' The great Chaos lord sounded resigned. 'No adornments, no embellishments, nothing to distract either of us. Does this satisfy you? Good. Then I'll say what I have to say and be done with it. The difference, Tarod, between the injustice that *might* be done to the girl Andraia and the injustice that Vordegh unquestionably *is* inflicting on the people he rules, is that one is the direct consequence of an action taken in this realm, and the other is not. I greatly dislike Vordegh's methods; in fact I greatly dislike Vordegh himself. But I seem to recall reminding you when we last discussed this that the first principle of Chaos is that we do not interfere in the lives of our worshippers. And I also reminded you that I firmly intend to uphold that principle.' He eyed his brother sourly. 'I sincerely hope you're not going to insist that I go over the reasons for that decision yet again. I'm starting to grow tired of repeating myself.'

Tarod shook his head in helpless frustration. 'No – no, I'm not asking you to do that. I'm not disputing our principles, and as I said before, under normal circumstances I wouldn't dream to suggest that we should intervene. But

170

the situation is *changing*, Yandros. These latest acts are being perpetrated *in our name*. Not in Vordegh's or the magi's; in *ours*. That's the difference, and if we allow it to continue we're as good as condoning it.'

Yandros considered this for a few moments. Then: 'No, Tarod. We're going over old ground again, and there's no point in it. I've already told you that I share your concern up to a point. But *only* up to a point. This quarrel, for want of a better word, is between Vordegh and the people he rules. It isn't our affair.'

Harsh lightning flickered somewhere in the depths of the cloud surrounding them as the fabric of Chaos reacted to the anger Tarod was striving to keep under control. 'And when those people start crying out to us to save them from Vordegh's depredations, what then?' he demanded. 'Will we still say that it isn't our affair?'

'Oh, *really*, Tarod! Now you're being tiresome *and* melodramatic. You know perfectly well that we're not and never have been in the habit of answering prayers, exhortations, pleas or any other means of petitioning which our human worshippers care to dream up.'

'The ordinary peasants don't know that. They believe, because the great and noble First Magus decrees it so, that we hear their every word and are privy to their deepest dreams, and that we mete out punishment to wrongdoers and reward to the faithful –'

'Then it's high time they learned that the First Magus's pronouncements aren't as infallible as he likes to pretend, isn't it?' Abruptly Yandros's mouth twitched in a distinctly malevolent smile. 'Some of the magi themselves – and I name no names – could benefit from the same lesson.'

'By the time they learn it, the damage may have gone too far!'

'And if we force it on them we'll be setting a dangerous precedent! Tarod, I'll say this once more and ask you to

171

think on it. If we interfere now, how much easier will it be to find a plausible excuse for interfering the next time something happens that isn't to our liking? And then a third time, and a fourth, and so on until our principles are a mockery? I won't risk that.'

Tarod sighed sharply and turned away. He was aware that he was losing the argument. 'The risk in doing nothing might be greater,' he said.

'I don't think so.' Yandros smiled again. 'As matters stand, the greatest risk is to Vordegh himself. If he continues with his present tactics and refuses to heed the warning signs, I suspect his fellow-sorcerers might find their own means of resolving the problem.'

Tarod frowned. 'Has a First Magus ever been deposed? I can't recall.'

'It happened once, though the circumstances were different – the man went publicly rather than privately mad, and was removed more to save face than for any other reason. In this case, however, I imagine the magi will resort to less overt means. Vordegh may outmatch any of them as a sorcerer, but there's no arcane answer to a knife in the back.'

Yandros had hinted at that possibility before, Tarod recalled, and he wondered if Pirane might have put such a thought into his mind. Of all the magi she was the most likely candidate for an assassin's role; she or Croin, the physician. But though Yandros seemed at ease with the idea, Tarod was not, for in his view it left too much to chance.

He said, 'If we were to make contact with some of the disaffected magi – quietly, of course –'

'No.' Yandros cut across him. 'We've both had enough contact with the mortal world of late. In fact in your case I'd say a little more than enough.' He eyed his brother slantwise. 'Your midnight call on Vordegh wasn't wise, and if I'd known about it beforehand I would have vetoed the idea.'

Tarod had the grace to look faintly abashed. 'I wasn't aware that you knew about it at all.'

'Then you underestimated me, didn't you? I don't, however, know what you gleaned from the venture – though I assume it wasn't of any value, or you would have told me about it after your return.'

Tarod stared through the clouds. 'It wasn't of any value.'

'Then all you've done is alert Vordegh to the fact that we are dissatisfied.'

'That *I* am. I didn't speak for you and I wouldn't presume to do so.'

'You, I, all or any of us; the effect is the same. I don't want that exercise repeated, Tarod. We will *not* take any part in this. I have no intention whatever of helping First Magus Vordegh in his activities, but I also have no intention of curtailing them. For good or ill he is to be left to go his own way, and anything that is done about him will be done by the magi, not by us. Do I make myself clear?'

'Yes,' Tarod said tersely.

'Then there's no more to be said.' Yandros stood up, flicked the chair out of existence and started to walk away. His footfalls set up multiple echoes, and as he neared the cloud-bank's edge his form began subtly and gradually to metamorphosize into something stranger. Suddenly he stopped and looked back.

'Bear in mind that this will probably work to our advantage,' he said. 'Vordegh's approach may be barbaric, but it's also likely to have the desired effect. And if, in disposing of the fools who are trying to revive the cult of Order, his methods goad the magi into disposing of him, that will be a highly satisfactory outcome for us on two counts instead of merely one.' He saw that Tarod wasn't convinced, and laughed softly. 'Think about it, my dear brother. You'll see that I'm right.'

The clouds rolled back and away, revealing a sharp and geometrically perfect edge where the floor ended in an impossible precipice. Gold reflections shivered briefly around Yandros's frame, then he stepped over the edge of the precipice and walked away.

Dawn was barely breaking when the horseman arrived at the farrier's shop. Kaldar, who had been sleeping in the hayloft above the barn, was jolted awake by the rapid clatter and, crawling to look cautiously through a knothole in the loft doors, he saw a sweating, dapple-grey horse in the yard, its rider already dismounted and in urgent discussion with Stiv Pollander.

Not a customer at this hour, Kaldar thought. And there was something furtive about the rider's movements; he kept glancing over his shoulder as though afraid that someone might have followed him and be watching from the cover of the early mist. The horse was led away, out of the narrow field of view afforded by the knothole, then with an echoing, grinding sound the barn doors below opened and Stiv's voice called out in a wary but carrying hiss.

'Kaldar! Kaldar, are you awake?'

Kaldar scrambled across the hay-bales that formed his bed, hauling on boots and belt – he had slept in his clothes – as he did so, and peered over the edge of the loft platform. Mist was curling damply into the barn, and the horse steamed in the warmer air. Other animals, Stiv's own which he kept for hire, shifted restlessly in their stalls; in the dawn glimmer their bulks were just visible.

The farrier beckoned. 'Come down. There's news.'

Kaldar's pulse quickened as the possibilities raced through his mind. A message from Simbrian? Word of

Benetan Liss? Or – but he pushed that down, knowing that to hope for any report of Iselia was irrational. Simbrian, most likely, for there could be little doubt that by now the sorcerer would have relayed orders to search for him in the wake of his flight.

Kaldar had feared that the order would precede him, and had half expected to find trouble waiting when, two days ago, he had walked into Stiv Pollander's shop and made himself known. But he had been lucky. Stiv, who ran a small but active rebel cell in the arable lands of the southern plains, had welcomed him like a blood brother, for his name and his story were widely known among Order's followers. The cell had heard nothing from Simbrian, and Kaldar had said only that he was searching for 'a friend', letting Stiv assume that he had left Summer Isle with their leader's full knowledge and blessing. Now, as he scrambled onto the rickety ladder and climbed down to the barn floor, Kaldar hoped fervently that the messenger wasn't about to expose his deception.

Stiv had closed the doors and was lighting a lantern. Returning with it he gravely indicated the dapple-grey's rider.

'Kaldar. This is Ryfern, a loyal friend from another of our groups further north.'

Kaldar was about to nod to the burly young man when the nature of Ryfern's appearance, and its implications, suddenly registered and put the other fears out of his mind. This man was no peasant. His clothes were far too good, his horse too well-bred, his manner too confident, and in sharp alarm Kaldar turned on the farrier.

'Stiv, he's –'

He got no further, for Stiv had realized what he was thinking and interrupted quickly. 'It's all right. Ryfern is one of our cause's most devoted disciples; Simbrian Tarkran knows him personally, and trusts him. In fact,' the farmer gave Ryfern a hard smile, 'he's put himself at considerable risk by coming to us.'

'I've taken greater risks under my father's roof,' Ryfern said, then returned Kaldar's gaze. 'My father is Overlord Anscom, of a demesne some fifty miles to the north-west. I'm sorry if that troubles you, Kaldar, but none of us has the power to choose our parentage.'

Kaldar hesitated, then acknowledged the rebuke. 'I apologize,' he said a little tersely. 'If Stiv vouches for you, that's enough for me.'

Stiv cut in. 'It had better be enough, Kaldar, because you'll want to hear what Ryfern has to say.'

His voice had an edge and the other unease came back. 'Something bad?' Kaldar asked cautiously.

'Very.' Stiv had unbuckled the dapple-grey's saddle and now slid it from the animal's back. 'Take Ryfern to the house while I see to his horse. He'll tell you while you get the fire started and get him something hot to eat and drink.'

'I'd appreciate that – and the safety of a barred door between me and the outside world,' Ryfern said with feeling. 'I may be many miles from where my face is known, but that doesn't make me feel any the more secure.'

'You weren't followed?' Kaldar's disquiet flared further.

'No, no; my father doesn't suspect me and I've given a plausible enough reason for being away. But from now on we're all going to have more than any overlord's scrutiny to worry about.' He relinquished the horse's reins to Stiv. 'I'll tell you everything when we're safe in the house.'

Ryfern's message did not come from Simbrian Tarkran, but any relief Kaldar felt at that vanished when he heard what the overlord's son had to say. Word of what had happened as a result of the First Magus's edict had spread fast through the rebel network. Stiv had already heard the bones of the story, but when the three of them sat down at the rough table in the kitchen, Ryfern had grim detail to add. More than a thousand people had been executed because no one in their districts could – or would – denounce a neighbour as a heretic. But not all demesnes had failed to meet Vordegh's demands, and no one was in any doubt that some of Order's genuine followers had been caught up in the net. Whether they had been betrayed by someone who suspected their true allegiance or whether the denunciations were sheer bad luck, Ryfern couldn't say, but either way the dangers were the same. All supposed heretics were now in their overlords' cells awaiting questioning, and everyone knew the form that the 'questioning' would take. The captives would tell what they knew; no one could expect otherwise and in all humanity no one could hold them to blame. The chances were, Ryfern said, that none would know enough to endanger the entire rebel network, but the ripples were sure to spread and some of their friends would be unmasked. That though, he added, sipping at the mug of hot beer that Kaldar had put into his hands, was likely to be the least of their worries in the days to come. For there had been a new development at the Star Peninsula.

'The First Magus's decree arrived four days ago,' he said, 'and it's the reason why I'm here. We have to get word to as many of our followers as we can, and above all we have to get word to Simbrian. Because, you see, I don't think our people will hold out for long against this. I don't think they *can*.'

He told them then what the First Magus's new edict contained. When he finished, there was silence for a few moments. Then:

'*Aeoris!*' Kaldar's knuckles were white on the table edge. 'He can't – he surely wouldn't –'

'You've never seen First Magus Vordegh, have you?' Ryfern said grimly.

'No, but –'

'I have. I accompanied my father to the Star Peninsula for the inauguration festivities earlier this season. I was presented to Vordegh, and I looked into his eyes.' Ryfern's shoulders twitched. 'Believe what he says, Kaldar. He'll do it. And if you're the sorcerer that I've heard you are, you'll know far better than I do what it means and how much power he truly has.'

Kaldar knew, and the full savour of it was coming home to him like ice slowly freezing him to the marrow. Vordegh had made one gesture to the overlords' authority and that was enough for him. Now he intended to take matters into his own hands.

Stiv spoke slowly, uncertainly. 'I don't properly understand. The First Magus speaks of "visitations" – what does that mean? Who are these "visitors"?'

'Not who,' Kaldar said. 'What.' He met the farrier's gaze. 'Beings from Chaos. Demons. Monstrosities. Things that I doubt if you can even begin to imagine. Vordegh is going to send them out into this world, without any forewarning, to pick off victims at random and . . .' He stopped.

'And what?' Stiv prompted.

Kaldar looked away. 'Mutilate their bodies, minds and souls in all the different ways that such abominations can devise. Most will probably be devoured and their souls annihilated. They'll be the lucky ones.'

Colour left Stiv's face. 'Isn't there some way to protect ourselves? You're a sorcerer, Kaldar; surely you must know –'

'No. Don't waste time and energy thinking about it, for there's *nothing* we can do.' Kaldar looked at the farrier again, trying to keep the quiver of bitter rage from his voice. 'Think about it in this way, Stiv. I have some sorcerous ability but it's nothing compared to Simbrian's. *None*

178

of our friends has a skill to match his. Yet Simbrian will be the first to tell you that he isn't a match for First Magus Vordegh. Not when First Magus Vordegh is reinforced by the entire might of Yandros and his loathsome brothers, and all that their vile world contains.' With a sharp spasm his hands clenched into fists. 'The only power that could stand against this is the *full* power, unencumbered, of our Lord Aeoris. And he is still held back by Chaos's barriers.'

'By the time those barriers are destroyed,' Ryfern said softly, 'it may be too late.'

Kaldar turned on him, eyes furiously alight. 'Don't *say* such a thing! We can't afford to tolerate that sort of talk!' He swung out from the table and paced across the floor. 'Simbrian must be told of this as quickly as possible. What arrangements have been made for getting word to him?'

'There's no one in my demesne with the ability to make direct contact,' Ryfern said. 'That's why I'm to ride on southwards – to carry the message to another group who have a trained psychic. It was the quickest way.'

Kaldar shook his head. 'There's a quicker. I'll do it.'

'Can you?'

'Yes.' The gods alone knew what manner of verbal scourging Simbrian would give him when he made contact, and it might well wreck his own plans, but this was too urgent for any personal considerations to get in the way. Compared to this, Benetan Liss meant nothing. Even – though every spark in Kaldar railed against acknowledging it – Iselia's safety must mean nothing.

'Give me a few minutes to prepare what I'll need,' he said, then glanced at Ryfern. 'Has there been any word yet of these . . . visitations beginning? If there has, Simbrian must be told.'

'We don't think so,' Ryfern replied. 'But there is something afoot. A rumour –'

'What rumour?'

'You've heard about the attempted uprising, north-west of here?'

'I've heard.' Kaldar's voice was grim. Stiv had told him of the rebellion, of how it started and of the methods the magi had used to suppress it.

'Well,' Ryfern continued, 'there's a tale going about that a Chaos rider was involved; one who came to the district secretly, ahead of the magus. We'd already had word from a group further north that he was travelling alone on the road, and we were asked to set people to follow him if he came our way. But he didn't. He turned west instead, to where the trouble was, and we think he had arranged to rendezvous with the magus when she arrived.'

Kaldar's heart was beating very slowly and painfully. 'What happened to him?' he asked.

'He was seen during the uprising. The message we had said that he was commanding some Chaos beast, something that could kill a man just by looking at him –'

'Never mind that! What happened to him *afterwards?*'

'No one's sure. One story says he went back to the magus's citadel before it vanished, and another says he left the district on horseback, going south. Either way, our friends have lost track of him since the night of the rebellion; though there was one unconfirmed sighting. But we think he – and others of his kind – are going to be Vordegh's instruments.'

'They're that already,' Stiv put in bitterly. '*Scum.*'

Ryfern cast a quick glance in his direction. 'I mean specifically for this new onslaught. We think that Vordegh will use the Chaos riders to control and direct the horrors he plans to release against us. We think he's sending the riders out – Aeoris alone knows how many of them – to spread themselves throughout the land, ready to carry out his new atrocities.'

Kaldar sat very still. Could that be true? Or had rumour

piled upon rumour, until the reality of one man riding on a solitary mission became garbled into the fiction of an encroaching host armed with the full power of the magi? The lone Chaos rider must surely be Benetan. But if the nature of his mission had changed . . .

He thrust the thoughts down. There was no time for doubt; he had to gamble that Benetan was not now acting under new orders from the Star Peninsula. *And even if he is,* an inner voice added, *that doesn't alter what I intend to do.*

He turned quickly back to the table. 'Ryfern, are our people still looking for this rider?'

'Yes.' Ryfern grimaced. 'Him and any more of his kind. It's a slender chance, I know, and will probably gain us at best just a little time; but if we can kill a few of them before they begin their work –'

'*Kill?*' Kaldar's voice shot up the scale. 'Our people mean to kill him? For Aeoris's sake, *who gave that order?*'

The young man looked blank. 'No one gave any order. But –'

Kaldar interrupted savagely. 'You're telling me that our friends are looking for him, and that if they find him again they'll . . . oh, *gods!*'

'I don't underst –' Ryfern began.

'No – no, of course you don't; how could you?' With an enormous effort Kaldar dragged his violent emotions under control. 'I'm sorry, Ryfern, I'm sorry.' He sucked in a deep breath. 'There isn't time for me to explain everything, but it's *imperative* that that Chaos rider stays alive! I've got to get word to our groups further north, tell them to hold back. If they kill him –' He paused, looked quickly at his two companions' uncomprehending faces and knew that he had to risk the lie, whatever the consequences later. 'If they kill him, it could bring about the ruin of our entire cause!'

CHAPTER XII

Kaldar and Ryfern left the farrier's shop midway through the morning, heading north astride the best two horses that Stiv Pollander could provide. Kaldar was no rider but he clung grimly to the saddle, determined to keep up with Ryfern and not delay them in any way. If Benetan Liss's life was to be preserved, they couldn't afford to waste a single minute — and in the light of what he had just learned, even the fastest pace their mounts could give them might not be fast enough.

He had made contact with Simbrian in great trepidation, and had been so astounded by what the sorcerer had to tell him that he had almost forgotten his own news. A direct command from Aeoris himself, vindicating Kaldar's personal mission and urging him to find Benetan with all haste. Simbrian had been horrified to hear of the trap being laid for the Chaos rider and had exhorted Kaldar to do anything and everything he could to contact their groups to the north and warn them off. He himself, he said, would also try to reach as many of their followers as possible with the same message. Beyond that, they could only hope.

That might have been enough, but for one small but zealous and proficient cell of Order's followers. Immediately after his contact with Simbrian, Kaldar had performed a second ritual, and the group he communed with told him that Benetan Liss had been seen again, riding south-eastwards and apparently intending to pick up the main tithe-road once more. Yes, they were following him, but their cell had neither the numbers nor the appropriate skills to risk an ambush and so they had sent a message-runner to a group whose territory the Chaos rider would soon be entering. *They* had the means to dispatch him and had been urged to do so — and there was no risk of repercussions, for the group's leader was the son of the local overlord and could ensure that the body disappeared without trace.

'Gods!' Ryfern said when Kaldar told him. 'That's my own group — it *must* be! But it's a three-day ride south from that cell's district, and two days north from here, which is little better!' He knew, now, of Aeoris's visitation, and the thought that his own people were about to put their god's plans in jeopardy horrified him.

'And you said there's no one in your demesne capable of making telepathic contact?'

'No one. We can only reach them by physical means. But there isn't enough *time*.'

Kaldar felt exactly as he did, but for the sake of his own sanity he didn't dare let himself acknowledge it. 'There'll have to be time,' he said tersely. *Because if there wasn't, Iselia's only chance of release would die with Benetan.* 'Somehow. *Somehow*.' So now they were on their way, cutting across wild country for the sake of saving time, and praying fervently that the rough terrain wouldn't lame their horses. Ryfern knew the area well enough to be sure of their direction, and they stopped only when absolute necessity demanded. Two changes of mounts — Ryfern had the money and the authority to commandeer, and get, the best available — and on the second night, as the first moon set, they reached a slow and shallow-banked river that meandered across flat, open country.

Frost crackled under the horses' hooves as they reined in, and fog was beginning to creep up from the river. Ryfern pointed ahead. 'See the pack-bridge, at the river's next bend? That marks the boundary of my father's demesne. It's guarded, but the bridge-keeper is one of our own. He'll know how the situation stands.'

They moved on. In the thin starlight the indistinct shapes of the bridge and its toll-house had the look of a strange, giant beast lying motionless across the river's width, and Kaldar shuddered, thinking of Chaos creatures and the First Magus's plans. Then a light flared in a window of the house, banishing the illusion, and moments later the noise of a door scraping open cut loudly through the cold air.

'Who's there?' A man's voice, with a suspicious edge. 'Neighbour or stranger?'

'Neighbour,' Ryfern shouted back. 'Anyone else about tonight, Bellser?'

'Sir!' Relief and surprise replaced the suspicion. 'No, there's no one abroad that I've seen. Come you in.'

Ryfern glanced at Kaldar. 'This won't take more than a few minutes. Stay and keep watch, if you will.'

Kaldar nodded, and Ryfern slid down from his horse's back and ran towards the toll-house. He and Bellser disappeared inside, and Kaldar let the horses graze while he stared watchfully around and tried not to speculate on what news Bellser would have to tell. Then, within two minutes, the door of the house opened again and Ryfern came out at a run.

'Kaldar!' He raced up, making the horses shy back nervously. 'There's trouble. The message reached our group this morning, and an ambush has already been set for your friend.'

Kaldar's skin crawled. 'When?' he demanded.

'Tonight – in fact it'll be a bloody miracle if it hasn't already happened.' Ryfern was gathering up his mount's reins and thrust one foot into the stirrup, hopping round after the horse as it began to dance nervily. 'But there may be a chance of saving him, if – stand *still*, you stupid brute! – if the ambush hasn't gone exactly according to plan, and as these things rarely do –' He swung into the saddle at last, shortened rein and turned his horse's head towards the bridge. 'Bellser's coming too, but we can't afford to wait for him to get his horse saddled; he'll follow. Come on!'

Kaldar's mount whinnied sharply. It was tired, and objected to being forced onwards against its will. Kaldar felt a moment's sympathy for it, but the feeling lasted only a moment before he drove his heels ferociously into its sides and set off in Ryfern's wake.

Benetan's suspicions had been aroused when the landlord of the tavern refused him a bed for the night. The man had claimed that all the rooms were taken and some customers were even having to share, but the lie had been obvious, for the taproom was half-empty and this wasn't a market or claim day. They argued for a while, but the landlord remained obdurate and at last Benetan gave up. The only option would have been to use his rank to secure lodging, and he didn't want his rank to be known.

Though he took care to appear nonchalant, his senses were sharply alert as he re-mounted his mare and rode out of the tavern yard. Still no shadow dogging his steps, and he had detected none since yesterday. There had been a lull once before, when Order's devotees apparently lost track of him after his departure from Magus Pirane's citadel, but this second hiatus was different. Until this morning they had been trailing him; now, suddenly and for no apparent reason, the followers had disappeared. And the fact that he had been turned away by the keeper of the only tavern in miles – more significantly, perhaps, the only one he could hope to reach before dawn – suggested that something was afoot.

If they intended to set a trap for him, they had certainly chosen the place well. This was open land, fertile but flat and all but devoid of trees or any other form of cover. Whether he rode through the night or stopped and made camp, he would be exposed. That also put potential enemies at a disadvantage, of course, for they would lose the element of surprise. But they knew the country; he did not. And with only the stars and both moons waned to the third quarter to light the surrounding terrain, there was every chance that they could get close enough to strike before he was aware of their presence.

He decided to ride on until daylight. It was unfair on the mare and he himself was bone-tired, but keeping on the move would be the lesser of two potential evils, for if he rested he probably wouldn't be able to stop himself from falling asleep. Even in the saddle there was a risk of dozing, but a mounted man taken by surprise would at least have a chance of getting away. As well that he hadn't eaten since morning; the gnawings of hunger would help him stay awake.

The land was empty, with few distinguishing features, and it was easy to lose all sense of time. The mare plodded on, her muffled hoofbeats hypnotic in their rhythm, and Benetan sang songs under his breath, or invented strategic puzzles for solving, in his efforts to remain alert. He watched the first moon set and saw the pale drift of fog rising over the river whose course paralleled his half a mile eastward. Cattle were bellowing beyond the river in the far distance, their noise carrying clearly and eerily in the cold air, and with the first moon now sunk below the horizon the starlight played tricks and created phantoms; fence posts appearing and vanishing, shapeless forms slinking out of nowhere and back into nothingness; even, once, a man in a flapping cloak and wide-brimmed hat who signalled to him from the darkness ahead before resolving into the harmless contours of a dead bush. That delusion shook him and he bit the back of one hand hard through his glove, trying to wake himself up with the small shock of pain. The crescent of the second moon glided in the sky, seeming to keep pace with him, and as he looked at it he thought how quickly it was westering. Another hour, possibly less, and it would be gone: then there would only be starlight to show the way home. No, not *home*. He shook his head to clear the fantasy from his mind; of course he wasn't going *home*. But to show the way. Only starlight . . .

The mare stumbled, and Benetan jolted awake. *Gods, where was he? How long had he dozed in the saddle?* Grasping at his confused senses and trying to haul himself back to coherence, he looked around. The second moon had set and the landscape around him was visible only as a tricky haze of gloom and shadow as the creeping fog from the river began to obscure the stars. Benetan scrubbed at his face, trying to clear his vision, but only succeeded in scratching a loose strand of hair across one eye which made matters worse. What *hour* was it? And how many miles had he covered? The mare seemed as mesmerized as he was, plodding steadily on without urging, but her pace was slow and rationality suggested that they had travelled by no means as far as he hoped. Perhaps he should stop, and damn the risk for the sake of a few hours' rest? If he didn't, then at this rate by the time dawn broke he would be a sitting target for a child, beyond any ability to –

The thought was truncated and a shock went through him as, from the direction of the river, a bird uttered a piercing call. The mare's ears went back and she tossed her head. And in the tingling aftermath of surprise Benetan listened, as some sense which he couldn't define – perhaps it only awoke on the border between dream and reality? – warned him that something wasn't quite right.

He could hear the river from here. A gentle *hush*, calm and steady. The track must be veering towards it, which might mean there was a crossing not far ahead. And a crossing could make a good place for an ambush.

Then the bird-call came again, and suddenly he knew what was wrong. That wasn't a real bird but a mimicry, albeit skilled. And the mare was uneasy, her ears flicking back and forth as though trying to place something. She wanted to halt and he let her, sitting motionless and tense in the saddle and wishing his night vision were better.

Either that, or that he was riding something less mundane than a horse . . .

Slowly, silently, he felt for the longer of his two knives. If his enemies could see him, they weren't yet close enough to identify him. And if they couldn't see him, then neither would they hear him until and unless he made the mare walk on. They wouldn't risk a bowshot, not while they couldn't be certain that he was the man they wanted. They would have to get closer to be sure. And that gave him the advantage.

Something slithered a few yards away and was followed by a faint crackling sound, like frosted grass blades breaking. Benetan's hand was on the knife now and he slid it noiselessly from its sheath. Couldn't risk the other; he'd need to keep one hand on the reins. Adrenalin was driving out his weariness, and his eyes, narrowed, stared hard into the darkness.

And suddenly the night was split by an ululating yell as two figures came hurtling at him out of the dark.

The mare reared, whinnying, and Benetan grabbed a handful of her mane as the yelling shapes charged headlong towards him. The mare's forehooves came down with a bone-jarring thump — and the two figures swerved, one to his right, the other to his left. Almost too late he realized the trick, and at the same moment there was a rush of feet behind him —

Benetan shouted a command, yanking on the reins, and

the mare cat-jumped around to meet the five men who were coming at his back. Starlight glittered on a blade and Benetan brought his own knife round to meet it – but these attackers were more adroit than the farmers of his last encounter, for they too swerved, ducking under his thrust; metal flashed and he felt the cut reins fall slack and useless in his grasp. At the same moment hands grabbed his stirrups, wrenching them away from his feet. Benetan kicked out, but his balance had gone and he was sliding sideways out of the saddle. At the last moment before he fell he brought the knife round and flailed out – he felt the strike connect, heard a stifled gasp of pain – then he hit the ground, hard, the mare's hooves only just missing his skull as she reared again.

Trained reflex brought him instantly to his feet and he found himself poised in a semi-crouch, the mare dancing, pressing against his back as he had trained her to do, while seven men ranged out facing him. One was wounded – the blood running down his arm looked black under the starlight – and but for the rasp of breathing and the mare's snorting and jingling there was no sound.

None of them had swords, or any long weapon; clearly they had intended their attack to be brief and efficient and had thought knives would be enough. Now that they had failed to dispatch him with their first strike they were less sure of themselves. Hadn't planned what they would do if he should still be alive and ready to fight when he was pulled down, and hadn't expected his horse to play her part, blocking them from coming at him from behind. Good. That meant the ambush must have been hastily organized and probably hastily conceived in the first place. Untrained men, out of their depth. He had a chance, at least.

But it wasn't a good chance, and as his gaze flicked from one shadowed form to another and another, Benetan knew

189

that the odds in his favour were ones which not even the most dedicated gambler would take. Even if he killed them all – which was unlikely in the extreme – how many more might be out there, invisible in the dark, waiting? Bowmen perhaps, who wouldn't chance a shot into the middle of a fight but would have a clear aim if their comrades fell.

He knew he couldn't afford to think about such hazards; the immediate danger was the only one which must concern him. The seven men were keeping warily out of knife range but they had closed their semi-circle to ensure that he had no chance to break through the cordon. Under cover of his coat Benetan palmed the second and shorter knife, at the same time feinting with the first blade to distract their attention from the movement. He thought he knew what their tactic would be; it was an obvious one but dangerously effective for all that, and to draw them into making their move he turned his head a little, appearing to focus his attention on the men to his left while obliquely keeping a careful watch to his right. Any moment now . . .

He had the warning he'd anticipated; a swift, furtive glance as a silent but clear signal was exchanged. They came at him fast, one from the left, shouting, two silently from the right with knives upraised. Benetan whipped the shorter blade out from under his coat and saw the shouting man jump back in surprise; then he spun, the knife in his right hand shearing through the air in a vicious arc. There was a jar, a scream; a dark shape fell – but the second man had ducked the strike and suddenly a flying body hit him in a ferocious tackle. They crashed to the ground together, rolling and struggling; the man had dropped his knife and was trying to pin Benetan's arms to stop him from using his own blades. They rolled again; now his attacker was on top but Benetan jerked his left knee, driving it savagely upwards, and with a yowl of pain the man fell away, clutching at his groin. Benetan twisted his body and sprang to his feet, but before he could straighten, a figure rushed at him from behind and leaped on his back, clinging with one arm round his neck and the other hand grasping for his right wrist. Fingers clamped, the nails gouging, and his assailant twisted and shook his arm, striving to force the knife out of his grip. Benetan tried to throw him off, but his foot slipped on the frosty ground, and suddenly the rest of them came piling into the mêlée. He heard a voice yelling hoarsely, heard the mare's shrill whinny and another horse answering – then his legs were kicked out from under him, and cold grey metal flashed towards his face and there was a sudden thump and thunder of hooves –

'*Stop! For all the gods' sakes, LEAVE HIM!*'

The voice roared shockingly out, and at the same moment a horse smashed into the tumult of the fight. There was a whistle of displaced air, then a whiplash cracked across Benetan's back, dislodging the man clinging to him and sending them both rolling. As he started to scramble to his feet Benetan saw more horses, men on their backs – one rider was brandishing a sword, while another couldn't control his mount and was about to fall. *If he could take that horse* . . . With the speed of desperation Benetan sprang at the panicking animal, grabbing for the reins. The horse reared, shrieking, and the rider pitched from the saddle to land flailing at Benetan's feet. He was up again in an instant, and with a yell he tried to grab Benetan's arm; Benetan had lost both knives but his free hand clenched and he hurled a punch at the shouting face. He hit the man in the left eye, not devastatingly but hard enough to send white-hot pain through his knuckles, and then he clawed for the horse's flying stirrup, pulling himself up, tensing for a leap to the saddle –

'*Benet, you bloody, three-times-damned idiot! It's me, it's Kaldar – we're on your side!*'

191

Astounded, Benetan spun round, colliding with the prancing horse's flank. '*Kaldar?*'

Blood was pouring from Kaldar's nose and his left eye was already half shut — but the other eye glared furiously as he grabbed Benetan's arm again and shook him with all his strength. 'Yes, Kaldar! And still in one piece, no thanks to you!'

Behind them, the fight had collapsed. Five of Benetan's seven attackers were sitting on the ground nursing their injuries — one had taken a kick from Ryfern's horse, another had been cut by Bellser's whip and Benetan had accounted for the other three — and the others stood huddled before Ryfern, who was cursing them roundly for their stupidity. Hearing him, Kaldar called, 'Leave it, Ryfern. If they'd been wiser, they'd probably have succeeded in their task before we could arrive to stop them.'

Ryfern paused in his string of obscenities. 'He's all right?'

'Not a scratch on him by the look of it.' Kaldar glanced witheringly at Benetan. 'He's got the luck of the Seven Hells.'

Ryfern's posture relaxed. 'Thank the gods for that! So, no harm done.'

'No harm?' Kaldar echoed sourly. 'Only five men disabled, and me with an eye I won't be able to see out of for the next month. No; no *harm*.' His good eye raked Benetan again. 'Maybe we should have stayed back and left you to finish the job for yourself. You seemed to be doing well enough — and what are seven lives worth, after all?'

Benetan rubbed a hand over his face, expelling a long, heavy breath. 'Don't be ridiculous, Kaldar. I didn't want to kill anyone — and I couldn't have done anyway. They'd have had me within another minute or two at most, and you know it.' He paused. 'So I owe you and your friends my life.'

Kaldar gave him an acerbic smile. 'That must rankle.'

Benetan sighed. 'No, it doesn't rankle; but if it gives you any satisfaction to think it does, that's up to you.' He flexed the hand that had thrown the punch, which still hurt. 'I'm just *confused*. First your people – I presume they *are* your people – set a trap for me, and quite an elaborate one from what I can judge. Then you and your friends come riding to my rescue at the last moment. What caused the change of heart – orders from on high?'

He was more right than he knew, Kaldar thought, but didn't comment. Instead he walked towards Ryfern, who was helping one of the wounded men to bind up his bleeding arm. 'Are there any serious injuries, Ryfern?'

A shake of the head. 'Nothing that won't mend quickly enough.' Ryfern looked up as Kaldar approached, and chuckled. 'By all the gods, you're a picture to frighten children with! Haven't you ever learned how to duck a flying fist?'

Kaldar ignored that. 'If all these men can walk, you'd best tell them to get themselves home before dawn starts to break,' he said. 'Bellser, too.' He nodded meaningfully over his shoulder to where Benetan stood. 'We may have saved his life but that doesn't mean I entirely trust him, and I'd prefer him not to get the chance to remember too many faces.'

Ryfern understood. 'I'll tell Bellser to get them away quickly and quietly. He'll return to his house by another route, and we can start back the way we came.' He paused. 'You want to take your friend south, don't you?'

'Yes. To the coast. Simbrian's sending a ship for us, and he'll meet us on the White Isle.'

'Mmm. The coast's a long way; several days' fast ride.' Ryfern glanced in Benetan's direction. 'Do you think he'll come willingly?'

'I don't know. I may need to do some very hard talking and bargaining.'

'It would save time if you didn't have to. I could arrange an escort, just to be on the safe side.'

Kaldar gave him a thoughtful look. 'That might be wise. Only . . .'

'Only what?'

'Simbrian instructed me to say nothing to Benetan about the uprising or the First Magus's newest threats. But your men will know about recent events, and they'll know who Benetan is. The temptation to make him aware of their feelings –'

Ryfern interrupted with a chilly smile 'Don't worry. I'll remind them there are other ways of showing their contempt for the magi's servants. They'll say nothing untoward – in fact, I imagine they'll have nothing to say to your friend at all.'

'Very well,' Kaldar returned the smile grimly. 'Then I accept. And I thank you.'

He turned away and walked back to where Benetan waited. The black mare had returned to her master and was exchanging cautious sniffs with Kaldar's horse while Benetan made temporary repairs to the cut reins. Kaldar took hold of his own mount's bridle and said tersely, 'Better get mounted. We're leaving.'

Benetan stopped what he was doing. '*We?*'

'Yes. You're coming with us – and I'm not going to waste time explaining why. You'll find out when we reach our destination.'

'I see.' Benetan looked at the ground, touching his tongue to his lower lip. 'And what if I have other plans?'

'I don't think you have. In fact, I think this suits your plans very well indeed. And if it doesn't . . . well, I'm afraid that choice isn't yours to make.'

Ryfern approached, leading his horse. In the background, concealed by the darkness, Bellser and the other men were making their discreet departure. Benetan looked from Kaldar to Ryfern and back to Kaldar again, and knew that he was in no position to argue. Besides, wasn't this what he had wanted, what he had promised Iselia? A meeting with Kaldar, a message delivered — and Kaldar had no intention of harming him; on the contrary, it was important to Kaldar that he should stay alive, as tonight's events had proved beyond any doubt.

He turned back to his mare. 'Very well. Since you put it that way, I accept your invitation.'

Ryfern said something under his breath, but Kaldar had seen the fleeting, wry smile on Benetan's face, and laughed.

'Do you know, after all these years I could almost begin to like you,' he said.

Benetan put one foot in the stirrup. 'I doubt it, Kaldar.' He swung up into the saddle, settled himself. The smile was still there but now it had an unquiet edge. 'I doubt it very much.'

CHAPTER XIII

Though his companions made a show of pretending otherwise, Benetan knew that he was going to his unknown destination as a prisoner. And even after six days in Kaldar's company, he still had no idea what the followers of Order wanted of him.

They had ridden hard across country, accompanied by six of Ryfern's men whose dour silence left Benetan in no doubt that his presence disgusted them. The route had obviously been planned in advance, for provisions and fresh horses were waiting for them at certain places along the way and whenever they stopped to snatch a few hours' necessary rest there was always a house or farmstead apparently forewarned and ready to offer them shelter. The extent of the heretics' network of friends astonished and dismayed Benetan – they were, it seemed, far greater in number and far better organized than the magi dreamed, and the thought of what First Magus Vordegh would do if he knew that his spy had uncovered such information and failed to report it brought a cold, crawling sweat to his skin.

Then on the sixth day they had reached the coast, and the ship that had been sent to meet them; a good-sized vessel at anchor off a deserted cove miles from the nearest habitation. Ryfern's men were not to sail with them, but the strength of the ship's crew who came ashore to escort Benetan aboard put paid to any ideas of resistance he might otherwise have had. So they had sailed, and after what Benetan judged to be two hours or thereabouts a dark smudge appeared on the horizon, growing and resolving into the stark, inhospitable contours of a barren island which, it seemed, was to be their destination.

Now, as the ship nosed into a narrow inlet and began to glide between sheer rock walls, he stared up at the volcanic crater of the White Isle towering into the sky ahead, fighting the twin miseries of claustrophobia and apprehension. The crew were not overtly unfriendly, as Ryfern's men had been, but they treated him as the stranger he was, and their reserve hadn't encouraged him to ask any questions. So throughout the voyage he had sat on deck with his back against the mainmast, staring at the endless water and wondering what lay in store for him. He had a grim and growing suspicion that once he landed on this bleak island he would be facing the prospect of a long stay. He didn't think they would leave him here to starve, but it seemed likely that Kaldar had in mind some form of ransom. Perhaps even an exchange; his life for Iselia's freedom. If that was so, Benetan reflected acidly, then Kaldar's judgement of the magi was a very long way wide of the mark.

He fingered the star amulet, which lay hidden on its chain under his shirt. In the early stages of their ride Kaldar had teased him, none too kindly, about his Chaos rider's accoutrements, but had assumed the amulet was just one more badge of rank and hadn't troubled to investigate it any further. Benetan didn't want to use the star for its intended purpose, but if the worst came to the worst it would give him the means to get out of trouble.

He saw the narrow gorge opening out ahead of them, and minutes later the ship sailed into the huge, quiet pool at the foot of the central crater. At the pool's edge a solitary figure was waiting; a big, bearded man with a bear-like look about him. A rope was thrown to shore, the ship eased in close to the weed-grown wall, and as a gangplank was slung across the divide Kaldar approached along the deck.

'Journey's end.' He smiled thinly. 'Are you feeling all right?'

'I'm not seasick, if that's what you mean.'

Kaldar grinned, then flicked an assessing glance over Benetan's spray-soaked coat and hair. 'You look like a scarecrow, but I don't suppose the rest of us are much better. Come on; time to find your land-legs again.'

Benetan got stiffly to his feet and followed Kaldar over the deck. They crossed the gangplank, and as they stepped onto solid ground the bear-like man came forward.

'You're Benetan Liss?' Dark eyes regarded him calmly, then the stranger extended an open hand. 'My name is Simbrian Tarkran. Welcome to the White Isle.'

Sheer courteous reflex made Benetan reach out and exchange the traditional wrist-clasp before he could even think what he was doing, and words came involuntarily as he stared at the man in astonishment. 'Then you're the leader of the heret –' He stopped himself.

'The leader of the heretics, yes.' Simbrian smiled wryly. 'I'm surprised – and a little daunted – that you know my identity.'

'Iselia told me. The idea was that your name would be a safeguard if I should run into any trouble from your followers.' Benetan glanced at Kaldar. 'As matters turned out, they didn't give me the chance to invoke your name or that of anyone else. Even Yandros.'

He mentioned the great Chaos lord deliberately, wanting Simbrian to know that he was neither cowed nor in a mood to be tactful. However, Simbrian only laughed. 'Oh, yes – I've heard that Ryfern's group were over-zealous to say the least, and I hope that you'll accept my apologies for their behaviour. Still, I gather that you gave a very good account of yourself.' He looked at Kaldar. 'How's the eye?'

'Well enough,' Kaldar said.

'I'm glad to hear it.' Simbrian looked at Benetan again. 'I imagine Kaldar approached you with his usual subtlety, did he?'

Despite his wariness Benetan smiled at that, remembering both the ambush and earlier encounters. 'You could say so. Although for once it was probably the wiser course – otherwise he might not have survived to tell the tale.'

Simbrian laughed, and Kaldar wondered how long the sorcerer would choose to maintain his easy and genial manner. He was aware that Simbrian's every word and nuance were calculated to test Benetan and probe the real man behind the Chaos rider's guise, and he also knew that Benetan was unlikely to be taken in by the pretence. But he suspected that Simbrian would learn a good deal before Benetan ran out of patience.

Simbrian's laughter subsided and his expression became sober once more. 'Well, Captain Liss, there's not a great deal of point in our standing about in this bleak place when we could exchange pleasantries in at least a modicum of comfort.' He indicated the long, steep slope of the volcano's flank stretching upwards and away behind him. 'It's a long climb, I'm afraid, but we can offer you some semblance of hospitality at the end of it.'

He turned as if to lead the party away, but Benetan said sharply, 'One moment, sir.'

Simbrian turned and met the challenge in the younger man's eyes. 'Is something wrong?'

'Yes, something *is* wrong!' Benetan sounded angry. 'I think that before you talk any more about pleasantries and hospitality, it would be the barest courtesy to offer me some kind of explanation!'

'Ah.' Benetan wouldn't realize the significance of the sudden glint that came into Simbrian's eyes, but Kaldar knew its meaning well and he suppressed a smile.

'I fulfilled my promise to Iselia,' Benetan said, 'when I gave Kaldar the message she asked me to carry and the news that she is in no danger at the Star Peninsula. Kaldar's — and his friends' — response was to effectively make me their captive and bring me against my will to this . . . this *place*, for some apparent purpose which they refuse to reveal and which I can't fathom. I imagine you don't intend to kill me, for if you did, there would hardly have been any point in transporting me all the way here to do it. And I'm sure you know enough about the magi not to believe for one moment that they'll be interested in bargaining for my life — or that I know enough about their plans for your demise to be worth torturing for information. So why have you mounted this charade? Why — to be blunt about it — are you pretending friendship towards me when you must know that I'm no friend to you?'

Simbrian continued to look at him for a few moments. Then he nodded.

'You're quite right, Captain Liss. Firstly that in all justice we owe you an explanation, and secondly that this is a charade. Not entirely a charade, I will say, because I have no reason to dislike you personally — rather the opposite, in fact, as the help and protection you have given to Kaldar's wife tells me that you're a very honourable man. But you have been brought here for a reason, and that reason does have a bearing on our cause.'

Benetan exhaled a sharp sigh. 'If you're going to try to convert me —'

'I'm not. Our cause is one of the heart, not of intellectual argument, and I respect your right to choose your own loyalties — although I hope you might also respect my right not to share them.' Benetan didn't answer that and Simbrian continued. 'To be blunt with you in my turn, Captain Liss, I will tell you that I don't yet know the full reason why you have been brought here. I gave the order, but I gave it simply because I have been instructed to do so.'

'Instructed? By whom?'

'By one greater and wiser than any of us – one whose judgement we do not question under any circumstances.' Simbrian paused, then smiled again, composedly and quite implacably. 'My instruction came directly from our Lord Aeoris of Order.'

Benetan felt as though his gut had twisted within him. '*Aeoris?*' His voice was an incredulous hiss.

'Yes. The barrier that exiled the lords of Order from our world has been breached – there's hardly any point in hiding that when you'll soon see the truth for yourself – and our Lord Aeoris has commanded us to bring you here. That, for the present, is all I can tell you, for it's all I know.'

He didn't believe it. It wasn't *possible* – this must be some subterfuge, some trick of sorcery intended to intimidate him. Yandros and his brothers had dealt with the demons of Order centuries ago, and the idea that any power could countermand the gods' work was unthinkable. Yet as he stared at Simbrian Tarkran, Benetan couldn't shake off the terrible feeling that the sorcerer wasn't lying to him.

'You need not fear our Lord Aeoris,' Simbrian said, misinterpreting – or pretending to misinterpret – the horrified expression on Benetan's face. 'He knows your allegiance but he is also aware of your integrity, and that is a quality which Order holds in high regard.'

Benetan gave him a smoulderingly hostile look. 'I don't *fear* your master, sir!' he retorted sharply. 'I serve one far greater, and I have had the ultimate privilege of standing as close to him as I am now to you. To me – as to anyone who has shared my experience – I assure you, your demons are of no consequence!'

Kaldar drew breath violently at what was, to him, a

blasphemy that couldn't be ignored, but Simbrian shot him a warning look and with an effort he subsided. The sorcerer's composed expression didn't change, but he was interested by the revelation that this young captain had met Yandros of Chaos face to face. Unlike many of his fellow rebels, Simbrian acknowledged that Order and Chaos were two faces of the same coin, and didn't for one moment underestimate Yandros's stature or his ability to invoke – and merit – the devotion of his worshippers. But it was just possible that the effect on Benetan of a personal encounter with his god might be turned to advantage.

Aloud, he said, 'I apologize, Captain – I didn't mean my words to sound patronizing.' A faint smile. 'But you'll appreciate that, to us, it is a little . . . unusual to encounter a man who doesn't hold Lord Aeoris in awe.'

Benetan made a brusque, cancelling gesture. 'As you said, your loyalties aren't a matter of intellectual argument. And neither are mine.'

Simbrian inclined his head in acknowledgement. 'Then as we seem to have agreed to differ without coming to blows over it, may I again offer you our hospitality, such as it is?'

There was a long pause. Then, a little curtly and very warily, but with a glimmer of reluctant respect in his eyes, Benetan nodded.

'Very well. Thank you.'

Simbrian smiled again, more openly. 'Thank *you*, Captain Liss.' He turned; then – the move was carefully calculated, but only Kaldar was aware of it – 'Oh; one small matter. Your talisman, Captain. The seven-rayed star that you wear on that iron chain around your neck. I know something of its properties, and I think it will be better for all of us if you give it into my safe-keeping while you are here.'

Benetan stood rigid. 'That talisman is –'

202

'I know what it is, Captain, which is why I ask you to surrender it. As a matter of courtesy.'

Simbrian extended a hand and Benetan realized that courtesy had nothing to do with it. If he refused the request, the amulet would be taken; and this man had the power to take it without any ceremony.

He put a hand to the chain, pulled it over his head – one link caught in his hair as though protesting, but he wouldn't let himself consider what that might imply – and dropped it into Simbrian's open palm.

'I'm obliged to you, Captain.' The sorcerer's fist closed over the star jewel, then he turned and indicated the long, tortuous climb ahead. 'Shall we be on our way?'

Benetan sat alone in a small cave, one of many that riddled the volcano's ancient crater, and wondered how long he would have to wait for the heretics' next move. They had made him as comfortable as circumstances allowed, providing him with light, sustenance and even bedding, but he was in no mood to eat or sleep and had eschewed the beer left for him in favour of water, wanting to keep his mind clear.

Night had fallen, and Simbrian and his friends had lit candles and set them in a wide circle on the bowl floor before settling themselves in the ring of light to talk and keep vigil. They had invited Benetan to join them but he refused; not because he wanted to be alone – far from it, in fact – but because he couldn't bring himself to accept the hand of friendship that they were apparently trying to offer him. Simbrian had brought a number of others to the island, among them several women, and from the moment he set foot in the bowl they had treated Benetan as though he were simply one more friend come to join the company. They smiled at him, spoke pleasantly to him, and there was no sign of the hostility and distrust, let alone hatred, that he had come to expect. It was, of course, impossible to know what deeper feelings the smiles might be masking, but outwardly at least it seemed that if Simbrian was prepared to make a Chaos rider welcome among them, the others trusted him enough to follow his example.

Simbrian himself was a conundrum. He had drawn Benetan into a little more conversation since his arrival – nothing contentious, simply the courtesies of a host to a guest – and despite the implacably opposed views which should have made them mortal enemies, Benetan couldn't help liking him. Simbrian was a warm man, utterly devoid of vanity, and it was obvious that his followers' unstinting loyalty to him had been earned rather than demanded. It was dangerously tempting to make invidious comparisons with the magi, for while there could be no doubt that the magi fully merited the respect accorded them by their servants, that respect had nothing to do with love or even liking but was based solely on fear.

Yet fear did have its place here, as for all the sorcerer's apparent gentleness Benetan had little doubt that he could, if he chose, be as dangerous as any magus. The incident with the amulet had been a small warning not to make the mistake of underestimating him, and on the broader canvas the tally of his abilities was formidable. To have developed such skills in the first place without coming to the magi's attention, and then to have used them to mastermind the entire heretic network and conceal it from the most intense scrutiny of Chaos and its servants, added up to an achievement which should have been beyond the power of any mortal man.

And perhaps was; for surely *no* man, whatever he might be or claim to be, could have enough power to deceive Yandros himself? That was what sent a chill, like the touch of something centuries dead, through Benetan's flesh and into his marrow. For it could only mean that the exiled forces of Order had indeed awoken and returned to the mortal world. And this island was their stronghold.

He wondered what the sorcerer and his followers were doing now. He could hear a low murmur of voices in the bowl, punctuated by an occasional ripple of muted laughter, but no words were discernible and Benetan still couldn't bring himself to leave the solitude of the cave and go outside. So he sat on the rock floor, the untouched food beside him and the forebodings continuing to gnaw at his mind, until a sound of footsteps and the flicker of light and shadow at the entrance warned him that someone was approaching.

Benetan got quickly to his feet. Earlier, prompted by some half-fledged impulse to make a defiant show in the face of Chaos's enemies, he had discarded his mundane clothing and dressed once more in the full regalia of his rank, but as his visitor appeared he felt suddenly foolish and a little shamed. A girl, slight and dark and no more than eighteen years old. He had seen her earlier, with Simbrian; she seemed to be attached to the sorcerer as closely as a shadow and he surmised that she was perhaps his niece or even his daughter. She had smiled at Benetan once, though nervously, but now as she took in the change in his appearance he saw the tautening of her body, the flicker of fear and repugnance in her eyes.

'I'm sorry.' He took a step back. 'I didn't mean to alarm you. I thought . . .' He didn't finish the sentence in the hope that she would give him some reassurance, but she didn't speak, only indicated the dish of dark bread and fruit on the floor.

'I wasn't hungry. I'm still not. If you want to take it . . .' He bent, picked up the dish and held it out to her, wishing that she would say something, anything. But she didn't. She reached for the dish, stretching her arm to its full extent rather than risk moving any nearer to him, and Benetan sighed.

'Please, don't be afraid of me. I've no wish to harm you or anyone else. These clothes are only –'

'Nanithe.' A voice spoke from the entrance and Kaldar came into the cave. 'Simbrian's looking for you; I said I thought I'd seen you come in here.' He smiled at the girl, then cast a quick, inscrutable glance in Benetan's direction. 'And Benet's telling the truth; for all that appearances suggest, he's harmless enough.'

The girl looked at Benetan again, her expression still uncertain and tinged with distaste. Then her shoulders relaxed, she nodded, patted Kaldar's arm in an odd, almost sisterly way and hurriedly left the cave. Benetan stared after her until Kaldar spoke again.

'You're curious about Nanithe.' His tone suggested that for once he wasn't in the mood to cross verbal swords, and Benetan felt relieved. Despite the flashes of bitter antagonism between them he at least shared some common ground with Kaldar, and at this moment he felt in dire need of a friend of any kind.

'I tried to reassure her,' he said despondently, 'but she wouldn't even speak to me.'

'Not wouldn't, Benet. Can't. She lost the power of speech when a band of brigands had some sport with her three years ago.'

Benetan glanced quickly at him. 'Sport?'

'The usual gamut of entertainments.' Candlelight reflected in Kaldar's eyes and made their colour hard. 'Rape, torture, a little mutilation ... She was the only survivor of a carter's party travelling between districts, but the murderers, of course, were never brought to justice. I don't doubt the local overlord had more important matters to occupy his time – such as counting the profits from his newest tithe.'

A month ago Benetan would have flared up at that, but in the wake of his recent experiences he felt, instead, a painful pang of remorse. Memories of Overlord Leyan, and Magus Pirane's indifference to justice, were too recent and too sharp. And Andraia's refusal to understand.

'Gods,' he said aloud, 'what a filthy mess . . .'

Kaldar, unaware of the full spectrum of his thoughts, was surprised by the bitterness of his tone and put the wrong interpretation on it. 'Oh, it's not that unusual, I assure you. But then you're safe in the castle, surrounded by all the comforts a man could wish for, so you no longer need to concern yourself with the way people live – and die – outside those hallowed walls.'

Benetan sat down, resting elbows on knees and staring unhappily at nothing. 'Maybe that was true in the past. But not now.'

'Because of Nanithe?' Kaldar sounded sceptical. 'I hardly think that –'

'No, not because of Nanithe; though what you told me has . . .' Benetan broke off and made an impatient gesture. 'Ah, what's the point? I don't want to explain it to you. I don't even want to talk about it.' He sought quickly for a way to steer the subject from its present course. 'So Nanithe and Simbrian aren't kin? I thought perhaps she was his daughter.'

A recent wound had been re-opened, Kaldar realized, and he wondered if it had some connection with the uprising in which Benetan had become embroiled. However, he didn't press the matter but only replied, 'No, they're not kin. But in recent days . . . well, you've seen for yourself.' Kaldar smiled wistfully. 'He loves her. And she adores him.'

Benetan nodded. 'Then he's a fortunate man.'

That bitter edge again. Oh yes, something was very wrong in Benetan's world. Kaldar knew that if he probed they would quarrel and he'd learn nothing more. But Simbrian would be interested to hear what had been said.

'Why don't you come outside and join us?' he suggested. 'You'd be made welcome.'

Benetan laughed humourlessly. 'When did you learn to be a diplomat, Kaldar? No. Thank you, but I won't sully your gathering with my presence. Go away and make your plans.' He looked up suddenly, and there was hurt and resentment in his eyes though Kaldar had the impression that it was directed at something – or someone – a long way from the island. 'And perhaps when you've decided my fate, you might have the decency to tell me what it's to be.'

Kaldar started to open his mouth, then realized that he had nothing to say. He shrugged. 'As you please.' Two paces from the cave entrance he paused and looked back. 'You never used to be one for self-pity. I wonder what made you change?'

He went out.

A hand touched his shoulder and a quiet voice said, 'Captain Liss.'

Benetan started awake. The flame of a lantern was flickering near his head, and by its weak light he made out the shape of someone leaning over him. For a moment reality became confused with the unpleasant dream he'd been having and he thought he was in his own room at the castle, being roused for some emergency. Memories of Savrinor on the night the old First Magus had died ... but his visitor wasn't Savrinor, and he wasn't in the castle.

'I'm sorry to disturb your rest,' Simbrian Tarkran said softly, 'but there is someone here who wishes to speak with you.'

'With me?' Benetan's mind was still fogged and it didn't occur to him to wonder at the statement. He sat up, rubbing his eyes. 'Gods ... what hour is it?'

'Daybreak's not far away.' There was tension in Simbrian's manner, Benetan realized now, and an air of eager impatience; with a sigh he climbed stiffly to his feet and followed the sorcerer towards the cave entrance. They walked down a narrow passage, an offshoot of the main tunnel that ran through the crater, and emerged into the pre-dawn gloom of the bowl. The air was chilly enough to drive out the last remnants of sleep, and as his brain cleared Benetan blinked, taking in his surroundings. Everyone else, it seemed, was sleeping, their recumbent shapes vaguely visible, and the circle of candles had been extinguished; all but one which glowed like a feral eye on the bowl floor. But then he realized that it wasn't a candle, for the light was too brilliant, the circle it encompassed too wide and too steady. And the flame was hanging, unsupported, in mid-air.

Simbrian took his arm, not a hard grip but one that allowed no room for challenge. 'If you please, Captain.'

They walked down the steep slope to the bowl floor. Benetan felt his way blindly, unwilling – perhaps even unable – to take his eyes off the light. It seemed to grow as they descended, and uncertainty began to give way to something stronger. There was more than a whiff of sorcery about this – what had Simbrian conjured? And what did he intend to do?

His arm was released as they reached the floor. Instantly he stood still but Simbrian walked on, moving towards the hovering flame. He took six paces; then to Benetan's surprise he dropped to one knee and lowered his head as though in obeisance. His voice carried clearly in the quiet as he said, '*My lord.*'

The light shimmered, shivered – then flashed into searing brilliance that made Benetan swing away, covering his eyes and uttering an inchoate protest. The brilliance lasted only an instant, and as the darkness seemed to redouble in its wake Benetan lowered his hands and, with after-images dancing before his vision, looked at the bowl again.

The figure of a man, unnaturally tall, stood where the flame had been. He was surrounded by a clear, cool aura, its edges so sharply defined that it looked, disconcertingly, as though it had been impressed onto the surrounding gloom, and his silver-white hair, held back by a simple circlet, flowed over his shoulders and seemed to merge with his long white cloak. But it was his eyes that riveted Benetan. They were clear, featureless orbs, filled with golden light. And although by their very nature those eyes could hold no expression, he felt their gaze focusing on him and the power of the serene scrutiny flooding his mind like a strange, warm balm.

The figure smiled, and Benetan felt as though something within him were catching fire.

'Captain Liss.' A hand stretched out, palm open in a gesture of friendship. 'You are welcome among us.'

Benetan couldn't move but only went on staring. The intensity of the figure's gaze was pulling at him, threatening to swamp him, and instinctively he fought against its lure. *It wasn't possible – this was heresy, it went against all reason* – Yet even as he recited the mental litany he knew that it carried no conviction. The sheer *power* of this being – it was immense; it was unhuman; as if the world into which he had stepped was too small to contain him.

'Benetan.' The smile was gentle now, so gentle that it hurt. 'This is not sorcery, and I am not a phantom. Come forward, my friend, and see the truth for yourself.'

Benetan didn't want to, but his feet moved against his will, propelling him towards the shining figure. Simbrian rose to his feet and stepped back, watching intently, but Benetan was oblivious to him as he approached, halted, stared again into the unearthly eyes. The figure's hand was still extended; he raised it then and brought it to rest on Benetan's shoulder.

A tingling charge of shock went through Benetan. The hand was real, solid; he could feel the pressure of the fingers through his clothing and a sensation of heat that seemed to penetrate his bones. Light from the being's aura flared on the badges of rank clipped to his tunic, chilling the silver flashes and igniting cold fires in the quartz pendants.

'You know my name,' Aeoris said with quiet certainty. 'And though you want to doubt my existence, I believe you can no longer do so. Am I right in that belief?'

Benetan's mind was rioting – but one certainty stood out as starkly as a rock in the raging sea of his confusion. He couldn't deny the truth, not to himself. And nor could he shame himself, and throw his fundamental integrity and honesty to the winds, by pretending otherwise.

He took a step back, so that Aeoris's hand fell away from his shoulder. A part of him wanted to send out a prayer, a call to Yandros to help and support him, but, for reasons which he didn't comprehend, he couldn't bring himself to do it. He forced himself to meet the lord of Order's gaze again, then tautly and very formally made the bow of the trained Chaos rider.

'Yes, sir,' he said. 'You are right.'

CHAPTER XIV

'And so I assure you,' Aeoris said gently, 'that what I have told you is true. The First Magus *will* unleash this horror on the world, and no words or pleas will sway him from his course.' He sighed. 'As captain of his riders, Benetan, you know Lord Vordegh's ways far better than any other mortal here. And you know that the value the magi set upon human life is small enough for them to care little for any innocents who stand in their way.' A pause. 'Your own recent experiences have been proof of that, I think.'

Benetan turned his head away, his expression tight with pain and his eyes bitter. He didn't want to believe this. He didn't *want* to. Yet could he deny it and be sure that he wasn't deceiving himself? Aeoris was right: he knew Vordegh's ways well enough. When it came to ruthlessness the First Magus had no equal, and since his elevation that ruthlessness had been growing. First there had been the matter of the newborn child – Benetan didn't know all the details of that travesty, but Savrinor had told him enough to sicken him to the pit of his soul. Then the first edict and the brutal, pointless executions. And now this second proclamation. Creatures summoned from Chaos and loosed on an innocent populace, preying at random, slaughtering, annihilating. A stratagem to root out the champions of heresy no matter what the cost. Oh, there was every chance that it would achieve its desired end. For all their strength, for all their god's protection, the heretics had done nothing to help those caught in the recent uprising. They hadn't had the power to stand against Pirane's citadel or to stem the murderous tide of Overlord Leyan's vengeance, and Vordegh's new onslaught might well succeed in smashing their movement forever. But for every heretic to die, how many others would lose their lives — and their souls — in this monstrous cull? How many of Chaos's own faithful, how many who had given lifelong fealty to the magi and believed, in their innocence, that the magi would return their loyalty in kind?

He couldn't find an answer to that question. But he knew that, whatever the answer might be, it would make no difference to Vordegh.

'Benetan.' A voice spoke and he sensed Simbrian's presence at his side. 'Benetan, none of us can be sure of what will happen, but —'

'No!' Benetan jerked aside as the sorcerer seemed about to reach out to him. 'No.' He took a pace away, keeping his back to Simbrian, not wanting him to so much as glimpse his face. 'He won't do it. The other magi won't permit it; they won't sanction such a thing.' Surely they wouldn't. *Surely?*

'They may have little choice,' Aeoris said quietly. 'The First Magus wields absolute power, and his word is law. I would put just one question to you, Benetan, and I do not ask that you tell me your answer; only look into your heart and decide what you yourself believe. If Vordegh has his way in this, which of his servants will he choose to be his instruments? And will those servants dare to disobey him if even his own peers cannot?'

Benetan's face turned dead-white as he realized what Aeoris was implying. It was hideously logical. He and his riders were trained for such work; they knew how the denizens of Chaos could be controlled and directed and used . . .

A surge of desperation rose in him and he swung round to face the lord of Order. He *wouldn't* accept this, wouldn't even acknowledge the possibility! Whatever Vordegh might do, whatever he might wish, there was another and higher authority; one which no man, however powerful, could defy.

'No,' he said again, his voice sharp with anger. 'You are wrong, sir, for you have overlooked one thing.' Confidence grew; suddenly he was no longer drowning and his certainty was more than a spar to clutch. 'The First Magus does *not* wield absolute power, for he – like all of us – is subject to the will of the gods. *Our* gods.' Deliberately, and reverently, he made the sign of the Seven. 'And I know – I *know* – that Lord Yandros will not sanction the slaughter of his own worshippers!'

The pupilless golden orbs of Aeoris's eyes continued to regard him steadily for a few moments. Then, softly, the lord of Order sighed.

'Ah,' he said, and there was a wealth of sadness in the word. 'Yandros.'

Benetan's jaw tightened. 'Unlike most, sir, I have had the privilege of meeting Lord Yandros, and I know –'

'No, my young friend, you do not!' The words cut across his, startling him into silence. Benetan floundered suddenly and the colour of Aeoris's aura lost its momentary furious edge.

'You have met your god once, Benetan, and briefly. But I have been acquainted with Yandros, and his brothers, for a time which you or any other mortal would be hard pressed to comprehend. We are the oldest of enemies, which in one sense means we are also most intimately acquainted. And one encounter, as I think you are honest enough to admit, does not compare with the knowledge of millennia.'

'Also the prejudice of millennia, sir,' Benetan countered. 'As you said, you and Lord Yandros are the oldest of enemies.'

'Oh yes; I am biased. But then, so are you.' The golden

light in Aeoris's eyes darkened hotly. 'After all, you claim that Yandros would not sanction the slaughter of his own worshippers. But has he not already done so? Or were the Chaos creatures that stalked the streets on the night of that unhappy uprising instructed to kill only heretics and leave the faithful unharmed?'

The little colour that had returned to Benetan's face drained once more. He couldn't reply. He wanted to deny it, refute it, but the words wouldn't come, for a denial would also have been a lie.

'There were some who prayed to me in their extremity,' Aeoris continued, his voice sombre. 'I could do nothing to help them; my power is not enough. But for every poor, stricken soul who cried out to me, how many do you think cried out to Yandros?' He paused. 'Did you see your god on that night, Benetan? Did he intervene, and protect his own worshippers from the magi's retribution?'

Memory snatched Benetan back to a forest clearing. A stench of burning on the air, clogging his nostrils and bringing sickness to his throat as he knelt in desperation, calling out, praying, imploring Yandros to break his silence and stop what was happening . . .

Aeoris spoke again, more gently. 'There is a very great deal that I could say to you about Yandros, and about the way in which Chaos chooses to impose its rule on mortals. But I am not here to win you to our cause, for I judge that you are a man of honour and integrity, and – quite rightly – such a man does not change his allegiance on the strength of words alone.' He paused. 'However, I also believe that you have other, more personal loyalties. And one in particular which does not accord with the homage that you pay to your gods.'

Simbrian, who was watching and listening intently, saw the dismay in Benetan's expression and the sudden high colour that came to his cheeks. The sorcerer's eyes narrowed as he wondered what the young man's obvious chagrin implied. Guilt? Shame? Fear? Kaldar insisted that Benetan Liss was a man of unshakeable honour, but Simbrian still had grave doubts. Infatuation was a powerful drug that could undermine the noblest principles — and twelve years at the Star Peninsula must change the perspectives of any man.

'Tell me, Benetan,' Aeoris said gently, 'why did you agree to keep Iselia's secret, and to help her?'

Benetan's shoulders quivered as he drew an unsteady breath. 'She was . . .' He faltered, tried to collect himself. 'We were childhood friends, and when I discovered what she . . . I couldn't . . . my conscience wouldn't . . .' He gave up.

Aeoris continued to watch him. 'There is nothing to fear in the truth, Benetan. Is the truth not that you helped her because you love her?'

The golden gaze was steady on his face. Benetan returned it and realized suddenly that he couldn't lie. It wasn't that he thought Aeoris could see into his mind and read his thoughts — he didn't believe the lord of Order had such power. But somehow, whatever his allegiance to Yandros, he couldn't bring himself to look this being in the face and speak anything other than the truth.

'Very well,' he said resignedly. 'There's no point in denying it . . . Yes. It was because of that.'

'And is love something to be ashamed of?'

'She's Kaldar's wife!' Benetan's voice rose in angry emotion. 'I have no *right* to love her; no right to —' He stopped.

'To desire her?'

Breath hissed sharply. 'Yes, to desire her. But that's *all* I have done! I wouldn't do anything to harm Iselia.' His head came up sharply and his eyes glittered combatively. 'I have not taken advantage of her, and I will not do so!'

Simbrian knew then that he was concealing something.

For all the defiant words there was painful remorse behind Benetan's eyes, a secret that he was unwilling or afraid to reveal. Perhaps he himself had done nothing to harm Iselia. But *someone* had.

Aeoris nodded. 'I recognize and acknowledge your honesty, Captain Liss. You are a man of honour, and I see that Iselia has a true friend in you. For her sake, therefore, I have a service to ask of you.'

A warning sounded in Benetan's mind as he noted the return to a formal mode of address and wondered what it presaged. 'A service?' he repeated uneasily.

Aeoris inclined his head. 'When you return to the Star Peninsula, the First Magus will be awaiting your report. As a loyal servant of Chaos, your duty is to tell him all that you have seen and learned: to unmask Simbrian and his friends and reveal the location of this stronghold. I have the power to shield my people from discovery, as you know; but if that shield should be broken, my strength is not great enough to stand against the forces that the magi can summon. The might of Chaos will smash us – and the magi will not be content until the soul of every mortal who has ever dared to whisper my name is consigned to the Seven Hells.'

Overhead, in the circle of sky high above the crater's rim, a faint glow was blotting out the stars as dawn began to break, but Benetan was unaware of the change. He stared at Aeoris, his eyes hunted and sickness churning in him. But he couldn't speak.

'Yes,' Aeoris said, so softly that his words were barely audible. 'I see that you understand.' He cast his gaze down. 'I do not ask this for my sake, Benetan. I have no right to do that. Nor do I ask it for the sake of those others whose lives you hold in the balance. But for Iselia, I ask you – entreat you – not to betray the secrets of this island.'

A shuddering spasm went through Benetan and he shut

his eyes, fighting the mental images that flooded the barriers he tried to raise against them. To report failure to Vordegh ... it was, in truth, nothing less than he had promised Iselia; and suddenly he could see her face again, stark in the moonlight on the beach below the castle stack. He could feel her fear, feel his own longing to comfort her and more, so much more. And he could hear the words she had spoken to him – *'Did you think I could change so much? Or that Kaldar could ever truly take the place that you once held?'*

But when he had made his promise he hadn't thought, hadn't *dreamed*, that he would find this. The lords of Order returned. Chaos's ancient enemy, summoned back from exile to manifest in the mortal world ... to keep their secret would be to betray not only his masters but also his gods. And he loved the gods. He had looked on the face of Yandros.

But he had also looked on the face of Aeoris, and though he fought the emotion with all his strength, a part of him – a part of his *soul* – was moved. He didn't know why he felt as he did; perhaps it was the quiet humility of Aeoris's appeal that touched him, or perhaps it was simply the warmth that, somewhere in a deep and unreachable part of his psyche, he felt all around him in this place, like a calm and gentle flow of water. And at the heart of it lay the one thing from which he could not escape. Yes; he loved the gods – but he loved Iselia more. Her life depended on the choice he would make.

And he couldn't let her die.

Aeoris's voice impinged on his churning thoughts. 'Don't feel that you must answer now, Benetan. That would not be fair to you.' He hesitated. 'A little while ago, and for another reason, I asked you to look into your own heart. If you will look there again now, and be guided by what you find, I shall be content.'

Benetan was silent and, for a few moments, motionless. Then slowly he turned and gazed around. The faint light was gaining in strength; long, dim shadows reached out across the crater bowl and the rock walls were taking on hints of red and gold among the featureless grey. None of the sleepers had yet stirred, and would not do so until Aeoris willed it. And suddenly Benetan felt utterly drained.

'I can't . . .' The words faded as he realized that he didn't know what he wanted to say. Time. He needed *time*.

'Sleep for a while,' Aeoris suggested gently. 'Your mind is troubled and unclear. Rest, restore your spirit; there is no need for haste.' He moved towards Benetan, and one hand gestured towards the ledge and the caves beyond while the other came to rest across the young man's shoulders in an almost fatherly way. This time Benetan didn't flinch from the touch, and nor was he aware of the small, subtle change in his energies as the lord of Order exerted a little power. All he knew was that suddenly the weariness was washing over him, weakening his limbs, blurring his vision, filling him with a craving for dreamless sleep.

'Yes . . .' he said, responding to the advice which, it seemed, Aeoris had given him half a lifetime ago. 'If I may rest . . . just for a while . . .'

He walked towards the caves with the gait of an old man, head bowed, not looking back. Aeoris watched, the gold of his eyes shifting tenuously towards a deeper and more molten shade, then when Benetan finally disappeared from view the god turned to Simbrian.

'He has already made his decision,' he said.

'My lord?' Simbrian's voice was reverent but his face betrayed his doubts. Aeoris smiled, a far harder smile than any he had bestowed on Benetan.

'Kaldar was right; Captain Liss is a man of rare honour. And, perhaps more to the point, a man whose emotions run very deep.'

'Then he does truly love Kaldar's wife?'

'Oh, yes. He does.' The lord of Order looked towards the caves again then steepled both forefingers and touched them to his chin.

'When I came to you on Summer Isle,' he said, 'I told you that Benetan Liss holds a vital key. My only doubt concerned his willingness to use it, for what I have in mind would be impossible without his free consent. Now, though, I think that consent is assured. His love for Iselia is greater than his love for Yandros and his squalid brood; for her sake he will take risks that would be unthinkable under any other circumstances.'

Simbrian nodded. 'Then you want more from him than you have told him?'

'Yes.' Aeoris began to pace across the bowl floor, the sorcerer following at a respectful distance. 'You know, without my needing to tell you, that no matter how great your own and your fellow-sorcerers' efforts, and no matter how I and my brothers strive to aid those efforts, the barrier that Chaos erected between our realm and the mortal world has only been weakened. We cannot breach it entirely, and we will not be able to do so until and unless we stand on an equal footing with Yandros and his brothers.

'At present, Yandros's power in this world far outstrips ours. And the key to that power is the gateway between the mortal dimension and the realm of Chaos.' Aeoris's eyes burned hot and his expression became malign. 'They have the arrogance, now, to call it the Chaos Gate, but they did not create it, and in the old days it provided a link between this world and many, many others, our own included. However, when we were exiled Yandros usurped it for his exclusive use. He established the castle around it and set his own unhuman servants in the castle to be its stewards.'

'The Old Ones?'

'The Old Ones, as you call them; though I think there must be few if any of that foul race left now, for even their lifespan wasn't infinite. But whether or not the magi still carry that tainted heritage, the source of their strength is unchanged. Yandros used the gateway, and uses it still, to channel power from the realm of Chaos into the hands of his servants. That is how the magi keep this world in their thrall, and if they are to maintain their supremacy the power must continue to flow.'

Simbrian was beginning to comprehend. He said, 'But if Chaos should lose sole control of the gateway . . .'

'Then they would also lose control of this world, and thus the barriers which they have set against our return would be shattered.'

'And what of the magi?'

Aeoris smiled balefully. 'Without Yandros's strength to sustain them, the magi are nothing more than mortal sorcerers – and may be challenged on equal terms.'

'I understand you, my lord. But – forgive me – I don't see how Benetan Liss can be of use to us in this.'

'Oh, he can, and will.' Aeoris halted and looked up at the sky, which now was turning to a hard, vivid amber as the rising sun hurled its light across the world. 'The power which flows through the gateway from Chaos has a very precise focus in this world, in the form of a wand which Yandros entrusted to the Old Ones and which has been passed down through the centuries from one leader to the next. It is,' his lip curled derisively, 'their most sacred artifact, and the symbol of the First Magus's authority. In fact it is far more than a symbol, for it is the one thing that links Chaos directly with the mortal dimension.' Aeoris turned his face to Simbrian once more, and his eyes blazed. 'Without that wand, the link no longer exists.'

221

The sorcerer let out his breath in a long, slow exhalation. 'Then if one of our own faithful could find and take –' Abruptly he stopped as realization dawned. 'Sweet g–' Hastily he bit the oath back. 'Iselia.'

'Yes.' Aeoris began to walk again. 'If what Benetan Liss has told us is true – and I have no reason to disbelieve him – Iselia has a degree of freedom within the castle, and is therefore well-placed to find out where the wand is kept. However, with Benetan Liss as our only courier we cannot let her know what we want her to do. A written message is clearly out of the question; the risks are too great. And any code that Iselia and Kaldar might have devised between them in the past would not be clear enough for our purposes. Another way must be found – and I believe Benetan Liss can be persuaded to provide it.' He stopped and turned to face Simbrian. 'When our young captain returns to the Star Peninsula, he will take Kaldar with him. And Kaldar will secure the wand and bring it to us.'

Simbrian stared. 'Kaldar?'

'Yes. I know what you're thinking – his name and his allegiance are known to the magi, and you believe that to send him into that nest of vipers is an act of madness.'

'My lord, I didn't mean to imply –'

'Didn't mean, or didn't dare?' Aeoris interrupted with faint irony, then his expression relaxed. 'But this isn't madness, my friend. Someone must go to the castle, and Kaldar is the obvious choice. I and my brothers have the power, now, to shield him from the magi's psychic scrutiny even within the walls of their own stronghold. And, more importantly, he is the only one among you who has, in Benetan Liss's eyes, a legitimate purpose at the Star Peninsula – that purpose being to rescue his wife from the life she is being forced to lead, smuggle her away and bring her to safety here in the south.' He smiled. 'What Captain

Liss will not know, of course, is that when Kaldar takes his wife from the castle, he will also be carrying the First Magus's wand into our care.'

'Ah. Ah, yes . . .' Simbrian felt his arguments beginning to totter. Whatever his misgivings, the sheer logic of Aeoris's plan couldn't be faulted; if they were to enlist Benetan's unwitting help, Kaldar was the only possible choice. Yet the thought of the countless snares that lay along that road still chilled him to the bone, and his brows knitted together unhappily. 'But even with your protection, Lord Aeoris, the risks are *enormous*. It would take only one word from Benetan Liss to bring disaster.'

'True. But Benetan Liss will hold his tongue, for two very good reasons. Firstly, his sense of honour will force him to acknowledge the justice of Kaldar's mission. His heart may rail against it, but despite his love for Iselia – or perhaps because of it – his conscience will oblige him to help her gain her freedom. Secondly, and more simply, he will be aware that if he does not hold his tongue, he will be condemning her to a slow and hideous death at the hands of the magi's torturers.'

Simbrian didn't answer. For a few moments the lord of Order watched the battle of conflicting emotions on his face, then he spoke again, more gently.

'I understand your fears, Simbrian. But would you deny Kaldar this chance? You've seen the frustration raging in him and you know how he rails against the inaction that has been forced on him since his wife was abducted. A purpose such as this is what he craves, and I believe he has the strength and the courage to succeed.' He paused, watching the sorcerer's face. 'It may also be the only hope for our cause. Would you deny *us* that?'

The arguments the sorcerer had been preparing crumbled, and he sighed a sigh of acknowledgement and acceptance.

'No, my lord,' he said. 'I would not.'

'I'm thankful to hear that,' Aeoris said softly. 'Very thankful.' He laid a hand on Simbrian's shoulder, a comradely gesture and one that implied great satisfaction. 'Come. Kaldar is still sleeping. Let us wake him, and tell him the glad news.'

Benetan argued with them for three hours. It was pure insanity, he said; no matter what story they might concoct between them, *no* sorcerer could hope to enter the castle and hide his talents from the magi. Kaldar's secret would be discovered, and within an hour of their arrival he, Iselia and Benetan himself would be food for one of Yandros's lowest and hungriest creations! All right, all *right*; Kaldar had found a way into the castle once before and gone undetected, but the magi had been distracted then by the forthcoming inauguration, and he had made his escape quickly. To go openly, to present himself, as was being proposed, as a loyal subject with vital information about the heretics to impart, wasn't merely suicidal, it was *deranged*.

And all the while, as his protests fell on deaf ears, a small voice was whispering and whispering in the depths of his mind: *if this lord of Order truly has the ability to protect him, and to help him get Iselia away from the castle, how great has his power grown? I am loyal to the gods; I should tell them, warn them – but how can I, when the price is Iselia's life?*

He knew that they would beat him down. Kaldar, savaging his conscience with the painful fervour of a husband's love for his wife; Simbrian with his gently emotive reasoning and faith that honour would triumph; and Aeoris, saying little but presiding quietly over all with an aura of empathy and compassion that worked its own form of spell. Yet for all the sway of their arguments it was Kaldar who dealt the final blow, and one in which neither emotion nor honour had any part.

'You forget, old friend,' he said, putting an unpleasant emphasis on the words and meeting Benetan's gaze with a ferocious challenge in his eyes, 'that we have your amulet.' He saw Benetan tense, and smiled without the smallest trace of kindness or humour. 'What, I wonder, would become of you if someone were to use it to return to the Star Peninsula ahead of you, carrying news to the magi that the captain of the Chaos riders is a secret heretic?'

Breath caught violently in Benetan's throat. 'The magi wouldn't . . .' He stopped, remembering the First Magus. Vordegh would believe such a story. Or, if he didn't believe, he would take no chances. One man — especially a commoner — was expendable, and easily replaced.

Kaldar's smile widened. 'Wouldn't they?'

At last Benetan managed to expel the air that was threatening to choke him. 'You talk of *honour* –' he began.

'Simbrian might. I don't.' Kaldar glanced at the sorcerer, but Simbrian was watching Benetan with the keen attention of a hawk. 'Extreme measures, Benet; but this is an extreme situation. It's possible that I won't have the courage – or the ruthlessness – to do it. But do you want to put that to the test?'

Benetan didn't, for as he looked into Kaldar's cold and steady blue eyes he knew that the threat was real. Later, he tried to tell himself that there had been other reasons for his capitulation, but the grounds rang hollow – save for one. And he dared not think of her.

They would depart that night on the ship that had brought them to the White Isle, aiming to reach the mainland at an hour when any curious coast-dwellers would be asleep in their beds. From there they would return to Stiv Pollander's farrier's shop, collect Benetan's mare and then use the amulet – which Kaldar would keep in his possession

— to transport them through the Maze to the Star Peninsula.

Benetan didn't know what manner of tale Kaldar intended to tell at the castle, but Kaldar swept his fears dismissively aside. All he needed to do, he was told, was affirm that Kaldar had asked for his protection and told him that he had vital information for the magi's ears alone; Kaldar himself would do the rest. As for the fine detail of how and where they were supposed to have encountered one another, that could be worked out on the journey. 'This way will be far better for all concerned,' Kaldar told him. 'The less you know, the smaller the risk of your making a mistake. Don't ask any more questions, Benet — and don't worry!'

His advice meant nothing; for all the confident words, Benetan was plagued by a constant, chill sweat of foreboding. Yet, short of killing Kaldar once they were on the mainland — and even in the midst of his confusion he knew he couldn't countenance that — he could do nothing to alter or block the plan. He would simply have to see it through, and hope to all the gods . . . he checked that thought, aware that a plea to the gods might be highly unwise under the circumstances . . . that nothing would go wrong.

But while Benetan waited, with his gnawing dread for company, Aeoris had one more deed to perform before his reluctant courier departed. He had said nothing of his intentions, either to Simbrian or to Kaldar. But what he planned would serve a dual purpose, for as well as being a just reward for a devoted follower it would also give Benetan Liss food for thought on his journey north.

Those assembled on the island all knew by now that their god had manifested among them, but as yet they had not been privileged to see him, for he had withdrawn to one of the caves before lifting the spell of sleep. Choosing his time with meticulous care, Aeoris waited until the afternoon was well advanced before sending word through Sim-

226

brian that he would make himself known to his followers at sunset. And, he added, he wished Benetan to be among the gathering.

Benetan didn't want to attend, but he had also had enough of arguing, and there seemed little point in wasting further energy over such a trivial request. So, as daylight began to fade, he abandoned his dismal contemplations and walked morosely out into the bowl. The followers of Order were waiting, and their eager expectancy was almost palpable in the air. It gave Benetan a sharp and none too pleasant frisson, for there were uncomfortable parallels with occasions at the Star Peninsula when the gods had made their presence known to mortals, and yet again he felt like a traitor. He shut out the memory of Yandros's cool, assessing eyes – at this moment any thought of the great Chaos lord was enough to terrify him – and went to stand silently beside Kaldar on the edge of the gathering.

Aeoris appeared as the sun's last rays flared across the jagged crown of the crater, and as he stepped out onto the ledge above the bowl, Benetan suddenly had to turn his head away as a surge of incoherent but shockingly powerful emotion surged through him. The lord of Order had *changed* – he couldn't define the change, couldn't begin to assimilate it, but it was as though the golden nimbus glowing around Aeoris had been augmented by another, invisible yet overwhelming; a vast and all-encompassing aura of sheer tranquillity that stripped away barriers and, he felt, bared him through flesh and bone to his soul. Irrationally, memories flared into his mind; tiny things, long forgotten but suddenly alive again and hauntingly, achingly clear. He was filled with a smoky yearning, felt his chest constricting as breath refused to come. Foolishly, childishly, *stupidly*, he wanted to cry.

A hand came to rest on his arm. He turned his head, blinking rapidly, bewildered. Kaldar didn't speak, but his eyes were very intent and seemed to hold a measure of affinity. Or was it triumph? Benetan didn't know, and shook off the touch, focusing his gaze hard on the rock wall at the far side of the bowl.

He heard Aeoris speak to his followers, but later he remembered nothing of those minutes save for the feeling of sadness, and that yearning, which clung to his thoughts and would not let him go. He felt a terrible sense of loss, as though something very dear had been taken from him and, however hard he strove, he could not quite reach out across the gulf of his mind to bring it safely back. But when at last Aeoris was done, and reached out towards someone in the small crowd, Kaldar's sudden tensing at his side drew Benetan out of his unhappy reverie.

He looked up, the spell that had held him crumbling, and was in time to see Nanithe step forward. Her face was pale and there was desperate fear in her eyes, but she did not dare to disobey her god's summons.

Aeoris smiled, and reached out to take her hand. 'Nanithe.' His voice carried softly, and Benetan caught a scent of something strange and evocative as a light breeze sprang up suddenly in the bowl. 'Dear child, don't fear me.'

She tried to look down, but before she could move he touched a finger to her chin, tilting her head slowly and gently so that she couldn't avoid his gaze. Nanithe began to tremble, and the lord of Order said, 'So much fear; so many cruel memories. You long to be free of them but you have found no true escape, only a retreat into silence.' He saw her try to shrink away. 'Don't flinch, Nanithe; don't close your eyes. There need be no more darkness.' With flawless assurance his free hand rose and he laid the palm against her brow. 'There *will* be no more darkness.'

Nanithe gasped, and mingling with the gasp was a whimper.

'*Great gods . . .*' Kaldar hissed.

'No darkness, Nanithe.' Aeoris's voice carried clearly, quietly. 'No nightmare, no cruelty; only peace. Let the darkness go, dear child. Let it go forever from your mind, and be whole again.'

As he spoke his hands slid to rest lightly on her shoulders. Then he leaned forward, bent, and kissed her on the brow.

All present, even Benetan, saw the pale light that quivered momentarily at the crown of Nanithe's head and then shimmered down the length of her body. They saw the spasm that went through her, saw her fall to her knees at Aeoris's feet. And they heard her voice; the voice she had been unable to use, unable to summon, since the horrors of her long-ago ordeal.

'My lord . . . oh, my lord Aeoris!'

Kaldar's vision blurred as tears started into his eyes. He wiped them away with a quick, vehement hand, but it was only an instinctive reflex; anyone, he thought, might be forgiven for weeping at such a moment as this. Or for laughing, shouting, hugging everyone within reach – he wanted to do all that, and more! Gods, at this moment he could even hug Benetan!

The sudden resurgence of darkly wry humour prompted Kaldar to turn and glance at the Chaos rider beside him. And what he saw stilled him.

Benetan was dry-eyed, standing motionless, watching the scene with a stare that seemed to register nothing. But his face had a deathly pallor, and when Kaldar looked more deeply at his eyes he saw that they were not unfocused as he had first thought. Benetan was gazing at something which no other living soul could see. And the pain of it had brought a part of him close to breaking.

CHAPTER XV

'One survived.' Physician—Magus Croin reached the top of the main staircase, and Pirane noticed that he cast a quick, almost furtive glance over his shoulder before they turned together and walked towards the west wing. 'A boy; the son of one of the grooms, I believe. The entities found some flaw in him which made him unacceptable as an offering.' His voice was perfectly composed, but his eyes, as he raised them briefly to meet his companion's gaze, told another story. 'The First Magus instructed me to use him in a probing and search of the planes instead. I couldn't help but ask myself: if a High Oracular Communion has already failed, what could he hope to gain from a lesser working among the lower dimensions?'

Pirane was disconcerted. The ritual to release the first host of demonic beings into the world had taken place on the previous night; Croin, she knew, had prepared the twenty-one servants for their role, but the conjuration itself had been performed by Vordegh alone. She was unaware that there had been any further activity.

'You didn't speak your mind?' she said uneasily.

'No, I did not. Under the circumstances, I hardly think that would have been wise.'

'Quite.' A pause. 'And the search of the planes?'

'It paid no dividend. Lord Vordegh was not pleased.'

Daylight was fading, but the torches in their wall-brackets hadn't yet been lit; the corridors were gloomy and filled with echoes, and the castle felt uncommonly cold. The wind had veered into the north during the night, and

Pirane could smell the advent of frost on the air. But it wasn't the change in the weather that made her suppress a shiver.

'I understand,' she said, 'that he has ordered a second list of names to be made.'

'Yes.' Croin paused as they reached a junction in the passage; again Pirane saw the rapid, uneasy look, as though the physician half expected to find something less than pleasant waiting for him in the side turning. 'Twenty-eight this time. Twenty-one will feed a second legion when it is conjured, but the First Magus has not yet revealed the purpose of the remaining seven.'

They were passing a window, and as they did so they both heard a faint, harsh sound beyond the glass, as though something were scratching on one of the latticed panes and trying to get in. It might have been a bird or rat but probably not; during the past few days the activities taking place in the castle had attracted all manner of presences from other dimensions, and now Pirane began to realize what had stirred them to activity.

'I suspect, however, that you have an idea of what he means to do with them?' she said at last, quietly.

'Yes. I imagine my services will be required again, for a further probing. And when that fails, a third. And then a fourth.'

'If, by then, there are enough expendable servants left.'

'Quite.' They walked on in silence for a few moments. Then Croin spoke again. 'Master Savrinor has been entrusted with the choosing of the new list. I hope, for his sake, that none of the candidates are found wanting this time.'

In one sense it would please Vordegh if they were, Pirane thought. She knew that the First Magus disliked Savrinor intensely, and while one small error was not excuse enough, even by Vordegh's criteria, to be rid of the historian, two might be a different matter. Savrinor wasn't the kind of man to inspire sympathy, but at this moment Pirane almost pitied him.

'He was hardly the ideal choice to begin with,' she said. 'For all his tastes and that air of *sang-froid* he cultivates so carefully, in some matters he has a very queasy stomach. I know for a fact that he was very far from happy with the first commission. He'll relish this even less.'

As she spoke, she realized suddenly that for the past few minutes she had been instinctively pitching her voice low; almost whispering, in fact. Was she catching Croin's malaise, imagining spies at every turning, fearing to utter the most innocuous thoughts aloud? Hardly surprising if she was; these days a good number of the magi were beginning to feel as though their waking hours were spent walking barefoot on broken glass. And little wonder, in the light of Croin's latest news.

They reached another turning, a narrower corridor which led towards Croin's own apartments. There were few windows here and the passage had the unpleasant look of an open mouth with a black throat beyond, leading away into the unknown. Croin repressed a shudder, then stroked one seven-fingered hand across the back of the other, and a vivid white flame materialized in his palm. He held it up and the shadows retreated a little.

'Savrinor is extremely shrewd,' he said, 'but all the same I think a word to the wise might not go amiss. Simply to warn him that . . . well, let us say that he is not in the best of odour with the First Magus at present.'

Pirane suspected that Savrinor was already well aware of his position, but nodded nonetheless. 'Better still, perhaps I shall cast my eye over his list of candidates this time and weed out any who could prove unsuitable.'

'Yes. Yes, I think that might be a precaution worth taking. And not only for Savrinor's sake.' Croin waited and, when she didn't reply, took a step towards the dark corridor. 'I must take my leave – reluctantly – and go and begin my preparations. The First Magus has commanded me to attend him tonight, and he has also ordered me to take no food or wine beforehand.' A sigh conveyed his distaste for the stricture. 'You'll speak to Savrinor?'

'I will.' Pirane inclined her head in farewell, began to turn away – then hesitated. 'Croin . . . the great majority of the magi are convinced that this supposed heretic leader doesn't even exist. Even the gods are convinced of it. Yet the First Magus continues in his obsession, and will hear no argument to the contrary. I ask myself – I *must* ask myself – where will it end?'

It was a question which Croin would not have dared to voice, and he admired Pirane the more for her candour in their present situation. But, even had he had the courage, there was no answer he could give her.

'I think, my dear,' he said very quietly, 'that if we are right and the First Magus is wrong, then the remedy lies in the hands of our Lord Yandros alone.' He paused, then added, 'But you, perhaps, know that better than any of us.'

Pirane watched him walk away, his shadow gliding on the wall beside him as the unearthly flame flickered in his hand. Outside, the wind was moaning softly, like the voice of an old, old woman in mourning, and a bitter little draught blew along the corridor. It was almost dark. At last the magus turned away. Croin had disappeared, and from the direction of the stairs a servant was approaching with a brand, kindling the wall torches one by one. Their light, Pirane thought, had no warmth tonight; and, drawing the folds of her silk shawl with its moving patterns of embroidery closer about her shoulders, she glided away in the direction of her own apartments.

* * *

'For the last time, will you let it *drop!*' Benetan jerked his mare to a halt and twisted in the saddle, his grey eyes like flint through the strands of hair whipping across his face. 'You've been questioning me and baiting me turn and turn about for the past seven days, and I've had *enough!*'

Kaldar reined in beside him, his own eyes challenging. 'Temper, Benet! I thought your masters trained your kind never to show any emotion? Certainly from what I've seen and heard of the Chaos riders –'

He stopped, for in the space of less than a second Benetan had drawn one of his knives, and the tip was hovering inches from Kaldar's throat.

'One more insult,' Benetan said, 'and I just might not be able to resist the temptation. And I assure you it's a lot more painful than a black eye.'

Another powerful gust of wind rollicked across their path and set Kaldar's grey horse snorting and side-stepping. Grasping at the animal's mane Kaldar steadied himself in the saddle, and as the grey settled he made a pacifying gesture.

'Enough, enough. Maybe I've been taking more out on you than you really warrant.' The gust had flung grit into his eyes; he blinked it away. 'It's this damned wind; it unsettles me. I hate wind.' He glanced at his companion again. 'Whenever a gale got up we used to hear it in the mines, echoing through the galleries. It sounded like something coming for us out of the Seven Hells, and it's one of those things you never forget. You know what I mean.'

It was as close to an apology as Kaldar was capable of offering, and Benetan nodded. 'Let's forget it. Just as long as you promise to change the subject.'

'I'll do my best. But if there *is* anything that you haven't –'

'Kaldar, how many more times do I have to say that I've told you *everything I know* about Iselia?' The lie had been repeated so often that it came easily now, and the early attacks of conscience were all but gone. Benetan had reasoned that he could do nothing but harm by hinting at the nature of Iselia's 'apprenticeship' to Savrinor, and had bolstered his decision by telling himself that he wasn't even certain that his suspicions were right. It was disingenuous at best, treacherous at worst, but the thought of the havoc that Kaldar's reckless temper might bring about if he knew what Savrinor had done to his wife persuaded him that he had to hold his tongue at all costs. Once they reached the castle it might be impossible to go on hiding the truth, but Benetan would deal with that problem if and when it arose.

Travelling with Kaldar had been disagreeable enough without the extra burden of his constant cross-questioning. The voyage back to the mainland had been rough, and on the five-day ride from the coast to Stiv Pollander's shop Kaldar had insisted on schooling Benetan, over and over again, in every detail of the report he would make to the magi at the Star Peninsula, punctuating the exercises with lectures on Chaos's shortcomings and subtle but malevolent observations aimed at undermining Benetan's convictions. They had quarrelled often, the quarrels usually ending in bouts of sour silence, and Benetan had been thankful to reach the farrier's. Stiv's presence would at least distract Kaldar from his target for the space of a night, and once they were clear of this district they could at last use the amulet to bring the unpleasant journey to an end.

Kaldar, however, hadn't done with him yet, and now the farrier's shop and the demesne in which it lay were two days behind them and still they were on the northward road. Something was holding Kaldar back, Benetan knew, but his efforts to find out what it was met only with a sharp refusal to answer and a barrage of new questions, which had finally culminated in this latest and angriest clash. Now, to make matters worse, the weather was deteriorating. The wind had got up during the previous night, sending temperatures plummeting; by this morning a strong north-wester was blowing and it had continued to strengthen throughout the day until with sunset less than an hour off Benetan was aware, above the wind's noisy bluster, of the thin, ominous whistling that portended a full gale.

The horses were walking on once more, though the grey gelding – one of Stiv's – seemed to dislike the rough weather as much as Kaldar did, shaking its head and jinking whenever a new flurry of leaves and dust whipped across the track. Kaldar himself had fallen silent, and gloomily Benetan surveyed the landscape ahead of them, an open patchwork of brown and faded green tinged with gore in places as the sinking sun broke through ragged cloud. 'There's little chance of our having a roof over our heads tonight,' he said. 'No sign of any kind of habitation, and the last of the light'll be gone within an hour.'

Kaldar hunched his shoulders. He looked uneasy but his voice was level enough as he replied, 'Your eyes are better than mine; I'll take your word for it. What do you suggest?'

'There's some woodland half a mile or so on, by the look of it. Not the ideal place to make camp, but in this weather it'll be preferable to open ground.'

Kaldar grunted. 'I suppose if we have to choose between being blown away and having an uprooted tree fall on our heads, the tree's marginally less of a risk. How long –' He stopped.

'What is it?'

Kaldar shook his head, frowning. 'Nothing. At least, I don't think so . . .'

Benetan's patience began to ebb. 'If you're going to make more difficulties –'

'No,' Kaldar interrupted emphatically. 'No, it isn't that,

Benet. For a moment I thought . . . Ah, forget it. It's the memory of those mine-galleries; it's resonating in my bones, that's all.' He grimaced, shaking himself as though to slough something off. 'I can't say I'm going to relish lying out tonight.'

Benetan smiled drily and with a faint hint of fellow-feeling. 'Neither am I. Do you remember any of those old songs we used to sing? We'll probably need them, for I doubt if we'll get a lot of sleep.' He squinted at the sky. 'Let's only hope that it doesn't rain as well.'

The woodland was a conifer plantation; less pleasant than broadleaf for a camp site but also less likely to harbour wild animals of any dangerous size. The sun had set completely by the time they reached the trees, leaving only a dull, ominous pall of bloody light in the sky, and the wind roared distantly in the high branches as they felt their way through the gloom in search of a suitable place to settle.

'We're sheltered here, at least.' Echoes, and the sudden remoteness of the wind, gave Benetan's voice a peculiar timbre.

'Maybe.' Kaldar and his horse were no more than silhouettes among the tree-trunks. 'But I don't want to venture too far in. Better to stay relatively near the road.'

'As you like.' The wood was making Kaldar nervous, Benetan surmised; hardly surprising for a man who had lived among treeless mountains all his life, and he smiled a dry, private smile at the thought that Kaldar's confidence had a few cracks after all. 'There's a clearing of sorts – to our right, you see it? Will that do?'

'It's probably as good as anywhere else.' Kaldar sounded impatient but Benetan also detected a trace of fear in his tone. And he recalled the previous small incident just before they left the road . . . But Kaldar was already turning away, and Benetan made no comment as he followed him to the clearing.

237

There was little in the way of undergrowth here but the thick carpet of pine needles would be passably comfortable. They unstrapped rolled blankets from their horses' backs, then Benetan took food and water from his saddlebag while Kaldar stared restively around.

'We'll have a poor fire at best with this wood,' he said moodily. 'That's if we can light a fire at all; the wind's still tricky enough in here to put out any small flame.' He hugged himself. 'Gods, that *noise*. It sounds like . . .'

Benetan looked up. 'Sounds like what?'

'Wait.' Kaldar had tensed and there was the look of a hunted animal about him.

Benetan started to say, 'What do –' but a sharply raised hand silenced him.

'*Shh!* Listen! Beyond the wind; behind it, far off – can you hear it?'

Benetan realized suddenly that the horses were reacting to something, too; his own mare had jerked her head up and her ears were pricked, while the grey started to stamp restlessly.

'Oh, gods,' Kaldar said hollowly, and at the same moment Benetan heard it. Far away, far to the north, a new sound riding on the back of the gale; a thin, eerie and impossibly distant howling . . . Quickly Benetan looked up, trying to see through the confused darkness of the treetops. There was still a glimmer of light in the sky beyond but its colour was changing, the blood-red afterglow of the sun draining away and turning to an evil purple shot through with a flux of baleful green.

Kaldar's voice was harsh with alarm. '*It's a Warp!*'

Two violent and utterly opposed emotions hit Benetan at once. The first was fear – the primal, instinctive fear of his childhood years, crashing out of the past and turning him to a petrified shell. But the second – twelve years of experience, of training, of wild memories and wilder excite-

238

ment ignited like fire on the heels of the terror as he heard and saw the first, unmistakable signs of the supernatural storm, one of the great harbingers of Chaos. *Screaming out of the gods' own realm, howling with the voice of an infernal choir; the shock of white lightning and the vast, dim bands of colour turning, turning in the sky, distorting the moons and turning them to blood; and the dizzying climb into ecstasy as the magi's narcotics did their work and he was riding out, leading his warriors, howling with the storm, reaching up to catch the lightning –*

'BENETAN!' A voice smashed into his mind and he reeled against a tree as something sprang at him, grabbing hold of his arms and shaking him turbulently. Memory clashed briefly and horribly with reality, then reality took the upper hand and he saw Kaldar's stark white face inches from his own.

'Benet, don't you understand? We're going to be caught in a Warp!' Kaldar shook him again, frantically trying to bring him back down to earth. 'We've got to find shelter!'

Though the effort was almost beyond him, Benetan dragged his reeling mind fully into the present. Kaldar's eyes were wild; he might profess contempt for Chaos but words were no proof against the old, ingrained terrors. And he didn't know what Benetan knew; he didn't *understand*.

'Calm down!' Benetan flung up both arms, breaking Kaldar's ferocious grip. '*Listen* to me, Kaldar! We're as safe here as anywhere!'

'*Safe?*'

'Yes! All the legends about people being carried away on the Warps, all the stories we believed as children – they're not true!' With a rapid flick of one hand Benetan pushed his coat aside, revealing the black uniform with its silver and quartz adornments. 'Wearing this, don't you think I should know?'

Kaldar's mouth worked and a shudder racked him. 'All

239

right.' It was taking a tremendous effort of will, Benetan saw, for him to keep his voice – and his mind – on an even keel. 'I believe you – sweet Aeoris, I've got no choice, have I?' He swung away, clutching his upper arms again. 'Trapped here, nowhere to run to –' Another shudder, and he rocked on his feet. 'All *right*. I'll calm down, as you said. Calm down and *stay* calm. Don't think about running, don't think about *anything*.' He started to pace, hands pressed against his face, talking to himself, talking away the fear, though the sound of the approaching Warp was growing louder and against it his voice was barely audible now. Benetan glanced at the horses. His mare was dancing, tossing her head, excited. She wasn't afraid of the Warps for she knew them as well as he did – but the grey gelding was another matter. The animal was trembling, and sweat flecked its muzzle, neck and withers; as Benetan took a step towards it, it reared, whinnying in terror, and pulled with all its strength at its tethering-rope.

'Kaldar!' Benetan yelled above the rising noise in the sky. 'Your horse – help me, quickly; secure that tether!'

Kaldar swung round, but any reply he might have made was drowned by an unholy shriek from high above. At the same instant a colossal blue flash lit the forest, and the grey gelding screamed an answer to the storm, plunging and bucking. Benetan saw the rope start to give – then with a final, panic-stricken struggle the gelding broke free and bolted. It charged straight past Benetan, knocking him aside as he made a fruitless grab for its bridle, and raced away. Benetan rolled, winded, and as he started to pick himself up another figure rushed past him in the gelding's wake.

'Kaldar! Kaldar, you won't catch him! For the gods' sakes, *come back!*'

But Kaldar was already gone, plunging among the trees into the darkness. Benetan climbed to his feet, brushing leaves and earth from his hair, and stumbled to his own mare. She was too exhilarated to stand still as he fumbled with her securing rope, and there was no time to calm her enough to allow him to get into the saddle; instead, Benetan grasped hold of the bridle-bit, pulling her in his wake as he set off in pursuit of Kaldar and the gelding.

With no undergrowth and thus no trampled path to follow, Benetan could only pray that his quarry hadn't changed direction. He was heading back towards the edge of the wood, and now he could not only hear the oncoming Warp but could feel it, a vibration that seemed to shake his bones and reverberate through the ground beneath his feet. High and shrill behind the more natural wind, the voices of the storm were singing in eldritch harmony. It was said by those who knew no better that this awesome sound was the crying of tormented souls, those who had offended the gods and were doomed by Yandros to be carried on the Warps forever. Benetan had believed that, before the castle changed him. Listening, he could almost believe it again now, and he ruthlessly crushed the queasy sensation it brought to his stomach.

'KALDAR!' His voice rang through the wood. 'KALDAR!'

High overhead, a network of blood-red lightning shattered across the heavens as though the sky were a vast shell cracking into a thousand pieces, and the wood exploded with ferocious brilliance that threw everything into a bizarre, two-dimensional tableau. It lasted only an instant, but in that instant Benetan glimpsed a distant shape, running –

He lurched on, the mare at his heels. Ahead of him a vast shadow of malignant ochre was sweeping slowly through the wood, and the trees were thinning out. Benetan shouted Kaldar's name again, then suddenly saw him. He had reached the wood's edge, and his figure was a stark silhouette against a background of mayhem as he stood mesmerized, unable to move.

'Kaldar!' Releasing the mare's bridle and trusting her to follow, Benetan ran towards the other man. Kaldar heard him, and whipped round in the way that cornered prey might turn for a last desperate confrontation with the hunter. In the light of a bolt of howling blue fire that ricocheted through the heavens his face looked like the face of a corpse. Then his legs seemed to give way beneath him, and he sagged against the bole of a tree.

Benetan raced to him, and as he burst into the open his mind and body together took a battering assault. The full force of the wind hit him, a roaring gale now, tearing at his hair and clothes and trying to rock him off his feet. And as the bowl of the sky opened before him he saw the full grandeur of the Warp sweeping down out of the north. Titanic bands of dark and monstrous colour were wheeling across the sky, marching one behind another in the storm's unstoppable progress, and as Benetan momentarily froze with the shock of the gargantuan spectacle, a chain of lightning-bolts erupted across the entire horizon in silent, lethal symmetry. For one instant, just one, time and experience were ripped away from Benetan's mind and he was a boy again, cowering in his parents' house with his arms over his head and the age-old terror of the Warps devouring him. *To see it like this, with no drug to inspire and shield him –*

An ugly, choking sound close by, barely audible against the screaming, ramping voices of Chaos, snatched him back from the brink of derangement. The panic-stricken youth spun away into the forgotten past, and Benetan ran to where Kaldar was clutching the tree as though it were his only anchor in a world that had gone mad.

'Come on!' The words rasped savagely as he grasped

Kaldar under the armpits and dragged him back into what small shelter the tree-fringe provided. Kaldar made no effort to resist; the shock of confronting the Warp face-on had stripped his will-power to the bone and he was like a child's rag-puppet. None too gently Benetan dropped him into a semi-recumbent position with his back against a pine trunk, then crouched down in front of him and took his shoulders in a fierce grip.

'Kaldar! Kaldar, can you hear me?'

'Uh . . .' Kaldar tried to nod.

'Are you all right?'

'Y . . . yes.' There was spittle on his mouth and chin; he wiped it away. 'It was the . . . I didn't expect it, wasn't prepared . . .' Black light flared across his face as a spitting network of fire cut the sky in half, and convulsively he tried to struggle upright. 'My horse – I couldn't catch it, it got out onto the road –'

'It'll have to take its chance.' They were both almost having to shout now, Benetan realized; the noise of the Warp was dinning in his ears and the full force of it was almost on top of them. Kaldar had started to shiver with reaction, and abruptly Benetan pulled off his own coat – the wind almost tore it away as he did so – and slung it around the quaking shoulders.

'What about you?' Kaldar's voice was jerky as he tried to stop his teeth from chattering.

Benetan shook his head, hair flying. 'I don't need it.' In truth he was glad to be rid of the coat; he had started to sweat profusely, as if his blood was cooking in his veins, and the psychic pull of the Warp was calling to him with a power he found hard to resist. If he had any sense he'd get away from this open vista before the call became too strong, and he scrambled upright, tugging at Kaldar's arm. 'Come on! Back in among the trees.'

Kaldar started to get to his feet, staggering as the gale

blew him sideways. Benetan flung a glance back to the road — and froze.

Something was coming along the track. He couldn't hear it above the yell of the wind and the triumphant voice of the Warp, but there was a blur of movement in the darkness; something large and heavy, racing towards them . . . Then seven huge silver bolts, one behind another, blasted across the landscape, and through the stunning glare Benetan saw two galloping horses pounding towards him, a wagon rocking wildly in their wake. The wagon's driver was standing in his seat, his mouth a screaming black gape in the white smear of his face as he lashed the maddened animals to greater effort; beside him a woman and child were clinging desperately to any handhold they could find.

'*Yandros!*' Forgetting Kaldar, Benetan dashed to his mare and flung himself into the saddle. It was sheer instinct and he acted on it without pausing to think; the wagon was going at breakneck speed, and if he didn't stop it, it would crash —

The mare leaped forward like a coiled spring released. As she charged out of the wood another titanic flash split the sky, and the terrified wagon-driver's brain registered an appalling phantasm of black and silver, lit demonically by the shrieking storm, rushing at him out of the night. *A Chaos rider* — the man's yell of horror was lost in the cacophony of the Warp and he lurched backwards, hauling on the reins with all his strength in a frantic bid to swerve the wagon aside. The horses, hurled off balance as their heads were wrenched up, lost their footing; the legs of one went from under it and it fell, cannoning against its companion. Wood splintered, the traces snapped like whip-lashes, and the wagon's central shaft broke in two as both horses crashed to the ground in a tangle of kicking legs and flying manes and tails. Nothing could stop the wagon's momentum; it hit the fallen animals, slewed broadside and careered off the road. Benetan saw the wagon-driver pitched from his seat, heard a shrill cry that cut through the Warp's din, and in horror he drove his heels into the mare's flanks again, spurring her to a gallop in pursuit of the cart as it bucketed away out of control.

And out of the sky, out of the Warp's heart, a wail of monstrous laughter rang shatteringly across the land.

Benetan's mare skidded to a halt and reared, forehooves raking high. Overhead, an immense shape blotted out the dim, turning bands of murky colour, and a concussion of displaced air overtook the gale and hit them like a wall. The mare tottered; Benetan clung to her mane, turning his head aside and hunching his shoulders against the onslaught, and *something* swept over and past them, descending steeply. He had one glimpse of its outline, burned against the sky as the Warp renewed its fury in an explosive surge, and knew instantly what it could only be – a demon, conjured by sorcery to cross the bridge between dimensions and sail on the supernatural storm like a ghost-ship on a boiling sea. Its great, membranous wings cracked the air in an inexorable rhythm as it veered; then it changed course with awful purpose and suddenly Benetan realized that it was dropping towards the runaway wagon.

'*No!*' He screamed with all the power he could muster, but the wind ripped his voice away. A peal of wild, echoing laughter answered him, and in the glare of a livid mesh of lightning that filled the sky and made every hair stand on end, he saw the demon plummeting to earth –

'*Oh, gods* –' He pulled the mare's head round, turning her, trying to drive her after the demon. But she wouldn't obey him; she reared again, twisting around, and Benetan lost his grip and fell from the saddle. He hit the rough ground of the track; for a moment he lay dazed, then, convulsively, he started to scramble to his feet –

There was a wailing sound in the distance and, mingling

with it, the scream of a human being whose mind had been hurled through the barrier between sanity and madness. Benetan saw the huge wing of shadow rushing towards him and instinctively he flung himself to the ground again as the demon soared overhead. It was gaining height fast, but as it passed above him Benetan saw it clearly for the first and only time. A shape that defied belief, changing and transmuting with every instant, it was horse and pig and cat and serpent and bird and a hundred other, unnameable things. Only the vast, black wings kept constant form. The wings, and the face.

Benetan knew he would see that face again and again in his nightmares. It was a human face, many times human size, pure and perfect and awesomely beautiful; but its skin had the nacreous sheen of the grave, and it was eyeless, and black flames burned in its open mouth as its strange, grim, wailing laughter rang above the tumult of the Warp and echoed in Benetan's head.

And in the demon's grasp, hanging from its mouth by ropes of black saliva and clasped between what one moment were white, graceful hands, and the next became shimmering talons, and the next jewel-red hooves, two doll-like figures dangled. One was limp and still; the other – a girl-child – struggled and writhed as the huge denizen of Chaos climbed into the frenzied sky.

Benetan's gorge rose, and with it a fury and a misery and a sense of petrified helplessness that he had never before known. It wasn't the demon itself – oh, no; he had seen far worse and far lovelier beings and he knew this for what it was; a low creation, a thing of sorcery – but it was the knowledge that this was the magi's doing, Lord Vordegh's threat made brutal and pitiless reality. One small family, fleeing from something they couldn't hope to outrun; dying hideously, their bodies and souls devoured, and never knowing why they should have been chosen from among so many, for there was no reason, none at all save cruel chance.

Benetan's ribcage heaved hugely, agonizingly, but for several seconds his voice wouldn't come. When it did, when it finally did, it was out of his control, a hoarse, tortured scream of impotent rage. *He could do nothing! And the child was still alive, still trying to fight –*

'*YANDROS!! YANDROS, HELP HER, SAVE HER!! CALL IT BACK, DESTROY IT – OH, GODS OF CHAOS,* **STOP THIS MADNESS!!!**'

He felt as though his soul were being torn out of him by the sheer desperation of his plea as he screamed it. But his only answer was a faraway shimmer of laughter, blending with the eldritch choir of the Warp. The demon sailed on, receding into the distance, and the gods of Chaos had nothing to say.

Benetan tried to turn round but couldn't move. His body was beyond the reach of his mind, as though the nerve-centre had been severed. Around him the supernatural storm still raged, but suddenly it was remote, unreal. He felt that everything within him – reason, emotion, *everything* – was shutting down. And before his inner vision, unbidden, was an image of Aeoris of Order's face –

A shattering harmony glittered across the landscape, and the colours of the Warp wheeled massively, slowly onwards. It meant nothing.

Quietly, his mind simply surrendering, Benetan collapsed.

CHAPTER XVI

'You're not to blame.' Kaldar hunched his shoulders as though against bitter cold, though the gale had dropped and the night was quiet and almost warm now. 'Gods, if I'd had my horse don't you think I'd have done what you did? Anyway,' he shut his eyes, pushing away the images that tried to crowd in on him, 'at very worst you only sped on what was inevitable. They'd never have outrun that monstrosity. *Never.*'

Benetan said nothing. He knew Kaldar's arguments were right, but as yet he wasn't ready to allow himself the luxury of even that small comfort. All that mattered was that three innocent people had died horribly, and that he had been able to do nothing to save them. And the thought that, in their last few minutes of life, they had seen him and recognized what he was and taken him for an enemy had sickened him to the core.

Kaldar got up and took a few paces along the road. Benetan's mare was tethered to one of the trees at the wood's edge; she raised her head briefly at his approach then returned to her grazing. Kaldar stared up at the sky but the cloud-cover was thick, obscuring any sight of the moons, and after a few moments he paced back and looked down at Benetan's huddled figure where he sat with his back against a trunk.

'What hour do you think it is?' he asked.

Benetan shrugged apathetically. 'I don't know.'

Kaldar hissed between his teeth. 'At least the damned Warp's gone . . . Do you want to sleep?'

'No.'

'Then maybe we should go.'

That did provoke a reaction; Benetan looked up. 'Go?'

'To the castle.' Kaldar made an attempt at a smile but it didn't quite work. 'Get it over with. It's got to be done at some time, and now –' He had been about to add, 'would seem as good a time as any' but abruptly thought better of it. In truth it wasn't a good time, not in the wake of what they had just witnessed, for thoughts of the nature and extent of the magi's power were too fresh in his mind for comfort. But the memory of the demon, and the havoc it had wrought, had brought home the urgency of his mission with ugly emphasis. 'There's no point in delaying,' he finished.

'What's changed your mind?' A flicker of bitter animation came into Benetan's eyes. 'You've spent the past two days dissembling; why this sudden resolve?'

'Because . . . oh, damn it.' Kaldar squatted down beside him. 'If you must know, I've been afraid to say the word. Afraid to do it.' He glanced sidelong at the other man and his lip curled. 'Surprised? Well, I suppose I should take that as a compliment; but it's true. Not because I fear your magi but –'

'They're not *my* magi!' Benetan interrupted venomously.

Kaldar made a pacifying gesture but the significance of Benetan's protest didn't escape him. 'Very well, *the* magi. Not because I fear them but because I fear seeing Iselia again. Seeing her, and discovering that that infernal place has . . . changed her in some way.'

Benetan prayed silently that in the darkness Kaldar couldn't see the flush that he knew had come to his face. 'It hasn't,' he said tersely. 'I've told you that.'

'I know you have. But however much I want to believe you, there's a part of me that still doubts. And I'm afraid of putting those doubts to the test.' He paused. '*Do* you understand that?'

'Yes.' Benetan didn't meet his gaze. 'Yes. I do.'

'Well, then, that's why I've been holding back. But I can't dissemble for ever. Eventually we'll reach the Star Peninsula by normal means anyway. And now, after what happened . . .' Kaldar uttered a humourless laugh. 'The prospect of staying on this road is a lot less appealing than it was.'

Benetan nodded. Whatever Kaldar wanted, whatever he decided, he was too tired and sick at heart to argue or even discuss it any further. Wearily, he started to get to his feet. 'We'd best wait until dawn before we go through the Maze,' he said dully. 'It can't be long away, and if we go on along the road until it breaks there's a chance we might find your horse.'

'I doubt it. The poor beast will be long gone – or dead.' Like the two wagon horses, now lying on the track some way south of them. One had broken its back in the crash, the other two of its legs; Kaldar had led Benetan away, unable to bear the creatures' cries of pain and fear, but he hadn't had the stomach to put an end to their misery. Benetan had done that, later, when he had finally stopped shaking. One thrust of a knife in the right place, he had said, and if you knew what you were doing, death was swift and merciful. At least, Kaldar thought, the horses had been spared the fate of their master and his family.

The black mare whickered a greeting as Benetan approached, and he paused to stroke her muzzle before looping the reins over his arm. Then he glanced back at Kaldar. 'Are you coming?'

Kaldar hesitated a bare moment, then succeeded in pushing the apprehension away. 'Yes. I'm coming.'

Without a further word they set off along the track.

By the time dawn began to break it was raining, a fine, soft, cold drizzle as heavier clouds drove in from the west in the wake of the gale. They had walked four or perhaps five miles, and as the first dreary grey light spread across the world they saw the contours of a still, silent landscape, apparently empty of all life. A little way ahead a farmhouse was just visible, tucked into the fold between two shallow hills, but nothing stirred as they approached it; no dogs barked, no people appeared. The breeze carried what might have been the noise of cattle bellowing in a byre somewhere, but the rain muffled the sound and it was impossible to be sure. Knowing the direction from which the winged demon had come, Benetan and Kaldar felt foreboding about the farm's occupants but neither wanted to be the first to voice it; they walked on past, then when the hills had obscured the house once more Benetan said, 'The castle will be stirring by now. If you're prepared . . . ?'

Kaldar wasn't, not entirely, but that wouldn't change. He nodded.

Benetan turned to his mare. He spoke quietly to her, then swung into the saddle and reached down. 'You'd better ride behind me.' They had found no trace of Kaldar's grey gelding. 'It'll be safer – the Maze can be disorientating and we don't want to risk getting separated before we're through.'

Kaldar took the outstretched hand and scrambled up, settling himself as comfortably as he could. 'All right,' Benetan said. 'Give me the amulet.'

Kaldar directed a barren smile at his back. 'Oh no, Benet. The amulet stays in my possession – and don't worry, I know how to use it: its secrets were easy enough for Simbrian to fathom, and he instructed me very carefully.'

Benetan sighed. It wasn't that he had had any thought of using the amulet to abandon Kaldar, for he had made a promise and wouldn't go back on it. But he would have felt far happier – and safer – if he could have regained control of the stone. Especially once they were within the castle walls . . .

He heard the chilly clink of the iron chain as Kaldar drew the amulet from under his shirt. Then Kaldar's voice whispered something, familiar words which Benetan had been taught during his training but had never fully understood. He felt a sharp flicker of heat, and momentarily the landscape around him seemed to distort, as though something had delivered a violent jolt to his senses. The mare's head came up sharply, her nostrils flaring; she pawed the ground –

Benetan saw the light change, felt the surge coming, and instinctively tensed. The vortex erupted out of nowhere, rushing at them, and the scene shattered into a million fragments as the huge, blinding rush of it engulfed them. He heard the mare's shrill, challenging whinny, heard Kaldar shouting in shock and exultation together – then the world exploded into the image of a titanic seven-rayed star, burning through his body, through his mind –

And with an impact that flung him backwards and almost out of the saddle, they burst through on the far side of the Maze.

'*Gods!*' Kaldar's free hand was clutching at Benetan's shoulder, so hard that his fingernails had drawn blood. Then he doubled over into a spasm of uncontrollable coughing.

Benetan had managed to right himself and reached back to grasp the front of Kaldar's shirt and keep him from falling. 'It'll pass.' He could barely get the words out; his lungs were heaving, head spinning as the mare pranced and skittered in the wake of the transfer. Saying to her, 'Quiet, now, quiet!' he kicked his feet free of the stirrups and slid to the ground, still supporting Kaldar with his free hand.

'I'm all right . . .' The spasm was fading; Kaldar shook

hair from his eyes then also dismounted, though he hung on to a stirrup as though he didn't yet trust his legs to support him.

The vortex had vanished. They stood on the rock stack in the teeth of a fierce wind, with the dizzying mainland bridge behind them and the walls of the castle rising black and impenetrable directly ahead. There was snow under-foot, and a white carpet of it spread across the stack, obscuring the rectangle of peculiarly lush grass that marked the Maze's boundaries. The fall looked recent but had stopped now; to their right the sun had just lifted above the horizon, and its rays, breaking through a rent in the cloud, had turned the sea to a glittering blood-red that seared the eye. It looked, Benetan thought, like a huge, banked and hellish fire, and the distant scatter of islands, silhouetted, were black coals newly thrown into its heart. He pushed the fancy away, together with the sudden feeling of ill-omen that had accompanied it, and signalled towards the barbican tower where he knew the guards would have registered their arrival. Seconds later a slow, grinding rumble echoed from the gates, and they began to swing open.

Benetan glanced at Kaldar. 'Ready? You'd best give me my coat before we go in. And in the name of all that's sacred, hide the amulet!'

Kaldar did so, silently cursing himself for the oversight. As the north wind bit through his own thinner clothes he shivered, then eyed the shifting black gates apprehensively. 'I'm ready. You remember your story?'

'Yes, damn it!' For a moment resentment flared in Benetan's eyes. 'I just hope for both our sakes that *you* remember *yours!*'

It was a relief to escape from the wind, but that was the only sense of comfort Benetan felt as he walked under the imposing black arch of the castle gateway. Even the sudden noise of his mare's hooves sounded ominous, and his heart was pounding so heavily that he was half convinced the arch would pick up the sound and echo it hollowly back at him.

The guards stared at Kaldar in open curiosity, but Benetan's rank precluded any questions and he only nodded to the men, accepted their salutes and passed on. The light started to dim as the gates were hauled back into place, and the final clang of their closing reverberated menacingly. Kaldar was still shivering but he said nothing, and they advanced into the courtyard.

At first glance it seemed as if the castle was not yet awake. The courtyard was empty, the ornate fountain stilled and fringed with icicles, and with the massive bulk of the north wing to act as a bastion the wind was barely audible. But there were lines of fresh footprints in the snow, and light glowed softly from the great dining-hall and in a number of upper windows. As they stepped clear of the arch Kaldar stared up at the great spires towering giddily into the sky, and Benetan saw his jaw tighten as though he were taking a hard grip on his resolve. This was not Kaldar's first venture into the castle, but the previous visit had been swift, clandestine, and had taken place at night when the full, bleak grandeur of the ancient building was shrouded from view. He hadn't expected this, and it had shaken his confidence.

Benetan felt uneasy too, but for a very different reason. He didn't share Kaldar's discomfort, for the castle had been his home for twelve years and was as familiar to him as his own reflection in a glass, but this morning something was out of kilter. An atmosphere – he could put it in no clearer terms – of tension, of disquiet. Of *suspense*. All appeared to be normal, but Benetan knew in his marrow that the appearance was a mask. Beneath it, invisible but very real, was something far darker.

'Capun Liss!'

The voice hailed from his right, shattering the quiet, and Benetan turned to see Lotro, one of his junior riders, running towards him from the direction of the stables.

'Capun!' Slithering and almost losing his balance on the half-frozen snow, Lotro flailed to a halt and made an inept salute. 'Sir, you be back!'

Benetan was briefly tempted to ease his tension with a sardonic response to such an obvious statement, but quelled the impulse; sarcasm, anyway, would have been lost on Lotro. And besides, there was something in the youth's tone . . .

'I'm that glad to see you, sir, proper rightly I am!' Lotro hadn't waited for a reply. 'Thur's that much ado all over as none of us don't know what be comin' next, and Sarn't Averel says if Capun Liss don't belong to come back quick –'

'Wait, Lotro, wait!' Benetan interrupted the hectic flow of words. 'What ado? What's going on? And where's Sergeant Averel now?'

'Not to duty for 'nother hour-two, sir, but he did say as we was to wake en if you should come any time he's sleepin'. 'Twas orders from Master Savrinor, he say –'

'Savrinor?' Benetan's voice was suddenly sharp. 'What message did he leave?'

'That if you do come, he's to be tolden straight-way. Don't know why, sir, he didn't say, he jus' give Sarn't Averel the order.' Lotro shifted agitatedly from one foot to the other. 'Shall I go rouse Sarn't, sir?'

It would be quicker to go to Savrinor's apartments himself, but that was impossible with Kaldar in tow. And whatever the urgency of Savrinor's message, getting Kaldar into the castle and out of the way of curious gazes must take priority. 'Yes,' Benetan said. 'Wake Sergeant Averel, and tell him to go at once to Master Savrinor and let him know that I'm here. I – we –' he indicated Kaldar, who was listening intently, 'will be in my room, and Master Savrinor can find me there.'

"'Es, sir!' Lotro saluted again, more smartly, then hesitated. 'An' shall I tell groom to come 'n' take your mare?'

'Yes. Yes, do that.'

Lotro sprinted away, shouted to someone inside the stables, then ran back across the courtyard towards the main doors. Kaldar stared after him. 'What was that about?'

'I don't know,' Benetan said tersely.

'But you don't like the sound of it?'

Benetan didn't, but he wasn't about to confide in Kaldar. 'Whatever it is, it's between me and my riders,' he replied.

'But this Savrinor – isn't he Iselia's –'

'Yes. And before you ask, I don't know what he wants me for or why it's urgent.' A groom was approaching; Benetan gestured at the man to hurry up.

'But if it's something about Iselia –'

'Knowing Savrinor,' Benetan interrupted curtly, 'I imagine it's considerably more important than that.' He flung the mare's reins at the approaching groom and stalked away towards the castle doors.

The last thing Benetan wanted at this moment was Lotro's eager ministrations, but Lotro was thick-skinned as a bear and so anxious to please his captain that to argue with him was more exhausting than to let him do what he thought was right, however inconvenient. The youth was at Benetan's door less than a minute after their arrival, bearing an armful of kindling wood and three massive logs, and as he set a fire in the grate and put tinder to it he told Benetan proudly that he had instructed a servant to bring along food and beer, as he was sure the Capun and his guest – no questions, but Lotro was clearly agog as he glanced

256

covertly at Kaldar – wouldn't have had time for breakfast afore, the hour being so early as it was. Benetan let the ceaseless chatter flow over him, occasionally making a monosyllabic response and warning Kaldar with a look not to give vent to his own impatience. He was aware, as Kaldar wasn't, that beneath the cheerful exterior Lotro was worried and afraid and this babble was simply the only means he knew of keeping the disquiet at arm's length.

Breakfast arrived as the fire was beginning to roar, and Lotro insisted on staying to serve it. He was heaping two plates with food that neither Benetan nor Kaldar wanted when there was a rap at the door and, before anyone could respond, Savrinor entered.

The historian glanced briefly, glacially at Lotro and said, 'Out.'

'Sir.' Lotro came smartly to attention, looking helplessly in Benetan's direction. Benetan gestured assent and the young man fled. Savrinor slammed the door on his heels with uncalled-for savagery and paced across the room to pick up the beer flagon.

'Gods, the swill your kind will drink . . . Isn't there any wine in this damned room?'

'In my cupboard,' Benetan said. 'If my sergeants haven't helped themselves during my absence.'

'I'll personally see them flogged if they have.' Savrinor wrenched the cupboard door open and took out a dusty flask. 'Better than nothing . . .' He snatched up one of the two cups Lotro had brought and filled it to the brim. Half the contents disappeared in one draught and, watching him, Benetan realized that never before had he seen Savrinor in a mood like this. He was, as ever, immaculately elegant, but there were heavy shadows under his eyes and it was obvious that he had been over-indulging in stronger narcotics than usual. And underlying it all was an aura of pent fury which, Benetan realized, had been induced by fear.

'So.' Savrinor finished the wine and refilled the cup. 'You've *finally* deigned to return from your gadding in the south. You've cut it very fine indeed, Benetan – if I didn't know you better I'd almost think you had developed a sense of humour.' He swung round. 'But as –' And the words cut off as, for the first time, he saw Kaldar.

His pale eyes seemed to turn to stone and he snapped, 'Who in the sacred name of our Lord Yandros is *this*?'

Kaldar had no experience of Savrinor, and Benetan saw his furious reaction to the question's arrogant tone. Before Kaldar could court disaster by retaliating in kind, he said swiftly, 'His name is Kaldar Tarkran.' Kaldar was a common enough name and they had decided that to keep to it would minimize the risk of any mistakes, while as Simbrian's identity was unknown at the castle, Tarkran could be used in safety. 'I've brought him from the south. He has information for the magi.'

Savrinor's eyes came back to life again, dangerously, and he raked Kaldar with such a baleful look that Kaldar involuntarily flinched. 'What information?'

'He won't tell me.' They had rehearsed the lies so often that they came with ease, and for good measure Benetan glanced at Kaldar as though in resentment. 'Apparently I don't rank highly enough to be trusted with it.'

'Don't you, indeed?' Savrinor pivoted slowly on one heel until he was facing Kaldar square on. 'Well, my good farmer or fisherman or blacksmith or whatever tiresomely worthy trade you follow, it may interest you to know that I outrank Captain Liss by a considerable degree. So I suggest that you might find it in your own best interests to grace *me* with your trust.'

Kaldar's jaw-muscles set hard. 'No,' he said, then at a

rapid warning look from Benetan forced himself to add, 'sir. I'll tell what I have to tell only to a magus.'

Savrinor's eyes narrowed to slits. 'Good gods, Benetan, what manner of lunatic have you dredged up from the depths? Does he have the *least* idea of what he is saying?' Then, to Kaldar: 'I don't think, my peasant friend, that you can know very much about our magi, or you'd not be so eager to keep your secrets for their ears alone. I spoke of your own best interests, and that was precisely what I meant. Waste my time, and you might lose some of the skin from your back if I happen to be in an intemperate mood. Waste a magus's time, and you'll find yourself –' He broke off and uttered a short, vicious laugh. Benetan had never heard anyone laugh like that before, and it chilled him. 'Well, if you care to learn where you'll find yourself, I can arrange for your name to be added to Lord Vordegh's next list.'

Benetan broke in quickly. 'What do you mean, Savrinor? What list?'

Savrinor made a sharp gesture. 'This is neither the time nor the place – you'll find out soon enough. And so will your friend here, if he continues to insist on putting pig-headedness before sense.'

Kaldar started to say, 'I don't –' and Savrinor turned on him. 'I have no interest whatever in anything that you do or don't think. I will ask you one question, and if you have any regard for your own neck I strongly advise you to answer it. What is the nature of your information?'

Kaldar's mouth set in a stubborn line, but before he could repeat his insistence on seeing a magus Benetan said, 'It's all right, Tarkran. Answer Master Savrinor's question – tell him what you told me.'

To his great relief Kaldar caught the urgent warning note in his voice, and a little of the angry tension ebbed from him as he brought himself under control and recalled the role he must play. Pretending to be intimidated he stared down at his own feet and said, 'What I told B— Captain Liss is that I know someone who is close to the heretic leaders. And I know how they can be rooted out.'

Savrinor stared at him. His face was impossible to read; in the space of a moment it had lost all expression and become utterly inscrutable. At last, quietly, he spoke.

'I see. And how have you come to possess this information?'

Be careful, Kaldar, be careful, Benetan prayed silently. *Don't underestimate him, whatever you do.*

Kaldar chewed at his lower lip, then drew breath as though bracing himself for an effort that would cost him very dearly. 'The man in question is – was – my master, sir. He –' Another deep breath. 'He's one of their number; trusted by them.' Quickly he looked up. 'But he doesn't know that I know – if he were to find out, if anyone were to tell him –'

Savrinor ignored this. 'And what is your master? What trade does he follow?'

'Not a trade, sir.' The indignation in Kaldar's face was convincing, though Benetan hoped he wouldn't overdo it. 'He's a tutor of children, and scribes for people who haven't learned their letters.'

'Ah. A scholar.' Savrinor's expression was still impossible to decipher. 'And you're his apprentice?'

'Assistant, sir.'

'I note the distinction. So we may take it that you have worked closely with this master of yours. Mmm.' A pause, then abruptly the historian's eyes glinted slyly. 'Does it not seem a little churlish – I might even go so far as to say *ungrateful* – to betray the man to whom, presumably, you owe your livelihood? To put it bluntly, Assistant Scholar, what do you hope to gain from it?'

This, Benetan knew, was the first test, and he held his

260

breath. Kaldar gazed levelly back at Savrinor for a second or two, then with an abrupt movement turned his head away and replied, in a voice that carried a hard and bitter edge,

'I want only one thing, sir, and if I can get it, it'll be reward enough for me. I want *revenge*.' He made an odd, rough sound deep in his throat. 'For my woman, and for what he did to her!'

It was convincing; oh yes, it was convincing, for Benetan knew exactly what – and who – was in Kaldar's mind as he uttered the words. Savrinor didn't and couldn't know, but he said quietly, 'Ah. I begin to understand a little better.' He set down the refilled wine cup, which he hadn't yet touched, and walked slowly, thoughtfully towards the window. 'One last question, then, Master Tarkran. Do you claim that the information you have come to offer to the magi will lead to the discovery and capture of the heretic leader?'

'That,' Kaldar replied, 'will depend on the magi. Sir.'

Savrinor turned and regarded him for a very long, speculative moment. Then he raised one hand and beckoned to Benetan.

'Benetan, my friend. A word with you in private.' He moved towards the door, touched the latch, looked back at Kaldar. 'You have considerable confidence in yourself. I sincerely hope that it's justified.' He opened the door. 'Stay here. I'll not detain your benefactor for long.'

Outside in the corridor, with the door firmly shut, Savrinor looked hard at Benetan and said without any preamble, 'Well? What have *you* got to say?'

'I?' Benetan asked cautiously.

'Yes, you! If I take word of this pet informer of yours to the magi, will it earn me their eternal gratitude or a place in the queue for Physician Croin's experimenting-block?'

'Don't be melodramatic, Savrinor!'

'Melodramatic? Ah, but of course; you don't yet know, do you?'

'Know *what*?' Then Benetan recalled an earlier remark. 'What did you mean about Lord Vordegh's lists? Has this something to do with –'

'*Keep your voice down!*' Savrinor cut in. The ferocity with which he said it brought spittle to his lips and he wiped it away quickly. Suddenly he looked haggard, and wearied to the limit of endurance. 'You have a short memory, my friend. You've forgotten what I said to you on the beach, on the morning following our beloved First Magus's inauguration: that in the days to come, walls might develop a distressing tendency to have ears. A trite little prophecy, I admit. But unfortunately it seems to have been fulfilled.'

'I don't understand.'

Savrinor sighed heavily. 'Dear gods, is that *still* your favourite phrase? No, Benetan, you don't understand, and if I began to explain now we'd still be standing here at sunset. Just answer my question, *please*. This scribe you've found and tamed and dragged out of the hinterland – is he just another fool looking for advancement, or *can he deliver what he claims?*' He met Benetan's gaze again. 'Believe me, under the present circumstances both our lives might depend on your judgement!'

Benetan knew he had no choice but to commit himself. He said: 'I believe he can.'

Savrinor tapped an immaculately manicured nail against his teeth. His expression was introverted. 'And this business with the woman; the revenge he alleges to be seeking. What did his master do – steal her from under his nose?'

'Something far worse. You remember Lord Vordegh's first edict?'

'All too well.'

'The girl also worked for the scholar. When the local overlord began demanding the names of suspected heretics, the scholar decided it would be wise to safeguard himself from suspicion. He denounced her.'

'And this brass-headed youth was enamoured of the girl?'

'They were pledged to marry.'

'Mmm. Then I suppose revenge is a plausible motive. At least he doesn't try to pretend that he's doing this for reasons of nobility and spotless loyalty to the magi. But it strikes me as a little convenient that he should suddenly have this information at his fingertips whereas he knew nothing before.'

'I think he did know,' Benetan said. 'Or at least, he suspected.'

'But didn't act on the knowledge until he had a personal reason to do so ... well, that's believable. Far safer to turn a blind eye, after all.' Savrinor gave another peculiar, truncated laugh. 'Let's hope for his sake that the magi take a lenient view of that laxness.'

'Then you'll tell them?'

'I think I must take the risk. I'll go to Croin. He'll extract the truth without terrifying your protégé entirely out of his wits, and if the information proves worthless we'll have a better chance of keeping our skins intact than if we've troubled Lord Vordegh with it.' Savrinor nodded towards the door. 'Go back and entertain him with some tall tales of your warriors' exploits until Magus Croin decrees what's to be done.'

Benetan nodded, wishing that he didn't feel so sick. 'Good luck.'

'I don't doubt I'll need it. Oh, but before I take my leave – what happened between you and Andraia in Magus Pirane's citadel?'

Benetan tensed, thrown by the rapid change of tack. 'Why do you ask that?'

His tone didn't deter the historian. 'My simple but insatiable curiosity. Stimulated by the fact that Andraia seems to have been living within her own personal stormcloud, complete with frequent bolts of lightning, since her return.'

Benetan turned away and stared at the wall. 'That's her privilege. And my privacy is mine.'

Savrinor smiled, but the smile was bleak. 'You really are a fool, Benetan.' He paused. 'But if it's of any comfort to you, you're not alone.'

He walked away towards the west wing.

CHAPTER XVII

'And that, my friend, is the entire sorry tale from beginning to end.' Savrinor drained his glass, tilted the flagon on the table between them and, finding it empty, looked about the hall for a servant. There were fewer in evidence than was usual at this evening hour, and now Benetan understood why.

A girl came, belatedly, at Savrinor's signal. She was about ten years old, clearly had no experience of dining-hall duties and was intimidated both by her surroundings and by the high-ranking people she had been bidden to serve. Savrinor had little doubt that she would bring the wrong vintage, but his senses were so saturated with wine and narcotics now that he was past caring. Benetan, by contrast, had hardly touched drink or even food, and if he had been in a state of mind to find anything amusing Savrinor would have thought their differing reactions wryly funny.

'Three times now I've compiled those damned lists.' He was, shockingly, stone-cold sober still, and kept his voice low, though their table was isolated enough to prevent any eavesdropping. 'Three times; and I assure you, Benetan, I am running out of *names*. But he still wants more. More souls for his experiments. More lives to be wasted in the pursuit of this vain, useless, *futile* hunt. Because, to my certain knowledge, our beloved First Magus's endeavours have yielded absolutely nothing.'

Benetan didn't want to ask the question but he couldn't stop himself, for it held a morbid fascination. 'What becomes of them all, Savrinor – how does he use them? Do you know?'

'Yes, I know, and you don't want to. I wouldn't readily inflict that information on an enemy, let alone a friend.' Savrinor sucked air between his teeth. 'Do you know, he has even sacrificed his own servants? With the exception of the indispensable Verdice, of course. As an example to others, he said. After all, if the First Magus himself is willing to suffer the *inconvenience* of doing without servants, who then can complain if they, too, are asked to make the same noble gesture? So now you know why even those of us who have thus far survived Lord Vordegh's cull do not lie easy in our beds at night. Damn it, where's that brat with the wine?'

'You've had too much already.'

'I've not had anything like *enough*, thank you. And don't fear that I'm in any danger of getting drunk and proclaiming my discontent to the rafters. I've never made that mistake in my life and I most certainly don't intend to start now.' He stared moodily into the empty glass. 'I'm only surprised that you haven't followed my example.'

'It would curdle in my stomach.' Benetan slumped back against the cold wall.

Savrinor's gaze slid sidelong. 'I can give you something that won't, if you want it. It will make the waiting easier, too.'

'One of your drugs? No, thank you – I've seen what they do to you.'

'As you please.' Savrinor shrugged, then drummed his fingers on the table. 'So; we continue to wait. Wait and wait, without knowing how much more time will pass before we hear any word.'

Benetan didn't answer; there was nothing to say that hadn't already been said a dozen times, and even the meticulous Savrinor was starting to repeat himself for the

266

sake of filling the silences. There had been no word of Kaldar since he was conveyed to Magus Croin's apartments early that morning, and all day Benetan had vacillated between bouts of cautious hope and dire pessimism until he felt his nerve could stand little more. He wanted desperately to see Iselia but was too afraid, for he knew the question that she would ask him, knew that he wouldn't be able to lie to her, yet couldn't bring himself to tell her the truth while Kaldar's fate hung in the balance. So instead he had barred his door, refusing to admit servants or Lotro or Sergeant Averel or anyone else, and, bone-weary after nights of little or no rest, lay down on his bed. He had slept, but fitfully, and as the afternoon waned to gory evening he had woken from yet another bout of hideous dreams and, unable to face the prospect of more, left the room and sought refuge in the hall. There he had found Savrinor, alone and glad for his company, and from him had had the full story of the events that had taken place at the Star Peninsula during his absence.

Now Benetan understood what lay behind the tension and foreboding that he had sensed immediately on entering the castle gates. The feeling hadn't abated as the day wore on, and even here, with the hall at its busiest as people took their evening meal, the atmosphere was palpably ominous. Unnaturally quiet, too; few diners seemed to wish to talk, and the few who did spoke only in whispers, echoless and peculiarly muted, as though the black walls were quickly soaking the words away into silence.

Yet the hush carried an undercurrent, and though he was no psychic Benetan was as aware of it – and of its cause – as anyone else in the huge chamber. It was, and would remain, unspoken, for even the group of magi who occupied one of the tables nearest to the hearth would not have taken the risk of voicing it aloud. But Savrinor had told him enough for the dark intimation to be clear.

Fifty-six people – nearly half of the castle's low-ranking servants – had died during the past few days, to serve the First Magus's purpose. Fifty-six lives sacrificed in the obsessive quest to unmask the heretic leader; and though their deaths had brought him no answers, Vordegh would continue, no matter how great the toll or how futile the campaign. No one could sway him from his course; no one, so Savrinor said, could even plead a case for cessation, for during the past few days the First Magus had permitted no one to come near him. He had moved from his chambers to the east spire, and there in a cold, empty room towering vertiginously above the sea he worked ceaselessly, sleeplessly, fixedly. More lives, more souls, ever more powerful sorcery. And until he had what he wanted, there would be no respite for him or for anyone.

And this obsession, as Benetan and Savrinor and so many, many others in the castle knew but dared not say, was carrying the First Magus along the road to insanity.

'Savrinor.' Benetan leaned forward suddenly. 'Hasn't anyone asked the gods for help?'

Savrinor shook his head. 'I don't know. I've prayed for Lord Yandros to intervene – Seven Hells, in the few spare moments I can steal, I've done little *else!* But I'm not a magus: why should the gods listen to me?'

'Or to anyone,' Benetan said under his breath.

'What?' Savrinor frowned, but his eyes had a drug-induced vagueness now and he obviously hadn't taken the words in. Benetan made a cancelling gesture. 'Nothing. It was nothing.' But he was remembering the citadel, and the demon on the road, and his own desperate appeals to which no answer had come.

The child returned then with a fresh flagon. Her grip wasn't sure and the flagon rocked as she set it down; Savrinor caught it before it could tip over and gave the girl a look that sent her scurrying away with an ashen face.

'As for the magi,' Savrinor said, dismissing the girl's clumsiness from his mind, 'who can tell what efforts they may or may not have made? But I doubt that any of them have done more than I have tried to do. Under the present circumstances I doubt that any of them would dare.' He started to tap the table again, an odd cross-rhythm that set Benetan's teeth on edge. 'However, at least we now have the consolation of your return, don't we? To save our skins, if not our sanity.'

'What do you mean, save your skins? And stop *doing* that!'

Savrinor gave him a look of mild surprise, but the tapping ceased. 'You haven't spoken to your Sergeant Averel?'

'No.'

'Oh. Well, I'm surprised you haven't fathomed the logic of it for yourself. When Lord Vordegh has entirely divested the castle of its menial servants – and that day isn't far off – he will have to look elsewhere for his raw material. I imagine that even he will find it more convenient to cull that material from the outside world rather than from our own less expendable ranks.' He smiled a very strange, grim smile. 'Sergeant Averel has been living in constant terror of the call to action. I think he is a little reluctant to take the responsibility on his own shoulders and has been praying for his captain to return in time to save him from it. As, I suspect, have a great many others within these walls.'

Little wonder Averel had been so anxious to see him, Benetan thought. The established gleanings were one thing: those taken from the villages at least had the chance to turn fate to their advantage, as he and most of his men had done in their time. But to cull for experiment, for *sacrifice* ... the idea of it turned his stomach, and he started to regret not having shared the wine; not, in fact, having had the wisdom to drown his senses in it to the point where this whole insane nightmare faded away.

Savrinor, perceptive still despite his own condition, reached for the second, pristine glass on the table, filled it and pushed it across. 'It does help,' he said.

'Yes. Yes. Thank you.' Benetan picked up the glass, took a mouthful. It made his throat burn but he didn't care. Then as he raised the glass a second time he saw that Savrinor had focused suddenly on the doors at the end of the hall, and his expression had changed.

'What is it?' Thoughts of Kaldar sprang up and Benetan turned, half expecting to see Magus Croin, in a towering fury, approaching their table.

Someone had come in, but it wasn't Croin. It was Andraia.

She was on the arm of a good-looking young man whom Benetan recognized as one of Qenever's most favoured protégés, and a second admirer was at her other side, his manner eager and solicitous. Even by her own standards she looked extraordinarily beautiful tonight; she was animated, vibrant, sparkling. Then she saw Benetan and the mask slipped. She halted, and for just one moment he saw the truth behind the veneer; the naked helplessness of desperate anger and deep pain. Instinctively he started to his feet, not knowing what he could say or what he could do, but compelled by a violent upsurge of emotion to make some move –

Andraia blinked, and instantly the mask was back in place and with it a bitterness as cold and clear as glass. Briefly she held his gaze, then with an exaggeratedly deliberate gesture she turned to her nearer companion and whispered something in his ear. His snort of laughter was clearly audible, and Andraia laughed too, sweeping past Benetan and heading pointedly towards the furthest free table she could find.

Slowly Benetan subsided back onto the bench, and Savrinor, who had absorbed every detail of the brief confrontation, sighed. 'Oh, dear. I surmise that it will take a little more than sweet words to mend the rift this time.'

Benetan turned on him, confused and therefore angered by the feelings that had been stirred within him. 'It won't *be* mended this time!' he retorted savagely. 'Whatever she and I' – he couldn't even bring himself to utter Andraia's name – 'might have been to each other in the past, I assure you it *is* past!'

'Oh, come! Surely –'

'Surely nothing! It's *done* with, and I'll thank you to keep your thoughts on the subject to yourself.' He hunched his shoulders, tension radiating from him in a hot psychic wave. 'If you'd seen what I saw, if you'd heard the things she said –'

'I'm thankful I didn't, if this is the effect they had on you. No,' as Benetan made to erupt afresh, 'no; hold your temper! I'll make no further comment. Though I still think you're a damned fool.'

'You're in no position to judge that.'

Savrinor smiled thinly. 'To my great regret, that's true.'

Yes; Savrinor had always had more than a passing interest in Andraia . . . and abruptly the other preoccupation, the deeper preoccupation, struggled to the surface as Benetan realized that he might turn this to his advantage.

He looked covertly to where Andraia was now being helped to a bench by her two attentive escorts, and thrust down the stab of hurt. He owed her nothing. And it would bring some satisfaction, albeit grim, to take a hand in ensuring that the break was finally irreparable.

Keeping his tone careless, he said, 'If you regret it, Savrinor, then the solution's in your hands. Don't imagine for one moment that I'd have any objections.'

That surprised the historian. Knowing both Benetan and Andraia as he did, he had been convinced that the violent acrimony wouldn't last and that this incident, like so many before it, would blow over. A misjudgment, he now realized. Something more than a lovers' quarrel had alienated them at Pirane's citadel, and his curiosity was honed. But to ask direct questions of either of them would achieve nothing. He had other, subtler ways of finding out the truth. And he couldn't help wondering if the truth had something to do with Iselia.

He was about to turn the conversation to a less contentious topic when the hall doors opened again. Reflexively Savrinor glanced up to see who was entering – and his face lost its colour.

'*Gods* . . .' The word was a hiss, choked off, and he got hastily to his feet, at the same time jabbing Benetan's arm in silent warning. Benetan turned his head, and felt as though his gut had twisted and inverted inside him as he saw the figure of First Magus Vordegh standing in the doorway.

Others in the hall had also seen, and there was a quick, harsh scraping of benches as the entire company rose. Faces expressed shock and chagrin; since the night of his inauguration festivities Vordegh had not set foot in the great hall, and no one could – or wished to – imagine what might have prompted him to do so now. Then the hiatus broke in a hasty *hush* of movement as everyone bowed. Vordegh ignored the salutations and his steady brown eyes scanned the gathering. He looked aloof, disdainful; shadows cast by the wall torches seemed to gather around him like a threat, and Savrinor would have been prepared to swear on oath that the torches themselves dimmed as he looked at them. The temperature in the hall seemed to drop.

Then the First Magus's gaze lit on Benetan.

'Captain Liss.' Though he spoke quietly, his voice carried in the silence that had fallen. A hand rose, beckoned laconically, and Benetan found himself moving out from the table, into the aisle, answering the summons with no more ability to resist than a moth lured to a flame. The First Magus's stare flicked briefly beyond him to Savrinor; another succinct gesture and the historian, shaking, followed Benetan. They stopped together; Savrinor bowed low and Benetan managed to collect his wits enough to make the Chaos riders' salute.

'Captain.' Vordegh was half a head taller than Benetan; his eyes, remote and intense in a very disturbing blend, focused on him in a way that made him feel as if his skull was being cut in half. 'I understand that you are responsible for bringing Master Tarkran to the castle.'

His tone gave away nothing, and Benetan knew that within the next few seconds his life might very well come to an end. His terror was so great that it numbed him beyond all feeling, and he heard his own voice, as though from a vast distance, reply, 'Yes, my lord.'

Vordegh nodded. Savrinor, equally horrified, was about to shut his eyes but suddenly registered something else by the doors. Three figures. One was Verdice; only to be expected, for she attended on the First Magus like a shadow. But the others were Croin and Pirane. And Croin was smiling.

Vordegh spoke again. 'Your judgement was sound, Captain Liss. You are to be commended.' He said it as disinterestedly as though he were making a passing, irrelevant comment about the weather, and as the significance of the words sank in, a wash of prickling heat flooded Benetan, followed by a wave of numbing cold. He struggled with his tongue, trying to form an appropriate response. 'I . . . th . . . thank you, my lord . . .'

Vordegh paid him no heed; he had already turned his gaze on Savrinor. 'As are you, Master Savrinor, for bringing the matter promptly to our attention.'

Savrinor, with more self-possession, bowed again. 'You honour me, sir.'

For a moment the First Magus continued to regard them both, thinking his own thoughts. Then, without a further word, he turned and stalked from the hall, taking Verdice and the shadows with him.

As the First Magus's tall figure passed through the doors Savrinor sat down, abruptly and heavily, on the bench beside the nearest unoccupied table. 'Yandros . . .' he whispered. His face was grey.

Benetan had pressed both hands over his eyes. 'I thought he was going to –'

'Don't say it.' People were staring at them, Savrinor realized, and with an effort he rose again, intending to return to their own, less conspicuous table. Before he could move, however, Pirane intercepted them.

'Madam.' They both bowed to her, though Benetan was unable to meet her gaze.

'The young man will be returned to your room, Captain Liss,' Pirane said quietly. 'Separate accommodation is being arranged, but for tonight I think it will be as well if you continue to take responsibility for him. The testing was . . .' the corners of her mouth flicked briefly, '. . . arduous.'

Benetan nodded, though he still didn't raise his eyes. 'I'll look after him, madam.' At last he gathered the courage to look at her directly. 'Thank you.'

Pirane gave him a chilly and faintly cruel little smile. 'No, Captain Liss; I thank you. You might well have achieved far more than you realize today, as Master Savrinor understands and will doubtless explain if you ask him.' Her slanting eyes flicked knowingly, briefly, to the historian, then she scrutinized Benetan again, with the air of someone examining the results of an experiment which had failed to live up to its early promise. 'In the light of the stance you chose to take during your stay in my citadel, I must admit that this demonstration of your loyalty is gratifying – and surprising.'

Benetan flushed to the roots of his hair. Fortunately, however, Pirane didn't appear to expect an answer to that; she was already taking her leave and turning away to where Croin waited for her by the door. Benetan stared after her, too disconcerted to move until Savrinor took a firm hold of his arm and steered him back towards their table.

'Sit down.' The historian refilled their wine-glasses and pushed Benetan's into his unresisting hand. 'And for the sake of your health and mine, drink that!'

Benetan's mind surfaced out of its paralysis; he looked at the glass he was suddenly and inexplicably holding, and shook his head.

'No. No, I'd – better see to Kal . . . to Tarkran.' He put the glass down, spilling wine on his hand and the table. 'Gods, Savrinor . . .'

'Quite.' Savrinor slumped on the bench. 'But you're not going anywhere until you've answered a question. What did Magus Pirane mean by "the stance you chose to take"?'

Benetan looked away. 'It's a private matter.'

'Between you and Pirane?'

'No. Between me and Andraia. But I'm not prepared to talk about it, and it isn't even important any more.'

'Oh but it is, my friend, if it means your loyalty to the gods has been called into question!' Savrinor's eyes were narrow, and as hard as flint. 'Wasn't that what the lady magus was implying?'

Their gazes met, held. 'If she was,' Benetan said calmly, 'then she's mistaken.'

He was aware that all eyes in the hall were watching him as he left, and the minds behind the eyes were wondering, speculating, guessing. Savrinor wouldn't lack for company through the night: let him answer their questions as he chose and be thankful for the fact that he was in good odour with the First Magus. That, Benetan knew, would

275

be enough to relieve Savrinor's fears, at least for a while. But as for his own . . .

He glanced back, only once, to where Andraia and her companions were sitting, but she had turned her head away and wasn't looking at him. He shut her from his mind, shut Savrinor and Vordegh and Pirane from his mind, and walked out of the hall.

Kaldar was brought back to Benetan's room by two servants, one of whom also carried a written note from Magus Croin. Kaldar couldn't walk unaided; his feet kept going from under him and his legs didn't have the strength left to support his body. Lowered onto Benetan's bed he lay supine, breathing raggedly, staring at the ceiling with blank, shocked eyes.

As the door closed behind the servants Benetan crossed to the bed and leaned over him. 'Kaldar, can you hear me? Can you speak?' There were no marks on him, no sign of any physical damage. But then Croin was an expert –

'In . . . in a minute . . .' Kaldar's voice was a mumble, but relief swept over Benetan as he realized that his sanity was still intact. 'Be all right in a minute . . .'

Benetan tried to give him wine but he wouldn't take it, only shut his eyes and began to work slowly and deliberately at his breathing. Benetan broke the seal on Croin's note; it said merely that Tarkran's full vitality would be restored by rest, and instructed Captain Liss to ensure that he was given a substantial meal, tonight if he could stomach it, tomorrow if he could not. Bemused by the message's prosaic tone, Benetan was still staring at it when there was a sound of movement behind him and Kaldar said,

'Gods, Benet . . . if you've got that wine . . . ?'

He spun round and saw Kaldar trying to sit up.

'Lie back, you idiot!' Benetan pushed him down again, reaching for the cup with his other hand. Kaldar had started to shiver violently, and as he drank the cup's contents Benetan wrapped his own fur coat and two spare blankets around his shoulders.

'I shall pr-probably be unable to – to keep this down.' Kaldar drained the cup, almost dropped it and managed a weak smile. 'Sorry . . . but it's w-welcome at this moment.'

'What did they *do* to you?'

A shake of the head. 'Nnn. Doesn't matter; you're not a sorcerer, you wouldn't understand the way they work.' A massive shudder ran through Kaldar's torso. 'The thin one, the one with the s-seven fingers . . . not so bad; he was almost . . . *kind*.' An attempt at a laugh turned into an unpleasant spasm. 'But then he took me to the spire. T-to that monstrous . . . that monstrous . . .'

'The First Magus.'

'Unh. First Magus. Yes. Gods, he's –' But Kaldar could only shake his head again, finding the right words beyond him. 'Simbrian told me what I might expect, but . . . he doesn't know half of it. Not *half*. Not what he – what he really is.' He shuddered again, but there was suddenly a new light in his eyes, a spark of excitement, and he gained better control of his voice as he added, 'But I *passed*, Benet! I passed all the tests he inflicted, all the ordeals, every *one*! Lord Aeoris's protection was strong enough, and even your First Magus suspects nothing!'

'Keep your voice down!' Benetan said hastily. 'Sound can carry, even through these doors!'

'I'm sorry, I'm sorry.' Another shiver, and Kaldar pulled the coat and blankets more closely around himself. 'Seven Hells, it's so *cold* in here.'

'Magus Croin says you should eat.' Someone, Benetan realized, had brought food here during his absence, doubtless on Croin's orders. Cold food, but in quantity; he piled several items at random onto a plate and carried it to the bed. 'Here. Try.'

'Not now; not yet.' Kaldar waved the plate away then took hold of Benetan's arm. His grip was weak but determined. 'Benet, listen, listen, *please*. Iselia – have you seen her?'

'No. I didn't want to, until I . . . knew what had become of you.'

'Uh, yes. Yes. But now – you've got to tell her, go to her and tell her, *now*.'

'I can't! She'll be –' And the protest broke off as Benetan thought: *but she won't be with Savrinor; Savrinor's in the hall, and he'll have enough questions to answer to keep him there for a long time.*

'*Now*, Benet.' Kaldar wouldn't let go of his arm when he tried to pull it away. 'I daren't waste any time. What I told them, what I said – it won't hold for long, because when they follow the trail they'll find out soon enough that it doesn't lead where they think it will. I *have* to get word to Iselia tonight!'

Benetan wavered. 'I can't bring her here!'

'I'm not asking you to. Only help us to arrange a time when we can meet, and find us a place that will be safe. I promise you, beyond that you needn't be involved at all.'

Maybe he was prompted by compassion for Kaldar after the ordeal to which Vordegh had subjected him, or maybe it was his conscience again, or maybe something else which he couldn't and didn't want to delve into any further, but Benetan surrendered. 'All right,' he said. 'If it's as urgent as that, I'll go to her.' Kaldar squeezed his wrist, conveying thanks. 'Tonight or tomorrow,' he said fervently. 'Try to arrange a meeting for tonight or tomorrow.'

Disquiet flared. 'You think the First Magus will find out the truth *that* quickly?'

'No. No, he won't; we'll have a few days at least. But Benet, she's my *wife*.'

Those last words were a body-blow. Benetan snatched his arm free, turned towards the door. 'Eat something, if you can.' There was a catch in his voice. 'I'll not be long.'

When he had gone, Kaldar lay back on the bed and closed his eyes, trying to will the fiery ache out of his bones and the last of the disorientation from his mind. What he had been through today had taught him two very valuable lessons: firstly that anyone who underestimated the magi's cold-blooded ruthlessness was a fool, but secondly that for all their reputation these Old Ones were neither god-like nor infallible. He had sensed from the beginning of his ordeal that First Magus Vordegh *wanted* to prove his story true, and as he was tested – not an experience he wanted to think about now that it was over – he had realized, with the small part of his mind that was shielded from the massive psychic assaults, that the tests were slanted to encourage the answers that Vordegh hoped to hear. So now the First Magus had enough to keep him occupied for a while, and it was time for the second stage of the plan to begin.

In a way, Kaldar felt sorry for Benetan. The look on his face when reminded that Iselia was Kaldar's wife had spoken volumes, and it had also goaded him into doing what the plan required. Poor Benet; he didn't know – probably never would know – how transparent his feelings for Iselia were to a shrewd eye, or how easily he could be manipulated because of them. And thanks to those feelings, and to his sense of honour, he was playing his part in this to perfection. If the plan was successful – no, *when*; it must be *when* – Kaldar hoped that Benetan might break the shackles of Chaos that had held him for so long, and be won to Order's cause. Though the chances were slim there had been small signs, like green shoots in a desert. Benetan had been roused to bitter fury and disgust by the evils that the First Magus was perpetrating, and though he still wouldn't speak about it Kaldar knew that *something* had happened during the abortive uprising; something which had driven a spike of disillusionment hard into his heart. Whether that first breach could be widened, Kaldar didn't yet know. But he wanted to try, for he knew — and Lord Aeoris knew it, too — that Benetan would be a valuable and worthy ally.

Besides, Order owed Benetan a debt. And when the magi learned that they had been duped, as they surely would before many more days had passed, only Kaldar and his friends would have the power, and the will, to save Benetan from the full fury of Chaos unleashed.

Iselia recoiled from the cabinet with a violent start when she heard the light, cautious knocking at the outer door. For three seconds her heart crashed agonizingly against her ribs and panic began to surge; but then reason struggled to the fore. It couldn't be Savrinor; he would never, ever knock at the door of his own apartments. But who, then? Who else?

She shut the cabinet door, fumbling in her haste and fear. Gods, was she going to be sick again? Pray not; the new dose should begin to work within a few minutes and then the nausea would pass. Next time, she mustn't leave it so long before taking more.

Another knock came; she forced herself to take two deep breaths and walked to the door.

'*Benet!*' Her eyes widened as they focused, a little unsteadily, on his face, then suddenly she looked wildly over her shoulder. 'Savrinor isn't here —'

'I know.' He crushed down the emotions that had surged in him at this first sight of her after such a long absence and stepped into the room, closing the door quietly behind him.

'You can't come in! He might return at any moment, and he'll think –'

'He'll not return. He's in the dining hall and he'll stay there for a good while yet; possibly all night judging by the condition he was in when I left him.' Benetan stared harder at her. 'Iselia, are you all right?'

'Yes – of course.' Thank Aeoris, the sickness was fading at last. She swallowed, trying to get breath past the constriction in her throat. 'I was – reading, and I must have dozed, I think. I didn't expect to see anyone. Least of all *you*. I – I didn't even know you were back!'

As she spoke, her hands moved distractedly, gesturing but without any co-ordination or purpose. Benetan caught hold of her fingers, forcing them to be still. 'Iselia, listen.' There was no time for preamble or to temper the shock. 'Kaldar came back with me.'

'*Kaldar?*'

'He's in the castle now.'

Astonishment and hope turned suddenly to horror and her voice went shrilly up. 'But the magi – if they see him, if they –'

'Hush! It's all right, I *promise* it's all right.' And he told her the bones of the story; the deception that Kaldar had planned and the protection that the powers of Order had been able to grant him. He avoided the subject of his own involvement and journey to the White Isle, only saying at last, 'He's come to take you out of the castle and away to the south. I couldn't deny him the chance, Iselia. I couldn't deny *you* the chance. And I swear, I swear to everything I've ever held sacred, that I won't betray either of you!'

Iselia nodded very slowly, her gaze fixed blindly on the middle of the room. 'I know, Benet. I – trust you.' And as the renewed effects of Moonwrack cleared and sharpened her mind she knew, too, that there was far more to the story than he had told her or even knew himself. A sudden and terrible lurch of excitement assailed her stomach and her breathing became rapid. *Hope – hope, in the darkness of this place. They must have a scheme, a strategy; Kaldar and Simbrian Tarkran wouldn't let such an opportunity as this pass . . .*

'Kaldar needs to see you, alone and soon,' Benetan was saying, and she snapped her concentration back to take in his words. 'But it must be somewhere safe; you and he can't take the risk of being seen together or it might arouse curiosity if not outright suspicion.'

'Yes. Yes, I understand.' She paused, thinking rapidly. 'The beach – at the foot of the stack, where you and I –'.

'I remember.' And he wished she hadn't reminded him of it, because it also brought back the memory of what she had said on that night. 'It's as good a place as any other.'

'There, then. Can Kaldar move about freely?'

'Freely enough, at least for now. But can you?'

'With a little care, yes. Savrinor allows me a certain amount of free time and he has no reason to mistrust what I do with it. Yet it would be safer if I could be sure of *his* whereabouts.' For a few moments she was still. Then: 'You said he's in the dining hall, and his condition is –' She let her expression say the rest, only colouring it with a bitter little smile. 'Is he drinking wine as well?'

'He was on his second flagon when I left.' There was no point, Benetan thought, in explaining why.

Iselia considered. If Savrinor hadn't returned to her after augmenting his narcotics with two flagons of wine, then it was unlikely that he would return at all before morning. Twice in recent days that had happened; she didn't know where he went and didn't care, for she was only thankful for the respite his absence gave her. But she would need to make absolutely sure.

282

'Benet, if you're right then tonight is the perfect chance for us.' Her fists clenched eagerly. 'I'm going to find out what's become of Savrinor and what's likely to become of him – I can do that easily enough. And if he's in the condition you say, he'll not care, or even know, where I am.' She started to pace, her body tense with a strange, animal energy. 'Can you see this window from your room?'

Benetan frowned, feeling that events were being snatched out of his control. 'Yes.'

'Then go back, and tell Kaldar to keep watch. If it's safe for me to slip away, I'll set a lantern in the embrasure. Tell Kaldar to come then. To the beach.' She stopped and looked at him, a look that made him feel as if the ground were falling away under his feet. 'Will you do it for me, Benet?'

He didn't need to tell her the answer, and desolation filled him as he nodded.

'Oh, Benet.' She came towards him, and suddenly her arms were around him and she was drawing him close to her. When she kissed him it was with a lover's kiss, deep and lingering, shocking him to the core as he felt his own emotions responding and spinning out of control. The fact that the kiss also bore a skill and expertise worthy of any courtesan escaped him entirely; he only knew that the woman he loved more than any living soul in this or any other world was giving him a boon that he had guiltily craved since the night his men had brought her to the castle.

She broke away at last and laid her head against his chest. The crown of her hair, scented with a faint, smoky fragrance, reflected lamplight into his eyes. 'Oh, my dear, dear Benet, thank you. I *must* do this, you know I must. But if only . . .'

She didn't say the rest and a part of him didn't want her to; though another part, by far the stronger, yearned and yearned for the words to be uttered. But she was Kaldar's wife.

Benetan forced himself to step back. 'I'll go now,' he said indistinctly. 'And I'll tell Kaldar. I'll – we'll watch for the lantern.'

For perhaps a minute after he had gone Iselia stared at the door. Her eyes were calm, her mind rioting. Then, when she felt sure that he would be out of sight, she cast a shawl around her shoulders and went quickly, quietly out into the corridor.

She had cultivated some useful acquaintances among the castle's senior servants, and it was easy enough to persuade one of those acquaintances to bring her news of Savrinor. Two hours passed before word came that he had left the dining hall, and when Iselia learned where he had gone, and with whom, she was both surprised and ironically amused. A very unexpected development . . . but she took care to give the appearance of hurt and jealousy before thanking the messenger and wishing her a good night.

The first moon had risen, but the sky was overcast and the moonlight spread no more than a faint, nacreous and featureless pallor above the castle walls. Well and good; darkness would be a friend tonight. Iselia suppressed a shiver, not of cold – for she felt warm now, warmer than she had been for many, many days – but of excitement. Then, lighting a taper from the sluggish fire in the hearth, she touched it to the wick of a lantern and carried the lantern, her beacon, to the window.

CHAPTER XVIII

Andraia wasn't at peace with herself and the world, but for the first time since the unhappy episode in Pirane's citadel the harder edges of the bitterness had blurred a little, to leave if not contentment then at least some small easing of the hurt. And though yet again she couldn't sleep, tonight it didn't seem to matter.

She sat on the window ledge, looking out at the familiar contours and shadows of the courtyard. A few lights still burned in the castle, and in the faint glow from one she could see an occasional drifting sparkle that told her it had begun to snow again. The night was bitterly cold and the fire in her room had sunk to embers, but though she was naked save for a silver-fringed wrap she wanted nothing more, for the aftermath of pleasure had sparked another kind of flame within her.

Now and then she turned her head to look towards her bed and the slight figure of the man sleeping now among the disordered blankets and pillows, and her mouth curved in a wry smile. Strange, the twists and quirks of fortune . . . had any seer predicted this even a mere few hours ago, she would have laughed aloud. It wasn't that she had not considered the prospect of a new lover; if circumstances hadn't changed, she would have spent the night with her two escorts and that would have been preferable to solitude. But circumstances *had* changed. The First Magus had made his unprecedented appearance, seeking out Benetan and Savrinor, then Benetan had left Savrinor alone to face the avid curiosity of everyone in the dining hall. And she had lingered at Savrinor's table while others drifted away, and then something in his eyes – perhaps, too, in hers – had warned her two would-be paramours that they were no longer welcome. And a little later, with no need for any questions to be asked or answered, Andraia and Savrinor had left the hall together and sought the privacy of her room.

She leaned her head against the stone of the window embrasure and smiled a different smile as she savoured more recent memories. She knew Savrinor's reputation – everyone in the castle knew Savrinor's reputation – and was honest enough to admit that there had been a strong element of curiosity in her desire to invite him to her bed. What she discovered had surprised and gratified her; a blend of finely-tuned inventiveness, extraordinarily sensual skill and, strange though it seemed in such an outwardly cold man, intense passion. But then Andraia had good reason to know that Savrinor's coldness was a mask of convenience under which other aspects of his nature were carefully concealed. She still recalled with bruising clarity their encounter in the library, when she had been close to the point of despair, and that other nadir at Magus Pirane's revel, when for the second time she had found a kind of solace in his company. And now . . .

Well, logically perhaps it could only have been a matter of time before the weft of events led to this. Yet although there was a tacit understanding between them that tonight was only an interlude, with no ramifications, Andraia had sensed a need in Savrinor for something more. Where the need sprang from, or why it was there, she couldn't tell and wouldn't ask, but it echoed a nameless emotion within herself. For her that emotion had been assuaged, or at least buried, by the satisfying of another kind of hunger, and she was a little surprised by the strength of her hope that it had been the same for him.

286

A draught snaked through a crack in the window frame, stirring the fringe of her shawl and raising gooseflesh on her bare skin, and Andraia stretched her arms. Perhaps she could sleep now, and even if she could not, the bed would at least be more comfortable than this hard ledge. She started to move – then paused as, in one of the windows opposite, a light dimmed, brightened, repeated the pattern twice more and then went out altogether.

Her eyes narrowed. It was possible that that odd little sequence was nothing but chance, perhaps someone having trouble with the wick of a lantern, but she doubted it. That pattern had looked like a careful and deliberate signal.

Who could want to send such a signal at this hour, and to whom? Andraia felt a peculiar, cold contraction as a possible answer came to her, and quickly she tried to locate the window again. She couldn't be sure of its exact position now but certainly it was in one of the upper rooms of the main wing, where a number of high-ranking people had their apartments. Including Savrinor . . .

Then a movement below caught her eye, and she looked down to see two figures emerging from a side door into the courtyard. Her first reaction was one of startled interest, for one of the figures had hair that even in the moonless dark showed vividly and fierily red. To the best of her knowledge no one in the castle had hair of that colour, and her interest burgeoned and quickened as she wondered who the stranger might be. Certainly his appearance so soon after the clandestine signal was no coincidence –

Then suddenly all other thoughts were eclipsed as Andraia recognized the red-haired man's companion.

In a moment she was pressed close to the window, hands cupped to block out the reflecting firelight, eyes straining as she strove to confirm the truth. Yes – she knew him too well for there to be any mistake; knew his figure, his walk, the set of his shoulders. Benetan. He was leading the other man, hurrying him, and there was something furtive about the way they moved, keeping close to the wall as they headed towards another small door which, Andraia knew, led to the castle's extensive cellars.

She exhaled a soft, hissing breath between clenched teeth and leaned back against the embrasure once more. Fragments of a puzzle: a signal from a window which might be Savrinor's, now Benetan and a stranger heading for the privacy of the cellars and taking a roundabout route less likely to attract the notice of any servants still abroad. To Andraia's mind the two events had a clear link, and the link was Iselia.

The two men had disappeared when she looked again, but she was just in time to glimpse the door to the cellars swinging shut. Final confirmation would come if Iselia herself emerged. But then she might take the inner stairway behind the entrance hall; as a servant of sorts herself, her presence would be less likely to arouse curiosity.

She would count to five hundred, Andraia decided. By that time the little heretic bitch should have made an appearance if she was going to appear at all. Lips moving silently, she began, the count falling into a steady rhythm that matched her own heartbeat. She had reached four hundred and twenty-seven when, down in the courtyard, another door opened.

Iselia moved like a deer wary of hunters. She had covered her hair with a shawl but the edges of it glimmered faintly under the snow-clouds' flat glow, leaving Andraia in no doubt of her identity. Andraia's body stilled instinctively and she watched as the girl followed the path that Benetan and the stranger had taken. Once or twice Iselia glanced back at her own footprints, but the snowfall was already beginning to obscure them and within minutes there would be no trace of her passing. The door to the cellars opened, she slipped through and was gone. And at last Andraia withdrew from the window.

She stared at the opposite wall, but blindly, not registering what she saw. The room felt hot suddenly, *too* hot; or perhaps she was sweating for another reason. *Was* this proof that Benetan was a traitor? Or could it be (please, a part of her cried out silently, let it be!) that he still didn't know of Iselia's perfidy? Andraia began to pace the room, light-footed, hugging the silver wrap tightly around herself as she tried to wrest her tumultuous thoughts into some semblance of order and reason. Since discovering Iselia's allegiance to the heretics she had tried to convince herself that Benetan couldn't possibly be implicated, and, clinging to that conviction, had refused to probe any deeper. She could have confided her suspicions to Savrinor, or she could have confronted Benetan himself. But she had baulked, and the reason why she had baulked, as she now acknowledged, was because her conviction had been more of a hope than a belief. Hope, though, was no longer enough. She couldn't ignore this – couldn't *afford* to ignore it, for her own sake and possibly for the sakes of many other people. Even Benetan – if he *was* acting in ignorance, then he must be warned and made to see and accept the truth about the evil little whore who had ensnared him. And if he was in league with the heretics . . .

'Oh, *gods*.' The imprecation came involuntarily, breaking the silence, and in the bed Savrinor stirred and murmured something. Andraia turned quickly and looked at him, then ran to the bed, climbed onto it and clasped his shoulder, shaking him urgently.

'Savrinor! Savrinor, wake up!' She acted on her resolve before cowardice could make her change her mind. This time she *had* to tell him, and he was the one human soul she knew she could trust. There was another, but he wasn't human and she dared not think of him, though even in her confusion she felt the pull of a love and a loyalty that transcended anything else and made this more urgent still.

'*Savrinor!*' Her nails dug fiercely into his skin. He moved suddenly, breaking out of a dream. Hair fell back from his face; then, unnervingly, his eyes snapped wide open.

'What is it?' He sat up. Andraia had never seen anyone wake so rapidly before and it almost frightened her. Then she looked more closely into his eyes and saw the hard glitter in them, the strange, unnatural and almost manic energy, and she knew that this was no normal awakening but a violent after-effect of drugs. Savrinor's mind was as sharp as a newly-honed knife, but the knife was brittle and could snap at any moment. Andraia had a sudden, shocking insight into the very private and perilous edge on which Savrinor's mind and body existed, and she tried to draw back from the brink – but she was too late. He was aware of her agitation, and his hands came up, gripping her wrists, making it impossible for her to pull away.

'What is it? What's happened?'

She tried to dissemble. 'You – you're –'

'I'm well enough. Tell me.'

She told him all of it. Her discovery of Iselia's true loyalties, her suspicions about Benetan, the cause of their final quarrel in Pirane's citadel and, lastly, the small scene she had witnessed only minutes ago in the courtyard. Savrinor listened intently, silent and motionless, his hands still clamped on her wrists, and only when she finished did he at last move. His hands dropped away. Then, his face expressionless, he climbed out of the bed and reached to where his discarded clothes lay on the floor.

Andraia watched him uneasily as he picked up his coat. 'Where are you going?' she ventured.

'Going?' He looked back at her. His face was dead-white. 'Nowhere. Nowhere at all. Unless, that is, you have

290

it in mind to turn me out?' He tried to put his habitual bantering tone into the question but for once it didn't convince.

Andraia shook her head violently. 'No!'

'I'm grateful.' He took something from the coat pocket, made as if to fold the garment neatly, then changed his mind and simply dropped it to lie where it would. Andraia eyed the phial in his hand and he smiled, a reflex without meaning.

'There are times,' he said aridly, 'when sheer sanity dictates escape as a better alternative to confrontation. This,' he unstoppered the phial, 'is one such moment.'

As he took a sip of the phial's contents she continued to gaze at him, pain in her eyes, wanting to share her own hope with him. 'It might not be true, Savrinor. I might be wrong.'

He set the phial down. 'Yes. You might. But then again, you might not. And at this moment I don't think I want to find out which is true.' Suddenly he put a hand over his face. 'Gods, I feel so *tired!*'

'I could go after them. Find out for certain.' Andraia didn't know quite why she said it; it was an impulse and the words were out before she could consider them. But he uncovered his eyes again and made a negating gesture. 'No. Why should you? Why should either of us? Better to let them slip the noose around their own necks . . . oh, Yandros *damn* them! Damn them *all!*' Suddenly, ferociously, he flung himself back onto the bed, lay back and shut his eyes. 'I don't want to know. Not yet, not tonight.' His eyes opened again. The pupils were dilating as whatever was in the phial began to take effect, but there was a sharp challenge in his look. 'I don't doubt that surprises you. The ever-curious Savrinor, turning his back on an opportunity to gain knowledge that might be used to his own advantage.'

'I'd hoped you might have begun to know me better than that.'

Savrinor uttered a husky laugh. 'Perhaps I have. But perhaps I also feel obliged to don my disguise again, for the sake of my reputation. It isn't wise to allow oneself to become *too* vulnerable in the eyes of others.'

Andraia smiled sadly. 'We can't always do the wisest thing, Savrinor. Besides, it's a little late to try now, isn't it? For both of us.' She hesitated, then decided to risk the question. 'You love her, don't you?'

To her surprise he didn't dissemble; perhaps, she thought, he had taken her words to heart. 'Yes,' he said, then fixed that sharp, strange glance on her again. 'As you love Benetan. But it seems that I must cure myself of the affliction.'

'It *is* possible that I'm wrong,' Andraia persisted. 'If I mistook what I heard —'

He touched a finger to her lips, silencing her before she could say any more. 'Your ears hear as well as anyone's. Why doubt what they told you? You could be lying to me, of course, but there's no reason why you should.'

Andraia cast her gaze down. 'No. There's no reason at all.'

'Then, on balance, it seems likely that your suspicions are true.'

There was silence for perhaps half a minute before Andraia said, very quietly, 'What will you do?'

He didn't answer immediately, only smiled. Then one hand reached out and touched her thigh. His fingers stroked lightly, making her skin tingle, and at last he looked at her. His eyes were growing cloudy now, almost other-worldly, and their look carried a very frank implication.

'About the wider concern, I don't yet know. And at this moment I don't want to consider. I don't want to care about her, about Benetan, about anyone who may be involved in this. I want – I *need*, at least for now – to care only about myself. And I would advise you to do the same.'

She turned her head away. 'I wish I could.'

'You can, if you will. There are ways.' Leaning across the bed, Savrinor picked up the phial. 'Not a cure, but a step upon the road to a cure. A step that can block out the pain and the uncertainty, lend strength where there is weakness, and ...' his hand moved again, intimately, 'focus all that you are, and all that you wish to be, only upon the here and now.'

Andraia stared at the phial with a restive blend of fear and longing. If what he said was true – and she believed him – then to be able to forget, to cast away everything but the moment, would be a blessing almost beyond price. Yet she also knew that such a blessing couldn't last.

She said softly, 'But tomorrow ...'

'Tomorrow will come, yes. But if we can postpone it for a little while, we might help each other to at least begin to break the spell.'

For a moment Andraia hesitated. Then, slowly, she reached out towards the phial.

Savrinor drew her into the bed and, as she lay back among the pillows, let four drops fall from the phial onto her tongue – no more, he said; she must have no more than that. Between every drop he kissed her, each kiss more vehement and demanding than the last, and as the phial was set aside once more Andraia felt a new warmth suffusing her body and spilling over, as though by some strange alchemy, into her mind. She told herself it must be imagination, anticipation; that surely not even Savrinor's esoteric potions could take effect so swiftly. But the logic of it was losing its meaning, if it had ever had meaning, and besides, there was another diversion for her consciousness now: the heat of a man's body against hers, the fierce hunger of his hands and his mouth, rekindling the fire in her and lighting a new spark of ecstasy. For a moment he raised his head, his eyes hooded and strange in the half-light. Then his eyes closed.

'Andraia, the spell can be broken. I know it can.'

Andraia uttered a soft, low moan. Benetan was nothing. Iselia was nothing. Perhaps tomorrow it would be different and the dilemmas and confusions would come back; but now, as her consciousness closed in and the room seemed to swim away into an infinite distance, there was only Savrinor, and that was enough.

Iselia's heartbeat was rapid and painful as she groped her way as fast as she dared down the winding stairs inside the castle stack. A few more minutes and she would reach the foot of the flight and the beach beyond, where Kaldar would be waiting. And though this was the moment for which she had longed since her fateful wedding-day, a part of her mind was dreading the reunion.

He would know. She felt the awful, leaden certainty of it; one look at her, at the changes that her months in the castle had wrought, and he would know what she had become. Not the fresh, innocent girl to whom he had pledged himself before the Chaos riders came, but another creature entirely; an influential man's whore whose existence was becoming increasingly governed by narcotics. No matter that she had had no choice if her sanity and even her life were to be preserved; Kaldar knew nothing of the castle's ways and she couldn't expect him to understand why she had taken the path she had. To face him now, and to bear the brunt of his condemnation, was a worse prospect than anything Savrinor had ever inflicted on her. Yet vying with her fear was the yearning which had been her constant companion during every waking moment in the castle. She loved Kaldar. She *loved* him. And that, together with her devotion to the cause they shared, had been the spark of light in darkness which had enabled her to cling on to hope. She couldn't lose that hope now. Somehow, *somehow* she must make Kaldar see that she was still his, and that all they had been to each other was not lost beyond redemption.

Her lantern, which she hadn't dared to light until she was on the stairs, cast a bobbing pool of illumination that showed her the flight was almost at an end. The air was growing fresher and much colder, and she could hear the sea now, a dull murmur that set up echoes in the stairwell. Iselia's courage faltered and she slowed, finally coming to a halt with one foot hovering over the last stair. The cave mouth was visible ahead, the outside world a vague, featureless blur beyond as the snow, falling harder, obscured all detail. No sound or movement in the cave . . . forcing herself to press on, Iselia stepped down onto the rock floor and walked slowly, hesitantly towards the entrance.

He was standing at the cave mouth, his back to her, gazing out at the night vista of sea and falling snow. She saw the colour of his hair first, and her indrawn breath was amplified by the cave, reaching him even above the rumble of the sea. He turned with the quick reflex instilled in him by his years as a fugitive, and as her lantern illuminated him Iselia braced her mind for the agonizing rush of emotion as she looked, for the first time in months, on his face.

'Iselia . . .' Kaldar choked on her name. Hectic colour flared, died, flared again in his cheeks – then as though some invisible force had violently propelled him he ran to her and caught her up in his arms. The lantern was knocked from her grasp; the flame went out as it bounced and rolled across the cave floor, and, stupidly, in that moment Iselia's only thought was to retrieve it, re-light it, make sure it was undamaged. But then Kaldar's mouth was seeking hers and he was kissing her with all the passion that he had forcibly banished from his thoughts since her abduction. She felt the roughness of his hair, the lithe, spare strength of his body as he crushed her against him – he was trying to kiss her and whisper her name at one and the same time, and his face was wet with tears that he couldn't control.

'Iselia, Iselia . . . oh, my love, my wife . . . I thought I'd lost you forever!'

Iselia held him close, returning his kisses, clinging to him. But a terrible tide was rising from the dark depths of her mind; a tide of realization, sweeping over her, drowning her. For her responses to Kaldar's passion were the responses of carefully practised skill and not of love. She knew what would please him, she did what would please him. But he could have been any man. Savrinor, Benetan, a passing stranger: *anyone*.

Kaldar buried his face in her hair, his voice breaking. 'Oh, my Iselia, I didn't believe it was possible to be so happy – I didn't believe it was *possible!*'

Iselia shut her eyes, teeth biting down into her lower lip. She made one vast effort to break down the wall in her mind, but even as she tried she knew that the stones were too heavy, and their mortar too hard-set, to be moved. The past was gone; she had travelled too far ever to come back. She was no longer the person she had once been. She did not know the man in her arms, her husband. And she did not love him.

'I still say it's too dangerous!' Kaldar's voice was pitched low, for they were close to the top of the stairs now and Benetan would be waiting in the passage just beyond the door ahead. '*I* should be the one to do it, not –'

Iselia laid a finger against his mouth before he could finish; a gesture she had learned, unconsciously, from Savrinor.

'And I say *no*, Kaldar. I know you're trying to allay the risk to me, but –'

'That's exactly what I'm trying to do!' He caught hold of her arms, trying to pull her towards him. 'Isn't that natural?'

She turned her head away, not wanting to stray into those murky waters again. 'Yes. Yes, it is. But you must see that for you the risk would be so *much* greater that we daren't consider it.' She paused. 'If we're to be sure of success, it *has* to be done this way. For the cause's sake.'

The cause was the one weapon that could defeat him, and Iselia saw immediately that he would capitulate. Quickly pressing home her advantage, she went on, 'I know that the First Magus has a special room where he keeps the trappings he uses for his sorcery, and I know where that room is. There's no secret about it; why should there be? That's where the wand is. And I have friends here who –'

'Friends?' He echoed the word in disgust.

'Yes! Do you think the ser– the other servants are any different from us? They're not castle bred; most of them are ordinary, decent people who were taken from small villages and forced to come here, just as I was – and like all ordinary, decent people, they gossip. They know what the First Magus does, where he goes, when he is or isn't in his chambers. All I need to do is listen and choose my time accordingly, and I'll arouse no one's suspicions. I've even won a measure of Savrinor's trust –'

Kaldar interrupted again, this time with pure vitriol. 'Ah, *him* –'

Iselia clenched her teeth together. To her profound relief Kaldar hadn't divined the truth about her association with Savrinor, for when, in the cave, he had wanted to lay her down on the sand and make love to her, she had found a way to dissuade him, telling him that for her safety's sake she must remain a virgin while she was still in the castle. Her own words rang in her memory: 'The magi find .... other uses for servants who are not virgins,' she had told him. 'And they have ways of knowing.' Then the second lie had come so easily: 'I love you, Kaldar, and I want to – to be your wife. But I dare not. Not until we're free.' Kaldar had accepted, believed she was still intact, and she prayed with all her soul that he might never learn how wrong he was.

'Sweet Aeoris knows, you can't loathe Savrinor any more than I do,' she said. 'But by behaving as a – a friend to him I've persuaded him to talk to me, and tell me things which he would not otherwise have done. And Savrinor, of all people, can be relied on to know a great deal about the First Magus.' She hesitated, wondering how much she dared say. 'I have learned how to manipulate and . . . and sway him. I've *had* to do that for my own survival – but it will stand *us* in good stead now. Please, Kaldar; in this you must be guided by me. *Please.*'

The piteous tone that so irked Savrinor had the opposite effect on Kaldar. He sighed heavily and released her, his hands falling to his sides.

'All right. I accept what you say. I see that in all reason I have no choice. But I won't know a moment's peace until the thing's done. If you should be discovered –'

'I won't be.' Iselia looked up at the last section of stairs curving away before them. There was an odd, strained expression on her face but in the lamp's inadequate light Kaldar couldn't see it. 'Kaldar, I have to go back now. If Savrinor should return –'

'You said he wouldn't show his face before morning. That he's with a woman.'

'Yes. But dawn can't be far away, and I'm so tired. I must sleep, at least for a while, or I'll be unable to do my work and Savrinor will want to know why.' She took a step upward, taking his hand, urging him to follow. 'We'll be together again soon, my love. And next time, we won't have to part.'

His last, long kiss meant nothing to her, but he didn't know it. They climbed the stairs, eased the door open. Benetan was waiting, as he had promised, to show Kaldar the way back through the confusion of passages; he had fallen asleep but a light touch on his shoulder woke him. They parted at the cellar entrance, Iselia flitting away like a ghost, Kaldar and Benetan following a minute later and taking a different route. Before they stepped through the door on the far side of the courtyard Kaldar paused and looked back through the snow at the chill, deserted scene. His face was hard and tense but he said nothing, and at length, with what might have been a small sigh, he turned and followed Benetan into the darkened castle.

CHAPTER XIX

'No, I won't confront him.' Savrinor studied his image in Andraia's looking glass, not liking what he saw, then focused his eyes on the reflection of the bed behind him. 'It would serve no useful purpose and might well work to our disadvantage. Better that he shouldn't glean the smallest hint of our suspicions, at least for the present.' He turned. 'As you said last night, there is a chance, however slender, that we're wrong. And I think we're both too . . . attached to Benetan to act against him without positive proof.'

'Only to Benetan?' Andraia returned his gaze from where she lay, wrapped in a tawny fur cloak, among the pillows. She looked, he thought, like some exotic and sensuous animal, and he held fast to his memories of that sensuousness as he said quietly, 'I've no interest in the fate of anyone else who may be involved.'

Andraia didn't answer that but rose from the bed, crossing to the hearth where a jug of spiced wine stood warming on a trivet near the newly rebuilt fire. Neither of them had touched the late breakfast that her servant had brought to them, but Savrinor had never been known to refuse wine and she poured two cups and carried one to him.

'Thank you.' He took the cup and with his other hand caught her fingers and touched them to his lips. Then he watched their reflections in the glass for a few moments before adding, 'Strange though it might seem, I still look on Benetan as a friend and I don't relish the prospect of his downfall. I suspect – and I hope to our Lord Yandros

I'm right — that he is for the most part an innocent pawn in this. Not entirely innocent, admittedly; that would be stretching credibility too far in the light of what you witnessed. But though he may be abetting Iselia and her copper-haired friend, I believe he knows nothing of her true allegiances.' He frowned suddenly. 'I *have* to believe that. The alternative is unthinkable.'

'Yes. Yes, it is.' The idea of Benetan in league with Chaos's enemies, betraying the gods themselves, was like a spike of ice striking into Andraia's heart. 'But if he isn't a traitor, what *is* his part in this? You said he brought that man — Kaldar? — to the castle, but he claims their meeting was sheer chance. That can't be true. He must have known the man had some connection with . . . with your . . .'

'With Iselia.' Savrinor smiled, though bleakly. 'It's kind of you to consider my finer feelings, dear Andraia, but it doesn't hurt me to hear her name spoken.'

Andraia coloured slightly. 'Yet last night —'

'Was night. The day brings a different perspective.' He leaned forward to kiss her lightly. 'It has to, or we'd lose our reason. And reason is what we must use now. Tell me, do you recall that some while ago I imparted a certain snippet of information about Iselia? Information that surprised you greatly?'

Recollection stirred, and Andraia's eyes were suddenly alert as she saw the greater implication. 'You said she was married . . .'

'Yes. The name and identity of the man in question are unknown, but I think we can safely assume he is from her home village. Which, of course, was also Benetan's home in the early years of his life.'

'So Benet would know him?'

'Indeed.' Savrinor took a sip from his cup. 'Benetan insists that isn't so, but I've never found his protestations entirely convincing. And now this informer of his, a man he claims to have encountered quite by chance, appears to be very well acquainted with Iselia. A singular coincidence, don't you think? In fact, *too* singular.'

'Gods.' Andraia sat down on the bed. 'He must be her husband. He *must* be!' Then quickly she looked up, horror dawning on her face. 'But Savrinor, that can only mean that Benet's in league with the heretics! If he's conniving with those two, helping them –'

Savrinor turned sharply on his heel. 'Wait. You're running too fast and too far. I agree that on the face of it the case against Benetan seems damning, but there's another conundrum to be considered. Kaldar Tarkran came here claiming to have valuable information about the heretic leaders. That could, of course, have been a lie – but for the fact that he was tested by Lord Vordegh himself, and passed the tests.'

'How could he have done? If he's one of them –'

'We don't know that he is.' Savrinor crossed restively to the window. 'In truth, we don't *know* anything with certainty; though I have a feeling in my marrow that tells me the story is a good deal more complex than we've yet guessed. But the fact that he passed Lord Vordegh's tests must mean one of two things – either Tarkran's information is genuine, or he's under the protection of a power capable of shielding him from the magi's most intense probing.'

Andraia stared. 'That isn't possible.'

'Quite.'

'But if he's not lying –'

'Then he doesn't share Iselia's devotion to the demons of Order.' Savrinor looked back at her. 'So the knot grows more tangled. But whatever the truth might be, I think Benetan's motive in helping them has nothing at all to do with how much he might or might not know about their loyalties.' He smiled thinly. 'He's attempting to salve his

302

conscience. His riders brought Iselia to the castle, after all, and even though he didn't find out about it until after the deed was done, Benetan feels personally responsible for her circumstances.'

Andraia shrugged a little defensively. 'In one sense, he is responsible. He could have let her go.'

'He could; though it wouldn't have been as easy as you think. The magi don't look kindly on those who make mistakes, however trivial. But he didn't release her, and as a result his conscience has plagued him mercilessly. Now, he sees a chance to make amends, albeit a little late in the day.' Another smile, slightly gentler. 'You of all people should know that's reason enough for Benetan.'

'Yes.' Andraia frowned, squashing a twinge of emotional pain. 'Yes, it is.'

'Then in his case I think we have our answer – and the reason why it would be wiser not to say a word to him. We must make our own investigations. And I would suggest we begin by –'

He broke off. Someone had knocked at the door.

'Damn the woman!' A scowl made Andraia's face petulant. 'I *distinctly* told her we didn't wish to be disturbed –' the words cut off in an exasperated hiss and she rose, went to the door and jerked it open.

'Lady, I'm sorry, but –' her maid began.

'Are you deaf as well as imbecilic?' Andraia snapped irascibly before the woman could say any more. 'I told you that under *no* circumstances –' She stopped. Standing behind the maid, her expression coolly cynical as she listened to the exchange, was Lord Vordegh's personal servant, Verdice.

'I'm sorry, lady,' the maid said again. 'But she insisted, and I couldn't . . . well, it wasn't possible to . . .'

'All right, all right.' Andraia didn't need an explanation; she knew Verdice's methods, and knew that if her maid hadn't complied with her wishes Verdice simply would – and could – have walked into the room, locked or no. 'I understand,' she said to the maid. 'You did the right thing. You may go.'

As the woman hurried thankfully away Andraia transferred her gaze to Verdice. 'Well?' Her tone was dangerous. 'What do you want?'

Verdice's expression didn't change in the least. 'It is not a matter of what I want, Lady Andraia, but what the First Magus commands. He requires Master Savrinor to attend him.' Her exquisite lips curled in a smile which might or might not have been intended to give offence. 'Immediately.'

Andraia's eyes grew combative, but she bit back the retort she would have liked to make. 'I will inform him,' she said coldly.

'Thank you. The First Magus is in his chambers. Kindly tell Master Savrinor not to waste more time than necessary.' Verdice inclined her head as she might have done to an equal – or an inferior – turned and stalked away, and, furious, Andraia slammed the door and swung round.

Savrinor had overheard and was rapidly straightening his clothes and trying to shake his hair into some semblance of order. He looked ill.

'Gods, a summons *now*, of all the times to choose . . .' He pivoted to face the glass. 'I haven't even time to shave, let alone go down to the bathing rooms.' He studied his face distractedly and Andraia said, 'You look well enough. Here, let me smooth your hair.' She took up her brush and made him sit. There was fearsome tension in his shoulders, and on impulse she kissed the crown of his head. 'Don't be afraid.'

He uttered a peculiar, truncated laugh and reached to catch brief hold of her fingers. 'I'd be a fool if I were anything else where Lord Vordegh is concerned. Sweet Yandros, what does he *want?*'

'You're in good odour with him. That won't have changed.'

'Perhaps. Perhaps.' A little of the tension eased. 'He might well want something from the archives, or another of his damned lists.' He shuddered. 'At least he's in his own chambers now. The prospect of climbing the stairs of that spire is more than I could countenance at the moment.'

Andraia stopped brushing. 'Are you feeling unwell?'

'Last night's little indulgence with the phial? No. Overuse takes its toll, but I don't seem to have been my usual profligate self of late.' He hesitated, then suddenly looked up at her. 'I hope you don't have regrets?'

He was referring to a great deal more than the drug. 'No,' Andraia said gently, and meant it. 'None whatever.' She set the brush aside, smoothed a crease from the collar of his silk shirt. 'There. The First Magus will have no cause for complaint.'

He stood up, turned to face her. For a few moments they looked at each other, then, very deliberately, Savrinor drew her to him and kissed her. It took her aback; last night there had been many kisses but not one quite like this.

'You're kinder to me than I deserve,' he said quietly when at last they drew apart.

Andraia cast her gaze down. 'I don't think so.' Her fingers clenched reflexively then relaxed. 'You'd better go.'

He started towards the door, and as he reached it she said, 'Savrinor . . .'

He turned.

'Come back to me.'

The haggard edge to his face softened a little. 'Yes,' he said. 'I shall.'

*   *   *

Work was a distraction that kept other thoughts at bay, and Iselia was sitting at her table, head bent over a sheaf of papers, when Savrinor returned from his interview with the First Magus. She looked up quickly on hearing the door open, and prayed silently that he wouldn't notice the tell-tale signs of the concoction she had mixed from the contents of his cabinet to sharpen her mind and keep herself awake. Savrinor did notice — to one of his experience her paleness and the unnatural glitter in her eyes told their own story instantly — but he ignored it, telling himself that he was uninterested in how or to what degree she chose to mistreat herself. Besides, he had other preoccupations.

He paused by the table to glance over her work and see what progress she had made. 'You're diligent this morning,' he commented.

'The work needs to be done, and I had . . . fallen a little behind.' Iselia didn't look at him.

And we both know why, Savrinor thought, but kept the thought to himself. Aloud, he said, 'When you've completed that fair copy, we have another commission.' He shook off memories of the shuttered, ice-cold apartment in the west wing, the sense of echoing emptiness and something more — a kind of hollow but implacable madness — that pervaded the atmosphere as the soft, relentless voice gave him his instructions. 'From the First Magus.'

Her head came up so fast that he knew he had struck his intended target with great accuracy. Yes, she had been waiting for this. Now, if his judgement was right, she would start asking questions.

'The — First Magus?' Iselia repeated. Though her facial expression was under control she sounded a little shocked. That also fitted with Savrinor's private predictions; she hadn't expected events to move quite so rapidly.

He gave her a smile that was not echoed in his eyes.

'Why so surprised, my dear? It's hardly a novelty these days.'

'No — no, of course not.' Ah; she realized now that her reaction was a mistake. She wouldn't make it twice. 'But I thought that we might have — well, a respite. That is, if the rumour I heard earlier is true.'

'And what rumour is that?' Savrinor picked up a stack of her completed papers and carried them to his own desk, pretending to be absorbed in examining them.

Iselia laid her pen down. 'I heard that Benetan returned yesterday and brought someone with him. An informer who has word of the — heretic leaders.'

'Well, well. News does travel fast.' He waited, and the question came.

'*Is* it true, Savrinor?'

'As a matter of fact, it is. I met the man for myself — some peasant from a southern demesne; hardly the type to strike anyone as the courier of vital information.' He watched her covertly as he said that but she was impassive, and he continued, 'However, he spent yesterday in the capable hands of Lord Vordegh and Magus Croin, and they are satisfied that his intelligence warrants further investigation.'

'Ah. Yes, that is . . . that is what I heard.' Iselia lifted her shoulders in a little shrug. 'I'd thought that the First Magus might be too occupied with this new matter to have more work for us.'

'Then you thought wrongly.' Savrinor flicked the papers with a fingernail and set them down. 'These are satisfactory. How long will it take you to finish the rest?'

'Another hour, I think. Perhaps a little longer.'

'Then we'll begin on this new commission immediately afterwards.' He started to walk towards the inner door, aware that she was staring at his back, and for a moment he thought that she might resist the urge to ask the question that he knew was in her mind. But as his hand touched the door, she said,

'The new commission . . . there's a connection with the informant?'

Savrinor smiled a private smile at her painfully casual tone. 'Oh, certainly. I'll give you the details later.'

A pause. 'Could I have them now?' He turned and she smiled at him ingratiatingly. 'It will be a great help if I can know beforehand how long the work is likely to take.'

Savrinor inclined his head graciously. 'Very well, my dear. You know I'm always willing to be of help to *you*. The First Magus requires two things: firstly, copies of the informant's deposition for all who have an interest in the matter, and secondly, messages commanding a number of the most senior magi to attend him in the council hall tomorrow evening.' He waited while she took that in, then played his trump card. 'By which time Lord Vordegh will have discovered the heretic leader's whereabouts. At least, we must hope for the informant's sake that he has done so.'

The colour left Iselia's cheeks. 'I don't understand.'

'Well, dear Iselia, you know the First Magus's ways well enough by now; especially in the light of our own recent undertakings for him. If this man is mistaken and Lord Vordegh is led on a wild goose chase, someone will pay a price, and I don't think we need to look far to see who that someone will be.' He continued to gaze at her for a moment longer, then gave a light, careless and perfectly calculated laugh. 'On the other hand, even if his intelligence does prove useless our informant still has another day to enjoy the castle's hospitality before his soul and his body are parted, so perhaps he'll count himself fortunate in either eventuality. Now, I'm going to the bathing rooms. I'll be back in an hour or so, and if anyone requires me in the meantime they will simply have to wait.'

The arrow, he knew, had gone home hard; he didn't need to look at Iselia's face to sense the tension – or perhaps even terror wasn't too strong a word – that his words had evoked in her. Savrinor tried to find pleasure in it, but the comfort was small and cold, for he was certain now that Andraia was right about Iselia and his own private hopes were unfounded. As he selected clean clothes from his chest and prepared to leave for the bathing rooms down among the foundations, he thought about those hopes and the emotions on which they had been based. Well, the basis must change now, and there was no point regretting it; calling down the moons had never been his way. He must simply close the door on the part Iselia had played in his life and the effect she had had on him. Close the door; break the spell. For his personal feelings didn't matter – Iselia had betrayed the gods, and for that he damned her without redemption. Savrinor didn't want vengeance; he wasn't the vindictive kind. But he would do what justice demanded, and do it with cold efficiency. The slate would be wiped clean.

She was intent on her work, or giving the appearance of it, when he left the apartment. He walked to the end of the corridor, and there he stepped into a side passage and waited. A few minutes passed – time enough, by her judgement, for him to be safely out of sight – then his ears caught the faint but distinct sound of a door opening and closing.

One look told Savrinor all he needed to know. She was heading in the opposite direction, and he had no need to guess where she was going – Benetan's room, where Kaldar Tarkran was presently lodged. The prey, it seemed, had taken the bait; Savrinor knew perfectly well that even the First Magus would need more than a single day to uncover Tarkran's little deception, but Iselia had believed the lie and was on her way to give warning. A pity, Savrinor thought, that he wasn't a shape-changer. A bird flying up to that window unnoticed and settling on the sill might be privy to a very enlightening conversation.

Iselia had disappeared now, and Savrinor left his hiding place and walked on towards the main stairs. His expression gave nothing away. But there was death in his eyes.

Iselia knocked for the third time, her heart thumping as fear and frustration threatened to swamp her. Someone *must* be there! Even if Benetan was absent Kaldar surely wouldn't be so reckless as to be prowling around the castle alone –

The thought broke off as she heard someone move on the far side of the door. Then a voice said cautiously, 'Who's there?'

'Kaldar? Kaldar, it's Iselia! Open the door, let me in, *quickly!*'

The door jerked open and Kaldar's astonished face looked out. Iselia ran into the room, shutting the door behind her, and looked quickly around. 'Where's Benet?'

'On duty. He told me not to answer anyone who came calling, but –'

She wasn't interested in his explanations. 'Thank the gods we're alone! Kaldar, listen to me. You've got to leave the castle.'

'*Leave?* But –'

'Don't argue, just *listen!* The First Magus summoned Savrinor a short while ago; he intends to call a meeting of the magi tomorrow night. And by that time, he'll know that the information you gave him is false!'

She repeated all that Savrinor had told her, refusing, though he tried, to let him interrupt. 'You *have* to leave,' she finished. 'If you don't, then by the time the meeting of magi begins you'll be shackled in a cell, or worse. And even Lord Aeoris won't be able to save you then!'

Kaldar was appalled. Despite Simbrian's warnings about the depth of the First Magus's obsession with rooting out Order's faithful, he hadn't dreamed that matters would turn about as swiftly as this. He had anticipated a respite of several days at least.

'But the wand,' he said urgently. 'We can't leave until we have it!'

'We shan't. I've worked out what's to be done.' It had come to her in a frantic tumble of desperation as she ran through the corridors to find him. 'You must go without me –'

'No!'

'*Yes!* Kaldar, please, you're wasting time by arguing, and time is against us! Listen to me. You must leave; there's no choice. Use Benet's amulet and go through the Maze, just as we planned to do together. I'll stay, and I'll take the wand. I'll have the chance tomorrow night, when Vordegh and the magi are in council. Vordegh's rooms will be empty –'

'What about his servants?'

'He has – dispensed with them.' Iselia suppressed a shudder. 'All save one, but she attends him wherever he goes, so she's sure to be in the council hall.'

'And Savrinor?' Kaldar asked.

'I think he, too, will be commanded to attend. If he isn't . . .' Iselia's mind raced, calculating. 'The meeting is to begin at first moonrise. That's also the time when most of the higher-ranking people will be taking their evening meal. If Savrinor goes to the dining hall, I'll have no difficulty. If he doesn't, there are other means. I'll find a way of evading him somehow.' *If all else fails*, she thought, *I'll put a knife through his heart – and sweet Aeoris, that would give me such satisfaction!*

'Wait,' Kaldar said suddenly. 'There's one thing you haven't considered, and it could be the greatest danger of all. It's possible – not certain but possible – that the First

311

Magus has a psychic link with the wand. If he does, then the moment you lay a hand on it, he'll know – and you'll have very little time to escape.'

Iselia stared at him. She had overlooked that prospect. 'How long?' she asked tensely.

'There's no way of knowing. But I'd say a few minutes at best – and less if Vordegh responds with any kind of direct magical attack.'

She was still watching him. 'Then I must make sure that I don't waste what time I have.'

'No.' He shook his head vehemently. 'There has to be a better way! I'll do it – I'll return, and –'

'Kaldar, you *can't!* Haven't you understood what I've been telling you? By tomorrow night the magi will know that you've tricked them, and if you set one foot inside the castle you'll *die!* Listen; listen to me, listen.' She crossed the room to him, caught hold of his hands and squeezed them with all her strength. 'I *can* succeed, and I *will*. Even if Vordegh knows that someone has taken the wand, he won't know immediately who that someone is and it will take him more than a single instant to find out. By then I'll have reached the gates. There's no watch posted after sunset and the gates are never barred; I can get out by the postern. Come back through the Maze and wait for me outside the wall. We'll be gone before the magi can even think of mounting a search for us!'

Kaldar hesitated. What she said was rational, *sensible* – and, he knew, their only hope of success. By tomorrow night there would be a price on his head and to venture into the castle again would be suicidal. If the wand was to be stolen, Iselia must be the one to steal it. But no amount of reason could eclipse the dread that had taken hold of him like a cold iron hand, for there were far too many uncertainties. So much could go wrong; and if it did, Iselia's fate would be too hideous to contemplate.

Then he looked at her and knew that no argument could sway her. She would only say again what she had said last night in the cave: that the cause must come before all else and no hazard was great enough to be allowed to jeopardize it. Anything else, she would say, would be cowardice. And she was right.

He pulled his hands from her grasp and laid them on her shoulders. 'The thought of you facing such dangers –'

'Don't think of that. Think of what we are achieving, and why.'

'Yes.' He closed his eyes. 'I know, love. I know.' With an effort he forced his lungs to expel pent breath. 'Very well. I'll return through the Maze just before first moonrise, and I'll be waiting for you, watching for you. But Iselia . . .' It was so inadequate, yet he had to say it. 'Be careful. Promise me you'll be *careful!*'

'I promise.' She let him kiss her, made the response he expected. 'As must you.'

'You'll be the one in peril, not me. I won't know a moment's ease until –' He broke off, knowing it was futile to say it, and sighed. 'I'll take care. I have every reason to. And I'll be waiting.'

Iselia nodded, then stepped back, breaking the contact between them. 'You should go as soon as you can. Have you still got Benet's amulet?'

Kaldar touched a hand to his neck and hooked one finger around the iron chain that hung there. 'I told Benet I'd relinquish it only when we leave the castle for good.'

'Then you needn't lose any time.' Iselia looked about the room and saw an unfinished meal on a nearby table. 'You'll need food. Take what's here; I'll wrap it for you. And water –'

'Water's plentiful enough in the mountains. But wait, Iselia. What about Benet?'

'What do you mean?'

313

'When this is over, what will happen to him? He brought me here; he'll be under suspicion. I don't want to abandon him to Vordegh's fury.'

'He knew the risk he was running when he agreed to help us,' Iselia said. 'And there's nothing we can do to help him without endangering ourselves.'

'I know that. But – all right, he knew the risk, but in truth Simbrian and I gave him little choice in the matter. I don't want him to suffer because of it.'

Iselia stopped and looked at him. 'I'm surprised to hear you of all people say that. You've always disliked Benet – and now that he's become what he is, I'd have thought you would dislike him all the more. Have you changed so much?'

'No! I still despise what Benet did – ingratiating himself with these scum, *choosing* to become a Chaos rider; it was detestable and cowardly. *I* haven't changed.' He paused. 'But I think he has.'

She resumed her packing of the food, but he saw the twist of her lips as she turned away. 'It's a little late for his redemption,' she said.

'It might not be. I think he could be persuaded to join us.'

She stopped again, and this time rounded on him so fast and so furiously that he involuntarily swayed back. 'Kaldar, are you *insane*? Are you saying that you'd risk everything for the sake of trying to change Benetan Liss's allegiance? He isn't one of us, and he never could be! He's a Chaos rider – you said it yourself, you said it not a minute ago! I know he agreed to help us, but that was because –' She stopped suddenly, horrified by the realization of what she had said, and a hectic flush suffused her face. But Kaldar only smiled sadly.

'Because he still loves you,' he finished the sentence for her. 'Even after all the years that have passed. Yes, I'm as aware of it as you are.'

314

She hunched her shoulders defensively. 'Very well, then. He does love me, or thinks he does, and that's why he agreed to help us. But it makes no difference; he's still a Chaos rider and we both know what that means. I could never trust him. *Never.*' Suddenly her shoulders slumped again. 'Oh, Kaldar, I don't wish Benet any harm! He's done the best he can for me here, and if he suffers now because of us I'll . . . regret that. If it were possible to warn him without putting ourselves in peril, I'd say yes, we should do it. But we daren't. We *daren't.*' She put a hand up to her face in distress, covering her eyes. 'Sweet gods, aren't we facing enough dangers without creating yet more?'

Kaldar's resolve crumbled. He said, 'Iselia, don't cry –'

'I'm not crying!' She evaded him as he tried to reach for her, and wiped angrily at her cheeks. 'Or if I am it's because I can't seem to make you understand that, whatever we both might feel, we *must* leave Benet to fend for himself.' She sniffed, then looked directly at him. 'One word to the magi. That's all it would take, and everything we've striven for would be in ruins!'

The last of Kaldar's defences went down. He said: 'I'm sorry. You're right, of course you're right. The idea was reckless, stupid; it would be sheer madness to take such a gamble.' He made a gesture as though shaking off something unpleasant. 'Let Benet take his chance. We owe him nothing.'

Iselia turned back to the table. She had gathered the food together and now wrapped it in the folds of her own shawl before bringing the bundle to him.

'It's little enough, but it will sustain you until tomorrow night.'

He took it from her. 'What will you tell Benet when he finds me gone?'

'I may be able to avoid him; Savrinor has work for me

315

to do and he doesn't brook interruptions. But if he does come searching, I'll tell him that we've made our plans and you'll be returning for me.'

'Do you think he'll believe that?'

'Yes.' Iselia didn't meet his gaze, knowing, as he knew, that she could make Benetan believe whatever she told him. Then she took a step towards the door. 'I must go, before Savrinor starts to wonder where I am.' She paused, looking back at him. 'Get away as soon as you can, Kaldar. And pray that all will be well tomorrow.'

'I'll pray for it with every moment!' Then, forcing himself to be practical, 'And I'll make contact with Simbrian; ask him to make whatever arrangements he can to get us safely away to the south. Iselia —' Suddenly he dropped the bundle and crossed the room to embrace her, burying his face in her hair. 'Oh, my love, my love — our Lord Aeoris protect you!'

The scent of her hair lingered in his memory when she had gone; a scent of woodsmoke and sea and something else, unfamiliar. Kaldar stared at the door until he could no longer hear her hurrying footsteps in the passage beyond, then, like a man coming abruptly out of a trance, he crossed the room to gather up the clothes he had brought to the castle. Among them was a heavy hide cloak with a hood that would conceal his hair. Wearing it, he could pass unnoticed across the courtyard, and no one would question his using the Maze; the magi frequently sent messengers through the supernatural gateway, and the watchmen were instructed to challenge only incomers.

Kaldar pulled the cloak on, hid the food bundle under its folds, then paused as his conscience stirred once more. Whatever the rights and wrongs of it, he couldn't make his departure without leaving some word, however cryptic, for Benetan. Yes, it was a risk, as Iselia had said. But Iselia hadn't been with them on the White Isle or, later, in the forest when the Warp and the demon came; she hadn't seen the changes that those experiences had wrought in Benetan.

There were writing materials on a small table under the window. For perhaps a minute conscience wrestled with caution, then Kaldar strode to the table and snatched up a pen and a sheet of rough paper. What to say? Nothing that might betray any hint of the truth. Yet he must give some form of warning.

It came to him and he began, smiling wryly at the thought that twelve years ago he could not have written such a message and Benetan could not have read it. The note was brief and simple: *Couldn't wait for you; time doesn't permit. Take good care – very good care. And thank you.* No names and not even an initial, but below the message Kaldar inscribed a small circle. To all intents and purposes it was the symbol for a kiss, so if anyone else should chance to see the note before Benetan returned, they would assume it to be from some lover or paramour. Benetan, though, would know that the circle had another meaning; that it was Order's secret symbol. Kaldar had done all he could, all he dared; and the subtle warning was there. He could only pray to the gods – *his* gods, who he knew would answer the prayer if they could – that Benetan would understand.

He laid the piece of paper on Benetan's pillow, gathered up his bundle of food once more, and went quietly out of the room.

CHAPTER XX

Dawn had barely broken when Benetan entered the great hall the next morning. The vast chamber felt dismal and unwelcoming; at this hour there were few diners in evidence, and the newly lit fire hadn't begun to lift the bitter chill. An elderly servant took his order for bread and a mug of hot beer – he didn't feel that his stomach would tolerate anything more elaborate – and when it was brought he sat warming his hands on the mug and watching the doors for any sign of Iselia.

His face betrayed the fact that he hadn't slept. There were shadows under his eyes, his skin had an unhealthy pallor and he would have given much to be able to lay his head down and sink into oblivion for a good few hours. But sleep, or peace of any kind, was beyond his reach and would remain so until the anxiety that had gnawed at him all through the night was resolved.

He had returned to his room late in the afternoon to find Kaldar missing and the note on his bed. The message explained nothing, but its cryptic implications had chilled him. *Take good care – very good care*; it was obviously as explicit a warning as Kaldar had dared to give, and Benetan's first, horrified thought was that the protection promised by Aeoris of Order had failed and the magi had discovered Kaldar's true identity. But there was no uproar and no rumour flying; in fact, with the First Magus closeted alone in his chambers and no apparent activity among the other magi, the castle was abnormally quiet. Yet something must have happened; something drastic enough to put

Kaldar to flight. And the one person who might answer the riddle was Iselia.

He had gone to Savrinor's rooms shortly after sunset, hoping that the historian would have completed his day's work and that Iselia might by great good luck be alone. Luck hadn't been with him; Savrinor was there, and in a strange mood, and Benetan had been obliged to invent a flimsy pretext for his visit which hadn't sounded convincing even to his own ears. He had retreated to the dining hall and sat there until well past midnight, praying that either Iselia or Savrinor would come in alone and give him the opportunity he so desperately wanted. Neither of them had put in an appearance, and discreet inquiries to the servants had yielded no word of their whereabouts. He could only assume that they were still in the apartment, still together, and at last he had given up and gone to his own room, where he had spent a miserable and wakeful night fretting over possibilities, imagining the worst, trying and failing to answer the questions Kaldar's disappearance had posed. He must have dozed over his breakfast, for he woke with a sudden start to find the beer cold and the hall beginning to fill with people. Two of his own sergeants were sitting at a nearby table with a mound of food between them; seeing him stir they grinned across and one made a very explicit gesture that also conveyed a mixture of congratulation and envy. Benetan smiled and nodded, not caring what interpretation they chose to put on his fatigue, and forced himself to start on his unappetizing meal.

He had finished the beer and half the bread when Iselia came in. She was alone, and she moved slowly and, it seemed, hesitantly towards a vacant table at the far side of the hall where the light was low. She hadn't seen him. Benetan swallowed the mouthful of bread he was chewing, hastily washed it down with a gulp from his mug as it threatened to make him choke, and got to his feet. The sergeants were watching covertly. Damn them, let them think what they pleased. He pushed the bench back, crossed the hall.

'Iselia.'

She looked up, started – then a wary expression crept into her eyes.

'I need to talk to you.' He sat down, not giving her the chance to argue, and after a few seconds' uneasy pause she sighed.

'Yes. I thought you would.' Gods, why hadn't she avoided the hall this morning? She should have known he would be here . . . but she had needed to get away, to have the distraction of other people's presence . . .

'Is Savrinor likely to come down?' Benetan asked.

'No. He spent the night with . . .' but she couldn't bring herself to tell him that, and finished, '. . . someone.'

Knowing Savrinor, that meant he wouldn't appear before midday. Benetan nodded, relieved. 'Then I should have come to you last night. Or perhaps you should have come to me?'

She looked at him, a painful look. 'I know, Benet. But I didn't dare.'

'Why not? Because Kaldar ordered you not to? Iselia, where *is* he? Where's he gone, and what is he doing? I think I have a right to know!'

That was the trouble, Iselia thought; in one sense, as Kaldar had said, he did have a right, for they had led him into danger and owed him the chance to save himself.

'He left a note.' Benetan produced the crumpled ball of it from a pocket and held it out to her. 'It explains nothing, but it intimates a warning to me to be careful. Why did he say that? What does he plan to *do*?'

She didn't take the paper from him but stared down at the table. 'Kaldar isn't going to do anything.' Her voice was low-pitched but firm; that, at least, was the truth. 'He left because of something Savrinor told me.'

'What?'

'That the First Magus has summoned a meeting of the senior magi tonight – Savrinor knows because Vor – Lord Vordegh ordered him to prepare the messages. Savrinor said that they'll know by then whether Kaldar's information is accurate, and that if it isn't . . .' Her head came up again and her eyes pleaded mutely. 'I had to warn him, Benet! He couldn't stay here, not with such a threat hanging over him!'

'You mean that they're going to discover the deception? That your god's protection isn't enough to . . .' Benetan broke off and turned away. '*Yandros!*' Reactions seethed; chagrin, confusion, anger and fear. 'Why didn't Kaldar *tell* me this?'

'He didn't dare. He thought you might stop him from leaving.' She hesitated. 'Would you have done?'

'I . . . don't know. But that's not the *point*, Iselia! Simply to go, and leave me to face the consequences without even knowing what's afoot – I thought Kaldar had *some* sense of honour!'

She looked away again and her voice was very quiet. 'Don't blame Kaldar, Benet; blame me. He wanted to warn you but I stopped him. I said that we couldn't take the risk, and I *made* him go.'

'I see.' Benetan didn't know whether or not to believe her; it seemed more likely that she was trying to excuse Kaldar's behaviour, shoulder the burden herself for his wrong. But then he sighed heavily and leaned back against the wall. What did the whys and wherefores matter? The facts were all that counted now. And his own prospects, which at this moment looked very bleak indeed.

Iselia said hesitantly, 'He's coming back for me.'

'When?'

'I'd – rather not say. But it will be soon, and then we'll both be gone.' Suddenly her voice caught and she put a clenched fist to her mouth. 'Oh, Benet, I didn't want this to happen! Neither of us did! We thought, we truly thought, that we'd have more time before the magi discovered the truth, and that we could use that time to find a way of ensuring that you wouldn't be in trouble because of us.'

In trouble was an understatement, Benetan thought bitterly. But then, how could she know that? To her gentler reasoning, it would be the merest justice for the magi to acknowledge that if Kaldar had been able to dupe them he had also been able to dupe a mere Chaos rider. She couldn't know that justice had no place whatever in Lord Vordegh's thinking.

'I don't blame you.' The words came wearily, resignedly, but with a new kindness. 'Though Kaldar . . .' But no; there was no point in expressing his feelings on that score. Kaldar had done what he had done out of love for his rightful wife, and Benetan had no right to censure him for that. If their positions had been reversed, wouldn't his desire to be reunited with Iselia have eclipsed all other considerations? Honour had nothing to do with it. As his own conscience had known at the very beginning, when he had kept her at the castle instead of letting her go free.

She said almost inaudibly, 'Kaldar wasn't at fault. Oh, Benet, please don't blame him – I couldn't bear it if you hated him when you should hate me.'

'No!' Without thinking he put an arm around her, pulling her close to him. 'No, Iselia, I won't hate you, I never *could* hate you! And for your sake, I won't hate Kaldar either. How can I, when he's only doing what he can to save you both? I'm not that much of a hypocrite!'

He realized suddenly that her head was resting against his shoulder and he was kissing her hair, distractedly, driven by an emotion that had spun momentarily out of control. It horrified him, and instantly he released her. 'I'm sorry. I shouldn't have done that.'

She laid a hand softly over his. 'And I shouldn't have wanted you to. No,' as he made to pull his hand away. 'Please don't, Benet. Let me touch you, just for a minute, just like this.' Her fingers tightened abruptly. 'After all, this might be the last time we ever see each other.'

Benetan knew then that he couldn't leave it unsaid. If there was to be nothing more – and there never would be anything more, for that would be so wrong – then he needed at least to have spoken what was in his heart.

'You know I love you,' he said. 'Don't you?'

'Yes.' It hurt him and gladdened him together to hear her say it so emphatically and with no hesitation. She looked at him, tears in her blue eyes. 'And I know, too, that you remember what I said to you that night on the beach, before you went away. It was true, Benet. And Kaldar's return hasn't changed it. But –'

He shook his head before she could say any more. 'No; no *but* or *if*. We both understand, but it's kinder if we don't say it.' Her hand was warm on his; he could feel the pulse in her wrist, rapid, fluttering. 'And if we're not to meet again I'd rather simply remember this and nothing more.'

She acquiesced with a small nod, and for a minute they sat unmoving and silent until at last Benetan said, 'Will it be tonight? When Kaldar returns for you?' She hesitated and he added, 'You can trust me. Don't you know that?'

She knew it. 'Tonight,' she said. 'When the magi are meeting. Savrinor will be with them in the council hall, and so there's no danger that he'll see me go.'

It hurt, it hurt badly, but Benetan dared not let himself acknowledge that. 'If Kaldar comes into the castle, he'll risk –' he began.

'He won't. He'll come through the Maze and I'm to meet

323

him outside the wall.' She flicked him a quick, anxious glance. 'My only fear is that I might be challenged at the gates. The watch will be ended, but –'

He interrupted her, as she had hoped he would. 'I'll issue an instruction to my men.' Some of them were sure to be in the vicinity of the stables; she couldn't avoid being seen by them as she left, and this would be a last service, something tangible to help her. 'I'll tell them not to question you; I'll say that you're on an errand for Savrinor – they know he and I are friends after a fashion and they won't be curious.'

Iselia cast her gaze down. 'That's . . . very kind of you.'

'Not kind.' He smiled bleakly. 'Call it my form of farewell.'

'Thank you. And you – when we're gone, will you be safe?'

He didn't know the answer to that, and felt now that to speak of it to her would be unkind. If the worst came to the worst, he thought, Savrinor would be an ally; he, after all, had also been involved in Kaldar's deception, however unwittingly. He was about to say something that he hoped would be both dismissive and reassuring when a flicker of movement near the doors drew his attention. Looking up, he saw that two more people had entered the hall. Savrinor – and Andraia.

Iselia saw him tense and followed the direction of his gaze. Overtly there was nothing in either Savrinor's or Andraia's manner to suggest any intimacy between them, but when Iselia glanced sidelong at Benetan the flush that came to her cheeks told him the truth.

He said nothing, only watched the approaching pair with an expressionless face, and at last Iselia whispered, 'I'm sorry.'

'You knew.' There was no condemnation; it was simply a statement.

'Yes.' But there was no point in elaborating. 'Perhaps I

should have told you,' Iselia continued, 'but it seemed . . . cruel.'

'Cruel?' Benetan tapped the table with an extended forefinger, then abruptly and curtly laughed. 'No. After our last quarrel I can make no claims on Andraia. Nor do I wish to. I'm simply surprised by her choice.' He rose abruptly. 'They've seen us. I'd best go; I'm on duty soon in any case.' He looked down at her. 'I'm only sorry that we can't say a more private goodbye. But there is one last thing.' Let Andraia, Savrinor and anyone else who might see him think what they would; he didn't care any more. And the chance would never come again.

He bent and kissed her, gently, lingeringly, lovingly. She didn't pull away; instead she raised one hand and held tightly to his sleeve, and when he finally released her she looked at him for what seemed a very long time.

'Goodbye, Iselia.' His voice was a whisper that no one would overhear. 'And . . .' He couldn't wish her the gods' blessing; in that, his mind was already too confused. 'Good luck go with you.'

He had to pass Andraia and Savrinor as he left the hall, and though he was determined to ignore them he couldn't overcome the compulsion to glance obliquely in their direction. Andraia's face was like stone, Savrinor's thoughtfully impassive. Then the historian put a proprietorial arm about Andraia's waist and drew her away. Iselia, watching, was terrified that they would approach her, but they didn't. Savrinor did look at her, once, but the look was unreadable and he showed no further interest in her as he escorted Andraia on towards the tables by the fire.

'It was satisfactory by some standards, but not by mine.' Savrinor dropped the paper he was holding onto Iselia's table. 'And if it doesn't pass muster with me, it certainly won't please the First Magus.'

'I'm sorry, Savrinor.' Iselia's voice was indistinct; she didn't look up at him.

'Sorry is as sorry does. And what you will do, my dear, is prepare two more copies for the archives and count yourself very fortunate that I had the foresight to make an extra document in case of an eventuality like this.' He crossed the room and she heard the familiar sound of his cabinet door opening. 'Pour me some wine, if you please. And while you pour it, reflect on the one golden rule that must never be broken in our particular vocation; that personal diversions, however alluring and absorbing they may be, must *never* be allowed to affect the quality of the work we are required to do.'

He looked over his shoulder as he spoke and saw the tensing of her shoulders. She feared retribution in some form; she knew perfectly well that he had witnessed Benetan's dramatic but pointless gesture and doubtless she thought him jealous and thus angry with her. Savrinor's lip curled cynically as he wondered how she could be so naive as to think he knew nothing of Benetan's unrequited longings, but he made no comment as he selected two glass bottles and a silver measuring spoon from the cabinet. She brought the wine in silence then retreated to her table once more, and as he measured and mixed his concoction Savrinor ran an expert eye over the cabinet's contents. Yes; the supply of Moonwrack was considerably diminished, even allowing for the level to which her addiction had grown lately. In fact a good deal had vanished since yesterday, suggesting that she had spirited it away and hidden it somewhere. That fitted with his suspicions, and he closed the door and glanced towards the window. The sky had turned blood-red and long shadows stretched across the courtyard; sunset was approaching and a north wind was getting up, likely, he thought, to bring cloud and with it more snow. She would need some time to prepare, of course, and would feel safer if she could be sure of being uninterrupted . . .

'I shall be in the dining hall for the next hour or two,' he said carelessly. 'After that, anyone who wants me will have to kick their heels until the First Magus's meeting has ended.' He sighed theatrically, and gathered up his case of writing materials. 'These matters are extremely tiresome and not a little exhausting, so you'll please me if you ensure that I have no questions to answer or problems to resolve when I return.'

She too was gazing at the window now, and he caught a glimpse of the peculiar blend of nervousness and eager impatience in her face. 'Yes, Savrinor,' she said meekly, and bowed her head to her work once more. She didn't look up as he went out.

Andraia was waiting. She had dismissed her servant for the night and was sitting by a well-made and welcome fire when he arrived; a flagon of excellent wine stood on a table beside her. She greeted him with an embrace but their kiss was almost perfunctory, a salute not of lovers but rather of friends – or, Savrinor thought, co-conspirators.

He closed the door and locked it. 'I've made what inquiries I can without alerting Benetan to anything amiss. There's no doubt of it; Tarkran's gone. And the evidence suggests that Iselia means to follow him.'

Andraia sat down on the fur rug before the fire and he crouched beside her, warming his hands at the blaze. 'When?' she asked.

'Impossible to say, but I'd surmise tonight.' He glanced at her. 'She thinks I'm bidden to attend the magi in the council hall, which removes one obstacle, and as she also believes that time is about to run out for her paramour, or whatever he is, I imagine she'll take the first chance that comes her way.'

327

Andraia mused over that. 'Yes. Yes, it would be logical.' She paused. 'Does anyone else know of Tarkran's disappearance?'

'I doubt it.' Then Savrinor smiled thinly. 'Apart from Benetan, of course — and the fact that he's failed to alert anyone appears to confirm our belief that he's helping them.' His hands were warm now and he lay back, his head in Andraia's lap. She stroked his hair, but although the sensation was delightful he was too preoccupied to enjoy it fully. His pale gaze, restless, roamed across the ceiling and he continued, 'In truth, Andraia, if it wasn't for this unresolved conundrum I'd be inclined to say let her go, let them both go, and be damned to them. Certainly it would be far simpler and less disheartening than this tangled subterfuge we're creating for ourselves.'

Her hands stopped moving. 'But you can't say it, and neither can I. And we both know why.'

Savrinor closed his eyes, acknowledging the truth of that statement. Last night, when he had come here to her room for the second time, his motives had been clear-cut; he had wanted to fulfil a promise and also to find sanctuary in the diversions she offered him. But without warning the mood between them had undergone a subtle, strange and almost unnerving shift. He didn't know quite how it had happened, but somehow their talk had turned to more arcane matters, and the name of Yandros of Chaos had been spoken. Savrinor knew the secret that Andraia kept close to her heart; the secret of her brief liaison with Yandros's brother and the joy and pain alike that that encounter had brought her. But what he had not known — though perhaps he had sensed it and, for complex reasons of his own, quashed the intuition — was that underlying that more intimate emotion was another, and one with which he was very, very familiar.

Savrinor's life was a mass of contradictions, illusions

and pretences, but through the twisted skeins ran one incorruptible and unbreakable thread. His dedication to the gods was absolute. Not through fear, though he was wise enough to fear them to the core of his soul; but through a love that ran as deep as any terror. Why it should be so he didn't know and had never questioned; it was simply a fact of his nature. But it set him apart – even from the magi, whose dedication all too often seemed to him to be laced with a little too much pragmatism. The First Magus might loathe the heretics who followed the cult of Order, but Vordegh's hatred was based on the threat that Order might one day pose to his own power. For Savrinor, such questions had no relevance: every part of his being was pledged unshakeably to Chaos, and he reviled Order as an evil abomination which tainted all it touched and whose principles utterly negated all that was right and good in this or any other world. He had made it a personal rule never to speak to anyone about the intensity of his beliefs; it was a private matter and no concern of others. But last night, while he and Andraia sat together just as they were sitting now, he had broken that rule, for he realized that he had found a like spirit.

It was possible that Andraia didn't know the depth of her own dedication to the gods; for all her sharp intelligence and broad experience there was a streak of artlessness in her that blinded her to many of her own qualities. It was also possible that the brief liaison with Yandros's brother had changed her, striking flame from what previously had been merely a spark; but Savrinor didn't believe that. If ever the gods should call upon her to do so, Andraia, like himself, would walk willingly into the Seven Hells for their sakes. And that was a devotion which could only be inborn.

He heard a faint rustle as she moved, then her lips touched his, gently but emphatically.

'I wish that we could forget them, too,' she said softly. 'I wish . . .'

When she didn't continue he opened his eyes again and looked at her. 'What do you wish?'

She shook her head. She had been about to say; *I wish they were dead, all three of them, and could be forgotten*, but she didn't mean it — not all of it — and if she spoke the words he would know she was lying. And there was something else, a feeling of foreboding that was casting a shadow over them both.

'It could be,' she continued at last, 'that she *will* simply go to join him wherever he is, and that we'll never hear of them again.'

'But you don't believe it, and neither do I.' He paraphrased her own words of a few minutes earlier, taking the edge from them with a faint smile. 'If they serve the demons of Order, then their masters won't have missed such an opportunity to plan mischief, and they won't leave without putting that plan into action.' Suddenly, startling her, he sat up. 'That's what's at the root of it, Andraia, nagging my mind like a disease. What *can* they be planning? What hand could they play, here in Chaos's stronghold, with any hope of winning?' Twisting around he reached for the wine and filled two glasses. 'I have an instinct which tells me I should speak to Croin —'

'Savrinor, no! We agreed —'

He held up his free hand. 'I know, I know; and I've no intention of suggesting we reverse that decision.' His shoulders hunched. 'There's still a faint chance that we're wrong, and I don't wish to light the fires of wrath by leading the magi on a dance that takes us nowhere. But that doesn't mean I can ignore what my sixth sense is trying to tell me. *Something*'s in the wind.' He stared hard at the fire for a moment, then with an abrupt movement drained the wineglass in one mouthful and stood up. 'We must go.'

His hand caught hers, and with a strength that surprised her he pulled her to her feet. For all her own volatility Andraia wasn't yet used to Savrinor's rapid and mercurial changes of mood and she said, 'Go? Where?'

'To the dining hall. If Iselia decides to make sure of my whereabouts, I want them to be publicly obvious.'

That made sense, but she knew he had something more in mind. 'And what then?' she demanded as he swung round in search of her cloak.

'I'm not sure yet.' He found the cloak and cast it over her shoulders; from ingrained habit the gesture was meticulously courteous despite his obvious distraction and Andraia was both amused and a little touched. 'But if she's planning to leave tonight, every fibre within me feels that she means to do something more before then. And we must find out what it is.'

Andraia didn't argue. Savrinor, unlike Benetan, was not an easy man to argue with, and besides, his words had brought her own unease back into sharp focus.

At the door he glanced back over the room and said, 'You'd best rouse your servant and tell her to tend the fire. The gods alone know how long we'll be gone.'

Andraia thought, *I wish they did, and could tell us*, but only nodded and went to the small chamber next door to issue her instructions. Savrinor waited in the corridor, and when she returned he shivered.

'Damn this freezing weather. I'm never at ease in the cold; it gets into my bones and won't be dislodged.'

'It's snowing again.' Andraia had seen the fall beginning beyond her window.

'I thought it would.' A torch further along the passage guttered in a bitter draught, setting their shadows dancing along the floor like grotesque marionettes. 'I'll be thankful when spring comes, and . . .' Savrinor's voice faded and Andraia looked at him keenly.

'What is it, Savrinor? What's wrong?'

He smiled, briefly and strangely. 'Nothing. Just a stray thought; a ghoul passing by in the night.'

She began to feel a chill that had no connection with the temperature. 'Tell me.'

He sighed. 'Very well, if you insist; though you're making consequences out of nothing. It merely occurred to me to wonder where we might all be when spring does finally come.'

Andraia continued to stare at him. 'We'll be here, living our lives as we've always done.'

Her words were intended to reassure, but something in Savrinor's look suggested that they had failed to do so. His smile had faded; for a moment his lips twitched and she glimpsed an echo of it, but the echo didn't last.

'I pray so,' he said and, taking her arm, started towards the main stairs.

CHAPTER XXI

Iselia's hand was shaking as she measured the dose of Moonwrack, and the thought of wine or even beer made her stomach churn so queasily that she forced herself to swallow the drug without diluting it. The bitterness made her gasp and brought tears to her eyes, but relief came quickly and with it the now familiar and potent sharpening of her mind.

Everything was ready. She had packed no clothes – she had only what Savrinor had given her, and didn't want to carry with her more of his taint than she must – but she had stolen nearly half his supply of Moonwrack, which was now in the pocket of her coat. When it was gone she would have no hope of getting more, but she prayed that once they were safe in the south, Simbrian or even Lord Aeoris himself would help her to break free from her addiction. And for all her self-disgust at that addiction she owed Moonwrack a debt, for without it she couldn't have maintained her sanity in this place.

For the twentieth time since sunset she crossed to the window, lifted back the curtain and looked out at the sky, but the cloud-cover was so dense and the snowfall so heavy that it was impossible to judge whether or not the first moon had risen. Kaldar would surely be waiting for her by now, and in this bitter weather the wait would be hard, dangerous. She *must* go soon.

From here she couldn't see the windows of the council hall, so didn't know whether or not the meeting had begun. The First Magus's apartments and surrounding rooms were in darkness, but that signified nothing; Vordegh rarely showed a light at any hour. Iselia let the curtain fall, turned, and took three deep breaths in an effort to steady her racing nerves. She couldn't delay any longer. This was her one chance, and it must be taken.

'Sweet Lord Aeoris, guide and protect me tonight!' She flung both arms out and the words choked from her in a desperate, heartfelt plea to the great master of the powers of Order. Hope and determination surged, lending her strength, and as the walls swallowed the echoes of her prayer she pulled her coat tightly about herself and ran out into the corridor.

There was no one in sight. Unnerved by the sound of her own ragged breathing, Iselia turned and headed towards the stairs; not the main flight but a secondary staircase that would take her to the west wing without needing to pass too close to the dining hall. In case the meeting hadn't yet begun; in case Savrinor was still there. That was her worst nightmare now, the prospect of turning a corner suddenly and finding herself face to face with him . . .

She was unaware of the shadow that moved silently and at a discreet distance behind her. Once she turned and saw a figure at the far end of the passage, but the figure wore the grey, hooded cloak of a servant and was, or so she thought, moving away and not towards her. She didn't look back again, and so didn't see the 'servant' turn a corner, stop, wait, then follow more cautiously once the quarry was out of sight.

To wait for Iselia and follow her had been Savrinor's idea, the disguise Andraia's; and Andraia had also insisted that she should be the one to carry out the surveillance. She could be light-footed as a cat when she chose, and now her soft shoes made not the smallest noise, while the cloak she had borrowed from a dining-hall menial was voluminous enough to entirely conceal the richer clothing beneath. As yet she had no inkling of where Iselia was going or what she intended, but her furtive manner was evidence enough that something, as Savrinor had said, was in the wind. And her first suspicion was that Iselia was making for Benetan's room.

Iselia reached the staircase and began to descend. The way was poorly lit but she knew it well enough to keep her footing as the steps curved round and steeply downwards. The foot of the flight opened onto another passage which then branched, one way leading to the kitchen stairs, the other towards the west wing. She tiptoed down the last few steps, turned into the corridor – and collided with two men.

'Careful!' There was laughter in the taller man's voice and he caught her arms to stop her from stumbling as she recoiled from him in shock. Then he peered harder in the gloom. 'Iselia? Good gods, you're not about to venture outside in *this* weather?'

He was a clerk, one of those whose services Savrinor had commandeered when the First Magus had given the order for his first edict to be prepared. Iselia felt hot colour coming to her face in a prickling rush and nearly bit her tongue as she tried to dissemble.

'I – ah –' *oh, dear gods, help me now!* And abruptly the glib explanation came. 'Not from choice, Venner, I assure you!' She injected a wry and weary note into her voice. 'But when I'm told that an errand can't wait until morning . . .' A shrug said the rest, and Venner made a sympathetic noise.

'Master Savrinor's a slave-driver, as I well know!'

'Yes.' Dared she ask the question in her mind? She decided to take the risk. 'In fact I – need to find Savrinor. Do you happen to know where he is?'

'Well, he was in the dining hall earlier. But Lord Vordegh

and all the senior magi went into the council chamber a good while ago, so I'm afraid you've come seeking him too late.' Venner grinned. 'Unless you're planning to interrupt them, of course!' Iselia pretended a shudder and joined in his laughter, and he added, 'If you can't complete your errand, why not join us for your evening meal? Better than sitting alone, and the hall's good and warm.'

'Thank you, but I – still have to deliver some documents.' She patted the wrappings of her coat, implying that papers were concealed beneath it. 'When that's done, though, I might well seek you out.'

'We'll watch for you.' Venner raised a hand in salute as she started to hurry away. 'And we'll have some hot beer ready to help you thaw your bones!'

In the stairwell, Andraia continued to listen. Venner and his companion were moving off; Iselia had gone in the opposite direction and her footsteps were diminishing rapidly. She wasn't going towards Benetan's room after all, or she would have followed the two men. Where, then? Andraia racked her mind, trying to recall exactly where the passage led. Then it came to her, and with it the uneasy feeling that, though she couldn't yet fathom her purpose, she knew at last where Iselia was going.

It took her five minutes to discover that her suspicion was right. Iselia grew more cautious as she neared her goal and once Andraia thought she had lost her altogether, but she took another way which, if she hadn't miscalculated, would intersect again with Iselia's route. She hadn't miscalculated. And in this part of the castle there were no lights in the corridors, no servants scurrying on their business, only a preternatural and ominous quiet; the quiet that the First Magus demanded at all times in the vicinity of his rooms.

Andraia watched Iselia turn the final corner. She could hardly bring herself to believe that the girl could be so reckless – or so resolute – as to do this, but there was no room left for doubt now. Savrinor's intuition had been right.

She drew back, retreated until she could be sure she was out of earshot. Then, throwing the encumbering grey cloak aside, she hitched up the skirt of her gown and ran, faster than she had ever run in her life, towards the dining hall.

Savrinor was surprised to see Benetan, but not, he realized an instant later, as surprised as Benetan was to see him. Benetan's face blanched as he recognized the historian, and for a moment his dismay was painfully obvious before he wrested back his self-control. He would have walked past Savrinor's table and on into the more crowded section of the dining hall with no more than a nod of acknowledgement, but there was a demon in Savrinor tonight and he held up a hand, beckoning the younger man across.

'Savrinor.' Benetan approached, wary. 'I ... didn't expect to find you here tonight.'

'Didn't you?' Savrinor smiled foxily. 'Whyever should that be, my dear Benetan? Even I have to eat from time to time, strange as it may seem.'

'I thought you were with the magi.'

'Oh, the business in the council hall? Yes, I was to have been, but Lord Vordegh sent word that my presence wouldn't be required after all. I don't mind admitting that I was relieved.' He studied his fingernails. 'These conferences can be very wearing.'

'There's ... nothing wrong?'

'In what way wrong?'

Benetan nodded in the vague direction of the council hall. 'The purpose of this ...'

'Ah, I *understand*. And I agree; it is somewhat unusual for our good First Magus to consult his fellow magi on

337

any subject these days. But as far as I'm aware, there's nothing wrong. Lord Vordegh is simply apprising his colleagues of the details of young Tarkran's intelligence, and giving instructions as to what's to be done about it.'

Ah, that threw him. He had expected trouble; Iselia must have passed on the little snippet of disinformation. Which version of the story, Savrinor wondered, would Benetan believe now?

'They may well decide to send for Tarkran at some stage of the proceedings,' he continued. 'I presume he's still safe in your room?'

A pause. 'Yes. Yes, of course.'

'Good.' Savrinor pretended not to notice the fact that Benetan's face had turned ashen, and continued carelessly, 'It must be most inconvenient for you to have had him foisted on you.' Another smile. 'I imagine he isn't the most entertaining of companions . . . oh, and speaking of companions reminds me; there's something I think we should clear up between us before it turns sour.' He pointed to the bench. 'Sit down, Benetan, for all the gods' sakes; you put me out of sorts towering over me like that.'

Benetan subsided onto the bench, but very reluctantly. 'I really haven't the time –' he began.

'She'll wait, whoever she is.' Then abruptly Savrinor's eyes turned flint-hard. 'Especially if she is who I think she is.'

Benetan half-rose again. 'No! It isn't –'

'Calm *down*. I'm not about to challenge you to a duel – I wouldn't be *quite* so asinine as to take on someone with your training. Nor am I about to upbraid you, or sulk, or demand that you never lay hands on the girl again while I still have breath in my body. After all, I'd be nothing less than a hypocrite if I objected, wouldn't I?'

'I don't know,' Benetan said whitely. 'Would you?'

'Yes, I would.' Savrinor lifted a pale eyebrow, making his meaning clear. No obvious outward reaction, he thought, but a change in the younger man's eyes betrayed the fact that that remark had hurt. Benetan still loved Andraia, in his fashion. And, more interestingly, he had abandoned his attempts to curtail this conversation – in fact, now that he realized Savrinor had no intention of picking a quarrel with him he seemed more than willing to stay and talk. So, whatever Iselia was doing at this moment, Benetan had no direct part to play in it. Though perhaps he *did* have a vested interest in ensuring that Savrinor stayed put for a while.

'I have no claims on Andraia,' Benetan said, a little sourly.

'Quite true; she's perfectly capable of making her own decisions and it would be a gross insult to her to suggest otherwise.' Savrinor's sly gaze focused on his face again. 'We don't follow the peasant custom of marriage here. Or perhaps I should say, most of us don't.'

His aim was perfect. Benetan blanched, his jaw dropped, and Savrinor saw the truth written on his face. 'Yes,' the historian said softly. 'Yes, I thought so. It's time, isn't it, that you and I had a small talk about your supposedly new-found friend Kaldar Tarkran?'

Benetan stared at him, his mind rioting. He couldn't tell even a grain of the truth, not to Savrinor of all people; one word and he'd condemn Iselia, condemn himself too . . .

'Silence,' Savrinor said with quietly ominous deliberation, 'often signifies guilt, in my experience. Or am I being overly cynical?'

Benetan drew breath. 'Silence signifies nothing whatever.' He turned his head aside. 'And I've nothing whatever to say.'

Real anger didn't come easily to Savrinor, but suddenly he felt a rush of hot fury, driven by frustration at Benetan's seeming determination to be obstructive no matter what the cost.

'Damn you, Benetan, what kind of stubborn insanity *is* this? Who are you trying to protect – Iselia? Her husband? Oh yes, I know who Tarkran really is; do you think I don't know about the clandestine meeting between the three of you and that I'm not capable of working out the implications for myself? You brought him here, you spun a pretty tale to the magi – where in all the gods' names did you think it was going to *lead*? Because if you're such a fool as to believe for one instant –'

'*Savrinor!*'

The cry cut across his furious outburst, cut through the hum of noise in the hall. People looked up, and in the sudden hush Andraia's footsteps thudded echoingly as she ran towards Savrinor's table.

'Savrinor, she's –' Andraia stopped. 'Oh, gods . . . Benet . . .'

For the first time since their quarrel they faced each other directly and with no possibility of avoidance. Tension built like a rising Warp – then suddenly Andraia's voice came harshly.

'You know, don't you? You know where she's gone and what she's planning to do!'

Benetan didn't know, but the burden of the secrets he had kept showed starkly clear in his face. 'Oh, gods,' Andraia said again. 'He's part of it, Savrinor . . .' She made as if to lunge forward –

'Wait!' Savrinor moved fast, catching hold of her arm. 'What have you seen? What have you discovered?'

She whirled to face him. 'She's going to the First Magus's chambers.'

'*What?* She can't –'

'She *is!*' Andraia turned again, bitter rage in her eyes. 'And he knows it, and he knows why!'

'No!' Benetan protested. 'That's not true!' He felt bewildered, horrified – the *First Magus's* rooms? But Iselia had said –

'You're lying!' He returned Andraia's glare with a fury of his own. 'This is some ruse to trap them –'

'Oh, *them* is it now?' Savrinor's voice was dangerous. 'At last we seem to be getting closer to the heart of it.' His gaze flicked sharply round the hall; for all their anger none of them had been shouting, and the other diners, unable to overhear, were rapidly losing interest and returning to their own concerns. It was imperative, Savrinor knew, that matters remained that way at least for the moment, and he stepped out from behind the table, placing himself between his companions and the rest of the hall.

'Andraia. Forget Benetan; tell me what happened.'

She told him. Twice Benetan tried to protest but a fearsome look from the historian silenced him, and when Andraia's brief account was complete Savrinor said, 'Very well. We don't know – yet – what she intends to do, but we know where her allegiance lies and that's enough. I'm going to the magi.'

Benetan said, 'No! You can't –'

'*Can't?*' Savrinor rounded on him ferociously. 'That lying, devious, traitorous *slut* is at this moment breaking into our First Magus's private rooms, and you tell me I should do nothing to stop her?'

'Benet, she's a heretic!' Andraia hissed desperately. 'Don't you understand? She isn't what you believed her to be; she's a worshipper of the demons of Order! You didn't know, you didn't guess, but –'

'Oh, he knew,' Savrinor broke in. 'In fact I think he's known for a very long time. Haven't you, Benetan?'

He didn't speak, but they both saw the answer in his eyes. Andraia began to shake; then her mouth distorted and she broke down in tears.

'Oh Benet, Benet!' She hated herself, hated the pain she felt at his betrayal, hated the terror for him that filled her, but the tears wouldn't stop and the grief was like fire burning her alive, devouring her. 'Do you love her so much that you'll – you'll turn your back on *everything* you've ever believed in, for her sake? You're betraying us all, Benet, and betraying the gods, and – and –' She covered her face with her hands, sobbing.

'Andraia –' Benetan started to reach towards her, but Savrinor pulled her back, putting a protective arm about her shoulders. 'It isn't like that!' Benetan said desperately. 'Not a betrayal, not in that way! I didn't know that she was – that she intended – oh, gods, I don't know what she's doing, and I don't want to know!'

'Oh, you don't *want* to know!' Savrinor fired back with savage contempt. 'For once in your miserable life, *tell the truth!*'

'It is the truth! I'm not part of this; I had no knowledge of it! Yes, I wanted to help her to leave the castle, but that's *all*.'

'So you brought her husband here, engineered a meeting between them – and what else?'

'Nothing else!'

'Nothing, he says. But Tarkran has gone – yes, I know about that, my friend; I have my own methods of finding such things out. And his wife means to follow him, doesn't she?' He paused. 'I've been wondering how they plan to achieve that, but now I think I know – for I've noticed something missing in your garb tonight, Benetan. Your amulet. The seven-rayed star, which has hung round your neck since the day you joined the riders as a raw recruit. Where is it now? Have you left it behind in your room by sheer oversight – or did you give it to Tarkran, to enable him to flee the castle and then come back for his wife, just as soon as she's completed the task that her masters have set her?' Savrinor's face twisted. 'Are you one of them, Benetan, is that it? Have you sold your soul to that filthy demon cult, with Iselia's favours as your price?'

'You vile-minded –' Benetan's hand went to his knife. Then, realizing what he had been about to do, he froze.

Savrinor had flinched back but his eyes were steady. 'Killing me will achieve nothing. And it certainly won't save her.' Andraia had moved away from him and was trying to regain her self-control; he took another step backwards and his hand touched her arm. 'We have no choice, Andraia. The First Magus must be warned.'

Andraia raised her head. Her expression was desolate. 'But if Benet's one of them –'

'He isn't.' Benetan's violent reaction to his goad had proved that to Savrinor's satisfaction. 'He's not a heretic, he's simply a weak fool who allowed himself to be manipulated by a clever and unscrupulous woman. He's not alone in that failing, as I know only too well. But the great difference between us is that my first loyalty, and my first love, is for the gods. And I won't compromise that for any woman ever born.'

He released Andraia's arm, took a step towards the door. Benetan's jaw set angrily and his body tensed. 'Don't Savrinor. I don't want to have to harm you.'

The historian's eyes followed his hand as it went again to the knife hilt. 'I don't think you'll try. Not in this public place.' He took another step. 'You could help us to put things right. The trap hasn't closed on you yet; you could still redeem yourself – and I have no wish to see you come to ruin.' A quick, oblique glance. 'Nor has Andraia.'

'Benet, please!' She ran to him, grasping his sleeve. 'Help us! Don't turn your back on the gods, don't make me believe that you're a traitor!'

For a moment he was distracted, and in that moment Savrinor turned and strode towards the door.

'Savrinor!' Pushing Andraia aside, Benetan went after the historian. Andraia stumbled painfully against the table edge, regained her balance and stared after him as what she had seen in his eyes in the moment of her plea came fully home to her. The gulf between them was too vast; he didn't understand her, he couldn't move to meet her. All he felt, all he knew, was the pain of a love that negated everything they had ever been to each other, and for the sake of which he was ready to throw his own future – even his own life – away.

Savrinor had gone; Benetan was vanishing through the doors. Behind her, a voice said, 'Andraia, are you all right?'

Someone was at her elbow, curious and solicitous, and throughout the hall people were staring again. Andraia didn't even look round, let alone attempt to answer the question. Her hand, groping, found an empty flagon on the table; she snatched it up – for defence, for attack, she had no idea; it was simply a spar to clutch in a wild sea – and ran after Benetan and Savrinor.

Benetan had caught up with the historian and they were arguing face-to-face in the corridor that led to the main entrance-hall. As Andraia emerged, Savrinor tried to push past the younger man but Benetan was too quick for him, catching hold of his arm and twisting it in a practised lock. Andraia didn't pause to think; raising the flagon she launched herself at Benetan and hit him with all the strength she could summon. The flagon struck the back of his skull and the force of the blow sent him stumbling against the wall. For a moment his fingers clutched at the stonework; then he slid senseless to the floor.

Andraia dropped the flagon and stared at him in horror. *Great Yandros, had she killed him?*

Savrinor crossed the floor and dropped to a crouch at Benetan's side. One hand went to the younger man's neck, feeling for a pulse, while the other explored his skull. After a few seconds the historian looked up.

'Stunned, but still breathing.' He rose, looking at her with a mixture of appreciation and surprise. 'Thank you.'

'I didn't mean to hurt him,' Andraia said in a very small voice.

'I know.' Savrinor rubbed his wrenched arm and gazed down at the unconscious man again. 'You'd better get him moved to his room. Have someone tend him – not Physician Revian; the magi don't need to know of his involvement yet. Send for one of the herballers.'

Andraia was starting to shiver. 'And you?'

'I'm going to the council hall.' He looked at her, steadily, and she nodded.

'Yes. Go, quickly.'

Savrinor made to move away, then paused. 'We might still save him,' he said. 'If only the thrice-damned fool will *let* us.'

Andraia tried to tell herself that she didn't care any more whether Benetan lived or died, but it wasn't true and they both knew it. Suddenly, impulsively, she ran to the historian. 'Oh, Savrinor, what are we to *do*?'

'Hush!' He kissed her quickly, almost savagely. 'Be calm. Only one thing matters now; to stop whatever evil the heretics are trying to perpetrate tonight. Look after Benetan, but if you value any of our souls don't let him speak to *anyone* when he comes round.' A pause. 'And have faith, Andraia – this is a matter for the gods now, and they'll see that justice is done.'

As his footsteps faded rapidly in the direction of the council hall Andraia turned again to Benetan's prone and inert form.

'You fool,' she said through clenched teeth. 'You blind, faithless, perfidious, gullible *simpleton* . . .' The words ended in an ugly, racking sound deep in her throat, and her fists clenched until the nails dug agonizingly into her palms. Then she turned and strode back towards the hall, her voice clear and calm as she called for servants to attend her at once.

CHAPTER XXII

Two Chaos riders were on guard at the door of the council hall. Savrinor hadn't expected that, and his stomach gave an unpleasant twist as he approached; such a precaution would not have been taken unless the First Magus was utterly adamant that there should be no interruptions tonight.

'Master Savrinor.' The men had recognized him and both made a bow; the elder, who had spoken, ventured a smile which quickly faded as he realized where the historian was intent on going. 'Sir –' He stepped out, barring the way, one hand extended across the door. 'I'm sorry, sir, but the First Magus has given strict orders that no one may enter.'

Savrinor's breathing was more rapid than he would have liked it to be. 'I'm aware of that,' he said levelly. 'However, this is an emergency that must override any instructions you've been given. I must see Lord Vordegh, and I must see him now. Step out of my way, if you please.'

The rider knew Savrinor's reputation and recognized the force of the warning in that tone, but he held his ground. 'Sir – with respect – I can't countermand what the First Magus –'

'The First Magus,' Savrinor interrupted, 'will consign your body to an elemental and your soul to the Seven Hells if the message I carry fails to reach him within the next minute. Do I make myself *clear?*'

Under other circumstances he might almost have felt sorry for the man; as it was he had no time for anyone's finer feelings and certainly none for reasonable persuasion. 'Allow me to pass,' he said. 'I take full responsibility, and you may make any excuse you please to our masters; tell them, if you wish, that you were unable to stop me because I came here with a full complement of armed men at my back.' His pale eyes fixed malevolently on the rider's face. 'Which I shall assuredly do if you continue to hinder me.'

His gaze held hard and steady, and he saw the man's will crumbling. The First Magus might have given his orders, but at this moment the First Magus was not here to enforce them. Authority suddenly had a new face, and the rider hadn't enough confidence to defy it.

He hesitated, then very slowly moved back from the door. 'Sir, I can't endorse – '

'I'm not asking you to endorse anything, my friend. Stay here; you may be needed.' He laid his hand on the door then nodded courteously, though his eyes were still dangerous. 'Thank you.'

As he turned the handle of the door, Savrinor felt a lurch of sick, vertiginous fear. *If Andraia was wrong . . .* But she wasn't wrong. This must be done.

He pushed the door open.

There were some twenty magi in the hall. They were gathered by the raised dais at the far end, their figures lit starkly by two globes of cool, nacreous fire that hung, burning steadily, above them. Savrinor glimpsed Croin's ascetic profile, Pirane's eldritch beauty, Menniam's cruelly intelligent features; and amid the ever-present shadows, presiding over them all, Vordegh.

The First Magus raised his head slowly, and even at this distance Savrinor saw the light that ignited and grew in the dark, deceptively mellow eyes. Behind Vordegh's high-backed chair Verdice stood, staring, and now the other magi were turning their heads.

'Master Savrinor.' Vordegh was rising to his feet, gracefully, almost languidly. The shadows around him grew darker; in their depths something horrifying seemed to stir. 'I trust that you are aware of my instructions?'

His imperturbable voice seemed to take on tangible form in Savrinor's mind, like the touch of something dead. Ghouls passing by in the night . . . 'My lord.' Savrinor spoke before his nerve could desert him, at the same time executing a deeply reverent bow. 'I can do no more than throw myself on your mercy. This interruption is unsanctioned, I know – but it is also necessary.'

'Necessary, Master Savrinor?' Vordegh's face was dead-white now in its shroud of dark, and Savrinor was dimly aware of Pirane's horrified, pitying stare. He steeled himself against the appalling psychic charge that was beginning to build up in his head as Vordegh's fury, though with no outward sign, rose like a slow tide.

'Yes, my lord.' Sweat broke out in a prickling wave; he could no longer meet the First Magus's stare. 'I have to tell you that – that at this moment, an intruder is in your private chambers. And the intruder is a heretic.'

The tide of rage ripped away, vanishing from Savrinor's mind and leaving every bone in his body aching. Silence gripped the hall. The First Magus stood utterly still. Then, at last, he spoke.

'You are sure of this?'

He used the same calm tone with which he might have inquired the hour of the day, and Savrinor shuddered inwardly. 'I'm certain, my lord.'

'And do you know the heretic's identity?'

'I do. She is . . .' *Gods, he had to say it.* 'She is my own servant, Iselia.'

The hall erupted into clamour. Croin was on his feet, Pirane too, others following. Questions came at Savrinor like arrows, but abruptly Vordegh's voice cut through the confusion, silencing them all.

'Attend me.' His eyes made Savrinor feel as though he were being flayed alive. 'I will have the full details from you later, Master Savrinor; for the moment answer only two questions. Firstly, do you know what this woman's intention is?'

'No, sir.'

'Secondly, is she alone?'

'She is, my lord, but . . . I believe she has an accomplice, who fled the castle yesterday and may now be waiting for her.'

Voices began to rise once more and were hushed with a gesture. 'Very well,' Vordegh said. 'Furnish my colleagues with everything you know of this accomplice; they shall deal with that matter while I deal with the intruder.' He stepped down from the dais; instantly Verdice made to follow but he forestalled her. 'You will wait.' Then he glanced at the physician. 'Croin. With me, if you please.'

The crowd around him parted as he walked towards the doors, Croin at his heels. Drawing level with Savrinor the First Magus paused and looked once more at the historian.

'Yet again, Master Savrinor, your diligence is commendable.' But there was no approbation in the statement, and Vordegh's eyes were like deep wells that contained nothing.

'My lord.' Savrinor's voice was barely audible. He watched as the two magi left the hall, wondering how long it would take to shake off the cold that seemed to have penetrated his bones. Then at his elbow a voice spoke.

'My dear Savrinor, you continue to surprise us.' Pirane was standing beside him. Her tone was bantering, but her face, when Savrinor looked up, wore a dire expression.

Savrinor shivered. 'I wish to all seven of the gods, lady, that I hadn't had to do so.'

'Mmm.' Pirane continued to study him, thinking her own thoughts. 'Well, the girl was clever enough to dupe

350

us all, so you can hardly be held accountable, can you? Now: her accomplice. Tell me what you know.'

Savrinor did, though he made no mention of Benetan's part in the affair save to say that he believed Kaldar Tarkran – or whatever his real name might be – had stolen Benetan's amulet and used it to escape from the castle through the Maze.

'If Tarkran has fathomed the amulet's function, then either he has some sorcerous ability or *someone* has instructed him.' Pirane's eyes narrowed. 'Whichever is the case, Captain Liss has been extremely careless.'

Sweat prickled coldly on Savrinor's neck. 'I believe Tarkran duped him, madam – just as he and Iselia have duped us all.'

'I take your point; though I must say your enduring faith in Captain Liss's calibre is beginning to stretch credibility a little. But the finer points of this affair may wait a while; we have more immediate matters to attend to. You say you believe that the girl's husband intends to return for her, and that they plan to use the Maze again for their escape?'

'I can't be sure, but it seems likely.'

'Indeed it does. And equally likely that he has arranged to meet her outside the castle wall; in which case he will be waiting at this very moment.' She smiled, a very hard smile. 'Come with me, Savrinor. I shall deal with this myself.'

The two Chaos riders were still at their posts outside the door. Pirane spoke swiftly and briefly to them; they saluted, and fell in behind her as she strode in the direction of the castle's main doors.

The snowfall had slackened but flurries were still whirling down from a featureless sky and the wind was bitter. Ignoring the cold, Pirane swept across the courtyard, Savrinor and the riders following. The magus halted some ten paces from the barbican; in the darkness under the great arch Savrinor could just make out the castle's gates, a solid wall of deeper shadow.

Pirane nodded to the riders. There was a cold, metallic sound, echoing in the quiet, as both drew their swords. Then, in unison, they walked forward. As they halted near the gates, Pirane raised one hand, spoke a word, and a chilly light sparked along the length of her arm. Her hand turned, the palm facing outwards in a forbidding gesture, and the light flowed to her hand, coalescing, taking the form of a huge, translucent key.

Savrinor had witnessed the rite that closed the Maze many times before. It was a trifling ritual for a magus, unspectacular and unembellished. But tonight, the words that Pirane spoke seemed to take on a new and ominous aspect. *Closing.* Like the jaws of a trap, Savrinor thought. Like the door of a cage, imprisoning them all.

Kaldar's body was aching with the cold and he felt that he was all but fused to the black stone wall against which he huddled. The castle's south side was at least sheltered to some degree from the worst of the weather, but even here gusts of wind curled spitefully around the edge of the spire buttress, driving into him like knives and flinging snow against his hunched figure, and no coat ever made was warm enough or thick enough to protect its wearer from such onslaughts.

His eyes, the lashes crusted with ice, were fixed unwaveringly on the small postern set into the castle gates some fifteen or twenty paces from where he crouched. He couldn't judge the hour, couldn't tell how long he had been waiting; but she must surely, *surely* come soon. Unless the plan had gone awry . . .

But he refused to consider that, just as he refused to look up a second time at the gargantuan spire towering into the night above him, like a black sword-blade aimed at the sky. For all his mountain upbringing he felt like a fly on a giddying wall here, pinned precariously between the spire's vertiginous bulk and the colossal drop of the castle stack such a short way off. Aeoris, how he loathed this place! It would give him such pleasure, one day, to tear it apart, pull it down stone by evil stone, blast and smash and hammer it into oblivion. His hands clenched convulsively on Benetan's amulet, still on its chain around his neck. Fingers going numb again; he worked them urgently, trying to restore circulation. When Iselia came –

The thought snapped off as his mind received a psychic jolt, and at the same instant the amulet pulsed suddenly.

Kaldar's hands stopped moving. The jolt had been brief, leaving no echoes, but he knew it was a premonition. He lifted the amulet to his face, peering at it in the darkness, and saw that the stones forming the seven-rayed star were glowing faintly, as though reacting to some external influence. But what?

Then he thought of the Maze. These gems had a link with the gateway; if anything should affect it, it would affect them too, and quickly he raised his head and looked towards the Maze itself. The odd, over-lush rectangle of grass was invisible beneath the snow, but Kaldar's trained eyes detected a subtle change in the air above the approximate spot; a peculiar clarity, a faint distortion . . .

With an oath he was on his feet as he realized what was afoot. *They were closing the Maze* – The amulet pulsed again, harder, sending a stab of heat through his palm, and Kaldar felt panic rise as he realized that something had gone terribly, hideously wrong. They knew – the magi *knew*; they had caught Iselia and now they knew he was here, waiting –

A sound cut the night; a deep, sinister rumble. Kaldar's head whipped round, and through the renewed flurry of snow he saw that the huge black gates were juddering as they began to move.

He had seconds, no more, in which to decide. The Maze was closing, the castle opening – and Kaldar knew with an ugly instinct that, no matter what the danger to Iselia if he abandoned her now, in the next few moments he must make a choice between life and death.

The air above the Maze warped violently, and reason fled. Kaldar flung himself across the snow-covered sward, the amulet gripped in his hand, his mind frantically forcing an image, a picture, *anywhere, it doesn't matter, just SEE it* – For an appalling moment he thought nothing would come, but suddenly memory flashed and there was a vista of mountains before his inner eye; a narrow pass with a high ledge, a cave where he had been safe –

The Maze snatched him as he hurled himself into its vortex. The world twisted, inverted; on the castle stack white light flared, changed through an awful spectrum into black, vanished – and the unearthly doorway slammed shut in Kaldar's wake as, seconds too late, the Chaos riders emerged from the castle.

The lock wouldn't break. Iselia didn't know how long she had been trying to prise it open, but the fear in her was close to becoming panic. It had been so easy to begin with – the First Magus's door was unlocked, the outer room empty; nothing human or unhuman had challenged her as she lit a single candle and groped her way by its unsteady light to the inner sanctum.

She had expected to find the First Magus's apartment frightening, but that had not been so. The rooms were so bare and austere that they evoked no atmosphere of any kind, nor even any sense of occupation; they were like the abandoned rooms of a dead man. There was no bed, no rugs, no chairs that offered any comfort; only the stark necessities of a stringently ascetic life. She had found the desk – unlocked; it seemed that Vordegh saw no need for locks of any kind – and had rifled feverishly through its six drawers to find that they contained only documents. A single cupboard in a corner yielded a similar harvest, and for an unpleasant minute she had thought that her quest was to prove hopeless. But then she had found the small door, set into an alcove in the wall and invisible until she had carried the candle close to it. And beyond the small door was the third and last room; the room she had been seeking.

The wand was here. She knew it the moment she entered, for the plain, black wood table that dominated the room was covered with magical implements. The objects were laid out with fastidious precision, each one to its place, all perfectly aligned. A knife with a bone hilt . . . she pushed away thoughts of what manner of bone it might be. Three clear crystals, perfectly faceted. A long cord of seven strands. A crucible. Other things which she could not name and whose function she did not know. And, at the table's exact centre, a long, slim box made from solid silver and set with fine-cut gems that formed the seven-rayed star of Chaos.

Iselia fixed her candle in a pool of wax and stooped over the box. At first she couldn't summon the courage to touch it. Visions of retribution filled her mind; demons erupting from the walls to tear her apart, shrieking voices giving warning to the powers of Chaos, a Warp striking out of nowhere – she forced the images away, telling herself over and again that she had come this far without catastrophe and if no horrors guarded these rooms then no horrors would have been set to guard the wand alone. And even if she couldn't make herself believe that without doubt, the risk must still be taken. For Lord Aeoris. For the cause.

No voices shrieked and no demons came when at last

she dared to lay her hands on the silver box. But this time there was a lock, and the lock would not yield. Iselia prised frantically at it, breaking her fingernails, then, dragging herself back to coherence, searched for a key. But if a key existed she couldn't find it. Perhaps it was not here, perhaps Vordegh carried it with him? Looking wildly around she grabbed the bone-handled knife (*ignore the feel of it; it isn't human bone, there's no reason why it should be!*) and attacked the lock afresh as her mind rampaged. *Oh, gods, how much time has passed? What if the meeting should end? And Kaldar – he'll be waiting, he'll think something's wrong, that I've failed, been caught* – Easier, it would be so much easier simply to snatch up the box and take it with her. But it was cumbersome and would be impossible to conceal under her coat. She *had* to prise the lid up.

'Open, damn you, *open!*' She hissed the words furiously, working the knife-point in the lock with a violence born of sheer desperation. Then suddenly there was a metallic cracking sound and the lid gave a little. Yes, she thought, *yes!* It was coming, it was yielding –

Suddenly the lock fractured. The lid flew back and its edge cut Iselia's hand, but she was unaware of the sharp pain or the blood that welled. She was staring, hypnotized, into the box's lead-lined interior and at what lay there.

The wand of Chaos, no longer than her forearm, shone a cold, dull and metallic blue. It bore no embellishment, displayed no sign of its nature, but bands of shadow moved slowly, steadily along its thin shaft, evoking echoes of the vaster shadows that wheeled across the sky when the lords of Chaos unleashed a Warp storm upon the world.

Iselia's hand hovered over the box and she thrust down the sickness of fear rising in her. Her fingers reached out . . .

And a voice spoke gently, lethally.

'No. *I think not.*'

Every muscle Iselia possessed locked rigid. She was rooted, like a tree, and the colour that exertion had brought to her face drained to a ghastly grey. The voice had emanated from behind her, but she couldn't turn; no matter how violently she needed to look and to see and to know, the strength was beyond her.

Though she waited, dreading, the voice said nothing more. But she could hear it – whoever, whatever was watching her – she could hear it breathing, steadily, gently. Such *patience* in that sound; and it told her that if the stalemate was to be broken, she must be the one to make the next move.

Slowly, propelled by a power over which she had no control, her hand withdrew from the silver box. She watched her fingers, saw that they were not trembling and wondered, with eerily detached fascination, if her fear had already bitten too deep for any physical response to be possible. If that was so, she told herself, if it was so, then she *must* make her body obey her and turn round.

Her foot slithered as she moved, and the sound made her think of a knife being slid from its sheath. *She* still held a knife, she realized; the bone-handled knife, gripped so hard that it hurt. *Mustn't lose hold of it. There might be a chance.*

She turned at last. The quiet, regular breathing continued to ebb and flow, ebb and flow . . . but the room was empty.

A tiny spark of hope stirred and she clung to it. She raised her other foot, ventured a single, faltering step . . .

'*I think not.*'

It came from the shadows, the dark swathe of shadows that suddenly were between her and the open door. Iselia froze again, eyes widening, not knowing what she faced. Then a hand, strong, graceful, seemed to form from the stuff of the shadows and with one serene gesture smoothed them aside. They fragmented, spread out and then began to re-gather, like a retinue of ghosts. And in their midst, his face accented by the still guttering candle and transfigured to a face from nightmare, stood the First Magus.

He didn't speak again. He merely looked at her, and in that look Iselia saw the prospect of a destiny that she knew she would be unable to endure. And as she recognized it, the image of his figure before her suddenly lost all relevance. She saw him, but it meant nothing; her senses knew only a terror that was too great for her to contain. She was going to snap. Mind and body; she was going to lose all control –

She felt the scream beginning somewhere in the pit of her soul, and it came up like a tornado. When it exploded it shattered the paralysis and blindly, shrieking, she raised the hand that held the bone-hilted knife and flung herself at the monstrous shape within the shadows as the knife-blade sheared for his throat.

There was a sound like the crack of a whiplash, smashing through her mind and searing up an impossible scale, and a colossal force flung her across the room. She crashed against the table, ricocheted, hit the floor face-first. Blood came from her mouth; she tried to vomit but there was nothing in her stomach, and her limbs were working, crawling, dragging her towards the door while the shadows closed in.

She reached the door, and it was open. *If she could get to her feet . . .* There was strength, little, but it would be enough, it *must* be enough. She began to rise.

'No.' The voice, so calm, gave the command, and at the foot of the shadows that surrounded him something took form and began to slither across the floor. She saw what it was, saw what it was made from, and the shutters of her mind tried to slam, to block out and repudiate the sheer horror of it. But it came on, flowing towards her, and something else was following it out of the dark, and

358

above her head the shadows were closing in, and a face, the face of abomination, coiled into manifestation and drifted downwards, gently, closer, smiling –

'Nnnn . . .' She found her voice but she had no control over it now; she was making noises, shrill, animal noises, insensate and meaningless. 'Puh – puh – ' She wanted to say *please*, but she couldn't make the word form and she no longer knew what it meant, what anything meant.

With a fragment of her mind that was still sane she heard Vordegh move, soft-footed, unhurried, and for a moment that fragment almost believed that reality would return and she might hold to it, *hold* to it. But the shadows still closed, and now they were sliding over her, engulfing her, and there were hands in the shadows, and faces and voices, and she was losing her hold, drowning under the onslaught of Chaos's horrors as the First Magus calmly exerted the power of his mind to conjure the delusions and magnify them, deepen them, drawing and coaxing her towards a height of terror that would tear her apart.

When Iselia's body went into violent spasm, Vordegh lowered his hand. Around him the shadows drew back, shrinking and fading in obedience to his will, and as the candle's wan flame brought a little light to the room he gazed down on the twitching shell of humanity at his feet. Blood and foam covered Iselia's mouth and chin, a sight which the First Magus found faintly distasteful. Her eyes were open, but she saw only unrelieved and illimitable darkness. And at last the spasms ceased and she was still.

Vordegh uttered a small sigh that might have conveyed either satisfaction or exasperation. Then he raised his head and looked in the direction of the door to the outer room.

'Croin.'

Croin had been waiting and watching. He approached, paused on the threshold, then stepped over it and looked down.

'She is alive,' Vordegh said, 'and her mind is still capable of functioning. Do whatever is needed to restore her wits sufficiently for interrogation, and have her taken to the Marble Hall.'

Croin was still looking at Iselia, with a physician's detached interest. 'Savrinor's protégée,' he said mildly. 'An interesting conundrum, my lord.'

'A protégée, a reputed heretic, a would-be thief and assassin.' Vordegh's expression didn't change. 'As you say; interesting. And I am beginning to wonder how many other traitors we have been harbouring in our midst.'

Croin smiled reservedly. 'With your leave, First Magus, I shall begin the process of finding out.'

Vordegh looked up. His eyes, half-hooded, contained a strange and ferocious spark. 'You have my leave, Magus Croin.'

☐	MAGICIAN Raymond E. Feist	0-586-21783-5	£6.99
☐	SILVERTHORN Raymond E. Feist	0-586-06417-6	£4.99
☐	A DARKNESS AT SETHANON Raymond E. Feist	0-586-06688-8	£5.99
☐	THE SILVER BRANCH Patricia Kennealy	0-586-21248-5	£4.99
☐	THE ELVENBANE A. Norton/M. Lackey	0-586-21687-1	£5.99
☐	MASTER OF WHITESTORM Janny Wurts	0-586-21068-7	£4.99
☐	THE DRAGON AND THE GEORGE Gordon R. Dickson	0-586-21326-0	£4.99
☐	BLACK TRILLIUM May/Bradley/Norton	0-586-21102-0	£4.99

These books are available from your local bookseller or can be ordered direct from the publishers.

To order direct just tick the titles you want and fill in the form below:

Name: _____

Address: _____

_____

Postcode: _____

Send to: HarperCollins Mail Order, Dept 8, HarperCollins *Publishers*, Westerhill Road, Bishopbriggs, Glasgow G64 2QT.

Please enclose a cheque or postal order or your authority to debit your Visa/Access account –

Credit card no: _____

Expiry date: _____

Signature: _____

– to the value of the cover price plus:

UK & BFPO: Add £1.00 for the first and 25p for each additional book ordered.

Overseas orders including Eire, please add £2.95 service charge.

Books will be sent by surface mail but quotes for airmail despatches will be given on request.

24 HOUR TELEPHONE ORDERING SERVICE FOR ACCESS/VISA CARDHOLDERS –

TEL: GLASGOW 041-772 2281 or LONDON 081-307 4052